HALL
OF THE
BETRAYED

HALL
OF THE
BETRAYED
HALEY D. BROWN

HALL OF THE BETRAYED

Tylor—

for whom I'd brave the unbravable

Cliffs of Chilital

V A L E

H E A V E N S

Oxcroft

Gloriala

E L E M

Mortis Hollow

A P H A

Alynthia

Fairshroud
(Castle Habren)

NCIA

Maedonia
(Wyndmere)

FLESH
and
BLOOD

Asena

ENTS

EDIA

CONTENTS

CHAPTER ONE

GLASS HANDS

*H*ow angry are you?

 The words were a plague, one that continued to haunt me long after Hrokr left me alone in my cell.

There were many things that should be occupying my mind. The last few hours—at least those I'd been conscious for—had given me more than enough to think about.

To stress over.

To grieve.

Calix's death at Hrokr's hand. My mother's death at Gar's.

But rage had become a blanket over my abused senses.

Though he'd long disappeared down the ivory hallway, I couldn't blink without seeing Hrokr standing on the other side of the gold bars now separating me from any hope of freedom or reunion with my family.

How angry are you?

He'd asked it openly—as if he truly awaited my response.

I'd not bothered to give one.

And after flashing me a knowing look—one that had my teeth grinding so hard they ached—he vanished.

Simply disappeared into a curling rift of grey smoke the drafty hallway eagerly swallowed.

How angry are you?

He had no idea.

And neither did the man—oceans away—with hands stained red in my mother's blood.

Gar.

Silas.

The man who'd cut my flesh, who'd locked my beautiful sister beneath the reach of the sun. The man who'd carved a hollow ghost out of the boy that used to be my brother.

It was a childish thought—an ill-worded plea, really—but I cast it out all the same.

Why me?

But the answer was gifted from my own thoughts, my own vile memories.

Because you're just as awful as him, Thea.

Just as awful.

Was I breathing?

A tightness pulled at my chest, and my breath came in shallow, broken pants.

A prick of pain in my palms as my nails broke my flesh into bloody half-moons.

A catch around the lump in my throat.

How angry are you?

How angry was I?

I'd never considered myself a particularly violent person. But the memories of everything I was—of who I used to be—fled me as I watched my hands reach out toward the table before me. As I watched my arms sweep across the surface, knocking a glass decanter to the floor where it shattered into countless, jagged pieces.

A broken, helpless noise filled the space—one I knew came from my own lips.

The table crashed into the floor, the chairs knocked over beneath the kick of my boot.

How angry was I?

My flesh was not a strong enough vessel to contain my fury. There were no words to describe the rage flowing within me, pumping from my stone heart.

My stomach turned with the knowledge that I'd kissed him, that I'd let his hands hold my skin. Hands that had bound my family, hands that had cut my mother's life short.

Smoke licked at my fingertips, and pinpricks of flame warmed my tingling palms.

And *Hrokr*.

Hrokr, who'd poured poison into my body, who'd snapped Calix's neck right before me. Who'd locked me as a bird inside a cage.

Hrokr, who thought *my* rage—*my grief*—was a weapon for him to wield.

Fragmented sobs wracked me, kicked me down to my knees. My hands braced themselves against the floor.

Glass cut my palms.

I cried.

Sitting in a puddle of glass and water, I cried.

I cried until the sun fled the world, until the pristine hallway outside lost the luster of daylight. I cried until my sobs were dry, and my body empty of all it could give.

I blinked my aching eyes against the night-dark room. Lavender moonlight stained the tile of the hall and cast a silvery sheen across the gold bars of my prison.

In a daze, I took in the room. The table and chairs I'd knocked over were a matching set, wrought iron and adorned with carvings of night-blooming flowers. The floor was so white the tiles were almost harsh to behold, even with only the faded night to give me sight.

The slate-grey walls were too smooth, unmarred and taunting me for being so defiled by scars and months of filth. A linen screen even hid a toilet and sink from view, as though such distasteful sights were not welcome in this glittering prison.

Glittering *crypt*—eager to house my dying soul.

But worse yet was the bed.

Crisp sheets of freshest cotton—untouched by tear or fade—and folded inside a navy duvet fit for a queen. Matching pillows with golden embroidery adorned the head, ready to tuck me in and never let me wake.

I looked down at the glass crusted into my palms, at the blood, sweat, and stain long-embedded into my tattered leathers.

It was as though all of Hrokr's grandeur was more than vain opulence. Looking around myself, I couldn't help but see it as another move on the proverbial chess board.

Hrokr saw himself as the sleek spider, spinning a web of glimmering silk.

And he thought me only a fly caught within it.

My lips peeled back from my teeth.

I slept—or something like it.

The poison I'd carried to the coal mines of Balaca was no match for the sickness festering within me now. I was ill with the poison of despair.

I hoped that in sleep I would find darkness, an abyss of reprieve.

I did not.

I found only dreams more wicked than the life around me. Only reminders that my mother was dead, I had no guarantee Mellian and Alek had made it home, and Sage—if she still lived—was in Oxcroft sleeping walls away from Gar.

My mind conjured a glimpse of her child-like grin on a long-dead face.

The sight was jarring enough to rip me from sleep. Caked in sweat, I lurched from the sheets and bolted across the room, falling to my knees before the toilet and vomiting until I couldn't breathe.

Just a dream, just a dream.

But how long would it be a dream? Was it real already?

I vomited again, filling the cell with the pitiful sounds of my retching.

When my body had wholly drained itself, leaving my throat raw and stomach cramping, I rested my cheek against the porcelain.

Then why me?

Because you're just as awful as him, Thea. Just as awful.

The sound of footsteps in the hall woke me. I still lay on the floor before the toilet, but the night had passed. Fresh sunlight filled the space, making my cell glisten like a sour gem.

I rose to my feet.

The glass had been swept away, the table and chairs sat upright. A fresh meal even sat atop it. I didn't allow myself the moment of fear and disgust at knowing someone had entered while I lay sleeping.

I was already at his mercy.

Hrokr stood on the other side of the bars, wearing simple finery. No garish adornments decorated him today, but the single stud on the tip of his ear remained. A long-sleeved, cashmere sweater clung to him, tucked lazily into dark pants.

Standing before him with my hair matted to my scalp and filth clinging to my body, I felt debased. Defiled.

"Hello," he said softly.

"What do you want?"

There was no life in my voice, only a rough scratch belying my night.

He took a deep breath that lifted his chest and broadened his shoulders. "We should talk about what happened."

"I have nothing to say to you."

There was a certain tiredness to him as he took a step closer and wrapped long fingers around the gold. "You can speak with me or you can have a real trial. You will be tried, convicted, and sentenced to death."

"I doubt speaking to you will make a difference."

A small, lopsided smile—though it was edged with melancholy. "I am not known for my mercy to foreign threats, I will give you that. But I'd still like to talk."

"Don't feign kindness," I rasped.

I could still see his hands twisting Calix's neck, leaving him a mass of empty flesh on the floor of the throne room.

Hrokr sighed—long and heavy—and even with the distance between us, the scent of rain and jasmine washed over me. "My feelings regarding your case are very strong, but I doubt devolving to that baser side will be of much use."

A pretty man of pretty words, and not a single one of them fooled me. Everything about him was artfully crafted, honed to pull the reactions he desired. I would not engage in it, would not believe for a *moment* he would choose to release me from Valencia with my heart still beating.

He wanted a moldable girl to wield as a weapon against a common enemy. Broken I may have been, but tamed I was not. "Poetic."

The only sign of his irritation was the slight narrowing of his eyes. "As I came here to say, I would like to speak with you about the nature of your crimes."

"You killed my friend."

He nodded, unfazed. "He was no friend to you."

"He was afraid—"

"He was *spineless,*" Hrokr growled suddenly. "And for all your apparent faults, cowardice is not one of them. I am willing to listen to your plight, but I am not interested in his. I had no need of him, and I do not like loose ends."

"All my apparent faults?" I croaked.

There was a heat building within me, and I tamped it down, trying to breathe it away. If I erupted in fire, he'd know precisely what I was. Hrokr was no fool, and Calix had already told him of my healing abilities.

Hrokr would not believe the lie Gar had, that I was born in Valencia.

He looked at me flatly. "Well, you're not very amicable, for one. You're reckless and arrogant—"

"Arrogant?" I hissed. "That's rich, coming from you."

He smirked, though I saw the flash of anger in his eyes. "I am Lord of the Hall. A certain level of elevation is required. I'm sorry that you weren't born with the same *gift*."

I wanted to laugh. Or scream and cry. The crest inked upon my hip ached like a fresh brand.

I was his equal, whether he recognized it or not.

But for all the rage pooling within me, a sliver of reality crawled in. I hadn't dared let myself feel the warmth of true hope, but if Gar had left Sage alive—I needed to go to her. I needed to get her out of there and take Mellian and Alek somewhere safe.

"Let me go," I said.

"Speak to me," he replied, letting his fingers fall from the bars. "Tell me why you were killing my men, and who sent you to do it."

I couldn't.

I couldn't send Hrokr to The Burning Arrow, because I knew he would raze it to the ground—if he hadn't already.

"I can't," I admitted, and hated that my voice sounded as defeated as it did.

Hated that I was as defeated as I was.

"I can pardon your crimes," he said gently. "I can let you go."

I remained only still, unable to accept his offer.

Unable to wholly refuse it.

To which waiting palm did I deliver Sagira's life?

Gar's or Hrokr's?

He met my gaze, the colors of his eyes seeming to swirl around his pupil, pinpricks of light bursting against a black sea. We watched each other for a long moment.

Whatever he was waiting for, he must have decided it wasn't coming.

He sighed and vanished into smoke.

The dark tendrils he left behind danced through the air until they thinned into nothing. With them went my only hope of saving people who may already be ghosts.

CHAPTER TWO

MILK AND RIPPLES

I mulled over Hrokr's ultimately useless offer for the rest of the day. I ate the warm food provided—seasoned eggs and diced potatoes. With it came enough bread, dried meats, and fruit to last me through the entire silent day. The meal was divine, and I hated myself for the speed at which I devoured it.

It felt like failing, somehow.

But I forced myself to remember that I needed my strength. Having the willpower to starve myself was not anything that would help me.

My mind raced with each passing moment, the only changing sight for my eyes the warm glow of watery sunlight fading into the deep hue of twilight.

Numb, I watched the night descend. But when I heard soft footsteps, my back snapped straight.

But I slumped back into my seat when the figure that came into view wasn't Hrokr. No, it was a thin girl with skin the color of alabaster and eyes that sparkled like cut emeralds.

"Hello," she said in a soft, musical voice.

I said nothing.

She didn't appear to be anyone of importance, nor did she look at me as if *I* were. Her full, rosy lips were held in a perfectly plump, uninterested line. As striking as the color of her iris was, the eyes themselves were unimpressed where they sat above sharply cut cheekbones.

She smoothed her hands down the front of her linen dress, an action that seemed more of genuine primping than any nervous tick.

She began unlocking my cell door.

I shot to my feet, hope and dread crashing over me in equal measure.

Until Hrokr appeared out of thin air behind her.

"Hello," he said, offering a grim, wary smile.

He looked just the same as he had yesterday, wearing only dark pants and a cream sweater pushed up his forearms.

As if he were only a man on a stroll down the hall.

"What is this?" I asked, narrowing my eyes.

He remained silent until the bars swung open. "You're not going home," he said. "But you're not going to your execution, either."

"No?" I said, taking slow steps toward the door.

"No," he confirmed.

But surely *something* was happening. My fingers shook as I stepped across the threshold and into the starlit hallway.

I didn't have a chance to take the second step before his fingers were curving around my upper arm. I tried to pull away, but he only tightened his grip. His touch was hard, but his eyes were careful.

"Please don't kill her," he said softly.

Horror—and a healthy dose of rage—rippled through me. "I'm not a killer," I snarled.

"No?" Hrokr asked, cocking one brow.

"No."

He released me slowly, fingers trailing against my skin. "Very well, then. Off you go, Shadow."

A burst of acute nausea roiled through me. "Do *not* call me that," I spat.

Gar's brand inked upon my being. A name that killed in his.

Hrokr cocked a dark brow. "What should I call you, then?"

I only narrowed my eyes, swallowed my instincts, and turned my back on my enemy.

The girl didn't seem at all fazed by the interaction, only silently leading me down the luxurious hallway. There were no other cells, but I wasn't sure if that should comfort me or not.

I was outside of the bars.

I should have been running for my life, cutting through everyone necessary to get to Sage.

But as much as it burned me, I knew better.

This was my chance to act the role of a perfectly dispirited, docile prisoner. To make him trust me, to let me out again.

I knew he likely had more sets of eyes on me than I even wanted to consider. Running now was foolish.

But maybe if I gave him the show he wanted to see, those eyes would lessen.

For all of Hrokr's transgressions, I didn't think he wanted me dead. But that didn't mean he didn't want me to suffer.

Hrokr will make you pray for death.

The words flowed through me, and I hated myself for the weakness of allowing them to haunt me even all these months later.

So I shut out the thoughts and tried to think of nothing as we continued down the hall.

We had only taken a few steps before the pain in my thigh was screaming—that nugget of steel buried in my bone and fighting against my flesh. That wound from the first day I'd met my captor.

I was thankful for it in this moment. It at least kept my thoughts from Gar. From Silas.

I followed the girl through the pristine hallway until we came to a dark wooden door on our right. We crossed the threshold and began the descent down a small, spiral staircase. Everything was made of stone, and the damp scent of water and earth swarmed around me.

It was a bath—if I could even call it that. An open cavern nearly the size of Castle Habrem's throne room, lit by some kind of magical essence. Tiny balls of blue, the light they gave soft and lulling.

The floor was polished stone, though some corners of the room were left untouched, sporting dripping stalactites and strong stalagmites. A large basin was cut into the rock floor, filled with clear water that rippled with drops from above.

Though twenty people could have bathed comfortably, the room was empty but for us.

I forced myself to take it all in in excruciating detail. It was smart to know even the smallest specifics of this castle.

The girl turned on me as soon as we cleared the staircase. As I slammed to a halt, she instantly began pawing at my leathers.

I ripped from her grip with such force that she flinched.

My ears roared, my blood pumping so quickly I wondered if I'd faint.

She wanted to strip me for the bath. I wasn't sure why I'd not expected it.

With slow hands, she reached for me again—but I took a step back. "Stop."

"This is my job."

"I don't care," I snapped. "Do not touch my clothes."

I would wear my filth for a century before I bared my tattoo to anyone in this wretched Hall.

She huffed a breath and gestured toward the bath. "Fine. Go."

"No," I said hoping desperately she could not hear the panic in my voice.

She snorted. "You will bathe. I can assure you, darling, you do not have anything I have not seen before."

I doubted that.

"I can do without the bath if you must watch me," I said primly.

She cocked a dark brow. "You are a prolific killer," she informed me. "And you're unashamedly asking me to turn my back to you."

"I am not a murderer," I said slowly, trying to keep my bite out of my voice. "I killed out of necessity. I won't harm you."

She watched me for a long moment before something softened in her gaze. "I have served many people of many ages, both men and women. You have nothing nefarious to fear from me. Lord Hrokr has asked only that I serve you here."

I summoned all the venom left within me, turning my nose up. "I don't think I'd like a bath."

Her face crunched into a wrinkle of unveiled disgust. "You need one."

My eyes slimmed into a cold glare. "If my scent is off-putting to you, you're welcome to leave me alone."

She wasn't moved at all by the crass response, only curiously cocking her head to the side. "You have a pleasant scent, actually. Strange, like snow and bitter coffee."

I blinked.

"It's not your scent," she continued. "It's your appearance. You look a mess."

A disbelieving sound was torn from my throat. "I'm in prison, if you haven't noticed."

She rolled her eyes, taking a step toward me.

I took two steps back.

"You're not in *prison,*" she sighed, exasperated. "You're in a holding cell awaiting trial. A trial that Lord Hrokr has been *very* benevolent in trying to spare you from."

"*Benevolent?*" I snarled, my ears twitching. "He killed my friend—"

"And you killed many of his," she snapped, rage sparking in her eyes like green fire. "And still, he offers you his mercy." She shook her head, grumbling beneath her breath. "I don't understand that man sometimes."

I opened my mouth to respond, but she took another step toward me, cutting me off. "Get in the bath," she commanded.

"I'm not stripping in front of you."

She looked young, barely in her twenties. But I could feel the age on her. She reminded me of a sour-tongued grandmother.

Irritated hands settled on her hips. "Fine. But you have to know I can't keep my back turned. Get stripped, get in the water." She turned around with a little huff, muttering "Prude."

My lips peeled back from my teeth, but I remained silent. I cast my eyes to the spiral staircase we'd descended, but I knew better than to hope. I would not escape this. I'd only find Hrokr on the other side of that door, arms banded across his chest.

Accepting this was the best I was going to get, I shucked off my dirty clothes and padded over to the water.

I dipped in a tentative toe, but the water was surprisingly warm. Sinking my body into the water, I found a natural ledge to perch on. The water came up to my underarms, wrapping its warmth around me.

I hated how good it felt, how my muscles immediately unclenched and relaxed in the hot water. I tried to shake it away and better position my body, contorting myself to cover up the tattoo on my hip.

Her footsteps were gentle and measured behind me. She had retrieved a small tray and pulled the stoppers off of a few glass bottles. She poured only a small amount of each, but instantly, a creamy lavender color began to spear through the water.

It filled the space, turning the water a milky purple color. Knowing she had done this to preserve what she believed to be my modesty, I whispered, "Thank you."

Thanking my captors...

She gave a tight nod as she sauntered over, tray in tow. My body seized as she settled herself behind me.

She couldn't see my crest, I knew. But still, I had to force myself to unclench my jaw and relax.

Scooping a small ivory bowl into the water, she poured it down the back of my head.

"You don't have to help me," I said. "I can bathe myself."

"It's my job," she said, her tone brokering no room for argument.

So I sat there, pressing my fingers into my hip until they ached as this stranger scrubbed my scalp with soap that smelled like milk and honey.

It was unnerving, as I knew I was naked with my back bared to an enemy, deep in the bowels of the castle of the most frightening man in the world. But as her fingers moved against my hair, and the scents and feel of the water wrapped around me, my body relaxed even though my mind wouldn't.

She washed as much of me as was above the water. My hair, my back, my arms and shoulders.

Her voice held a motherly croon as she asked, "Are you tender-headed?"

Without speaking, I shook my head. The only sound in the room was the clink of her rustling through metal tools beside me, choosing an iron-toothed comb.

My stomach twisted.

I truly thought I'd cried all the tears I had left.

As she began combing the months' worth of knots from my hair, pain radiated from the crown of my head. It hurt—

But that was not why warm tears spilled down my cheeks, salty where they met my lips.

Vain as it may have been, I shed my remaining tears for the mattes and tangles my fingers had not been able to tame in Balaca.

I lost hair.

Not enough to be noticeable by anyone other than myself, but enough to avert my eyes from the growing pile of dirty, split strands placed at my side.

Finally, she pressed a sudsy cloth into my hands. "I will give you a few moments," she said gently.

I dropped the cloth onto the craggy ledge, wiping the tears from my eyes only once I was sure she was gone. I ran shaking fingers through my hair, fresh tears collecting on my lashes when I felt it smooth and clean. Trying to bury my strained emotions, I scrubbed the rest of my body.

I sat in the silence of the warm water for a few minutes after I was finished, trying to collect myself enough to face the world again. She finally returned, silent as she handed me a thick, white robe and again turned her back.

I pulled myself out of the water, the tepid air biting against my skin. My fingers shook as I tied the sash around my waist.

She led me across the smooth stone until we crossed through the only door and into a small room. The same orbs of light hovered in the corners, but this space wasn't as raw as the bath. Rich, dark wood was smooth underfoot, the walls slate grey.

The woman gestured me onto a small stool sitting before a large, gilded mirror framed in intricate, curling wood. A massive armoire took up nearly the entire right wall, its surface holding many drooping candles and a stack of folded clothes.

The plush, forest-green stool was soft beneath me, and its place before the mirror offered me an uninterrupted view of the girl behind me. She combed through my hair with her fingers, twisting it into loose curls. My hair held the curl, drying beneath her fingertips.

"You have an air affinity?" I asked.

She didn't look up from her work as she murmured, "Yes."

In silence, she finished her work, leaving my hair loose but shapely and clean. "Your clothes," she said, gesturing to the right wall before turning her back on me. "I'll be outside."

I let out a long breath as the door clicked shut behind her. I stood, hesitantly approaching the mirror. I touched my fingers to my hair and studied the flush still coating my cheeks from the warmth of my bath. Slowly, I dropped the robe from my shoulders and draped it across the stool.

My ribs poked against my flesh, and even the jutting of my hips was far too sharp. My skin was paper stretched over glass bones.

Balaca had not been kind to me.

I ran delicate fingers across the Aphaedian crest, touching mountains and constellations, before I let my hand drop with a tight breath.

I didn't let the terror overtake me, but I felt it—nibbling—just behind my eyes. I wished I could carve the crest from my body, leave the severed flesh behind me.

But I knew maiming myself would bring no reprieve. Whether I bore the sigil of my people or not, I still was what I was.

The Heir to the throne of Aphaedia. The Lady of the Southern Hall, trapped in the basement of the keeper of the north.

The panic rose higher; I forced it down.

I couldn't think about it right now. Couldn't think about Sage or Mellian or Alek. I couldn't think about my dead mother or the fact that I was one broken neck away from damning the hope of an entire continent of people.

Since the War of the Twins, the Aphaedian people—*my* people—had become scattered refugees. They'd spent a millennium barred from their homeland, forced to leave the Hall in snowy ruin.

If I died, the bloodline would die with me. The hope of healing the land would be gone forever—there would no longer be a home to return to.

With a deep, shaking breath, I turned from my reflection. Atop the armoire sat a long, black dress. I slipped it over my head, finding the material flexible and form-fitting. Short sleeves gave me free use of my arms, though my legs were bound by fabric that flowed down to the floor.

It would be hard to run in—but not impossible.

I pulled on the small, black flats and slipped out into the bath.

The girl—whose name I still did not know—walked me back up the stairs to my cell in perfect silence.

Hrokr was waiting with his arms crossed, leaning against the wall before my cell.

His eyes traveled from my head to my slippered toes, cataloguing my every movement. "Things went well?" he surmised as we drew closer.

The girl snorted, and I threw an immediate glare in her direction.

But Hrokr seemed to be more relaxed than when we left, and a slight smile pulled at his lips. "She pitched a fit about the dress, I assume?" he said, watching me with mischief in his eyes.

I had enough anxiety and irritation to flay them both in this moment, but shredding his skin from his bones would not serve me now. I walked through the open door of the cell, knocking his shoulder with my own as I passed. Looking down my nose at him—as much as I could from a foot shorter—I said, "I like dresses."

What I wanted more was to slam my shoulder into his, to shred him apart with my nails. But arrogance, the assertion of social dominance—it was the only pride I had left. I would not win a physical battle within these walls.

His body remained still and cool, the slight widening of his eyes the only hint of any surprise.

Once I was fully in my cell, Hrokr locked the cell gate and disappeared down the hall with the girl in tow.

No parting words today.

I moved slowly as I seated myself at the table, trying for just a while to cling to the silent emptiness. I needed to consider my next moves, and soon. But for now, I was relieved to dwell in this empty cocoon.

A small moment of nothingness.

That is until Hrokr sauntered back through the hall to lean against the bars. I was resigned to being good—to playing nice—but Hrokr was wearing a lazy smirk, and his eyes were bright with fresh-born stars.

I narrowed my gaze.

"You didn't kill Gyda," he said by way of introduction.

"Were you hoping I would?" I asked, ears twitching.

He chuckled—a low, throaty sound. "On the contrary. I'm quite relieved you delivered her back to me in one piece."

"If you were so sure I was going to gut her, why did you send her alone with me?"

His lips twisted into a lopsided smile, showing one fang. "A small experiment of sorts."

My ears twitched again. "If she is so important to you, why would you send her?"

His smirk deepened, something glittering in his eyes. "She is of no importance to me in my personal life. But I care about all my people."

I didn't want to hear it—his praise of his own benevolence. "What do you want?"

"She informed me that you are quite the shy one."

My cheeks heated, but I refused to drop my head or hide in the curtain of my hair. "I don't see how that could be any concern of yours."

He chuckled, eyes bright. "It's only surprising, is all."

And even though I knew my reasons for modesty were far beyond his imaginings, I still took the bait. "Why is it surprising?"

"You can slaughter a room of strangers without an inch of remorse, but the thought of stripping in front of an eighty-year-old woman makes you bashful?"

Without an inch of remorse.

How angry are you?

Because you're just as awful as him, Thea.

Just as awful.

I tried to outrun the words and instead focus on the fact that she was *eighty*. I shouldn't be surprised. The man standing before me was nearing six hundred.

I took the moment to truly study him.

Even lazy and casual, the swollen air of invisible darkness that swathed him the first day we'd met still clung to him. It was as if a wave of black shrouded him, but was just beyond the veil—just outside of the realm of vision.

"You are full of surprises, Shadow," he said with the same mischievous grin.

Rage—acute and boiling—ripped through my veins, tearing me out of my soft reverie. Images flashed behind my eyes. Images of Gar and The Nock and Oxcroft Keep. Fantasies of all the horrors I hadn't seen with my own eyes.

"Don't," I said, deathly soft. "Don't call me that."

The humor in his eyes banked, replaced by something that—if I didn't know better—I would call concern.

"What is your name?" he asked softly.

I was tired. I was angry, and I was *done*.

"Thea."

Let him have my name, let him curse it if he so desired.

But I would wear Gar's no longer.

CHAPTER THREE
LESSONS IN REGRET

H rokr left me without further goodbye. The emotional weight of the last
hour bore down on me, making even my bones feel tired within my skin.
I collapsed on the bed.

I should have known better than to seek reprieve in sleep. My dreams were fierce
and fitful—gory masterpieces of my greatest fears. Sunlight was already spilling
onto the white tiles of the hall when I hurtled toward the toilet to empty my
stomach.

I let my eyes fall closed as I pressed my forehead against the porcelain, willing
my tears to dry on my lashes. When I found the strength to rise, I scrubbed my
mouth with fresh water from the sink.

As I twisted the faucet off, the sound of footsteps came tentatively down the
hall.

It was not Hrokr's strong, sure-footed gait.

A guard peaked her head around the corner. Short black hair fell only to her
shoulders, curling inward at the ends. She paused as if she hadn't expected to find

me awake and staring straight at her. A surprised, pink flush dusted her porcelain cheekbones.

Her dark eyes narrowed.

It was such a subtle gesture, but it had my fingers reaching for a knife I no longer had strapped to my thigh.

She wore a sleek, black cloak—one in pristine condition. "Without your keepers?" she crooned, tilting her head to the side.

I cocked a brow.

She dropped to her knees, producing a ring of keys that she quickly began unlocking my cell door with.

My heart instantly leapt into my throat, tangling with the questions I didn't know how to voice. I stood frozen in stunned silence as she pulled open the gate, shoving her keys back into her cloak pocket.

I took a tentative step forward, rasping, "Why?"

A brilliantly cruel grin turned her lips. "I'm a friend of Gar's. We have other plans for you, ones I'm sure you'll want to hear."

My entire body plunged into a hatred so cold it froze my veins.

Absolute stillness settled between us.

I should go.

I could let her lead me off this accursed Hall, let her lead me to Gar where I could gut him with my nails. I should have let her lead me through Hrokr's blind spots, should have let her deliver me to Gar with a knife in my hand and hatred in my heart.

But my emotions took control of my body.

Like a feral beast finally free of its leash, I leapt and tackled her to the floor.

She didn't scream. She *couldn't* scream, because she was somewhere that she was not supposed to be.

Who was she more afraid of? Me or Hrokr?

With some animalistic, feral rage riding my bones, I smiled down at her. Her brown eyes went doe-wide as she struggled beneath me.

I was wild.

Unhinged.

Shattered.

She wasn't Gar, but she was here. She would have to take the brunt of my pain. She was all I had.

I reared back, punching her directly in her upturned nose. She made a strangled sound as the bone broke on impact.

Rage contorted her fair features.

My head jerked to the side as she wrapped a fist in my hair and pulled. I cried out, even as I managed to land a knee in her gut.

"What is wrong with you?" she howled.

"Me?" I hissed, pulling her up to slam her back down into the floor. "He took *everything* from me. He *killed my mother!*"

I hit her again—across the lip—and blood spilled down her chin.

Even with the heat of battle and the rush of adrenaline pulsing through me, I felt an uncontrollable sob rising in my chest.

He hurt me.

He killed my momma.

I trusted him.

I loved *him.*

I was fighting almost uselessly now, crying and slamming my fists into her chest. She reached for her blade, but I pried it out of her hands—

And buried it in her stomach. She bit into her lip, trying to stifle the cry.

I pulled it out—

And buried it again.

And again.

Again.

She was crying now, begging me to stop.

The sounds of our wretched sobbing filled the room. But I kept going until the sobs began to fully take over me.

Only then did I drag the blade across her throat and end her cries.

I was straddling her body, caked in her sticky blood. I knew I needed to move, needed to run through the open door. But I couldn't.

I sat there—back bowed over her body—and wept until I couldn't breathe. Violent, hysterical sobs that blurred my vision and made my lungs feel like they were rupturing within my chest.

My fingers shook as I clung to her bloody cloak.

I can't breathe, I can't breathe, I can't breathe—

Rushed footsteps sounded down the hall, which only kicked me into a higher level of hysteria.

I knew I couldn't fight my way through an entire Hall—what was I thinking? What was I doing?

I'm going to die in here, I'm going to die in here, I'm going to die in here—

Gar did this to me, Gar got me involved in this. If I lived to escape Valencia, I was going to peel his skin from his bones.

I couldn't move, couldn't stop shaking and crying, even as the footsteps spilled into my cell.

I heard a sharp intake of breath followed by voices. I couldn't discern what they were saying, and I didn't care to. I couldn't stop shaking, couldn't stop—

Strong hands wrapped around my arms and began pulling me away from her body, but I fought it. I writhed and thrashed and pulled, but these hands were stronger than mine.

They had the strength to collect both my wrists in one hand, and then gentle, firm fingers were under my chin, turning my head.

Hrokr's wide eyes were inches from my own. "Thea."

But I couldn't breathe, couldn't catch my breath, couldn't speak, couldn't—

"Thea," he said again, starlight eyes searching my own. "What happened?"

He shared a concerned look with someone behind me.

Through my hiccuping sobs, I thought I choked out, "He killed my mother."

And collapsed.

I rose to consciousness but didn't dare stir. Voices were a low buzz against my ears, a messy dissonance that my addled mind couldn't comprehend.

Until one of the voices said my name, and everything snapped into hyper-sharp focus.

"I don't know," a raspy voice said. I'd heard that voice once before; it sounded like gravel and shifting sand.

Hrokr sighed heavily. "Council only."

"Of course."

Hesitantly, I opened my eyes, finding neither of them looking in my direction. Someone had deposited me atop the navy duvet, where I was still covered in blood.

The female guard's body still lay on the floor.

My stomach twisted in sour knots of regret.

Not guilt.

But regret.

I recognized the Gentry Fae speaking to Hrokr as the man who had restrained Fallon Blightbringer during our last encounter. I remembered his voice, those bands of lightning running up his arms, the pure white of his hair, and the electric blue of his eyes.

Hrokr pinched the bridge of his nose between his thumb and forefinger, glancing down at the body on the floor.

Another heavy, tired sigh from Hrokr. "Fetch Gyda for me, will you?"

They began to move, and I snapped my eyes shut immediately.

"You sure, Crow?" the white-haired man asked.

I could only assume this man was Ciro—the third in Hrokr's male trio—if he was speaking to the lord this casually.

"Yes, I'm sure. She'll be safe."

I felt a wriggle of shame.

There was no remorse to be found within me for taking the life of an *arrow*, but it still wounded something of my moral pride to be viewed as a ravenous killer. It was obvious that Ciro feared for Gyda's safety. From me.

But I supposed I looked as deranged as they believed me to be, as they had no idea why I would want their guard dead.

I suppressed a sigh.

"Open your eyes, love. It's rude to eavesdrop."

My eyes flashed open, ready for a fight, but there was not one to be found. Ciro was gone, only Hrokr standing before me with a smirk painted across his lips.

But as he beheld me, his eyes gentled into something like mourning.

"Did you know her well?" I asked, voice small.

"Hmm?" he hummed, blinking away the softness. "The guard? No." He shook his head gently, as if shaking away his thoughts.

He offered no other words.

He stood before me, creamy sweater smeared with blood. His dark eyes were tired, one hand shoved in his pocket. He took a soft breath. "Why?"

I said nothing.

"Did she hurt you?"

"What?"

"She was inside of your cell and did not have clearance to be. Did she come inside to hurt you?"

Yes, but not in the way he thought. I offered only, "She did not hurt me."

"But you killed her."

"Yes."

He sighed, pinching the bridge of his nose again. "Do you want me to kill you, Thea?" The words were tired, exasperated.

My voice had no fire when I asked, "Is that a threat?"

"It's a genuine question."

"No, I do not want you to kill me. Why would I want that?"

He didn't respond to the question but instead asked his own. "Did you have a reason for killing her?"

I shifted my weight, forcing myself to meet his eyes directly. "Yes."

"And was her employment with me the reason?"

"No."

"Did you know her?" he pushed.

"No."

He let out a sharp burst of air. "Thea, you have to give me some answers."

"I'm trying," I spat.

He watched me for a long moment, eyes running across every inch of me. I had no doubt he was cataloguing the blood soaking through my dress, the red stuck beneath my fingernails and flaking off my hands. The salt tracks down my cheeks.

Angry eyes gentled yet again.

"Gyda will be here any moment," he said quietly, turning his back to me as he made his way to the door. He paused in the open gateway, casting a final glance over his shoulder.

"My condolences," he murmured, "about your mother."

He didn't lock the door behind him.

I knew better than to follow him through it.

Gyda walked through the door only moments after Hrokr disappeared down the hall. She merely clucked her tongue at the corpse on the floor and motioned with a sharp hand for me to follow.

I let her lead me to the baths, let her lead me through the same motions as yesterday.

I was lost in thought—thinking of what I'd done, why Hrokr wasn't killing me, where Sagira might be—when Gyda laid my clothes beside me.

She returned me to my cell without speaking a single word. It was freshly cleaned, and a dinner for one had been arranged on a linen placemat.

I took it alone.

Alone—and with less hope than yesterday.

CHAPTER FOUR

BREAKFAST GUESTS

After my nightmares chased me across the cell to empty my stomach for the third time, I accepted defeat. Curling into a ball, I rested my head against the cool floor. I stayed there for long hours, unable to find the strength to cart myself back across the room and to the bed.

Thea, are you awake?

Hrokr's voice.

I sat up immediately.

A few moments passed before he added, *You need to learn how to project. It will make your life much easier. I'll be there in ten minutes with breakfast. I'd ask what you'd like, but, alas. Another reason for you to learn how to project.*

I narrowed my eyes at nothing. He was being nice today. Extra nice.

Pulling myself to my feet, I cleaned my mouth and washed my face in the sink. There was no reflection to face, and part of me was thankful for that.

I'd rather not watch myself wither.

After removing the tie from my braid and combing through the soft plaits, I seated myself at the table like a perfect lady.

I could only assume Hrokr's newfound hospitality meant something, and I was desperate enough to play along.

Especially after my errors yesterday.

He was true to his word, and ten minutes later he strolled in carrying a covered tray. Even wearing only simple, nondescript black pants and a grey button-down, he still looked like an intricately carved dagger of a man.

"Good morning," he said softly, setting the tray on the table. He kept the cell door propped open, and I had to force my eyes away from it. I wasn't sure if he was simply unconcerned about my escape—as he was here to cage me himself—or if he left it open to tempt me.

I tried not to think about it.

"Morning."

His lips twitched as he seated himself across from me. I vaguely registered the spread—eggs, bacon, waffles, toast, fruits, potatoes. But my fingers reached out to drag a warm mug to myself.

"Do you dine with all your prisoners?"

Though the skepticism in my voice was obvious, it didn't have much bite.

"I hoped that maybe you would be more amicable over a meal."

My eyes flashed up to meet his, and the thin sheet of civility I'd wrapped around myself crumbled. "Am I not normally amicable?" I asked, ears twitching.

But Hrokr was unfazed. He cracked a small smile. I noticed, again, how incredibly tired he looked. "You do alright."

"*Alright?*"

He sighed, leaning back in his seat. "You seem insistent on not trusting me, despite—"

"I'll remind you that you murdered my friend, in case you've forgotten."

He rolled his eyes. "Murder," he scoffed beneath his breath.

"It *was* murder. What would you like me to call it?"

He took a heavy breath, as if he were trying to steady himself. "Calix is not what I wanted to talk about."

I stared.

When he said nothing more, I waved a loose hand at him. "By all means, Your Highness, continue."

His lips twitched, the anger gone from his eyes in an instant.

I openly scowled.

"We can start with the easy things," he said. "Get comfortable with one another."

I snorted, picking up a gold fork to spear a piece of melon. Hrokr's eyes carefully monitored my every moment. As his gaze fastened on my hand—and the utensil within it—I asked, "Would you like me to use the spoon?"

"Pardon?" he asked, brow furrowing.

"Is my holding a pointed object making you uncomfortable?" I sneered.

He laughed out loud, the sound abrupt and surprising. "You do not frighten me, Thea." His eyes slid up to meet mine once more. "We are the same in that way, at least."

"How so?" I asked, pulling a waffle onto my plate.

"I do not frighten you."

I didn't bother to respond. I didn't bother to admit I had months' worth of nightmares of him taking my life. I didn't tell him his nameless faerie's words—*Hrokr will make you pray for death*—still sounded through my head every day.

I supposed I didn't speak to him as someone who was afraid.

That didn't mean I was brave; it only meant I was hopeless.

"Where were you born?" he asked.

I fought against the flush of hot panic racing through me and instead borrowed from Sage's history. "In the Hall of Flesh and Blood."

"When did you come to the Hall of the Elements?" he asked, pulling the other mug of coffee into his hands.

I could lie, tell him it was recently. That would keep Mellian and Alek safe from him, but—

I was much more likely to be caught in a lie if he discovered I knew nothing about Flesh and Blood.

"Shortly after my birth," I said.

"You're a healer." It wasn't a question.

"Yes."

"What's your second affinity?" he asked.

"I only have the one," I told him, meeting his eyes. If he ever found out about my control over fire, it would be the end for me.

Hrokr would not believe my lie of being born in his court. No, he'd know exactly who I was.

Though, I wasn't even really sure what I was worrying about anymore. He was never going to let me out of his Hall willingly, anyway.

He nodded slowly. "It will manifest sooner or later," he said softly.

My brow furrowed. "Why would it? Not everyone has two affinities."

He twirled a golden fork between his fingers. "You're far too powerful to have only one."

A shiver wriggled down my spine. "I suppose we'll see," I said noncommittally.

He smirked, one fang showing through his parted lips. "Planning on staying with me for a while?"

Leveling a flat look at him, I asked, "Planning on letting me go anytime soon?"

He laughed. "Fair."

I said nothing.

"I think I understand you more than you know, Thea."

Ice crawled inside of me, nestled up against my frozen heart. "Yeah?"

"Yes."

I studied him, watching the slow movements of his eyes scrolling across my face.

"Would you like me to tell you what I've deduced?"

A tight nod.

I prayed to the Elders he wouldn't know enough to get Sage killed. Maybe Calix's betrayal hadn't given Hrokr enough information to find Oxcroft.

He leaned back in his seat, crossing one long leg over the other as he watched me beneath heavy lashes. "Many people on Alynthia would like to see me dead."

When he added nothing more, I let my lips curl into a cruel smile. "I couldn't imagine why."

He huffed a small laugh, but there was no light in his eyes. "I can't begin to know how, but I think you found yourself caught up in a group dedicated to undoing me," he said. "That would explain both your blatant distrust of me and your presence at the Eclipse Fete."

I remained silent, forcing my face into perfect neutrality.

"You know nothing about what you've gotten yourself into." Before I had a chance to let my irritation show, he amended, "Or at least, you didn't. You appear to know a bit more now. Someone was using you," he said softly. "And you figured it out."

Color rose to my cheeks, anger boiling within me.

"It was a smart play, really, to try and secure my Orb of Dolga first. It would be best to pluck mine up before I saw the others being taken, as mine would be the hardest to secure." A pause. "Or perhaps Aphaedia's. But you didn't know they raise the dead."

I had nothing to say.

"The Orbs are almost worthless at this point," he said. "Dolga only granted us five, and each is only able to be used once. Still, all must be assembled in order to ferry the soul back from the Far Away. But there is only one living Orb left. Each Lord and Lady of the Hall holds their own very close. They've become nothing more than a stalemate." He ran his fingers through his loose, black curls. "No one is going to give up their own piece in case they need it someday. Therefore, no one has the power to do anything. They're worthless."

But Gar would do anything for his wife. If there was someone deranged enough to find a way, it was him.

"Anyway," Hrokr said, clearing his throat softly. "I know where the Guild is." My eyes flashed to his.

"Calix told Fallon, you'll remember. I know exactly where it is."

Even curled around the steaming mug, my fingers were suddenly cold.

But that couldn't be true, not really. Sure, he had a general idea of its location, but—

Every member of the Burning Arrow would be dead if Hrokr wished them to be. And if what he was saying was true, I imagined he very much did want them to be.

Were they all gone?

He must have read the fear in my eyes. "An ugly, drab building, that keep. One—maybe two—miles east of Oxcroft Fields, Vanadey."

The color drained from my face.

"Did you kill them?" I asked, voice small.

He sighed. "Politics are a messy, messy thing."

No.

Relief was a punch to my gut.

I forced myself to meet Hrokr's eyes. "But you would. You'd kill them if it were that simple."

He didn't blink. "Of course I would."

A shiver pulled my skin tight.

But Hrokr leaned forward suddenly, elbows braced on the table between us. "You'd kill them too, Thea. You killed my guard, not because she was mine, but because she was *theirs.* She was disobeying my direct orders to come to you; her allegiances were not to me.

"And you slaughtered her. Gutted her like a fish."

My fingers curled inward, threatening to crack the ceramic between them. He noted it.

"I can help you, Thea. I can help you kill them all."

I was shaking my head before the words left his lips.

A wide smile that bared his teeth. "And *there* is the catch. The reason you won't trust me. The reason you won't save your own life."

I waited, willing myself into stillness.

"You're protecting someone. Someone you believe to be innocent of the rest."

I clenched my teeth so hard my jaw ached.

"Is he your lover?" he asked softly.

My spine snapped to a painfully straight point, and Hrokr leaned back a fraction of an inch. "No," I growled, both grief and rage ripping through my throat.

I wondered if he saw even more than I wanted him to, as he nodded carefully.

"Just a friend you made there, then?" he pushed.

I closed my eyes. I didn't even know what I was saying, didn't want to think about the concession—the risk—I was making. But he already knew where she was, and she wasn't safe with Gar. "She's my closest friend."

My voice was nothing more than a broken whisper. As if maybe if I spoke softly enough, the Elders would snatch the words from the air before they reached his ears.

He took a deep breath, one he exhaled as a gentle sigh. "I'm not very confident in your ability to choose friends if Calix is any indication."

My eyes burned into his. "He is no indication," I said, deathly calm.

Hrokr's eyes were wide, earnest. "I'd like to meet her."

Heart pounding against my ribs, I asked, "Why?"

"I'd like to ascertain for myself if she is unlike your Calix."

Deep hooks of cold sunk into my chest like frozen talons. "I've had enough breakfast, thank you."

I was going to puke—or claw my skin from my bones.

I made a mistake.

I admitted to Sagira's existence, and now Hrokr was going to find her. He was going to hurt her. If he judged her as quickly and as finally as he judged Calix, there was no hope for her. My fingers were shaking, my palms full of sweat.

I needed him to go—before I puked all over the table.

Shooting to my feet, I mumbled, "Go."

Hrokr stood, tension filling his shoulders. "Thea, wait—"

"Please go," I said, hating the broken hitch in my voice.

I was not above begging, groveling, falling on my knees—

Not for myself—

But for my Sage.

He watched me, thousands of emotions flashing across his face. Anger, distrust, sorrow, something akin to regret. "Thea, I'm not going to—"

"*Please.*"

And then he was gone.

Vanishing, as he does, into nothing more than whispers of smoke twirling through the air.

My knees barely hit the floor before all the contents of my stomach came back up.

I had to get out of here.

CHAPTER FIVE

LUCKY

Three days passed, and Hrokr did not visit me again.

Gyda—unsupervised—collected me for baths. Nameless attendants wore iron courage as they opened my cell door, leaving me my meals.

I was a perfect, docile prisoner.

I didn't want to think about why it was that Hrokr was gone. I didn't want to think about him giving up on my freedom, of keeping me as a regular prisoner. Even worse, I didn't want to think about him making the trek to Oxcroft to collect Sage.

I was painfully aware that Hrokr *not* finding her could be just as lethal.

I thought, I planned, I dreamed, and withered.

At dinnertime, a tall, thin man pushed open the gold gate of my prison. He wore the same black Valencian cloak I'd grown accustomed to seeing. Dark ringlets fell to his shoulders, and his umber cheeks were stained a heady red from the cold.

"Just bringing dinner," he said with a small smile.

"Where has Hrokr been?" I asked, forcing a sad smile of my own.

He dragged yellow eyes across my form. "*Lord* Hrokr is away on business."

My heart sank. "On business where?"

A curling of his full lip. "I'm not sure he would approve of my disclosing his work with a prisoner."

Fair.

"Alright," I said meekly. "I'm sorry."

He huffed a noncommital acceptance as he set my dinner on the table and turned back toward the door.

Trying to slow my racing heart, I took a step toward him.

He stiffened but didn't turn. If he worked for Hrokr, he was trained—intelligent. He knew he shouldn't bare his back to an enemy, but perhaps he thought pulling a defensive stance would only escalate what might be nothing.

His mistake.

I would have felt guilty—would have, if I weren't doing this only to protect Sage.

I moved fast, slinging my arms around his neck and squeezing. It was hard with the height difference, but I had the advantage of the first strike. He fought hard, clawing at my bare arms and throwing a kick back into my legs. I only hissed through the pain and squeezed harder.

It took far longer than I hoped—long enough for him to project this to someone if he had the ability—before his struggling eased, and he went limp in my arms. I lowered him to the floor slowly, watching intently for any sign of movement. He was down.

But I had no idea how long he'd stay that way.

I knew I was acting rashly, but what other options did I have? Hrokr was away, and I didn't know when I would be given this opportunity again.

I had to go.

I should have stripped the guard and worn his uniform, but I wasn't confident I had the time. His uniform was solid black, and my current clothes were fairly similar. I pulled the cloak from his shoulders and draped it around my own, pulling the cowl up over my head.

Disarming him, I found a measly two daggers.

Slipping them into my pockets, I ran.

And stopped immediately.

Standing in the middle of the hall—not three feet from me—was Gyda.

She didn't look surprised or scared. She looked only angry—disapproving even. Grandmotherly hands were planted on her hips, her full lips pursed as if I had spilled wine on her favorite rug. Like this was nothing more than a child's fit.

We locked eyes, and I whispered the only thing I could. "He's not dead."

And then I was sprinting past her, trying to remember enough of Castle Habrem to get me *out*.

Though I had spent many months stalking places I was not supposed to be, this was by far the most terrifying. I was in an entire Hall full of enemies, an entire Hall likely full of projectors.

I was one wrong move—one wrong *breath*—away from death.

I moved through the wide, ivory hall, thankful to the Elders it was empty. But my footsteps sounded like thunder against the tile, and I feared it was only a matter of time before I was discovered.

After all, Gyda would tell someone.

But by some immeasurable mercy, my first turn put me in the entrance hall of Castle Habrem.

Running right out the front door wasn't the stealthiest move, but I was out of options.

I felt so small, dwarfed by the massive doors. They towered above me, nearly thirty feet tall. I pushed one open and slipped through, pulling it shut behind me.

Before me, the steps cascaded down, blinding beneath the orange glow of the setting sun. The spread of the city swelled out before me, pulsing with vibrancy and life.

If I could just get away from this castle and into the city, I could get away.

I knew it.

I took my first step, and stumbled as something moved in my periphery.

"Miss?" a guard asked, drawing my gaze to the right.

I turned slowly, cataloging the grounds around me. Everything was just as beautiful as it had been the last time I'd seen it, but it was nearly empty. Only two guards—one to my left, one to my right—stood by the doors.

"Yes?" I asked, facing him. I shrunk back into my cowl, praying that Hrokr had enough visitors that I could get away without trouble.

"Should I prepare a carriage?" he asked. He was young—at least he appeared to be—but had shrewd, green eyes and black hair that fell to his shoulders. He leaned in, squinting into the darkness of my cloak. Before I even had a moment to respond, realization dawned on his face.

I didn't give him the chance. I spun on my heel and launched myself down the steps, running blindly for the city. The guards behind me were shouting, but I still heard only two sets of steps.

I ran straight down the steps, nearly jumping to take them two at a time.

A sudden, wild, *searing* pain erupted in my thigh. I nearly buckled beneath it but managed to steady my stride.

The dagger tip Hrokr had healed within me was going to get me killed.

If I could just reach the city, if I could just find somewhere to *hide*—

But charging straight out of the valley city were four guards.

I twisted to the right, not knowing where I was going, only knowing I had to get away.

To the right spread more of Castle Habrem. And behind it, the mountains were far too close.

I hissed under my breath and whirled, ready to fight.

The two guards from the castle were hot on my heels, and I barely had a chance to spin out of the reach of the black-haired man. The other had his cowl pulled tight around his head, but I could see the rage in his shadowed eyes.

He reached for me, hand outstretched and vulnerable. I sucked in a sharp breath and grabbed his forearm. I ripped him forward, pulling and twisting until I had his arm pinned behind his back.

I applied pressure until I heard the pop of his shoulder slipping out of its socket. He howled in pain as I shoved him face-first into the grass.

Just in time for the black-haired guard to grab a fistful of my hair. I shrieked, instinctually reaching for my head as the searing pain of a dagger slammed into my gut.

He was grinning when he ripped the blade out and dropped it, only to bury his icy fingers into the wound. I screamed and my vision swam as something cold and oily overwhelmed my senses and throbbed around the wound.

I recovered enough to jab at his face. I went for the eyes, grimacing as one finger slammed into his right eye. He roared, releasing me to clutch his face. Red blood poured through his thick fingers.

The footsteps of the other guards were coming quickly. I palmed a dagger and readied my shoulders.

I hadn't wanted to kill today. I knew my recapture was not only possible, but likely, and I didn't want to give Hrokr any more of a reason to want me dead.

But I wasn't ready to die today, and blood was pouring readily from my stomach. I tried to heal it, but was struggling to stitch the wound together. I needed to get out of here *now*.

I felt a hand on my shoulder and lunged, burying my blade to its hilt in my attacker's stomach. He didn't so much as grunt, and my eyes flew up to meet—

Maddox.

His free hand gripped my wrist so hard I thought it might shatter bone as he ripped it away. The knife pulled out of his stomach, along with a stream of blood. He squeezed my wrist until the dagger fell harmlessly to the grass.

Up close, he was much larger than I remembered. He towered over me, his fingers overlapping around my wrist. The orange of his iris only made him look more threatening.

"Let me go!" I shrieked, kicking and pulling against him.

I managed to gain a few inches and his eyes went wide. *"Woah,* you're strong," he hissed, ripping me back to him.

My panicked eyes looked around to prepare for the rest of the guards, but they were all standing down. They didn't feel the need to do anything with their commander present.

He hauled me against his chest, and I bared my teeth, ready to tear into his neck if need be.

"Woah, *woah,*" he shouted, giving me room to pull away. "Put your fangs away, sunshine."

I scowled, jerking against his hold hard enough to let my wrist snap if he kept it up. I'd take the pain if it set me free.

"Are you going to quit or not?" he grumbled. And—more than anything—he looked... *irritated.*

As if I were some errant pet that he had better things to do than fetch.

"What do you think?" I hissed, spitting at his feet.

"Halls," he muttered. "Ciro!"

Ciro stepped out from behind me—when had he even gotten there?

Strong, cold hands grabbed my wrists, pulling me out of Maddox's grip. Ciro held my arms behind my back, securing them with rough binding. I struggled against the tether, but it was no use. I was tied well.

He released me, and I stumbled forward. Maddox stepped away, fully willing to let me fall on my face. I scowled at him after I steadied my footing, but he only smirked.

"Up you come," he chuckled, reaching for me. I jerked back, but Ciro's hands gripped my upper arms, holding me in place. Maddox swooped down and threw me over his shoulder.

My head bounced against his back as he marched me toward Castle Habrem, the wound in my stomach aching so fiercely my vision began to blur. If he felt my blood seeping into his shoulder, he did not comment on it.

Ciro fell in step beside Maddox, and I twisted to meet his eyes. They were empty and cold. Aloof. He looked away, appearing almost bored.

"Just a few minutes," he said softly.

"What?" I snapped, fighting Maddox's grip on me.

They ignored me, likely projecting to one another. I wiggled again, though my stomach begged me to be still.

"Would you quit?" Maddox grumbled. "You do understand that if you manage to get free you're only going to fall, right? And then I'll just scoop you right back up."

Rage filled me. *Being carted around like some sour child.* "Why bother with all the fanfare?" I hissed. "Hrokr's just going to kill me, isn't he?"

"If we're lucky," Ciro said under his breath.

I shook beneath the force of Maddox's laughter. "Halls, Ciro, you're so *mean.*"

Ciro rolled his eyes.

All too soon, we were back before the familiar bars of my cell. Ciro held them open while Maddox walked me through. Ciro cut the bindings on my wrist, and Maddox dropped me unceremoniously on my bed.

I swallowed the scream of pain as my stomach began pouring fresh blood.

But the two males didn't even spare me a parting glance before they locked the bars behind them and left me all alone.

CHAPTER SIX

GUILT AND MIRRORS

I n their absence, I forced myself to my feet and stumbled over to the table.

The pain in my leg had settled into a solid ache, though it wasn't half as bad as the agony tearing through the wound in my stomach. I peeled my blood-soaked shirt up, trying to get a better look.

Mangled and jagged.

My stomach turned.

I tried again to muster the healing magic within me, but the flesh would not stitch. Sweat as cold as bitter panic beaded against my forehead, running down my temples in defeated rivulets.

I tried to brush away the rapidly crusting blood to see better, but even the gentle swipe of my fingers nearly sent me to my knees. My flesh burned.

Infected so fast?

I tried to heal it again, and a sharp dizziness slammed through me. I stumbled, barely catching myself against the iron table.

Poison. There was *poison—*

I took a breath—one that went nowhere. A streak of terror barreled through me, cutting off every other thought.

My throat tightened as angry tears filled my eyes. I blinked against them, trying in vain to steady my shattered breathing.

When I finally regained some modicum of calm, I prodded the flesh again, wincing as pain speared through me.

"Taking the easy way out?" A cool, sardonic voice asked.

My eyes flashed up to find Hrokr in my cell, having materialized out of nowhere.

"What do you want?" I snapped, ripping my bloody shirt down to cover the wound.

"Answer me."

"What?"

"Have you decided to take the easy way out?" he asked, gesturing to my bloody abdomen.

"Are you hoping that I do?" I challenged.

He sighed, pinching the bridge of his nose. "I'm simply trying to understand why you've not healed your wound."

I said nothing, and his eyes darkened. A muscle feathered in his jaw, something dark and wild churning deep within his gaze. He took a step toward me, and I promptly took a step back.

Another step—another retreat.

My back soon hit the wall, but still he strode for me. Something unhinged, something full of *rage* shone in his eyes. But his steps were calm—measured—as if he had himself on a tight leash.

I had enough wisdom to feel fear. It slipped down my spine, wrapped itself around my bones. This face was the face of the Lord of the North, of the cold and vengeful man the world feared.

And he was livid.

I was caged by his presence, able to see nothing but the anger in his too-bright eyes, the steady rise and fall of his chest.

"Let me see it," he said softly.

I tried to pull away, but there was nowhere to go. His fingers were steady as he reached a hand toward me. His touch was gentle as he lifted the hem of my shirt, exposing the mass of tangled flesh and muscle already sporting the dark tendrils of poison.

Hrokr's fingers brushed against my skin, and I sucked in a shrill breath.

His eyes flicked to mine.

The moment was heavy, terrifying. "Who did this to you?"

I said nothing, shaking my head numbly.

He touched me again, fingers feeling suddenly cold as he pulled the poison from my flesh. Blissful relief flowed through me, and I would have sagged against the wall if it weren't for his touch against my skin.

"You didn't kill anyone," he said quietly.

"No."

"Why?"

I didn't have an answer for him, not really. So I said, "I relieved him of one eye."

His fingers stilled. "Good."

"You're not angry," I said, surprised.

His hands resumed their work. "Believe me, I am *very* angry."

I waited, silent.

"He'll be dead by nightfall."

"Why?" I blurted.

"My men are not to harm you," he murmured.

His hands moved to my waist, pulling the hem of my shirt back into place.

I don't know what spurred me to say it, why I would defend the man who'd hurt me. Perhaps it was only confusion, but I whispered, "He did only what he should have."

Hrokr's eyes were sharp with rage. His scent suddenly deepened, all-encompassing this close to him. I scented rain and lavender and something else. Something old.

Something ancient.

Primal.

"He disobeyed my orders."

"But, I was his enemy. I was—"

"My orders," he interrupted smoothly, "are *not* to be disobeyed."

As much as these words were spoken in my defense, I heard them also a warning I should heed.

As I stared, he took a measured step away from me. He spun on his heel and strode toward the door.

"Wait," I called out, taking a step forward.

He froze. Hrokr slowly turned his head over one shoulder. "Yes?"

"Where are you going?" I asked.

A ghost of a smile flashed across his face, but it was gone in a moment. "I'll send Gyda for you. I'll be back later tonight."

Then he vanished.

And I was left wondering what, exactly, was happening.

Gyda was calm and collected—as always—when she appeared a few moments later.

She clucked her tongue at me. "Must you always make a mess of yourself?"

I scowled at her. "You don't seem that surprised," I muttered. "It makes me think maybe all Hrokr's prisoners behave the same way."

She laughed out loud, gesturing me down the hall toward the baths. "Lord Hrokr does not keep prisoners."

I stopped walking. "But—"

"Hurry up," she hissed, grabbing me by the arm. I was too dazed to do anything but allow it.

"What do you mean he doesn't keep prisoners? He has cells."

"He has *a* cell. And it was unfurnished until your arrival."

I narrowed my eyes at her, finding myself enough to rip my arm away. "You expect me to believe I'm his first prisoner?"

She laughed again—a loud, boisterous sound. "I guess I should say the cell is not normally used for such gentle holding."

"What's it used for?" I asked.

But immediately, I knew the answer. Gyda didn't reply.

Torture.

"Why is it different for me?" I asked.

"Ask Lord Hrokr."

"I'm asking you," I hissed.

"And I'm telling you," she said, turning to narrow her eyes at me, "to ask Lord Hrokr."

I rolled my eyes, and settled into an angry silence.

When we entered the bathing chamber, I expected more of the same. And it was, to an extent. But she filled the pool with extra powders and liquids, and spent nearly three times as usual washing my hair.

The water around my body turned a cloudy red, and I grimaced at all the blood sloughing off me.

Gyda finished with my hair and plucked one of my hands up out of the water. She scrubbed and scraped at me, dragging caked blood out from beneath my fingernails. I allowed it, until I saw her reach for a small, black bottle.

I jerked my hand out of her grasp. "Is this really necessary?"

"Yes," she hissed, ripping my hand back toward her.

"Why?"

She wasted no time, smoothing black polish across my nails and summoning a cold wind to dry them.

"You have plans tonight."

My heart tripped in my chest, dread and confusion crashing over me in a solid wave.

"And these plans require me to be plucked and pruned?" I griped.

She rolled her eyes. "They do. If you'd like to fit in at all."

I pulled against her, but her grip was like iron. "I have no desire to fit in with you people. I want to go *home.*"

"Then be good," she snapped.

And despite the crass delivery, those words were the first that brought me any ray of hope.

I stood in front of the vanity mirror, shaking my head.

Gyda chuckled softly. "Suck it up, darling."

I had no problem with the attire—not at all. That was exactly what terrified me. *Horrified* me. I felt something akin to happiness blooming inside of me, and I did my best to tamp it down.

Because quick on the heels of that happiness, was a guilt so raw and wretched that it coiled nausea within me.

Was I truly so vain?

I brought my fingers up, watching the black shine of the polish glinting off the light as I dragged my fingers through my pin-straight hair. I had never seen my hair so straight.

The rich brown framed my face and fell down my back, bringing out the freckles dusted across my tan skin. My eyes looked wide, glimmering. The lightest lining of kohl was setting against my eyes, and Gyda had used a black cream and brush to darken my lashes.

I'd never had much exposure to cosmetics, but I now understood why girls back home made sacrifices to afford them. I looked beautiful—

And I hated the way it made me feel.

How angry are you?

Was I angry enough?

The dress Gyda had draped me in was ornate and glittering. The breast was intricately stitched, golden thread wound through navy fabric. It was tight at the waist, but a slit up the thigh would allow me to move freely.

Sage was in danger. Mellian and Alek had targets on their backs. Gar was still loose, still able to bring harm to those around him.

The thoughts sobered me, spinning me back toward Gyda with tight lips.

"What kind of plans do I have tonight?" I asked, reaching down to adjust the strap on my heels. Even my toes matched my fingernails; Gyda had spared no extravagance.

"Nothing too ornate," she said, leading me back toward my cell.

I cocked a brow at her back. "Then why all of this?"

Her delicate shoulders rose and fell with an easy shrug. "Lord Hrokr likes things to be pretty. His guests are no exceptions."

"His *guests*?" I repeated, laughing harshly. "I would hardly consider myself a guest."

She spun on me, stopping my steps short. "Not tonight," she said, voice tired. "I know you hate him, and I am old enough to understand you likely believe you have reason to. But he has shown you mercy. Tonight he will extend *kindness*. I would suggest you play nice and bite your tongue. He wants you out of that cell just as badly as you want to be gone."

"How can you even know that?" I snapped.

She turned around and continued up the stairs. "If not, he would have slit your throat by now."

CHAPTER SEVEN

MURDER AND CROWS

Gyda deposited me back in my room, and I was left to pace and wonder what I'd gotten myself into.

Maybe Gyda was right, and I should take her advice. Play nice, be friendly and answer questions so Hrokr would let me go.

But I didn't believe even for a moment it could be that easy.

Despite him healing me, despite him instructing his people not to harm me—

He wanted me only as a weapon to wield.

I paced as the thoughts nipped at me, doing my best to avoid chewing the polish off my nails.

Before I had enough time to truly descend into panic, smooth footsteps came strolling down the hall.

I stilled immediately, my spine tightening.

Hrokr appeared on the other side of the bars, looking as collected as ever.

He was in his finery tonight. Diamonds and chains dripped from his ears, rings embraced his fingers.

A button-down shirt in the deepest blue I'd ever seen clung to his frame, sleeves rolled up his forearms. It was tucked loosely into tight black plants, which were in turn tucked into knee-high, shimmering boots.

It wasn't fair how beautiful he was.

No one so wretched should be allowed.

He vanished into smoke only to reappear a few feet from me. I stumbled back a step, causing his lips to split into a brilliant, ornery grin.

"Nervous?"

I narrowed my eyes.

He rolled his own, but his easy smile remained. "I have a proposition, though it appears Gyda may have beaten me to it," he said, waving a hand at me.

"She didn't tell me anything."

He slid a hand into one pocket. "Well, I won't keep you waiting, then. Come—dine and dance with me tonight. No guards, no bindings. I will ask that you remain by my side since I know how much you love to run off," he said, a smile in his eyes. "I plan to show you that my Hall is not entirely wretched, in the hopes you will let me help you. I want to know who sent you after me. I am willing to offer amnesty to both you and your friend should you agree to my terms."

I wasn't sure I believed him, but I also knew I had no other choices. Perhaps I could feel him out for the night, see for myself if I could trust him *just* enough to let me go.

I raked my eyes over him again. He carried no weapons I could see, but—truth be told—he didn't need them. Faint scars peppered the ivory skin of his hands. His chest and shoulders were broad, defined by years, decades, *centuries* of training.

He was thoroughbred.

He was a *killer*. I had seen him snap a man's neck with no remorse.

But he wasn't letting me out without me giving him something, I knew that by now. I was terrified to risk Sage's life, but staying here and doing nothing was just as much a risk to her.

When I again dragged my gaze to his face, a comfortable smirk sat on his lips.

"My deal," he continued once he realized I wasn't going to respond, "is simple. Accompany me tonight. Give me the night to show you Valencia in all her glory. Tomorrow you will meet me in my office, and we will talk about whatever little misunderstanding has come between us."

"Misunderstanding?" I repeated, incredulous. "You killed my—"

He held up a hand. "Not tonight, Thea."

"Do *not* interrupt me," I snapped. Hrokr may be more pleasant on the surface than I had expected him to be, but I hadn't forgotten.

Images pelted me.

A knife in my thigh. Compulsion in my thoughts. A poison brand inked on my flesh. Hrokr's long fingers cradling Calix's face. A body on the floor.

His eyes widened with surprise, but he slowly grinned. "My apologies."

I watched him carefully, but his smile was pure.

"We can be friends," he said. "Just for one night. If you'd like to go back to hating me in the morning, that will be your choice. I have allowed you the opportunity to explain your actions. I would hope you would have the respect to offer me the same."

He held his hand out in invitation. "Accept my offer. I will bring you to the throne room tonight, and you will vow to be present tomorrow morning."

I eyed his outstretched palm. "And if I don't come tomorrow?"

He wiggled his fingers. "If you shake my hand, you won't have a choice."

"I'm sorry?" My eyes flashed to his.

"You won't be able to leave," he said. "You know how these things work, darling. Deals, bargains, promises."

"And you'd take me on my word?"

His brow furrowed now. "Are you serious?"

"Yes?"

"Have you never done this before?"

"What are you talking about?" I asked.

He chuckled softly. "Be careful of any deals you make in this world, Thea. They are unbreakable."

I remembered our teachers at school telling us not to trust Fae bargains, but I never believed them.

"What happens if I break it?"

"You can't," he said simply. "With the correct magic, the Elders involve themselves. They'll ensure you keep your vow or die trying."

I didn't like the idea of that.

"Maybe we should rely on old-fashioned honesty then," I said, a knot forming in my stomach.

Hrokr laughed. "Very well, Thea. But please be nice tonight."

He offered me his arm then, and I reluctantly took it. "What kind of event is this?" I asked.

He grinned. "Only our nightly festivities."

He led me through the bars of my prison, and immediately the roar of voices floated down the hall. I looked back at the bars, brow furrowed.

Hrokr followed my eyes, chuckling. "The cell is soundproofed."

"But I can hear it when you talk to me through the bars."

He shrugged. "Ether is a strange thing."

We continued in silence, though the music and laughter grew louder as we neared the entrance hall.

The room was not as barren as it had been when I made my daring escape earlier today. It reminded me now of the first time I'd been in the Hall, tightly packed with ostentatious bodies. Orchestral music poured down from the grand staircase at the far end of the hall. The mezzanine above the glittering fountain offered the sound of clinking crystal and dull laughter.

Most of the attendees were Gentry Fae.

But not all.

I spied the mortal curve of human ears, something that nearly had my heels stumbling beneath me.

Gar once told me that Apheadia was the only Hall in which the mortal and immortal coexisted.

I supposed Gar had told me many things.

There were other creatures, too. Ones with sleek gills cut into their necks, animalistic men with proud horns, and women with serpentine features and flowers in their hair.

Perhaps the strangest sight was a young man near the end of the hall, preoccupied with re-fastening his tie. His skin was a cool brown, a color deepened by the creamy white suit he wore. Black hair hung to his shoulders, but it parted around strange ears.

Strange, because they were not quite human... and not quite Fae.

I wanted to stop and marvel at such an impossible sight, but we'd come close enough to the entrance that eyes were beginning to spot us.

Awed staring spread like wildfire, and we commanded every eye in the room before we even crossed the threshold.

I refused to wither beneath it.

Their love for Hrokr was obvious. Many watched him with open admiration, ogling the glory that was their ever-ornate lord.

Despite their enamored eyes, there was a feeling of trepidation in the air.

The attendees stared at me with open confusion, but many even cast fearful, concerned glances at Hrokr.

They must have known exactly who I was.

The Shadow of Judgement.

And he had cloaked her in a pretty dress and carted her out in front of them.

An audacious, cheeky move.

Hrokr leaned down, and I jerked as his nose brushed my ear. "I have a present for you."

I slid wary, cold eyes toward him, but he only grinned and tugged me along.

He met every stare with his easy smile, convincing his people I was no threat at all with only the curl of his lips.

I'd not yet decided if I was thankful or offended.

At least it got them out of our way. People stumbled back to avoid even the threat of being in Hrokr's path, so we made it through the crowded room quickly.

We ascended the glistening stairwell, and the sound of chatter quieted enough that the burbling fountain was audible. Upstairs, the crowd was looser. We were met with sharp-toothed smiles and feral, excited eyes.

These people were the ones who adored him.

My eyes scoured the space as we moved, trying to find the key players I knew he'd have present.

Almost immediately, I spied Fallon lounging in a green slip on an ivory chaise at the far left of the room.

Her eyes were shrewd and cold. Careful.

I held them long enough for her to look away.

Hrokr led me through the throne room, which was as ridiculously lavish as it had been the night of the Eclipse Fete. The crowd parted around us, daring not even to brush either of our shoulders.

His people truly awarded him the reverence of an Elder. My stomach twisted into knots.

He cut a path through the dancing bodies all the way to the balcony doors, thrown open to let the crisp night air in.

I slammed to a stop.

Hrokr stopped with me, allowing me to take it in on my own time.

I'd expected to see the spread of the valley city below, the stars drooping down like low-hanging fruit—a glittering blanket draped over the town. And while that was indeed the backdrop of the scene painted before me, it was the centerpiece that had my body frozen to the pale stones below.

A soldier's body hung from a smoothly braided rope swinging from a pole at the edge of the balcony. The body swayed, limp and dead. A small murder of crows pecked at the corpse, plucking out gory chunks of flesh. Valencian guard clothes adorned him, tattered in the places the crows had become too eager in their feast.

He had no eyes, but I remembered they were green.

He was the guard who poisoned me.

The eye I'd injured was still in the socket, but it was shattered and cratered in on itself. The other was missing wholly, complete with a bloody gash across the brow.

Someone had carved it out.

My gaze slid to Hrokr to find him grinning, a wicked gleam to his starlit eyes.

It's okay, love, he said softly, squeezing my arm. *You can smile, I know you want to.*

"Why?" I whispered instead.

You don't like it? he asked silently.

"Why?"

He shrugged, grinning that lopsided smile that showed one long fang. "I'll remind you that you gutted a *stranger*. You were practically bathing in her blood when I showed up."

I blinked as if maybe the sight before me would blend into a new one. "She deserved it."

"So did he," Hrokr said, cocking his head toward the body swaying in the wind.

"Is this supposed to bring me joy?" I croaked.

"It would bring *me* joy."

Then why me?

Because you're just as awful as him, Thea.

Just as awful.

"That's wretched."

Another shrug as he steered me back inside toward a far table. "No more wretched than stabbing someone while they actively beg you to stop."

The words—or perhaps being away from the crow-carved corpse—sobered me enough to snap, "Why do you sound impressed?"

I couldn't stop hearing Gar's words play in my head over and over again.

Just as awful.

A wicked grin. "Because I am."

"I could just as easily gut you."

He laughed out loud, reaching out to pop the crystal stopper out of a decanter. "I swear it by the Elders, Thea. I *genuinely* wish you would try. It's been far too long since I've had any fun."

I eyed him, raking my eyes from his loose curls to his shining black boots, scouring his body for any tells of vulnerability. "I'll remember that."

He twisted his head and winked before turning back to the crystal.

"Why'd you do it?" I asked him earnestly.

"I told you already. I run a tight ship. People do not disobey my orders and live."

"But I was attacking him."

"No," he said, turning to face me fully. His eyes were penetrating and—if I could believe it—honest. "You were trying to escape and you *ran*. He should have waited for Maddox and Ciro to get there."

I chewed on the inside of my cheek. "Maybe he thought Ciro and Maddox wouldn't be able to apprehend me on their own."

I wasn't sure why I was pushing. I didn't know what it was I was trying to get him to say, what exactly it was that I was accusing him of.

Hrokr pursed his lips, but they quivered.

"What?" I griped.

A laugh broke out, and he reached a scarred finger out to flick my nose. I shirked away, swatting at him. "Halls, Thea, you're so *cute.*" He turned away, shaking his head. "Oh, the two of them are going to get a kick out of that."

"You can't be serious," I blurted.

They were two of the most powerful Fae on Alynthia, but I was—well, me.

You're an arrogant little thing, he purred, pouring himself a shot of something clear.

"Because you're so humble."

He smiled, knocking back his shot. "I've earned the right to be what I am."

"What is that supposed to mean?" I asked, brows flying up.

He just shook his head, dismissing the words. "I am going to have so much fun with you, Thea."

I snorted—a sound more snide than humored—and turned away from him.

His hand snaked out and wrapped around my forearm. "Drink with me."

His fingers slid slowly against my skin, turning me back to face him.

"No."

"Come on," he chuckled. "I brought you down here to play. What are you even going to do all night? I plan to have a very nice evening."

"Enjoy your nice evening," I sneered. "Maybe I'll head back to my cell."

This was a mistake. He was parading corpses, parading *me*. I didn't have the time for this.

But what was I to do?

I couldn't run. I couldn't stay. Was my only option to become his puppet until he gave my rope enough slack for me to slip away?

Or was he only giving me enough rope to hang myself?

I should be soft, docile. I should be silent.

But I ripped my arm out of his grasp. "Is this what you want?" I hissed under my breath. "To flaunt me like some trinket?"

His eyes danced.

"You're free," he said calmly, making a show out of stepping back. "Stay in the room, Thea. I want my eyes on you."

I waited for the catch, but it never came.

He slipped into the crowd, swallowed by his people.

CHAPTER EIGHT

TAME

T he party was one of the stranger events I'd ever attended.

The music, the dancing, the foods—much of it was foreign to me.

And, on any other day, I might have cared. I might have wanted to learn the steps of the Northern dances, to study the strange chords the orchestra played, or to marvel at the fashion of a Hall so far from my home. I might have wanted to study the meticulous, ancient paintings adorning the slate walls, or marvel at the crystal chandelier high above our heads.

But I no longer had the time to appreciate such insignificant, beautiful things. I'd lost that privilege long ago.

I found myself wrapped in the arms of a nameless stranger—one who'd gotten a little too grabby during the last number.

He was beautiful. Disgustingly, ornately beautiful—outshone only by the Lord of the North himself.

He'd whispered his name in my ear, but I'd promptly forgotten it.

I didn't care to hear it again.

Piercing blue eyes stared at me, half-lidded with either lust or drink. His hands played at my waist, and his white-blond hair—damp with sweat—curled around his temples.

He didn't seem to mind that I'd only met his gaze a handful of times since this dance started ten minutes ago.

No, my eyes—and my smirk—were focused solely on Hrokr, who was currently sifting through the crowd like water. Though he was obviously the main focus of the entire night, I noticed something strange.

No one ever touched him.

Not even a brush of the shoulder.

His eyes split the crowd to focus solely on me.

I couldn't stop hearing Hrokr's voice, hearing *Gar's,* over and over again.

How angry are you?

Because you're just as awful as him, Thea.

Just as awful.

I wouldn't be what either of them wished me to be.

If I had to be a prisoner, then a prisoner I would be. But I would *not* be brought down to Hrokr's cruelty. I would not gloat over a corpse or allow myself to become a crown to be worn.

Probably for the first time in his miserably long life, someone else in a room commanded as much attention as he did. He had wanted me to be a lion on a chain.

These people knew to be afraid of me, but he thought he could cart me around, hold my leash, and I would be tame for him and him alone.

Wrong.

I knew it wasn't smart to antagonize him, but I couldn't help it. I didn't *want* to help it. So I would show his court that he was not special, that I was my own force of nature.

"Are you even listening to me?" the blond asked me, nose brushing the shell of my ear.

Hrokr's eyes narrowed from across the room.

"Hmm?" I asked, twisting to meet his eyes.

They were equal parts hungry and irritated. "I asked," he drawled, "do you want to get out of here?"

I fought the urge to peel my lips back from my teeth. Instead I plastered a sickly sweet smile on my lips. "And miss all the fun?"

His hands were rough on my hips. "I have a feeling we'd have more fun somewhere else."

I'd wanted to push Hrokr, but I wasn't about to crawl out of here with some strange faerie. "We are having fun here, aren't we?"

Blondie's eyes narrowed, and I took a step back. He crowded me. He released one of my hips to brush the back of his hand across my cheek. It was instantly snatched away—long, white, scar-flecked fingers wrapping around his wrist.

"May I cut in?" Hrokr asked, sickly polite. "Gordon." Hrokr tacked his name on as an afterthought, a mark of intimacy that made the thinly-veiled threat in his voice a little more real.

Gordon blanched, though not before I caught the flash of irritation in his eyes. "Of course, Lord Hrokr," he deferred.

Gordon's fingers grazed my waist as he stepped away.

He cast one last look over his shoulder before he was swallowed by the crowd.

I turned my eyes to Hrokr's, the stars in them burning bright against his pupil. "Are you having fun?" he asked flatly.

I grinned, though it was more of a baring of teeth. "Would you be upset if I was?"

The snark seemed to jolt him back into the present. His scowl melted into a loose smirk. "Not at all, love. I do hope you're enjoying yourself."

"I *was*."

Hrokr narrowed his eyes. Halls, it was easy for him to blow hot then cold then back again. "By all means, enjoy the best of my people," he said, waving a loose hand to encompass the room. "But *him?*"

I swallowed my grin. "What's wrong with him?"

"Gordon Balhorn?" he growled, as if I should have known the answer to my own question.

I shrugged. "He's beautiful."

A slight grimace.

I laughed out loud. I moved to step around him, brushing my fingers across his chest. "Don't be jealous, Hrokr. It doesn't suit a man of your age."

He let me get past him before I felt his breath on my ear. The hair at the back of my neck stood on end. "You don't want to dance with me?" he asked, ignoring my quip.

"Not particularly."

He sighed, the scent of rain washing over me. I turned back, expecting him to look crestfallen, or at least angry. But he was grinning that lopsided smile, one long fang exposed. "Do enjoy your night, Thea. You're welcome for saving you."

Somehow the words felt threatening.

Hrokr left.

Slunk off somewhere. Alone, I noted.

That surprised me, as not even his Council followed. He strode—chin up and shoulders back—out of the hall and down a corridor with no one trailing him.

My initial thought was: *run.*

Run and don't look back. Get out of this castle, get out of this city, get off of this Hall.

But a quick glance around the room confirmed that all members of the Cardinal Council were present, conspicuously *not* watching me. Which I knew meant they were watching me more closely than any of the attendees openly staring.

Ciro and Maddox were engaged in some kind of game, cards and half-full glasses before them at a low table.

Fallon was cleaning her nails with a dagger, lounging like a cat on an ivory chaise. A small, brown-haired girl sat cross-legged beside her, muttering something that looked admonishing. It was the same small girl I'd seen dragging Fallon away from me the night of the eclipse ball. She must have been the last member of the Council, Haizea.

I stayed as long as I could stomach it. I'd kept up this night of charades just to appease—or antagonize—Hrokr, but with him gone, I had no reason to be here. I knew better than to think I could just walk out the front doors of the castle, but as I moved toward the hall, no one moved to stop me.

I caught a few curious looks, but no one seemed inclined to follow me. Once in the hall, I began to move toward my cell, but something caused me to hesitate.

Perhaps I *could* just walk out the front door.

I wouldn't run, not again so soon. But maybe I could at least poke around, feel the night wind brushing across my skin.

The entrance lobby was teaming with people, just as rowdy as upstairs. And while everyone turned to watch me, no one said a word or made any attempt to stop me. I expected the party to spill out onto the grounds beyond, but when I pushed open the towering, white doors, I was greeted with silent midnight.

The air was perfect, a crisp breath blown across the sweat coating my skin. And for a few heartbeats, the world was still.

Until, "What happened to old-fashioned honesty?"

Hrokr, leaning against the wall, eyes closed.

For a long moment I considered returning to my cell in silence. But I said, "Have I lied about something?"

His eyes flashed open, and even in the heavy cover of night, they were obviously bloodshot. The dark circles beneath his eyes were stark in the bare night, his skin washed alabaster beneath shafts of ivory moonlight.

"You tell me," he said, pushing off of the castle wall. "I thought you weren't going to run tonight."

I was still as he took my measure, his eyes lazy as they cataloged the loose brown hair blowing across my chest and shoulders.

"Am I running?" I asked.

He stalked toward me, and I was frozen as he crowded the space around me. Instantly his smell of lavender and night-blooming flowers was all-encompassing. There was something different in it tonight, something sweet and cloying.

Every nerve inside of me was jerked into hyper-focus as he drew a gentle finger down my upper arm. "Aren't you?" he whispered.

My heart lurched into my throat, surprised gooseflesh drawn in the wake of his touch. "Are you sober?" I croaked.

His finger fell, but I did not dare move. He studied me, and I could not begin to chase the thoughts spiraling behind his eyes. Finally, he said, "Perhaps we should both retire for the night."

But I couldn't help the flick of my eyes to the open Hall behind him. Warm, swaying grass before the first notes of structure. A blanket of open skies and stars lying across the valley city.

"I'll catch you," he said.

I wasn't sure he would. Not in this state, with liquor and sweet smoke clouding his breath. With drunk eyes and liberal hands.

I lunged.

With every ounce of speed and strength I possessed, I threw myself down the steps. Foolish, *foolish,* but a chance.

I made it to the last step before Hrokr materialized before me. I jerked to a stop, but when I tried to spin past him, his fingers locked like a vice around my wrist.

His eyes were brighter than the stars we stood beneath, wild with something I wasn't sure was pleasure or anger. "I thought you weren't running."

"I thought it had been far too long since you'd had any fun," I parroted.

His nostrils flared as his fingers tensed against my skin. But he had no response other than, "Why are you favoring your left leg?"

Immediate heat nipped at me. I tried to pull away, but he only held me tighter.

"Let me go," I hissed.

"What's wrong with your leg, Thea?"

I didn't like the way he spoke my name, here beneath the open world, here shrouded in the intimacy of heavy nightfall.

"You should know," I said darkly, ripping my hand away so sharply that he ceded.

Realization dawned in his dark eyes. "You're a healer," he said softly.

My lips peeled back, baring my teeth. "It's in my *bone.* "

I turned away, content to march back to my cell, but he appeared before me. I stumbled back a step, but he caught me. "Let me heal it," he said.

No.

The world very nearly tumbled from my lips. I didn't want his help or his mercy. I wanted to stomp my foot like an errant child, to wear my wounds with the pride I'd earned receiving them.

But that was foolish.

"Why?" I asked instead.

His brow furrowed, as if he wasn't quite sure himself. "It's only polite, I suppose."

Silence fell between us, broken only by the dull roar of conversation leaking from the castle.

Beyond words—beyond wanting to find them—I nodded.

His movements were slow and hesitant, but Hrokr did indeed sink to his knees before me. He met my eyes, and I immediately looked away.

His fingers were gentle as they found the long scar he'd carved into me. I jerked slightly as a small burst of pain cut me.

"I'm sorry," he whispered, but the pain was gone before his words cleared his lips. I glanced down in time to see him lick my blood from his thumb, a troubled expression carving his features.

When he reached for me a second time, I rasped, "What's wrong?"

It was perhaps the answering of a different question, but he said, "I can remove most of the scar."

"Don't," I said, taking a step away from him.

Because I needed to remember.

I *wanted* to remember.

I wanted to see my maimed flesh and remember what he'd done to me. I wanted to remember that he was not a gentle ghost in the middle of a valley night. I wanted to remember that he was a lord of rage and cruelty who had cut my flesh and sewn me back together like a split doll.

His eyes were dark as he met my gaze, as if the stars within them had banked. "Go to bed, Thea," he said quietly. "Lock your door behind you."

I opened my lips—to say what, I wasn't sure. But I never got the chance. He disappeared, becoming only a rift of smoke the night greedily swallowed.

My eyes cast up to the second floor balcony, empty but for a singular form that looked like Maddox. But after a blink, I wondered if I imagined it. The balcony was empty.

I wasn't sure what it said about me that I obeyed Hrokr's orders.

CHAPTER NINE

GROUNDS OF MEMORY

The sunlight was bright, and I could feel its heat trying to permeate my skin. But there was nothing it could do against the chill that seemed to always cling to the grounds.

I sat in a large, battered pavilion, staring out across the ruins of some once-great city. The homes looked like they'd once been warm and cozy, but now they housed only ghosts. Burn marks and smears of soot clung to their stone walls, wooden structures long rotted away and reclaimed by the dying ground. Shattered glass and eroded stone still littered the cobbled streets.

The sunlight refracted in brilliant gold and rainbows off the packed snow, blinding me.

I shivered, still in my grey nightclothes, and wrapped my arms around my knees. My toes were submerged in the snow, freezing them beyond feeling.

I wanted to go inside, to find somewhere warm. But I didn't even know where I was, much less where to go.

"Oh! There you are, Lady Starsea!"

My head whipped toward the voice, finding Letti waddling toward me, making tiny footprints in the snow. The locks of her brown hair blew wildly beneath her cap, and her little mushroom body shook violently in the cold.

I reached for her as she got closer, scooping her into my hands. My fingers were numb with cold, but I had to believe my grasp was at least warmer than the icy ground.

"Letti?" I said. "What's going on?"

"It's been so long," she replied, smiling at me. "You made it to Valencia."

I frowned. "I guess so. I'm being held prisoner there."

She shrugged her little shoulders, as if the *why* was of no importance. "You can save us all, now."

I shook my head. "Things weren't what they seemed."

She finally seemed to catch up to my mood. "What has happened, Lady Starsea?"

So much had happened since I'd last seen her. "I found my family, but my Momma was killed." A shadow of grief passed across her eyes, but I continued on. "My brother and sister are possibly safe, but I know nothing of Sage's fate. Gar betrayed me, Letti. He was the one who killed my mom. He goes by the name Silas, and—"

I broke off when she made a choked noise of horror. "Silas?"

I tried to ignore the pain that flared inside of my chest. "Yes."

"I am so sorry, my lady."

It was only a simple statement of sympathy, but my chest felt like it was being cleaved open from the inside out. "Thank you," I choked out.

"But you are in Valencia now," she said. "You can continue your mission. You can save the world."

I felt my face scrunch in frustration. "I don't see how I can save anything, even myself. I'm stuck behind bars, and—"

She stumbled suddenly, looking surprised. I caught her, pulling her closer to me. "Are you okay?"

"Something's happening," she murmured. She looked around, as if she could see things I could not. Her eyes flashed to my own. "I will see you again, Lady Starsea."

"But—"

She was gone. And *I* was gone. Between one blink and the next, I was transported between worlds. I traded the glaring sun and snow for the white, stone ceiling of my cell in Castle Habrem, dim with the muted light from the hall. My head spun from the sudden change.

What a dream.

I rose, rubbing sleep from my eyes.

Before I even had a chance to gather my bearings, footsteps sounded near the table. Hrokr.

"What are you—"

"What are you doing, Thea?" he growled, coming right up to me. His chest rose and fell erratically, his cheeks pinked with his anger.

All visage to a tipsy, brooding wraith long lost.

"*What?*"

He crowded me, leaning down to come nearly nose-to-nose with me. I began to pull away, but he snatched my wrist up and held me in place.

His hair was mussed, no jewelry adorning him. His clothes were black, plain, and soft. Had he come straight from his bed?

"Did you really think you could get away with that? Are you that ignorant?" he barked, his grip tightening on my wrist.

I ripped my arm free, baring my teeth. "I don't know what you're talking about," I snarled. "Keep your hands off of me."

Hrokr was feral. He was shaking, very barely holding himself in check. "Who did you bring here?"

"*What?*"

His lips peeled back from his teeth, showcasing fangs that were deathly sharp.

"I've been locked in this cell, in case you've forgotten," I snapped. "I didn't bring anyone here."

"Do not be coy with me, Thea. Did you think it wouldn't disturb the wards? *Who is walking in your dreams?*"

The air was sucked from my lungs. Walking in my dreams?

Letti.

But there was no way. She was just a dream, a figment of my warped imagination.

My silence only angered Hrokr more. He leaned forward again, grabbing onto my arm to haul me closer to him.

Before I gave myself a chance to consider the repercussions, I drew my hand back and slapped him across the face. The sound echoed through the small space.

His eyes went wide, his mouth parted in shock. He released my arm to gently touch his face where I had struck it. He worked his jaw, a muscle feathering in his cheek.

And the rage in his eyes could have leveled Alynthia herself.

A lick of reason flashed through me. One that had me blurting, "They're just dreams."

He rose to his full height and looked down on me, every inch the cold destroyer I knew him to be. He cast his eyes—eyes that were suddenly brighter than I remembered—away from me, even turning his back to compose himself.

The back he turned to me was rigid and strained. When his hand fell away from his face, the very last words I expected to hear were, "I'm sorry for grabbing you."

I studied his form as he slowly turned back to face me. "I shouldn't have struck you."

Silence deepened the corners of the room. After a long moment, he said, "Who is it?"

"I do not know who is visiting my dreams," I said, pulling my knees to my chest.

He nodded gently, his rage visibly ebbing. "You don't see them?"

"I don't know her," I admitted, and I wondered why I was even telling him the truth. "She has visited me once before. I didn't know about dream-walking. I thought they were only dreams."

His brow furrowed as he ran a hand through his ebony curls. "What does she want?"

"I—" I hesitated. "I don't know."

Save us all.

But what did that mean, really?

Hrokr regarded me carefully. "Thea, I would like to believe that—recent events aside—we have come into some semblance of peace."

"Alright," I drawled hesitantly.

"If you are leading people here, people to save you..." He took a breath. "They will not survive a raid on the Hall. You understand that, right?"

His tone was gentle, but the threat beneath them was very real.

"No one is coming to rescue me," I whispered. I hated that I sounded as pitiful as I did. I pulled my knees farther into my chest.

He was quiet for a long moment before he said, "Thea, I do not wish to be your captor." His voice was soft, gentle.

I met his eyes. "Then let me go."

He showed no reaction to the statement, as if he had expected it. "You killed many of my men," he said. "You slaughtered one of my guards. I am more than willing to pardon you, but you have to give me *something.*"

"What do you want?" I asked.

"Just tell me why."

I thought again of Sage, and prayed she still lived. I couldn't give Hrokr information that could potentially hurt her. I still wasn't sure Gar wasn't in Hrokr's employ. Though, the longer I stayed here, the more the theory began to dissolve. I hadn't encountered any slaves here, though perhaps Hrokr just didn't keep them at Castle Habrem. But why wouldn't he? And Hrokr hadn't been angry that I'd killed his guard.

"Tell me what you're thinking," he murmured.

I shook my head, my fingers curving tightly into the pants of my sleeping clothes. "My friend—she is in danger, and I need to go to her."

He did not look surprised by my words. In fact, his face only softened further. "I've already told you I will spare your friend."

I cut baleful eyes in his direction. "Forgive me if I'd figured you chose to renege on your kindness."

He flinched, brows high. "Why would you think that?"

I said nothing, and we sat in silence for a long moment.

"Let me go," I repeated.

He took a deep breath, his chest swelling with the movement. He tilted his head back, as if the stars in his eyes could see the ones swirling above Castle Habrem. "Alright."

My heart jumped and faltered in my chest. But—it couldn't be that easy, not with Hrokr. "Alright?"

He shifted his gaze to mine, looking at me from beneath long, dark lashes. "Is that not what you wanted to hear?"

"But—why?"

He perched himself on the edge of my bed. "You can go, for today only. I want you home by midnight."

Hope and hopelessness vied for dominance within me. "That's absurd. You know I can't even get to the other end of this Hall by midnight."

He chuckled, a light and easy sound. "I'd hardly be so wretched a host as to make you trek across the Halls," he said. "You can voidstep there; you'll end up fairly close to where you need to be."

I stared at him. "And if I don't come back?"

He reached forward slowly, unwrapping my fingers from their death-grip on my legs. He held his hand to mine, palms touching and fingers sliding against one another to their full lengths. "You will not have a choice," he said softly, watching the glide of my fingers against his.

"A bargain."

"A bargain," he echoed. When I was silent long enough that he interpreted it as consent, he said, "What is your last name?"

I fought against the stiffening of my muscles. "Why?"

He shrugged, a gesture that looked strangely delicate on his honed body. "Bargains are normally bound with first and last name."

"I don't have one," I lied.

He watched me carefully. "Unusual," he finally said, "but not unheard of."

"What is your last name?"

71

He grinned, though it was edged with something dark. "I suppose it does not matter, as our vow will be sealed with only our first names."

I blew out a long breath. "I suppose so."

"Thea, I propose to you a bargain of deference of leave from your state as my captive. You will be released and allowed to travel to Vanadey, the Hall of the Elements. You will return to me or to The Northern Hall of Valencia by the next midnight. You will vow to speak to me tomorrow morning, providing information not previously disclosed. Do you agree?"

I considered it—as if I had a choice. It was obvious he was trained in the art of bargains and deals and brokerings. His choice of words was quite specific. *The next midnight, providing information not previously disclosed.* But—he had only said I had to provide information, not answer every question truthfully.

I couldn't believe he had made a mistake, and could only interpret it as a small act of good faith—perhaps a mercy.

"Yes, Hrokr," I said, and instantly felt a zing through my palm as his name passed my lips. "I agree." The binding magic of the vow speared through me, nestling somewhere deep in my chest. Hrokr slowly withdrew his fingers, letting their tips drag across my palms.

He stood gracefully, reaching down a pale hand to help me to my feet. I took it and let him haul me up. "Let's go," he said. "I will provide gear and weapons. You'll be deposited about an hour's walk from Oxcroft Fields. Do remember that when you are preparing to make your way back to me."

Not even half an hour passed before I was armed and standing in the Portal Room. Hrokr and I were both silent throughout it all, lost to our own thoughts.

He outfitted me in sturdy leather plants, a tunic, a long cloak that fell to my calves, and boots that rose to meet its edge. All in midnight black. A weapons belt was slung around my hips, sixteen knives slitted into it.

I was surprised. I'd expected an old, chipped dagger if anything.

I stood surrounded by runegates—marked by the runes etched and painted onto the floor. Signs hung above them, indicating location.

Hrokr strode confidently for one, waiting for me to catch up to him. "Are you familiar with voidstepping?" he asked.

"Yes."

He nodded. Without another word, he stepped into the runegate on the floor, disappearing and leaving behind only the soft wisp of smoke that always accompanied his disappearances.

I took a tight breath and followed him.

Long distances were disorienting. For the brief moment my eyes were closed, I felt as if I were moving fast—very fast. And I supposed I was—the pieces of my body flying through the universe at unimaginable speeds. When my eyes finally opened, I felt suddenly too still. My body pitched forward as if trying to correct my speed.

Strong hands steadied me around my upper arms. Hrokr released me, and together we stepped off of the platform. We were in a dilapidated, stone building—bare except for the runegate and a stone door.

It was awfully similar to the runegate I'd once shared with Gar, though I did my best not to think about it.

I reached for the door, but Hrokr pulled me back by my shoulder. "Give me your hand," he said.

"No," I snapped immediately. "Another bargain?"

"No," he said soberly. He seemed to have lost his mirth as the hour went on. It was almost strange to see him without his smirk. "The door is warded. You will not be able to pass through unless you have been keyed in."

Same as with Gar.

Hrokr held his palm aloft, waiting for me to give him my hand.

Swallowing my trepidation, I slid my hand into his. He slipped a dagger from my belt. "The spell requires blood." He twisted my hand, palm up. "Would you like the honors or I?"

"Go ahead."

He set the tip to my skin and dragged it across my palm. I inhaled sharply, watching the blood well. When a puddle had formed, his magic speared through me, healing the cut. He pressed my hand against the door, smearing my blood onto the wood.

My skin tingled beneath his touch; magic flowed readily from him.

It was a short moment before he released me, handing me the dirty dagger, hilt forward.

I wiped the bloody blade on my pants before sliding it back into my belt.

Hrokr held the door open, and cold winter air snapped into the space. I met his eyes, finding they had regained some of their easiness. "Don't get lost," he winked, and took a step backward, disappearing back into Castle Habrem.

I turned away from the empty room and faced Vanadey. I stepped into the cold, pulling my hood up over my ears. The stars were bright tonight, shining down on me and staining the grass beneath my boots silver.

It was nearly morning, dawn readying on the horizon. The remaining stars told me to move northeast to find Oxcroft Fields.

CHAPTER TEN

REMEMBER

What am I even doing?

The thought struck me hard. What was I really going to do? Slaughter everyone in the Burning Arrow?

The thought wasn't exactly off-putting—and Hrokr had surely armed me well enough to complete the job. But somehow, I didn't think Gar would allow it to be that easy. I knew I could overpower him in a match of magic and brute strength—but would that be enough?

I had no idea what to expect at Oxcroft Keep.

I had no idea what exactly I would feel when I saw him again.

A sudden wave of regret washed over me. *Why had I agreed to go back to Valencia?* I wanted to be angry at myself for my shortsightedness, but I couldn't bring myself to hold onto the emotion. Hrokr never would have agreed to let me go otherwise.

I sighed, picking up my pace.

And what if it was all just a ruse? Gar wasn't innocent, but neither was Hrokr. Had I become a blade wielded by the both of them?

When Oxcroft Fields came into view, every one of my muscles tensed. It was strange, to feel the comfort of familiarity and simultaneously be aware that all this kindness had been facade.

My boots were silent on the cobblestone streets as I walked through the square. I tried to keep myself slow, so as not to draw attention if there were any late-night travelers out, but as I spied the gates of Oxcroft Keep, I broke into a run.

But as I got closer, my breath was ripped from my lungs. My chest was cleaved wide open, where my splintered heart tumbled out. The gate—broken—hung ajar.

Had Hrokr done this?

Had he truly any reason to send me here if he had?

My hands shook at my sides as I pushed through the gate.

The keep was decimated.

The building still stood, but some of the stones were crumbling, and black smears of fire damage licked around the doors and windows.

The training rings were disrupted, the weapons racks empty and cast aside. The vineyards were a mess, roots ripped from the earth, stalks cut, and spoils burned.

There was silence inside of me—silence and the white-noise of panic.

I stumbled my way to the front doors and shouldered them open.

The great hall was destroyed. It looked like a battle had been waged, though without any blood being shed. I spied no puddles or smears, but everything else was in tatters. The smell of smoke and ash still clung to the air, and the furniture that had not been wholly eaten by flame bore its soot. The far windows—the whole northern wall—were blown out. Jagged shards still clung to the frames, and a spray of glass lay before them.

Before I had a moment to even begin to collect my thoughts, soft footsteps began descending the stairs. I spun, my palms sliding to my knives.

I held myself still, willing my enemy to show themself first.

And show himself, he did.

Gilded by the glow of a wintry dawn pouring through the windows, he stood. A strong breadth of shoulder, a height that towered my own. His hazel eyes were wide with shock, his hands tight and rigid at his sides. He wore an olive-colored button down today, tight to a frame I knew all too well.

Gar's lips parted in a surprised breath.

And I was not prepared for the way I suddenly felt weak in the knees. For the tears that sprung to my eyes. For the way my heart fled, and a hoard of violent birds thrashed in its place within my chest. I was not prepared for a throat suddenly dry, and an ache so bone-deep I could not force it away.

Hate.

It was hate I felt for him, for what he'd done. But my hands—they remembered what it felt like to hold him. My flesh knew what it was to be warmed by his. And my eyes... They couldn't help but take him in.

He did not look like Silas, drowning in a sea of night-choked ash as I'd last seen him.

No.

No, he looked like the Gar I'd kissed on the steps of this very keep, the Gar I'd clung to in my last moments as an *arrow* and prayed they would not be the last.

They were.

Palms forward—as if I were a feral beast who'd slipped her leash—he took a step toward me.

I took a step back. And that single step was like wading through thick mud—hard and unnatural. While my mind could know hate, my body knew only memory. It knew only the desire to throw myself in his arms, to have him soothe away this nightmare as he had all my others.

"Thea."

His voice was rough with unshed emotion, tight with anticipating how I would respond. It was his old voice, the one he'd whispered sweet nothings with.

"No."

And, Halls, my voice wasn't my own at all. It was cracked and foreign, strained with hate and brittle from the rot of love.

He took another step forward, his boots and long stride closing the distance more quickly than I could handle.

"Don't," I rasped.

He paused. Hurt crashed across his features—those hazel eyes wide with surprise.

Silence descended between us—thick and sour.

"Thea, where have you been?"

My ears started to ring as if my body wished to shield me from the cadence of his voice. I only shook my head.

My cheeks were indeed wet with tears I'd never dreamed I'd shed.

He took another step.

Only a few feet separated us now. Cold wind from the shattered windows moved through the space, drying my tears and tickling my cheeks.

With the cold came a sense of clarity.

Mellian with hair shorn to her shoulders, coal smudged across her cheeks. Alek with a shaved head and purple bags beneath his normally bright eyes.

My mother dead.

Heat pulsed through me.

A cramped cell with moldy bread and stale cheese. My hair matted to my head, water that tasted of rancid poison. Lonnie and Ellie and the other humans—dead.

And countless soldiers burned into nothing by my own hand.

I'd faced Gar before. Hardly any time had passed at all, but it felt like another life. But I'd had poison in my blood to numb me then, and adrenaline to fill the void magic could not.

Now there was nothing.

Nothing but a few feet and a breath of winter air. Nothing but the ruins of a land I'd once called home.

"How could you?"

He flinched as if struck, confusion drawing his brows together. "Thea, what are you talking about?"

I searched his face, looking for any tells of the truth.

Heat licked at my palms, and his eyes tracked the movement carefully.

"Please," he said. "Tell me what's happened."

Fire—an element buried from childhood—was more than just the orange flames at my fingertips. It was the heat in my blood, the song that begged me to raze the world down to the bare earth floor. "Silas."

Gar shook his head, hazel gaze heavy. "What about him?"

A flush drew across my cheeks, one born of fury. "Are you going to pretend none of it happened?"

He swallowed, a soft movement in the heart of his throat. "I don't know what you're talking about," he said slowly.

But he'd made a mistake.

He forgot to feign surprise at my use of flame.

I waved a burning hand at him. "No questions about this?"

His brows rose, but I did not see the flash of regret or anger I expected. Only concern. "Quite," he said. "But there are much more pressing matters."

"Like?"

Another step in my direction. "Like the fact that I've not seen you in months, Thea. The fact that you're looking at me like you've never seen me before. That you're cloaked head to toe in Valencian armor," he said, dragging bewildered eyes across my form.

I knew—*I knew*—he was lying. But a wild piece of me wanted to believe him.

A naive piece of me.

I shoved it away.

"Where did you get this?" he asked.

I took another step away, letting my flame falter as my hand slipped toward the knife at my hip.

He froze.

I ignored his question, asking the only one that still mattered between us. "Where is she?"

He searched my face, his concern and confusion an artfully crafted mask. "Who?"

My teeth ached beneath the force I grit them. "Sagira."

He gentled further, the movement curdling my stomach. He nodded as if in a daze. "Do you want to see her?"

My heart leapt into my throat. "Is she here?" I asked, breathless.

"No one is here," he said with a half-smile that didn't reach his eyes. "Only me."

"Why?"

He took another step, close enough now that I could reach out and touch him. "Because I've been waiting for you, Thea."

I searched his eyes, trying to understand the new stage of this game between us. "What happened in Balaca?"

He shook his head again. "Balaca?"

Frustration tightened my spine. "You were there, Gar."

His brow furrowed. "I last saw you here," he said. "Months ago, now. Remember? You were going to Valencia."

"I made it," I snapped.

His eyes dragged across my body from cowl to boot, snagging on the dark polish painted on my nails. "I see that."

My lips threatened to curve back from my teeth, but I forced them still. I gave him what I had to. Anything, to get to her. "I was poisoned and you—you *took* me. Locked me in a mine, killed my mother."

"*What?*" he cried.

I let the tears fill my eyes. "You hurt me, Gar."

"Thea," he said, his voice choking on my name. "You were poisoned?"

I curled my fingers into fists at my side. "By Hrokr."

Realization—the act I was prepared for—dawned in his eyes. "He *poisoned* you? A dark mark on your flesh?"

"Yes," I rasp.

My tears flowed freely, and I wasn't sure if I was faking them or not.

"Thea, love," he rasped, stepping so close we were nearly chest-to-chest. I did not move. "Poison magic can cause vivid hallucinations."

But Gar's Thea would not fold so easily. "I know what I saw," I croaked.

He reached out slowly, brushing a lock of hair behind my ear. I stiffened, hating the way his callouses felt soft and familiar against my skin. "What did you see?" he asked gently.

"You're Silas," I breathed, my lip curling. "You kept my whole family captive."

A phenomenal actor. Heartbreak shuddered across his face. He leaned down, studying my eyes with such raw intensity. I wished I could believe it.

"Do you truly think me capable of hurting you so deeply?"

Yes.

Yes, a thousand times yes.

"I don't know what to think, Gar."

He scrutinized every inch of me. He was so close I could smell him. Warmth and sunlight and broken leaves. "We'll talk about it," he said carefully. "Thea, I'd—" His voice broke, and he cleared his throat to right it. "I'd never hurt you. I don't know what you saw or what happened, but..."

His fingers lifted to my face, cradling it in one warm palm. "I'd *never* hurt you," he repeated, eyes boring into mine. "But I can give you the time to remember that. Let's get you home. You can be with Sage, and I can—I can stay away until you're ready to see me again."

The words sounded so real. They sounded so much like everything I could ever want to hear.

And if any portion of his charade was to be believed—*Sage was alive.*

"Come with me," he whispered. "There's a runegate upstairs."

My stomach sank. This should have been my chance to save her. But I had no way of knowing where I was going, no way of knowing I'd get out on time.

"I can't," I croaked. And the heartbreak lacing my words was so horribly real.

If I couldn't get her out by midnight, I'd die—and then there would be no one to save her.

Confusion—likely the first true show of it—settled on his face. His fingers stilled against my cheek. "Why not?"

I searched his eyes, wishing I could draw the comfort I once did from them. "He's waiting for me," I whispered.

There it was: the flash of rage I'd been waiting for. His stubbled jaw worked as his fingers twitched against my cheek. "Hrokr?"

My voice was as silent as the wind beyond. "Yes."

"And you wish to return to him?"

I drew in a breath that went nowhere. "I have to," I admitted. "A bargain was the only way he'd let me leave."

His nostrils flared. "And what does your end of the bargain entail?"

"Only that I return," I whispered.

His eyes fell closed. "Thea—"

"But I wish I could," I rasped. And, Halls, I meant it.

His hazel eyes flashed open, surprise written openly in them.

"I don't know what happened in Balaca," I lied. "But I've missed *this,* Gar. I've missed what I left behind here in Oxcroft."

And perhaps it was true. I did not miss *him,* the monster who'd cut my flesh and slaughtered my mother. I did not miss Silas.

But I thought I might always miss this Gar. This man who never really existed, but was kind and sweet and kissed my bad dreams away.

He moved with hesitation as he dropped his forehead to my own. "I've missed you so much, Little Shadow."

My eyes fell shut.

I could feel his breath on my lips as he whispered, "Can you escape him again?"

A swollen moment of heavy silence.

"Yes."

Gar kissed me.

I allowed it because I had to, but oh, did my lips remember his. Guilt was a sour nausea in my stomach as I tasted him, as his hand slipped into my hair. He tilted my head back, kissing me deeply. My lips moved against his, and I wondered if he could taste the tears that leaked down my cheeks.

I wonder what emotion he thought they were borne of.

He broke from me sooner than I thought he would, but only to hold my face tightly against his chest. "How long can you be gone?"

"Not long," I lied.

"When can you come back?" he asked.

I cautiously wrapped my arms around his waist. "I don't know. But I will try."

"Where does he have you?"

Ever the soldier, ever the gatherer of intel.

Ever the man willing to exploit me for militant gain.

"In a cell," I said.

His arms tightened around me. "In the Castle?"

I wondered if, perhaps, I should be lying. But I did not know all that he knew. "Yes."

He pulled back and wiped the tears from my eyes. "Why did he let you go, Thea?"

"I don't know," I whispered.

Gar's brow furrowed. "Likely to gain your trust."

"He'll never have it."

His lips parted to speak, but I cut him off before he could. I wasn't sure how much more of this I could take. "I should go soon, Gar."

He nodded slowly. "Alright, but... I need to tell you something before you do."

My stomach tied itself in knots. "What is it?"

"I didn't want to tell you this way," he whispered, touching my face with the tips of his fingers.

I fought the tightening of my spine, the curling of my fingers.

"But I can't bear the thought of you going back without knowing," he whispered, gathering one of my hands to press it against his chest. Beneath my palm, his heart pumped steadily. "Can you feel how much I've missed you?"

Gar leaned down, his lips a hairsbreadth from my own. "Mates can feel what others can't."

I sucked in a sharp breath, but his lips were already on my own, moving fiercely.

My heart thrashed against my ribs, my body frozen beneath his touch.

Mate.

Mate.

Surely not.

Surely not.

But he was still kissing me, still clutching me to his chest. Some errant part of my mind remembered to kiss him back, to cling to him if only to avoid having to speak. But he pulled away too soon, and I was left floundering.

Staring.

He smiled.

"Come home to me, Thea," he whispered. "Be safe."

And while I was left gasping for air that wouldn't come, he only studied me with that satisfied smirk he so often wore. "Come back to me," he said.

"I will," I whispered.

I wasn't sure how real it looked, but I found it within myself to smile.

He backed away from me slowly, not taking his eyes off me until he reached the stairwell landing. "I love you, Thea," he said.

I swallowed a shattered breath. "I love you, Gar."

He disappeared up the steps, gone to voidstep to wherever it was that he held Sagira.

CHAPTER ELEVEN

QUESTIONS

I made it only far enough that I was sure Gar could not have eyes on me before I vomited into the bushes.

My mind was reeling, my steps uneven. I wasn't his mate. There was no possible way I was his mate.

But why had he said it?

Why had he said anything today at all? Why was he so wholly committed to his lie?

I had a reason for my performance. I had to stay close enough to get to Sage. But what did Gar gain from any of this?

What had he gained from it the first time?

I braced my hands against the bark of the nearest tree, trying to calm my racing heart.

I *knew* it was a lie. Even if there was truth in his claim about poison-induced hallucinations, that didn't explain enough. He hadn't been surprised about my use of fire.

He hadn't mentioned Calix at all.

Shouldn't he have been curious how I'd gotten back without my traveling partner?

I heaved again.

"Are you alright?"

I nearly came out of my skin, but the voice was only Hrokr's. A few paces down, he leaned against a gnarled oak, wearing gear that matched my own.

"Yes," I said curtly, straightening to my full height, trying not to cringe at the position I'd been found.

His cowl was down around his neck, pooling about his shoulders. His boots—though freshly polished—were splattered with dust from the dirt paths. Hrokr studied me, his dark eyes scouring every inch of my body.

"How did it go?" he asked softly.

I pushed away from the tree, making to move past him down the road. "Are you following me?"

He fell into step beside me. "Perhaps."

"Why?"

A beat of silence. "I asked you how it went."

"And I asked you why you're following me," I hissed.

The beginnings of Oxcroft Field came into view as he said, "I take it not well."

I said nothing.

His voice was softer when he asked, "Did you speak with anyone?"

"No."

We managed only a few steps in silence before, "Who was there?"

"No one."

Harsh fingers were suddenly in my cloak, ripping me backward to face him. Indignation ripped down my spine as Hrokr scowled inches from my face. "Do not lie to me, Thea."

I tore from his grasp, my lips peeling back to brandish my fangs. "Do not touch me. Did we not cover that last night?"

He smirked. It was a cold, cruel thing. "Do not lie to me. We covered *that* first."

Rage heated my cheeks. "What makes you think anyone was there, Hrokr?" I spit. "I was only inside for a few minutes."

His nose wrinkled as his eyes darkened. "And I can scent someone on you. That and a wealth of soot."

The thought of carrying Gar's scent upon my skin was nauseating. Enough so that I let the heartache show through my anger. "Do you think it's easy for me?"I hissed. "To be back there? Do you think I want to talk about it? With you?"

He narrowed his eyes, but his tone was soft when he said, "I only want to know why you'd lie to me. Do you think it's easy for *me,* Thea? To play keeper for the woman I met as she was invading my home? I've extended an overwhelming amount of naive trust in letting you out of your cell at all."

"Then don't bother playing keeper," I snapped, turning back down the trodden path.

"And let you die?" he called, keeping a steady gait beside me. "What if they'd taken you, Thea? And you hadn't gotten back to me in time?"

"Do you think I can't handle myself?"

"Do you think chancing it was a better call?"

I stopped, turning to face him fully. There was a wildness in his gaze, one I couldn't quite place. "Why do you care if I die?"

He looked back and forth between my eyes as if the answer lay somewhere between them. "Why don't you care if you do?"

The words hit me low in the stomach—a wound my already nauseous gut wasn't ready for.

Gentle wind ruffled his idle curls, blowing them into his dark, starlit eyes.

"Can you answer a single question without asking another?" I asked.

"Can you?"

I sighed sharply, the heat of my breath creating a small cloud between us. "Did you burn the keep?"

"No."

I studied his sharp features, looking for any tell of a lie within them. "How long have you known?"

"I found out when you did," he said.

"So you followed me the entire way there?"

"Yes."

I curled my fingers into fists, unsure of what to say. Unsure of what to feel.

Hrokr held himself preternaturally still as he watched me. "Was your friend inside?"

"No."

I could have sworn his eyes looked gentler. *Who was?* he asked silently.

My chest was suddenly too tight, my words clinging to the sides of my throat as if they could keep themselves contained within me. But I said, "Someone I never want to see again."

But I knew I would see him again.

As I marched off toward the south, Hrokr followed, but he did not speak.

It only took us an hour to reach the little hut containing the runegate back to Castle Habrem.

We moved in silence, Hrokr daring not to break it, and me having no desire to.

I was plagued with fears about Sage. I assumed she was likely alive—but what if she wasn't? What if this was all only a ploy to bring me back to being Gar's captive?

Not to mention the matter of my bargain. I wasn't sure what to tell Hrokr tomorrow.

I believed, of course, he had no allegiance to Gar and the Guild. But that didn't mean he didn't have allegiance to Silas. I knew Gar planned on attacking him, but would that attack be a betrayal? Or only another pain in Hrokr's side?

How deep would I have to dig to begin to understand what was going on?

My thoughts plagued me as Hrokr walked me back toward the cell. He paused next to the door leading to the bathing cave. "Would you like a moment?" he asked.

I looked down at my pristine clothes.

But I didn't want to carry the touch—the scent—of Gar upon my skin.

Want me to send Gyda down, or would you prefer some time to yourself?

"Some time to myself would be nice."

He smiled, though his eyes were worlds away. *Very well,* he said, gesturing to the door. *I'll have a meal prepared for you by the time you return.*

Without another word, Hrokr disappeared down the hall. I slipped through the door and down the stairs.

I lost track of time in the bath. When I emerged from soaking, I wrapped myself in fresh clothes from the dressing room. Black tights and a white wool sweater, comfortable enough to sleep in, but sturdy enough to be worn on a walk through the castle.

Upstairs, the hallway was full of the sounds of laughter, music, and the hum of mass chatter. Despite being exhausted, I wandered down the hallway once I made it to the top of the steps. It was strange—to be a prisoner without manacles.

I knew I couldn't leave, unless I wanted a repeat of last night. Yet—I was not bound. Despite my uncertainty of Hrokr, he did appear to wish me alive. He'd made that obvious by following me today.

It was likely only to glean what I knew about his enemy, but for now, I was safe from him.

And I didn't feel quite as much of a prisoner anymore. My cell door was propped open, and I didn't think it would be necessary to lock myself inside of it. Still, I wondered if I should, if only to protect myself from any wandering strangers.

I walked slowly down the hall, the thrum of voices growing louder. And once I rounded the corner—

Another party. I caught only a few glances as I made my way across the floor and up the grand staircase to the open second floor. I turned to face down the throne room. The balcony doors were open again, night air rushing inside and carrying the scent of snow even on the luke-warm breeze.

My eyes immediately found Hrokr, though he did not appear to notice me. His hair was wet—from a shower or sweat, I did not know—and falling into his eyes. Even from the distance I could tell his eyes were glazed with something that looked like aged boredom. Boredom and—definitely—liquor.

Those eyes were red-rimmed, half-lidded, and lazy. He was seated on an ivory chaise, white silk shirt unbuttoned to nearly his naval.

A gaggle of women were draped around him, though none appeared to be touching him. They were enraptured just being near him. And, of course, they were all beautiful. Dripping in pearls and diamonds, some even emitting a faint glow that had to be magic.

He outshone them all.

As he drew a glass to his lips, I turned and slipped down the stairs—praying he'd not noticed me at all.

CHAPTER TWELVE

AFRAID

I nightmared all night, far more than usual. I couldn't escape the feeling of Gar's hands around me, his lips pressed to my own.

I could not outrun the memories, even as I threw myself from the bed and vomited myself dry into the toilet. Even as I splashed cold water on my face and tried to wash away the burden of the previous day.

I kept hearing his voice, watching the ash sift through the sky around him as it had in Balaca.

When soft dawn light began to creep across the tile floor, I combed through my hair with my fingers. It wasn't long before I heard Hrokr's sure-footed steps coming down the hall.

He looked exhausted. After seeing his nightly activities, I found it wasn't hard to imagine why.

"You look awful," I said in lieu of greeting.

It wasn't true; it never was. He was in a white wool sweater and tight black pants, quite similar to my own. Despite the soft style of dress, he retained his warrior's boots. He looked quite nice, actually.

I scowled at the thought.

But his curls were mussed with recent sleep, and faint plum bruising hung beneath his eyes. He was tired.

His lips twitched open, exposing one fang in that lopsided grin. "Your charm is noted, as usual."

"I mean it," I said, folding my arms across my chest.

He glanced at me knowingly. "No. You don't."

Heat flared in my cheeks at the absolute arrogance in his tone. "Do you ever sleep?" I snapped.

His brow furrowed, bemused but entertained. "I'm sorry?"

"You always look exhausted. Do you ever sleep?"

His eyes narrowed, and the predatory angle of his body reminded me of a cat. "Do I dare believe you are concerned about me, Thea?"

I scoffed. "No. I just would have liked to see you awake and alert this morning, is all. Not exhausted from a night—*carousing.*"

He snorted. Somehow, he made even that sound graceful. "I can *assure* you, love, I am well-rested." He chuckled openly, mostly to himself. "There was no carousing for me."

I stared. He was lying. It wasn't that he didn't have the right to, but—*he was lying to me.* He was up late, I was sure of it.

"*Thea,*" he breathed, still grinning. "What did you tell me? *Jealousy is unflattering on a woman of your age.*" He winked before adding, "Besides, there is nothing to be jealous of. My heart is wholly yours."

I sighed—a sharp, angry sound. "Do not mock me, Hrokr. I don't care what you do in your free time. I had just hoped to be taken seriously this morning. Hopefully you stay awake through my tales," I added with more snideness than I probably should have been giving so early in the morning. "And for the record, I am *young.*"

That washed some of the humor from his face, though his eyes were still alight. "Define *young.*" He eyed me and held up a hand. "Wait—let me guess."

I scowled.

"You don't look older than eighteen or nineteen," he hedged. "*But* your phenomenal skill at committing murder leads me to believe you're likely older." He tapped a finger against his lips. "But Gyda is eighty and—"

"I'm nineteen."

He glared at me. "Way to ruin the game, Thea. And, also, no."

"I am," I said, blushing. "Why do you think I'm an old lady?"

He laughed, a warm, light sound that seemed at odds with his usual darkness. "You think eighty is *old?* Halls, I'd hate to know what you think of me."

"Yes," I agreed, "you would."

He didn't rise to the taunt; he only laughed. He leaned against the open doorframe, and something in his expression softened. "I don't know what you've heard or thought or seen, but I spend my nights alone. The throne room becomes a maze of chaos at night, I'll admit." He ran his fingers through his inky waves. "I would prefer you keeping this to yourself, as my court is unaware of my vices, but I was up late enjoying a fresh bottle and reading. A lonely, quiet night." He gave me a sarcastic bow. "I deeply apologize for arriving in less than pristine condition. It will not happen again, Your Majesty."

I highly doubted his court was unaware of his vices.

"Why hide it from them?" I asked, though not unkindly. "You're the lord of the Hall. Do whatever you want."

He sighed. "If only it were that easy, my Thea. People grow concerned over the tiniest things. It becomes an entire ordeal." But a hint of darkness crept into his eyes as he spoke.

I couldn't help but point out, "You think it is a burden to be loved by them."

His eyes suddenly showed his age. And his bone-deep weariness. "A great one."

A part of me wanted to pity him, wanted to tell him that he was wrong and being loved was a treasure. But was it, really?

"I can't relate," I snarked instead. "Most everyone hates me these days."

"Shall we bond over our solidarity of loneliness?" he asked sweetly, sarcasm a gentle lilt on his tongue.

I walked toward him, moving to brush past him in the doorway. "Better than how you bonded with your friends last night."

His fingers snaked out to wrap around my wrist. I turned to look at him, schooling my expression into innocence. But his eyes were wide, amused. "You're serious."

His fingers were warm around my skin, and I could feel his warrior's strength even in the smallest flexing of his hand.

"It's no trouble to me," I said. "Maybe you'll fall asleep, and I'll finally succeed in running away."

"Maddie and Ciro would catch you."

"I am not afraid of them," I responded quickly.

Too quickly, if the parting of his lips was any indication. "But you are afraid of me?" he asked softly. His voice was low, almost rough.

The smell of him was intoxicating, washing over me in waves this close. The rise and fall of his chest was strained through his sweater, the pulse point hammering away in the hollow of his throat. It unnerved me enough that I spoke freely.

"You are the first person I've encountered that I thought may win against me."

He was silent for a long moment, eyes ravaging my own. "By that logic," he said lowly, "I am afraid of you."

Heat flared down my spine and limbs, spread across my cheeks and chest. It was heady, disorienting.

I tugged against his grip. "Well, good thing we are friends today."

He chuckled darkly, and his fingers released my wrist. I started down the hall, but he appeared in front of me, leaning against the door to the bathing cave.

Cheater.

"Gyda is downstairs with fresh clothes," he said, holding the door open for me. "My Council wishes to be present for today's meeting, but I am happy to send them away if you're not yet comfortable with their presence."

A jolt slipped through me at the candor of the offer. But I already knew Hrokr would relay everything I said today anyway. I supposed it did not matter if they were there. "There's no need to send them away."

He nodded and gestured me down the steps. When I glanced back, he was gone.

Gyda was waiting in the dressing room, though she didn't have much to say this morning. She brushed through my hair and handed me a fresh set of similar clothes. Soft material that was easy to move in. A long-sleeved yellow shirt, and skin-clinging black pants.

She left before I could ask her to.

We are in the Council Room, Hrokr said, his voice brushing up against the walls of my mind. He projected an image of an ornately carved, wooden door. *You won't miss us.*

CHAPTER THIRTEEN

COUNCIL ROOM

As I neared the Council Room door, I expected Hrokr to be the one to greet me, but the doorway was empty. I straightened my spine and sucked in a breath before I pushed into the room.

They were all there, all five of them. And despite the nature of the meeting—what should have been an interrogation of a lethal prisoner—they were all at rest. In fact, *much* more casual than I had ever seen them.

Perhaps happy.

Even Hrokr looked different to me from his perch atop his desk. He sat on the wood, leaned back and propped on his hands. I knew they were Gentry Fae—that *I* was Gentry Fae—but it struck me suddenly how inhuman this room really was.

Hrokr didn't look human at all. He met my eyes from beneath long, thick lashes. Lashes any of the mortal girls in Ekin would have slaughtered for.

While his overall appearance was healthy and whole, his cheeks were gaunt, his eyelids thin and veined in lilac. His eyes rested in a bed of pale plum bruising. The insides of his wrists—they were delicate. And despite that delicacy, the lean muscle of his chest, arms, and shoulders—they spoke to the centuries he had spent as a warrior. As did the cunning, too-aware look in his starry-night eyes. Skin the color of living porcelain, hair darker than the night he ruled beneath.

He was as different to the Fae as we were to humans.

And the others in the room were not too far behind.

Ciro was a monster out of a child's scary story, and still he was breath-taking. Scars—or tattoos or birthmarks or runes, I wasn't sure—adorned his arms. It was like living lightning crawling up his flesh and across his throat. Snow-white hair fell unevenly into his bright blue eyes as he toyed with a skinny dagger, towering over the girl seated beside him at the breakfast-laden table.

Haizea, I still assumed. She was hunched over a book, scribbling furiously against the parchment. She had only glanced up at my entrance, offered a quick smile, and dropped her eyes back to her work. This was the first moment I'd had to study her from so close. Her eyes were the color of rich twilight, of fragmented amethyst. She had small bones—a tiny face with perfectly bowed lips and an upturned nose. A handful of pale freckles dusted her round cheekbones. She wore gear, to my surprise. A black cloak and equally dark leathers. I wondered where she was headed after this meeting.

Perhaps the most surprising of all was Fallon.

She looked half-asleep, curled up on a divan in a shaft of sunlight like a sun-bathing cat. Her silvery hair was in a messy knot atop her head. No shoes. Only thick, fuzzy socks over old, ragged leggings. Her brown sweater was aged-faded and torn. I had always imagined her—*seen* her—as someone pristine and perfect. But she looked comfortable. Lazy, even.

And last was Maddox, sitting with a fat grin across his face. He folded his arms across his leather-clad chest, the muscles near to bursting through his sun-darkened skin. His red hair was pulled back in a pony-tail, still falling to the middle of his back. And those orange, russet-colored eyes, burning with amusement.

"Hold on," Fallon grumbled into the stilted silence, holding up a hand and dragging herself to her feet. "I need food before this."

Hrokr sighed, but it was more a sound of endearment than true exasperation. He turned his eyes on me, catching me watching him. He smiled, a soft twist of his full lips. *What would you like to eat? Coffee? Waffles? Bacon? Rice? You can sit,* he said, gesturing to a chair beside Maddox.

I nodded as I moved on numb legs, a blush staining my cheeks at the uncomfortably silent room. Hrokr slid off the desk and gathered my breakfast as he addressed the room. "I suppose introductions are in order. This is Thea," he said, without gesturing to me in any way. We all knew who each other were.

"She will be telling us of her history this morning." He turned back to me, breakfast tray in hand, with a wink. He sat the tray on a small table between mine and Maddox's chairs. Maddox reached for a piece of bacon instantly, and Hrokr slapped his hand.

Watching his Council was strange. While they were just as terrifying as I had imagined—if not more—they reminded me of something like a family. I supposed after centuries, friends would no longer be friends. They would be family, indeed.

Maddox grunted, waving Hrokr away. Hrokr walked through a swath of sharp, dawn sunlight before resuming his perch on his desk. While Hrokr's back was turned, Maddox shot me a quick look.

Care to share?

Without waiting for an answer, he was stuffing bacon behind his lips, hurrying to swallow before Hrokr turned back around. Though, from the amused look on Hrokr's face, I had no doubt that he knew.

Hrokr did like to play, and it appeared his court did as well. At the very least, Fallon and Maddox did.

I pulled the mug into my hands, nestling its warmth into my lap. It was red and gold, painted with lanterns and wooden platforms and *cats* of all things. The tray was the same. In fact, the whole breakfast spread was settled on a matching set. It was one of the only splashes of color in the ivory room.

I met Hrokr's eyes, and his seemed suddenly heavy, aware at least to some degree of what was coming. "Start from the beginning, love."

"The beginning?" I echoed. Every eye in the room swiveled toward me. I fought the urge to fidget and instead focused my gaze on Hrokr.

"Yes," he said aloud. *Just tell us how you got involved with the group.*

"Well," I said, shifting in my seat. Halls, I had only said one word and already the images were swarming me—drowning me. "I grew up in a human village in Ekin."

A heavy silence pressed up against the walls.

"There was a raid. A group of Gentry Fae came into the village with slave wagons and started taking humans." My heart began to pound in my chest, and I took a deep breath to steady it. "My mother was taken, alongside my sister and my brother."

In the silence that followed, Hrokr said, "And they let you go?"

"No, I fought them. I killed five before one landed a blow to my head that dazed me. He cut through my calf badly enough that I couldn't walk, and then knocked me out."

Almost absently, I lifted my pant leg and eyed the scar I tried not to think about. It was pale and faded now, but the slash was still there. Beside me, Maddox sucked in a sharp breath.

Hrokr's eyes were dark with glittering rage, but his voice was soft when he spoke. "I assume he did not know you were a healer."

"I wasn't. At least, I didn't know I was. But my friend was. I crawled to her house, and she healed me. Days later, I crossed the border into Vanadey."

I chanced a quick glance around the room and was rewarded with steely looks of grim respect.

It softened me enough to say, "The person who took them, who hurt me—" Another break in my voice. "I should admit he has ties to your people. I do not understand the nature of them, but that is why I am... *hesitant.*"

Open shock colored their faces, and they all glanced around at one another, confused.

"And who was it?" Ciro asked, a low, gravel voice from the corner of the room.

"I didn't know at first," I admitted with a quick glance at Ciro.

I settled my gaze back on Hrokr, willing myself not to miss even his smallest twitch. I had to see his raw reaction to my next words. "He wore an iron mask."

Hrokr's face was hewn from granite—or ice. A depth of rage I couldn't even fathom brewed in his eyes, the lights of the stars winking out, being sucked into the darkness of his pupil. His lips peeled back from his teeth.

I swore I could feel it.

"*Silas.*"

The wealth of hatred in only a single word. Hrokr spoke it as if it were a poison, as if it burned him being dragged through his throat.

There was so much I didn't understand, but one thing was certain: there was endless hatred on both sides, and—if the look on Hrokr's face was any indication—it was genuine.

At the breakfast table, Ciro and Haizea were rigid. He reached a hand toward her, but she jerked away, shaking.

"He is not your ally," I said softly.

"*No.*" It was Haizea, voice withered and cold.

Maddox stood as if he were ready to confront Gar now.

"Sit down," Hrokr said, dragging a long-fingered hand through his hair. "I'm sure there is more you'll want to be present for."

Maddox grumbled something unintelligible and dropped back into the chair.

After the room was given a breath to collect itself, Hrokr murmured, "Continue."

"When I made it to Oxcroft Fields, I settled with The Burning Arrow Guild." Even though my next words were a surprise to no one, I had to steel myself to speak them. "I killed many of your people. I worked at the Guild hunting Valencians. I was told you were the slave trader, that it was Valencia stealing humans from the Ekin."

Hrokr's face did not change. If he felt anger, he hid it well.

"How do you know it wasn't us?" Haizea asked.

Hrokr silenced her with a look that could have withered stone.

"No," Ciro said gently. "It's a fair question. How did you figure it out?" He looked directly at me, bypassing Hrokr's angry gaze.

"I was captured," I said. "I was on my way back from your Eclipse Fete when a volley of arrows hit me," I said gingerly, looking at Hrokr through lowered lashes.

He looked sad.

"I was held in the coal mines of Balaca with human slaves for over a month until I escaped, and—"

"How?" Maddox interrupted, watching me with eager eyes.

"Don't interrupt her," Hrokr admonished softly.

"It's alright," I said, turning to face Maddox. "I fought my way out."

It was Fallon who asked, "And the humans?"

A lump formed in my throat. "I tried," I whispered. Looking down into the swirl of my coffee, I added, "Silas was the one who captured me. He came to me in there, visited me. He had nothing to say, really, other than that he hated me." I raised my eyes, meeting Hrokr's. "I found my family, though. My siblings are safe, but my mother had been killed by Silas."

Every head in the room swiveled toward Hrokr.

He looked murderous.

But it was more than rage, more than anger. He looked heartbroken. I wondered if he projected something to them, because suddenly every eye snapped away.

"And then?" Hrokr asked aloud, voice thick.

"And then not much of anything," I whispered, though that was perhaps the biggest lie in the world. "I escaped the coal mine, but members of the Guild had assembled nearby." I took a tight breath. "The leader of the Guild is Silas."

Silence. Pure and deafening.

And then a cacophony of noises.

Ciro and Maddox flew out of their seats, exclaiming words that fell on my deaf ears. Fallon, ramrod straight in her seat, looked back and forth at the movement across the room. Haizea looked like she had seen a ghost.

And Hrokr. An ethereal, otherworldly creature who looked like he would tear all of Alynthia apart with his bare hands if it would sate his bloodlust.

His voice cut through the chaos like a knife.

"He told you? He told you that he was Silas?"

"He took his mask off, I'm sure."

Hrokr's eyes darkened. "What did he say he wanted with you?"

I shifted uncomfortably. "He seems to have quite the fascination with you. He knew the people I killed."

"That doesn't narrow it down," Maddox grumbled.

Hrokr glared, but his anger seemed to be more directed at the situation than the commander himself. Hrokr shook his head, running his hand through his hair.

"He's a seer," I offered.

Hrokr watched me, thinking. "Did he tell you anything he saw?"

I didn't want to admit it, to face the implications of the words. But I admitted, "He said I'll hold the Orb of Dolga, here, beneath the eclipse. He said he would be there to take it from me."

CHAPTER FOURTEEN

HERO

H rokr moved our group to the dining table, suggesting that perhaps we would think better if we were fed.

Small bits of conversation swarmed around us, mostly between Ciro and Maddox.

I tried my hardest to tune it out. Though we'd moved, hardly anyone was eating. I nursed my coffee, but it had long since gone cold.

Fallon held a trembling Haizea, who stared down into her fruit, eyes unseeing. Fallon stroked her hair in silence, a strangely motherly gesture.

I studied Hrokr, but he did not meet my gaze. Seated diagonally to his place at the head of the table, I gently knocked my knee against his own.

His eyes flicked toward mine from beneath his furrowed brow. I could almost see the wheels spinning behind his eyes as he thought over all I had told him.

Are you alright?

I tried to whisper as quietly as I could, though I knew it was useless in a room of Gentry Fae. "You all know him."

He took a breath. *We do not know him. We know of him. While we've encountered the Burning Arrow before, they've never presented the kind of threat Silas does. It's quite concerning to learn they are the same entity. He has taken the lives of many people we have loved.*

"Why?" I whispered.

I don't know, he sighed, sounding defeated. *He is the one you saw yesterday, isn't he?*

I dropped my eyes down to my mug. It was answer enough.

You loved him.

Was it so obvious?

"I loved a lie," I whispered.

He smiled, though it was somber and melancholy. *I understand your hesitation in your trust of me.*

I nodded. I wasn't sure what else there was to say.

He cleared his throat to assemble the table, and even that sound was graceful coming from him. "It appears Silas wants the Orbs."

"Apparently," Maddox grumbled.

"But why Thea?" Ciro asked in his low voice, brows drawn together. "Maybe he needed her for the Orb, but there has to be more, right? Why else would he hurt her the way that he did?"

I tightened my fingers on my mug.

What do you know? Hrokr asked softly.

"He said that from what he sees of the future, I am... I am not a good person. He told me I am awful, just as awful as—" I cut myself off. Perhaps these were not good words to repeat.

"Us?" Haizea supplied in a small, sour voice.

I raised guilty eyes to Hrokr.

Me. The word was not a question.

A slight dip of my chin was the only response I would give.

"Was your relationship with Silas public?" Ciro asked.

I flinched, and a hiss slipped through Hrokr's teeth. Ciro leveled a flat look at his lord. "Let us not tiptoe around our feelings, Crow." He turned his crystal gaze on me, cocking a brow.

"Yes."

"How public?" he pushed.

I frowned. "I don't follow."

"Hrokr informed us your friend is with him." I nodded along. "Are the two of them close? Does your past love for him taint her view of him?"

The question was a kick to the gut.

Shadows curled around the tips of Hrokr's fingers. I glanced at them, and they vanished.

"Do not act like this is her fault, Ciro," he said in a calm, cold rage. As he spoke, his voice whetted itself into a sharp edge, slicing through the thick silence before him. "He has lived a millennium, and we have all been bested by him. Do not fault her."

Something in my chest seized to a painful degree.

"I'm not," Ciro said calmly. "I only wish to be prepared for all outcomes."

Hrokr opened his mouth, eyes swirling like pits of starlight. I spoke before he could. "It will be a concern," I admitted, though I prayed I was wrong. "I'm not sure what he's told the others, but he is claiming to be my mate."

The table recoiled in physical disgust.

"You are *not* his mate," Hrokr snapped.

"What if she is?" Fallon asked gently.

Hrokr's nostrils flared as he leaned forward. Everyone seemed to feel the fury leaking from his skin. "Mates are equal, Fallon Blightbringer. After everything she just divulged, you would accuse her of that? Of sharing the soul of the man who would do what he did to us? Who would kill—"

"Crow," Fallon interrupted calmly. "It was no accusation, only a question."

Haizea slunk farther into her seat, looking like she was only a moment away from crumbling.

Gar had cut this group of people deeply. It must have been years ago, and I found myself suffering through an entirely new wave of disgust for him. Whatever he did to them left its mark. And that mark was not a scar—it was a wound that had not yet closed.

"Well, did you ever do the ritual?" Maddox asked. Despite the tension building in the room, he was casually munching through a strip of bacon.

"What ritual?" I asked.

"Blood-sharing."

I shook my head slowly. "I am unfamiliar with many Fae customs."

Hrokr answered me. "A bond between mates is just a pull, a lure. It is not complete until the two share fresh blood, like pressing bloody palms together."

"Oh," I said. "No, we've never done anything like that."

"It doesn't matter," Ciro said. "If the group believes them to be mates, it could be advantageous to the situation."

"*Absolutely* not," Hrokr growled.

"I'm only suggesting that—"

"I am well aware of what you are suggesting, Ciro. And the answer is no. He cut her with *rowan* wood."

A collective intake of breath from the group.

"Halls," Maddox grumbled. "That *is* bad."

"Why would us being mates be advantageous?" I asked in the quick silence.

"You could go back," Ciro said baldly. "Bring your friend back with you, stab Silas in the heart."

"It would be easy," Maddox cooed with a fat grin.

"*Stop,*" Hrokr snapped. For the first time around his Council, I heard the raw power in his voice. The others heard it just as surely as I had.

You are free to make your own decisions, Thea, he said to me. *You are absolved of any guilt and no longer under any trial from me.*

But I would never, ever, *expect you to do this to yourself. You do not have to go back, you do not have to subject yourself to that. I apologize for them even asking.*

My chest tightened.

But more than kindness—I heard my out. There was a part of me—so small and naive—that felt guilt. Hrokr and his people had been something akin to pleasant in recent moments, but that didn't erase my truth.

Like a fool, I felt myself trusting his kindness.

I remembered what it had felt like to trust Gar, and just how far it had gotten me.

I would not make the same mistakes again.

Truthfully, I felt certain now. Hrokr and his people had no allegiance to Silas. But that did not absolve Hrokr of his own crimes; it did not prove the rest of his innocence.

I would not be their retribution. I would be my own.

"She should go," Ciro pushed.

"No," Hrokr snapped, with one final glance at me. "We aren't sending her."

It was only a moment—but there was a collective pause around the table. As if they expected me to argue, as if they expected me to be the hero I'd claimed to be.

But I turned to Hrokr and offered a pained smile. I whispered, "Thank you."

CHAPTER FIFTEEN

ORANGES

The meeting was quickly adjourned, every member of the Cardinal Council off to begin their preparations.

I knew it wouldn't be long before they were storming Oxcroft Keep, pouring into the runegates etched on the faded floor.

I didn't have much time.

Hrokr walked me back to my cell, thoughtful and silent beside me. As we reached the door, he caught me by the wrist. "Thea."

I raised my eyes to his and prayed he could not see the guilt within them.

His face was troubled. "Are you alright?"

My arm pulled from his grasp. "Yes."

His lips parted—and promptly closed. He did not know what to say.

"I'm fine," I whispered.

Something dark—something I might have called guilt—darkened his eyes. "I'm sorry if this was too soon. I'm—"

"I'm fine," I repeated, retreating within the bars of my cage. I offered as much of a smile as I could.

One long-fingered hand wrapped around the gold bar as he leaned into my cell. "Silas was... He was not good to us. But we decided long ago that unspent vengeance was a worthy price to pay if it meant protecting those of us who are left."

What had Gar done to them?

"You're safe here, Thea," he said. "We aren't sending you anywhere."

I nodded numbly.

Shadows stole the stars from his eyes, and I fought against the strained feeling in the pit of my stomach.

"Gyda is preparing a room for you," he continued. He studied every inch of me for a long, heavy moment. Finally, he took a small step into the heart of the hall. "She'll be down for you soon."

He didn't bother walking away; he disappeared into nothing.

Gyda knew something was wrong. I wasn't sure whether she could see it, scent it, or feel it—but she knew. It was obvious in the way she watched me, and the slow, precise way in which she moved. But she led me in silence, marching down a long hall past the Council Room and up a long, winding stairwell.

Ivory steps and slate walls—Castle Habrem was nothing if not consistent.

At the top, my eyes were drawn down the hall toward an open turret and a single door, but Gyda tugged me back toward the right.

"What's down here?" I asked.

"lord Hrokr's rooms," she said curtly. "Come now."

Gyda was normally warmer; she knew something was amiss indeed. Down the barren hallway was a single door—ornately carved from rich, dark wood.

Though as Gyda paused to take a deep, steadying breath, I wondered if perhaps her foul mood was not because of me.

"Is everything alright?" I asked.

She didn't respond. Her slender arms pushed the door open, revealing the suite beyond. Beautiful, as was everything in Valencia. The tart scent of fresh, grey paint immediately met me, chasing away the smell of cold nature that seemed to cling to everything else in the Hall.

Every piece of furniture was brand new, not a scuff or streak in sight. We entered into an ivory and gold receiving room with a perfectly polished oak table flanked by plush, white chairs. A marble fireplace took up the entirety of the left wall, a bare bookcase taking up the right. And on the far wall was a massive set of gold-gilded doors propped open to a golden canopy bed.

As I stepped into the room, Gyda remained beside the door. Her emerald eyes were skeptical and cold when she said, "The mercy he extends you is worth considering."

It was likely the guilt within me, but my back straightened to a painful point. "What is that supposed to mean?"

"Don't do anything stupid."

She was frank at least. She left without another word, and I was left to the raw silence around me.

I wasted no time rushing into the bedroom. It hosted a private bathing room in blinding white, and a walk-in closet I hoped housed what I needed.

Of course, it did.

One corner was a verifiable arsenal. I must have truly proved my allegiance if Hrokr had given me a private armory within the home of his people. Gear, boots, daggers, belts. It was as if he was prepared to lead me into war.

Perhaps he was.

But it was the far wall that gave me pause. A host of dresses each more wonderful than the last. Silks, satins, and chiffon all arranged by color. More concerning was the wall of lazy home clothes. Pants, shirts, sweaters—outfits for every season.

As if Hrokr expected me to be here a very long time.

Gar's words suddenly rang through my ears. *A hundred years,* he'd said. He had bet his entire operation on the belief that I would be in Valencia during the next eclipse.

I shook my head as if I could dislodge the thought. I believed in seering. I couldn't fight the truth that I would be here at the next eclipse. But that did *not* mean I would be here *until* then.

No, I had a life to live that had nothing to do with faeries or this accursed Hall. I would get Sage and I would go *home.*

I would be human, because human was all I was ever meant to be.

While I deliberated over knives and gear, Hrokr's soft projection filled my mind.

I'd like to speak with you over dinner, he said. *No prying eyes. Just me.*

A sour feeling bloomed within me. It was one that made my limbs tighten and my heart race, but I pushed it away as best I could.

I changed into a pair of dark leathers that I stuffed into combat-grade boots. As I was lacing them up to my knees, Hrokr's voice carried to me once more.

No task will be asked of you, he said, and something deep in my chest caved in on itself further. *I only wish to talk.*

I finished my boots and pulled on a billowing, white button-down. I secured a single dagger to my hip; Hrokr would not question it.

I had no security or keeper as I slipped down the empty, sconce-lit stairwell. There was a part of me that wanted to run *now*, to slip out of the heart of Castle Habrem while no one was watching.

But even though there were no eyes on me, I knew Hrokr waited for me. It would be smarter to leave while he was asleep or occupied.

There was a small part of me that thought perhaps it would be best just to tell him I was leaving. But as much as I wanted to escape Gar, I wanted to escape this life in the Folk lands altogether, too. I didn't need to give Hrokr a reason to follow me by announcing my departure.

My Fae heritage had served me well in Balaca, but that didn't mean I wanted to live this life. The only thing I'd wanted since this nightmare started was to make it home to Mortis Hollow with all my loved ones.

All my loved ones left, anyway.

No, my future had no room for faeries or Folk at all. No room for Gar and no room for Hrokr.

To preserve that future, I let my feet carry me down to the Council Room. I knocked gently.

Come in, Hrokr said softly.

Gingerly, I pushed open the door. Inside, the space was darkened with the impending night. The wall of windows to the left let in nearly no light, as the sun had almost fully fallen behind the horizon. Only a deep, bruised purple was visible outside.

Even the orbs of light bobbing in the corners were dimmed.

Hrokr sat—alone, as he had promised—at the head of the dining table toward the right wall. Before him was an elegant spread, nothing like the meals I was used to taking at the Guild.

He didn't rise, only gestured a slow, long-fingered hand toward the seat beside him. I made my way across the room, eyeing the meal instead of him as I neared. Dark wine, rare meats in thin strips, beds of rice, small vats of sauce. A bowl of fruit that looked too beautiful to be edible.

"Thea."

He said my name gently as his only greeting.

"Hrokr," I returned, sliding into the seat beside him.

When I finally forced myself to meet his eyes, he was studying me carefully. There was something guarded in his eyes—something I couldn't place. But still, I sat like a perfect lady and watched him just as openly as he watched me.

"I wanted to apologize for this morning," he said, leaning forward to pour two glasses of wine.

"There's no need to."

The bottle clinked against the lip of my glass as he poured. "I'd like to apologize all the same."

"Then I suppose you're forgiven," I said. My voice was light and easy, even though something dark prickled just beneath my skin. Something that tasted like betrayal, even though we both knew I'd sworn no allegiance to him.

If only to distract myself, I swiped up the glass of wine and downed it all.

He *laughed.*

It was a light thing, surprised and off-guard as if he himself had not expected it. His eyes were bright with it, his body loose and reclined.

I let a gentle laugh pass my own lips, and something in his expression shifted at the sound.

I didn't think he'd expected me to be amicable.

I wondered what exactly I would be if I wasn't planning on running from him.

I tapped my now-empty glass. "It's been a while."

His fingers—scarred and pale—toyed with the stem of his own glass. "Are you much of a drinker?"

"Only when things are bad."

He laughed softly. "Should I bring out a good bottle, then?"

I smiled, something that felt strange on my face. "Only if you're feeling generous."

His dark eyes touched my lips for a brief moment, as if the sight of them twisted up was a surprise to him.

He rose, and I studied the bowl of fruit before me instead of his form as he crossed the night-dim room. But I could hear him behind me, sliding open the drawer of his desk.

Hrokr returned with a bottle of clear liquor, gently setting it on the table before he slid gracefully back into his seat at my side. I remained still as he finished his own glass of wine in one swallow, and reached across me to pull an orange from the bowl.

He tore it in half with lethal fingers, a small spray of rich citrus breaking from its pores.

While I could imagine this thick silence would be uncomfortable to anyone else, there was something curiously easy about it. While he moved instead of spoke, I was not pressured to lie to him.

He juiced each half into our respective glasses—a rudimentary form of bartending. It was strange to watch him, to see him work so crassly within the heart of the most opulent castle on Alynthia.

Dropping the carcass of fruit within the glasses, he filled them the rest of the way with liquor.

It was a heavy pour.

As if entirely unburdened by the silence, Hrokr nursed his glass, propping one lazy elbow atop the table and ignoring dinner altogether.

The rough scratch of glass on wood filled the space as I slid my glass toward me and tasted it.

Sweet. Bitter.

Into the silence, he again said, "I apologize."

I sat the glass on the table, creating a dull thud. "What for?"

"For a few things," he replied, studying me.

I cocked a brow in response.

Hrokr eyes flared before a smooth smirk turned his lips. "I could go in chronological order if you'd like."

I chuckled, something that surprised me crawling up my throat. "Are you starting with cutting me the day we met?"

"No," he purred, twisting his glass by the rim. "You earned that one."

My lips twitched as I picked at the rim of my own glass.

Silence settled between us. Silence that had me asking, "What do you want, Hrokr?"

I knew it was more than a dinner, more than an apology.

He took a long drink, draining his glass to the dregs. My eyes slid up to him, finding him studying me as he poured another glass. "I want to know it all."

"Know what?" I asked.

"What he looks like," he said. "What name he went by. Where he went, where he came from. What he wants, why he targeted you. Who he spoke to, what he did. What drew you in, what pulled you away."

I took in a long breath before turning toward him fully. "Is there somewhere you'd like me to begin?"

He waved a lazy hand as if he didn't care, but said, "What's his name?"

"Gar."

His dark brows furrowed. He sat a little bit straighter. "What does he look like?"

"Brown-blonde hair. Stubble. Hazel eyes."

He nodded almost idly, theories and strings connecting within his mind, deep where I could not see them. "Where did you meet him?"

And so I told him.

Many things.

I answered all of Hrokr's questions. I didn't care if he had the means to find Gar. I planned on leaving Gar dead somewhere, anyway. If by some chance I failed—I would be glad Hrokr was following to cut him down.

But I avoided any mention of where I'd come from or where it was I planned on going. I spoke of Gar, giving Hrokr anything he would need.

I told Hrokr how sometimes I wouldn't see Gar because he was away, but I had no idea where *away* was. I told him about The Nock, about the Guild, about the *arrows*. I told him about Gar's dedication to killing Valencians and how he told me Silas *was* Valencian.

Hrokr finished another cup of liquor. I could now see a sheen of gloss across his eyes. His body was looser, reclined and lazy as he shot question after question at me.

It was only as he was filling a third glass that he asked, "Did you love him?"

Every ounce of ease I'd managed to garner fled immediately, locking my spine up tight. "Does that matter?" I asked.

He studied me from beneath long lashes. Rapidly approaching drunk, he looked at me differently now. He was not in control of himself enough to remember to cover up the shifting of his eyes, to pretend he wasn't studying my fingers against the rim of my glass, or my lips fighting against the words trying to slip free.

I tucked a piece of hair behind my ear, another movement he openly tracked. The smile that twisted his lips was melancholy. "I suppose that is answer enough."

I straightened. "I did love him," I said coldly, the warmth I'd brewed for the last hour slipping away from me quickly.

"Why?" he asked.

My eyes narrowed. "*Why?*"

"Yes, Thea," he breathed. "*Why?*"

I didn't like the way he said my name, the way he tasted it like the dark wine forgotten between us.

"Why does anyone love anyone?"

He smiled, his eyes lighting at the verbal sparring. "An age-old question, I suppose. But I'm asking *you.*"

I didn't want to think about loving Gar, didn't want to think about those early smiles and the way his hazel eyes would crinkle around their edges. I didn't want to think about his lips pressed against me or his arms tight around my waist.

So I didn't.

I thought about the innocent blood on my hands, the fact that I was *here,* thousands of miles away from my home because of what he'd done. I thought about the fact that I had no idea where Sage was, that my mother was dead, that my siblings were missing, that I'd gone through a wealth of heartbreak just for him to further his own plans.

"I don't want to talk about my relationship with him," I said honestly, my voice rough with unspent rage.

"What do you want to talk about?" he asked.

As if we had all night. As if we had all our lives, as if we had immortality stretched out before us to talk plans forever.

I supposed we did.

And the thought was more sobering than any other I'd had this night.

"What do *you* want to talk about, Hrokr?" I asked instead, infusing just enough charm into my voice.

He leaned forward, bracing his elbow on the tabletop. His glass—half-empty—dangled from his fingertips. I could smell the liquor and orange on his breath, smell it just as surely as I smelled thunder and jasmine and nighttime leaking off his skin. He bent toward me, as if we were two conspirators sharing a coveted secret.

As if we were two lovers sharing an untouched dinner beneath faded moonlight.

His voice was a sultry caress as he purred, "I'm going to kill him, Thea."

Gooseflesh chased chills across my skin. He noticed, his eyes tracking the pebbled flesh of my arms. He reached out—fingers still gripping the rim of his glass—to drag a finger down my forearm.

I held myself perfectly still, waiting for his vulnerable, drunk eyes to once again meet my own. When they did, he asked, "Does that bother you?"

"Do you think it would?"

"I suppose it might," he said.

"Why's that?"

Hrokr took a deep breath, leaning back into his seat. I relaxed immediately, not realizing how stiff I'd held myself until his close presence was gone. "Love—even rescinded—is often a powerful thing."

I pondered that, wondering what rescinded love drove him to his own conclusion. "Are you wed?"

"No." The answer was fast and hard.

But there was something more within it. I asked, "Ever been?"

His eyes went somewhere far away at the question. "Not really."

"Not really?"

He studied the table between us as if it held his memories within. "I was engaged once, a very long time ago."

And that girl was no longer here. It was perhaps too far to push, but I asked softly, "Where is she now?"

He smiled, eyes flicking up to my own. "If the Far Away has an Underbelly, I can only hope she is nestled firmly in the deepest pits of it."

I choked on my breath.

But he only laughed. "A marriage of alliance, but she attempted to lead something of a coup against me. She's been dead for a long time, Thea."

A chill worked down my spine. He didn't need to say it; I knew he was the one who killed her.

I considered that and decided to push my luck further. "Did you love her?"

He dropped his eyes once more, consulting the orange rind within his glass. "I really tried."

Silence fell like a thick sheet between us. "That isn't a yes," I murmured.

"No," he agreed, finishing his drink. "No, it is not."

I was curious, even though I knew I shouldn't be. "Have you ever loved?"

There was a hitch of hesitation, but he admitted, "Yes. Everyone has loved, Thea. I love Maddox, my parents. Fallon. Haiz and Ciro." A shadow entered his eyes. "Many others."

I could nearly taste his grief and had no doubt that 'many others' were dead. "So you've never been in love," I surmised, trying to wrap my head around an existence as long as his devoid of this most intrinsic interaction.

Another hesitation, longer than the first. Then, "No."

I studied his face, watching as he studied me right back. Cole had only brought me grief, and Gar only betrayal. My life would have been better without it. "You're not missing out much," I offered.

He tightened. I felt more than saw the shift in the room. He pursed his lips, nostrils flaring. He studied me for a long, thick moment, thoughts spinning behind his dark eyes. Then abruptly, he stood and slipped across the room to his desk. He opened his drawer as I turned, pulling out another bottle that he rested atop his desk. But contrary to his actions, he said, "It's late."

A dismissal if I'd ever heard one.

But that was fine by me. And while there was a part of me that perhaps felt guilty I'd let him drink himself into a stupor—and then drew his mind back to a bloody past—there was a greater part of me that knew my goal was outside of this room.

Outside of this castle.

Outside of this Hall.

I rose to my feet. "Goodnight, Hrokr."

He toyed with the neck of the bottle, not raising his eyes to my own. "Goodnight, Thea."

I made my way across the floor to the door in silence. I paused halfway through the doorway, casting my eyes back toward him. He was sitting at this desk, eyes on me.

I pulled the door shut behind me.

I knew there was a possibility I'd get caught. But I also knew that his Council was away—likely told to stay away by Hrokr himself. And he was nearly a bottle deep and expecting not to see me again until morning.

So when I turned toward the Portal Room instead of the stairwell, I told myself this was my best option.

I did not hesitate as I stepped into the runegate.

CHAPTER SIXTEEN

HOPE AND LIES

I ran.

As hard as I could, as fast as my feet could take me, barreling north. It made me feel wretched not to check on Mel and Alek first, but I had to believe Calix had told the truth about setting them free.

It was possible they were in danger, but I *knew* Sage was at the mercy of our enemies. I didn't know what I would find when I made it back to Oxcroft. I didn't know if Gar would be there, if he would bring guards or a new set of shackles.

I didn't know what I'd find at all, but I didn't care. Sage was on the other side of those runes, and that was enough for me.

I didn't dare slow, knowing what I knew of Hrokr's power. If he discovered me gone, he *would* catch me. It did not matter how fast I was; I could not outrun someone who could voidstep. There were a whole host of other things I was ill-equipped to endure, but I still had to try.

Namely, rowan wood.

Gar had once cut me off from the supply of fire and healing with nothing more than a glorified stick.

I would be at his mercy.

But was I not already?

Sage, Mellian, and Alek were all that I had left, and he had either one or all of them. And his vision of my future—however displeasing—gave me a sort of invincibility. If I was to be present in Valencia a century from now, I would not die today.

I no longer feared for my own life, only the lives of those I loved.

Quickly, the crumbling gate of Oxcroft Keep rose above me.

I'd barely stepped onto the grounds when the keep doors flung open, and out stepped a group.

I went through a myriad of reactions as they piled out of the charred doors of Oxcroft Keep.

Roderick, Dorin, Lorenzo, and Gar.

Immediate dread washed over me. Who was with Sage if they were all here? Was she even still alive? A thousand worst-case scenarios flicked like torrid daydreams behind my eyes.

And the small, threadbare strip of hope I'd held that I could slay them all and whisk Sage away was immediately shattered.

I'd have to further submit to Gar's will and allow him to voidstep me anywhere. I wasn't sure why I'd been foolish enough to hope at all.

I had hardly any time to react before Gar was bounding for me, sweeping me off my feet and crushing me against his chest. The breath was knocked from my lungs, replaced by the choking scent of his sun and citrus skin.

I buried my face in his chest only to give myself time to process. He held me tighter, saying my name over and over again. "Thea, Thea, Thea," he breathed. "You came back."

"Where is she?" I rasped against his chest.

"Home," he replied, holding me tighter.

I pulled away, not even daring to meet his eyes, but instead glancing behind him.

Lorenzo's lips sat in their usual smirk, his pale skin stretched like porcelain over his too-sharp bones. Emerald eyes stared back with shrewd understanding, bringing out the green brocade of his black tunic.

At his side, Roderick grinned cheerfully, the same look that he normally held. Dark arms were banded across his grey-clad chest, but his body language was open and welcoming. I looked for the spark of deception in his black-ringed, moonlight irises, but I found nothing within.

He had to know of Gar's deceit. But if their intention was to lie to me, Roderick hid his betrayal well. Unlike Lorenzo, who wore his cruelty only thinly veiled.

But it was Dorin who gave me pause.

His tall form was motionless in his quiet way, his corded arms resting gently at his sides. He was dressed the most casually out of the group, his broad, dark chest peaking above the loose neckline of a paint-splattered white shirt. His black hair had grown a few inches of springy curls, softening him.

I couldn't read much in the deep, green gaze beneath his strong brow, but I thought perhaps there was concern within it.

I wanted to trust it, if only for Sage's sake.

But I wasn't sure I could.

When I felt a gentle touch at my elbow, I finally turned my eyes to Gar. There was a subtle hardening of his eyes, one so slight I wondered if I was imagining it.

Maybe I didn't want to look at him—or maybe I was truly concerned about being followed—but I cast my eyes to the south from the way I'd come.

Gar moved with me. His voice had a sharp edge when he asked, "Does he know?"

If Hrokr didn't know I was gone, he would soon. And perhaps it would be better if Gar thought he was coming for me.

Coming for him.

Coming for us both.

"Yes," I croaked.

His fingers tightened around me. He tugged me toward the doors of Oxcroft Keep. Roderick and Lorenzo spun immediately, filing through the burnt doors without even a glance or word of affirmation.

But Dorin remained still. As Gar hauled me past him, we shared a long, heavy moment.

Oh, how desperately I wanted him to be ignorant of it all.

But I pulled my eyes away as I followed Gar.

Foolish hope would bring me nothing.

"Where are we going?" I asked as he released me only to sprint up the steps toward the Void Room.

It almost brought me a sick sense of joy. While Hrokr was hardly my friend—and I knew he posed a very large threat to my own plans—it stroked some dark place inside of me to see Gar so off-kilter at the thought of Hrokr finding him.

If it was not a killing blow I wanted myself—

If it was not Sagira waiting on the other side of those runes—

I would enjoy watching Hrokr tear him apart.

But I swallowed the angry bile and followed him down the hall. Gar pushed open the door to the Void Room, revealing a room that looked entirely the same as it had the last time I'd seen it.

There were no burn marks in here—as if it were too far away from the start of the fire to be affected.

It was a foolish move. Anyone hunting them would know better than to believe it had been accidentally unscathed.

Hrokr would be smart enough to know.

I felt guilty that the thought brought me comfort.

Roderick and Lorenzo stepped over the runes without hesitation, disappearing into wispy pillars of smoke as I watched.

But when Gar pulled on my hand, I tugged back. "Where is she?" I asked again.

"Home," he repeated, shooting a strained glance behind me where Dorin was likely standing.

"I know," I said, forcing a smile I hoped reached my eyes. "But where is that, Gar?"

There was only a moment of hesitation, but it was enough to confirm everything I already knew. But he was smooth as he responded, "I'm not sure, Thea.

Someone else laid these runegates. But it is safe, and she has been safe away from it all. Isn't that right, Dorin?"

Dorin stepped up beside me, his stance feeling more menacing than it ever had before. But his voice was the same low-toned, calm sound I was used to. "That's right."

Silence fell in the room.

"We'll be over soon, Dorin."

Dorin glanced at me—as if for permission.

Or perhaps that was only what I wanted his look to convey. But I nodded all the same and watched him disappear over the threshold of the runegate.

When it was only Gar and me, we watched each other for a long moment. It was he who broke the silence. "What's wrong, Thea?"

His eyes—they were soft with concern.

It was such a foolish, ignorant desire to believe the gentleness within them. I couldn't.

It was even harder to feign this kindness. As much as I hated him and everything he'd done to me—done to us all—I couldn't help but remember loving him.

As I stared into Gar's earth and honey eyes, Hrokr's words from only moments ago came back to me.

Love—even rescinded—is often a powerful thing.

I hated just how true it was.

"It's been a long day," I said softly.

It had been such a short time since we were lovers, and already I did not know how to talk to him. I didn't know how to remember what it was I would have said only weeks ago.

Perhaps the longest weeks of my life.

I must have done well enough to let his facade continue, because he pulled me into his arms in a rushed hug. "I can only imagine," he said. "But we should go before he finds us."

Pressed against the warmth of his chest—his heart hammering beneath my ear—I wondered how prudent it would be to kill him here.

To leave his body on the floor for whoever would come back to find him. To storm the runegate and tear her away from the home she thought she knew.

But I remembered words he'd told me long ago. He told me to be careful using just any runegate, lest I get trapped somewhere I was not keyed in to pass further. So I swallowed my rage and said, "Alright."

I held my breath as he pulled away, held my hand, and stepped us through the runegate.

The feeling of swimming through space was becoming familiar to me now. I landed in a small, barren room, empty of even Roderick and Lorenzo. The room was a rickety, wooden box only large enough for the black runegate etched on the floor. With Gar and I both pressed inside, there was hardly room to breathe.

He released the pressure by shouldering the door open.

A sudden mixture of surprise and despair washed over me.

I had no idea where I was.

CHAPTER SEVENTEEN
ON ALL SIDES

I t was hot. The sun beat down against my skin and cloak as if we were in high
summer, not the dead of winter.

It had been just a moment since we'd stepped out, and already sweat began to
bead at the back of my neck. My boots were standing in white, blinding sand.

And for as far as the eye could see—nothing. Nothing but the wind-whipped
sea, lapping against the shore in every direction.

I spun around to see the rickety closet of a building I had stepped out of. Behind
it was a structure of glass and wood, jutting out over the water. It was the size of a
large family home, not even a quarter of the size of Oxcroft Keep. Inside, figures
moved.

And behind it—

I put a hand over my mouth in horror, despair breaking against me as surely as
the sea broke against the shore.

Behind it was the ocean, surrounding us from all angles. The sun was oppres-
sive here. Suffocating.

But it was not the sun or the endless ocean or the sense of sudden hopelessness within me that had my knees buckling.

Sagira.

Her lavender hair was in a braided knot atop her head. She wore a faded apron that was stained in many colors as if she'd painted with it on.

Painting.

She was not only alive, but well enough to devote time to hobbies—just as Dorin had been.

My knees fell, hitting the bleached sand beneath me.

She was running—falling to her own knees before me—slamming into me with an eager force that I readily returned.

What I wouldn't give for the ability to voidstep, for the ability to fall through the earth beneath me and land anywhere—

Anywhere but here.

"Thea, Halls, *Thea,*" she cried, clutching me.

I held her, begging the earth to open and swallow us whole, to spit us out somewhere safe.

But the ground beneath me did not change, so I did only what I could, clinging to this fleeting moment of joy in which Sage was alive and in my arms.

"Gar said you were alive," she mumbled into my shirt. "But I couldn't believe him, not until I saw you myself."

I wondered if she could know just how much I felt the same.

I pulled away to look at her face. Her crystal eyes were swollen with unshed tears, her lips puckered and quivering.

We stared at one another for only a beat of silence before the tears spilled over, running in salty tracks down her cheeks. "I'm so sorry, Thea," she croaked. "I should have never let you go, I—"

"Stop," I interrupted, pulling her hands into my lap. I brushed away her tears, tucking a loose strand of lavender hair behind her ear. "You have nothing to apologize for."

Her face crumpled as she studied me back, squeezing my hand between her own.

A warm hand came down on my shoulder, gentle in touch. But I could not find solace in the soft touch knowing it came from Gar. Even as I stared at Sage, a sudden bloodlust overcame me, crashing over me in sour waves.

Maybe it would be worth it to shred this island into tatters, to gut him where he stood and rip Sage through the runegate behind me.

But when I twisted my head toward him, I felt the first lick of something that might be fear. Gar grinned openly at me, something akin to challenge in his eyes.

He smiled in a way that told me he knew exactly how much I did not believe his ruse. He smiled in a way that said he'd set just another trap I had gotten snared within.

The rune gate is still there, I reminded myself. *I can still get back.*

I would *not* spend a century trapped on this island with Gar; I would not allow him to turn it into my prison.

Gar stepped away, still grinning down at me. "Come on," he said. "We can start with supper."

Supper.

What time was it here? How far away was I?

I'd traded the cloaking night for blinding noon. I glanced up at the sky, wishing I had the stars to tell me something of where I might be.

"Are you alright, Thea? You—" Sage began.

"She's fine," Gar interrupted. "She just needs some rest."

I turned to him slowly, sudden ice sluicing through me even amidst the heat of the day. He helped me to my feet, and even though I wanted to tear his arm from its socket, I swallowed my pride and let him haul me to my feet.

The house was only a few yards away, but once we reached the sun-baked steps, my blood was boiling. Both from the disorienting heat and the rage burning inside me.

We stepped through the glass-cased front door into a large living area. There were multiple couches and a conjoined dining room housing two large tables. Things were too small, cramped. Too sun-bleached, too bright.

There was no reprieve from the heat. This home was obviously built to enjoy the summer, and most walls were covered in open windows.

The floors were faded wood, the walls the same. No art, no decorations. This wasn't a home; it was a base of operations.

Just as Oxcroft Keep had been.

We passed Roderick and Lorenzo—both grinning—on a faded green couch as we headed for the staircase at the far end of the room.

Upstairs the floor was carpeted in a yellowy fabric I suspected was once white. We pushed through a faded white door into a cramped bedroom. A large bed took up most of the space, and the floor was littered with clothes, both male and female.

My panicked eyes shot to Sage, who blushed delicately.

I knew she and Dorin were close, but *this* close?

Sage ducked her head and moved to a closet, dragging out a pair of thin grey shorts and a blue, cotton shirt.

Bewildered, I took the items and tried to offer my best smile.

"Here," she said, gesturing me toward another door. "You can change in the bathroom."

"Thank you," I murmured, dazed, but eager for a moment to escape Gar's eyes.

I hadn't been gone *that* long, had I?

Had I?

Inside, I locked the door and immediately sank to the floor, burying my face in my hands. I allowed myself only a moment to catch my breath—a moment that my tears leaked through my fingers.

What have I gotten myself into?

When I stepped out into the bedroom, it was empty. Though I changed into the clothes Sage offered, I kept my Valencian dagger strapped to my thigh.

"Sage?" I called.

No response.

Realistically, I knew she was probably giving me my privacy. But I couldn't help the dash of panic that rushed through me.

I peaked my head out into the hall and let loose a sharp breath of relief when I saw Sage sitting atop the stairs.

She turned around, smiling. "Hey. Are you feeling better?"

"I am," I said as she stood.

"Come on. I'll take you to your room so you can put your things away." She took off down the hall, where I hesitantly followed.

It was obvious as soon as I stepped inside that the room was Gar's. I wasn't quite sure why I expected anything less. It was a copy of Sage's, though his was barren. A perfectly made, green bed, and not a single item out of place. The only person effects were his weapons propped by the door.

"He has your clothes put away somewhere," she said, turning to me. "We can get them down now that you're back."

"I'll be sharing a room with him?" I asked.

Wariness flooded her features. "Don't you want to? He's your mate."

She said it so casually—as if it were a simple truth.

"I'd be livid with you for not telling me," she added. "But Gar told us you didn't know before you left."

I glanced around to see if anyone was watching, even though I knew the house was full of Fae ears. I whispered, "It doesn't have to be right now, Sage, but we need to talk soon."

She took a step away from me, and my heart pounded against my ribs. Something like despair darkened her eyes. "Gar was right."

My pounding heart leapt into my throat. "Right about what?"

"Something is wrong with you," she whispered. The words weren't an accusation; they were a lament.

Fear slipped down my spine. "We have to get out of here," I whispered so quietly I was nearly only mouthing the words.

Fresh tears began to well in her eyes. "They were afraid this would happen," she said, her voice so soft I could barely hear it. "That Hrokr would taint your mind."

Rage—acute and blistering—rippled down the lengths of my arms, pooling into burning embers at my palms. Had Gar not taken enough from me, that now he wished to turn Sage against me as well?

But my voice was deathly calm when I said, "I need you to tell me everything that happened while I was gone."

She balled her hands into tiny fists. "It was awful, Thea!" she hissed, more panicked than angry. "You were gone, and then everything fell apart. They say that Calix is dead, that Gar's friend saw it happen."

Nausea twisted inside of me. *Lies.*

"That isn't the truth, Sage," I said softly.

The only people inside of that room were Hrokr and Maddox, and I didn't think Maddox—who'd been more than ready to throw me out of Castle Habrem when we met—could possibly be Gar's ally. Especially considering he was the one who thwarted me from finding Valencia's Orb in the first place.

No, no one saw what happened in that throne room. No one other than Gar himself with his seer's visions from the Elders.

Her eyes were wide, frightened. "What did he do to you?" she asked, voice breaking. "To make you this way?"

I tried to ignore the words that pelted me like arrows. "I was there when Calix was killed. No one was around."

Sage shook her head. "That can't be true."

"It is. I was there." I let loose a harsh sigh. "What's going on between us? How can you not believe me?"

She shook her head again, pressing the heels of her palms into her eyes. "I don't understand, Thea. I don't understand how you could give up on him."

Ice ripped through me. "Give up on *Gar?*"

"Of course!" she wailed. When she looked up, her eyes were full of tears. "You didn't make a lot of friends at the Burning Arrow, Thea. I was a *disaster* when you were gone! And then you were gone again. And *again.* Always leaving." Her voice broke, and the tears poured readily. "Gar was the *only one* who loved you as much as I did. Dorin was there for me, but Gar was the only one who *understood.*"

My heart broke for her, her misjudgement, her victimhood.

I dropped the clothes and opened my arms as she hissed, "*No.*"

"Come here, Sage," I whispered, stepping closer. She froze, but I wrapped my arms around her anyway. She was angry, pushing against my shoulders. But finally she let me hold her, sobbing into my chest.

"I love you so much," she cried.

"I love you, too," I whispered, pushing her hair back from her face.

"You were gone. You were gone and now you're back, spouting all kinds of nonsense."

"I swear to the Elders, Sagira, it is not nonsense."

"It is," she sobbed.

"It *isn't*. When have I ever lied to you?"

She pulled back. She was a mess. Snotty and tear-stricken, with red, puffy eyes. "I don't think you're a liar, Thea. But you can be wrong, too."

I closed my eyes, trying to force away the blanket of terror that was very near to suffocating me. What if I couldn't reach her?

"Don't I know it," I whispered.

"Your mind is sick."

I sighed, though it had enough bite to be a sob.

"Why did you come back, then?" she asked, voice small. "If you just want to leave?"

I opened my eyes, tears spilling down my cheeks. "I came back for you, Sage. I'll *always* come back for you."

"How could you ever give up on Gar?" she asked, brow drawn in something I thought might be anger.

"Let me tell you," I pleaded. "Let's talk, let me tell you everything."

"No," she said firmly. "I think you need to spend some time with Gar. After that, after you give him *a real chance,* I will talk to you. Can you promise me that?"

I hated how easily the lie came to my lips.

"Yes," I whispered. "Yes, I can promise you that."

She was still angry, but looked appeased. "I don't know what that monster did to you, what kind of lies he filled your head with, but Gar loves you so much. He was terrified when you were gone. I overheard him speaking with The Nock, you know. He was *crying,* Thea. It was just him and The Nock in the office. He kept saying 'I miss her so much, I can't live life away from her any longer.'"

He had to know Sage was listening, it was the only explanation. Or it was his wife he was grieving.

But I wouldn't tell her that, not yet.

"I'll talk to him, Sage," I murmured. "Today. But tomorrow morning you promise to listen to *everything* I have to say."

She sighed a long breath. "Alright. The sun is going down soon. Come have dinner with us." She eyed me up and down, wiping her tears. "I'll wait while you put away your things."

I surveyed the room, noting the two end tables on each side of the bed. Only one was occupied, housing a small dagger. I walked to the other at the far side of the room by the window and opened the lower drawer, depositing all my clothes into it.

"Alright," I said. "Let's go."

I followed her down the stairs to a dinner set by my greatest enemy.

And prayed it wasn't a mistake that cost us our freedom.

CHAPTER EIGHTEEN

FAMILIAR

Downstairs, dinner was served.

"It'll be easy tonight," Sage whispered to me. "Some of the others are gone. It's only friends here."

Friends.

Dorin was sitting at one head of the table, watching me with shrewd eyes. I tried not to meet his gaze, as I wasn't sure what he'd see in mine.

On the far side of the table sat Roderick at Dorin's side, and Lorenzo at—

Gar's.

Fresh anger surged in me, but I did my best to shove it away. He smiled something fierce as we made our way across the room.

"I saved a seat for you, Little Shadow," he crooned, gesturing to the seat at his right, across from Lorenzo.

Sage hesitated before slipping into her own seat—as if his new tone gave her pause.

I hoped it had.

"You can call me Thea now, you know. Surely there is no need for secrecy anymore," I said, pulling my chair out. It scraped against the floor, the only sound in the suddenly silent room.

"Of course I can," he chuckled. "But you've always liked the alias, yeah?"

I tried to smile, though it felt like a grimace.

Every time I looked at him, I saw Alek. I saw my baby brother with his head buzzed and the whites of his eyes yellowed. I saw Mel with her hair shorn, her hands calloused and nails blackened with coal.

I saw the face of my mother—a face I would never see again.

I saw that dreadful day we met, when he slashed his blade through my calf, severing my muscles so severely I couldn't walk.

Whether it was by his blade or not, I saw Cole's cold, dead eyes staring across the Meridian. I smelled the sour scent of human terror.

I hated him—hated him with a rage that only grew more pungent with each moment spent in his presence.

And—despite the strained nature of the situation—I saw Hrokr's Council and the age-old rage that filled their eyes when I spoke of him.

I was going to kill Gar. It wouldn't heal all the pain he'd wrought, but it would at least stop him from bringing more.

I plopped down in my seat. Sage gingerly slid closer to me.

"Are you feeling better?" Lorenzo asked me, grinning his shark's smile.

"Very much so," I said politely. "Thank you for asking."

"You're in a unique position," Roderick said, pulling a chunk of charred fish onto an aged, chipped plate.

"How so?" Dorin asked sharply.

Roderick cut him a baleful glance but quickly returned his eyes to me. "Not many make it into Valencia and live to tell the tale."

My hands were slow—careful—as I reached for a plate and took a small slice of fish.

I wasn't sure I could bring myself to eat it.

"I guess not all can be as great as me," I said, giving Roderick a coy smile.

Gar chuckled at my left.

"So what's it like?" Roderick pushed. "You can give us details, layouts, weaknesses."

"She just got back," Sage snapped.

"That's never stopped her before," Lorenzo said softly.

"Sagira is right," Dorin said calmly.

I chanced a look at Dorin to find him staring at me with concern written openly on his chiseled face.

"You always think Sagira is right," Roderick groaned.

"My name is Sage," she mumbled.

I reached beneath the table and gripped her hand. She squeezed my fingers before releasing me and digging into her dinner.

"Just a little," Lorenzo pushed. "Anything you remember." When Dorin opened his mouth to protest, Lorenzo silenced him with a sharp look. "It is best to paw through her memories while they are fresh."

"I don't know anything," I lied. "I was in a cell the whole time."

I could feel Gar's eyes tracking my every breath, my every twitch.

"He kept you in a cell for weeks and then just cut you loose?" Lorenzo asked, cocking a brow. "That doesn't sound very much like The Lord of The North I'm familiar with."

I grinned openly. "Are you quite familiar with him, Lorenzo?"

"Easy," Gar chuckled.

I resisted the urge to slam my fork through his palm.

Lorenzo's eyes raked across me. "No, but it sure sounds like you are."

Sage dropped her fork onto her plate, its crude clattering the only sound in the entire house.

"Excuse me?"

"It's true," Lorenzo said, leaning back and shrugging to the room at large. "You expect us to believe you just waltzed out of the most impenetrable castle in Alynthia? You showed up bearing Hrokr's emblems. I say you're a liar, Thea."

I cast a quick glance at Gar, but he was stone-faced as he watched our verbal sparring.

I smirked, propping my elbows on the table. "So you believe it impossible that he cut me loose, but entirely likely that I've got him doing my bidding in a matter of days?" I laid a hand across my chest. "I am flattered."

But his grin was just as insolent. "I think you confuse who is the master and who is the puppet in your relationship with him."

"Enzo!" Sage snapped. Every eye swiveled toward the uncharacteristic spitfire in her voice. "Do not speak to her like that. He was her captor."

"Surely," Dorin drawled, eyes on Gar, "you have an opinion on how your mate is being treated."

Gar frowned at his dinner. "If they do not trust her, it is better to have this conversation now." He looked up, eyes burning with a false passion. "We will discuss it until she is absolved of all guilt."

"Perhaps," Lorenzo lamented, "only time will tell."

I curled my hand so tightly around the fork that the metal bent. This is what Gar wanted to gain: time.

But I would not lose this game.

I sighed. "If time is what it takes, then time I will give," I lied. "I just want my life back."

Gar leaned over to press a kiss to my cheek. "I'm sorry," he whispered, though it was far loud enough for all at the table to hear. "They'll come around. Isn't that right, gentleman?"

"Of course," Roderick mumbled, though Lorenzo only dipped his head in a reluctant nod.

In a decisively obvious attempt to change the subject, Gar leaned away, poking his fish. "Little Shadow, you haven't touched your dinner."

I was being paranoid. Everyone was eating the food, and I had selected my own cut. It was unlikely it was poisoned or tainted, but I couldn't bring myself to trust it.

"I don't have much of an appetite," I said demurely.

A muscle feathered in Gar's stubbled cheek, but he only murmured, "Of course. Forgive me."

The rest of the dinner was strained and awkward, but there were no more verbal brawls. After I complained about missing the feeling of fresh air on my skin, the group went out for an oceanfront walk.

Sage prattled on about all the things I'd missed, which turned out to be hardly anything at all. She'd taken up painting, but it was more of an outlet for her fear and grief than a joyful passion.

As she spoke, I gazed up at the stars, trying to figure out where I was.

Trying to figure out what I was doing.

I missed spending afternoons with Sage, playing my cello while she sketched. That life felt impossibly distant. It felt like it had ended, as much as I hoped that wasn't true.

Sage broke away from me, clinging to Dorin. I wanted to be happy for her, but I wouldn't trust Dorin just because of Sage's love for him, not after Gar's betrayal.

I faced the ocean, letting the smell of the water and salt-spray wash over me. I hadn't been to the beach in years, and even then it was a craggy, rocky thing in southern Ekin. While this view was beautiful, I was hot and sticky with sweat, and found myself wishing for the frigid winter I had left behind.

I heard his footsteps and forced myself to relax. Gar's arms banded around me as he nestled into the crook of my neck. "Are you ready for bed?" he murmured.

"You're welcome to sleep. I think I'll enjoy the water a little longer."

He straightened up, pressing a kiss to my hair. "Come on," he urged. "I've missed you."

I swallowed my bile and followed him up the steps to the house. I met Sage's eyes, and she gave me a tentative smile, remembering my false vow.

That I'd give him the chance to win me back.

CHAPTER NINETEEN

FOOL

Wˈe'd only just crossed the threshold of the bedroom when Gar spun me, clutching me against his chest. A small gasp was torn through my lips, my body immediately filling with the adrenaline of the fight.

But he was only smiling.

It was an old smile, one soft and tender that crinkled the corners of his hazel eyes. It was as if—for only a moment—this was all a bad dream. Only a nightmare I'd wake up from if I tried hard enough.

His smile said that he loved me, that I'd dreamt it all, that poison had eroded my brain enough to imagine all the horrible things he'd done to me.

Mellian in chains with hair cut unevenly to her shoulders. Alek with a shaved head and hatred in his eyes. My mother in a caravan, screaming for me to run and keep myself alive—the last time I'd ever see her.

Ellie's youthful face—dead.

Lonnie's foolish hope—dead.

Manacles around my ankles and wrists, cutting so sharply they drew blood.

The crack of marrow as I snapped my own bones.

My breath came too quickly, fighting my lungs so fiercely my head spun.

And then he was kissing me.

He pressed his warm lips to my own, moving with all the familiarity he'd grown between us over long months of lies. His stubble scratched my cheeks; his hands warmed my skin.

I hated that my body remembered him.

I hated more that he felt confident enough in my belief of his lies to crowd me backward until the backs of my knees hit his bed.

I stiffened.

He paused, sighing against my lips. As Gar rested his forehead against my own, I squeezed my eyes closed, trying to calm the heart racing against my guilt and disgust.

The sound of our ragged breathing filled the room, rivaled only by the ringing in my ears.

Bracing his hands beside me, Gar murmured, "You're probably tired, Thea."

"I am," I rasped, my voice choked.

He drew away slowly, studying me beneath heavy-lidded lashes.

Gar raised a hand, brushing gentle knuckles across the heady flush coating my cheekbone.

He left my side, and I sucked down steadying breaths, sitting in strained silence as he drew shut the shades against the now-dark night. I was still as he extinguished the light in the wall-sconces and came to stand before me.

"Do you want to talk about it?" he asked gently.

My stomach twisted into a tight ball. "Talk about what?"

He laughed softly, just a short breath of a chuckle devoid of any true humor. Gar wore his mask well. "Thea."

I studied his face, looking for the chinks in his armor. Finally I said, "I think I want to sleep, Gar."

He nodded solemnly, as if concern for me were a true motivator for him.

But I followed him as he pulled the duvet back and opened his arms. I swallowed my bile and lay next to him.

I hardly dared to breathe as his heat wrapped around me, as his scent assaulted me. I waited for the danger, for him to try and tear my physical heart from my chest just as he'd stripped me of my figurative one.

I wasn't sure how long we laid that way. It had to have been at least an hour of terse silence, silence in which I watched the stars outside the window and imagined myself anywhere but here.

Silence I spent hating my body for once treasuring the comfort of his.

Finally, his breathing evened out as he slipped into sleep. I thought I would feel better, but it only made my rage grow. He truly underestimated me enough to *sleep* beside me, to be wholly unguarded.

What made it worse was the fact I hadn't yet driven a knife through his chest.

Forgetting all caution, I reached for my dagger, warming the handle in my calloused palm. I crawled to my knees, positioning myself over him gently.

He was still as I straddled him, deep in his sleep.

I could do it. I could get to Roderick and Lorenzo—even Dorin, if need be—before they hurt Sage. I laid the blade flat across his throat.

One shot was all that I had, considering if I failed he would know for sure I did not believe his lies.

He shifted beneath me, and my heart lurched into my throat.

Gar's voice was thick with sleep when he rasped, without even opening his eyes, "Do it, Thea."

My fingers shook.

"You won't because you know you can't," he said, hazel eyes opening lazily. He was utterly unfazed by the cold blade against his throat.

Utterly unfazed of my calling of his bluff.

"I can," I whispered.

"Then do it," he urged, even raising his neck harder into the blade. "Kill me, kill Roderick and Lorenzo. Kill your friend's mate while she watches."

"Mate?" I croaked.

He smiled gently. "So oblivious you still are."

I pushed harder, and blood began to bead against the warm steel. He did not flinch.

"Kill me and die here, Thea. Starve. Drown trying to get home. He will not find you."

"I do not need him," I hissed. I watched in shame as tears—tears from *my* eyes—splashed across his chest.

"Does he even know you're here?" he asked. "I doubt it. You're always so reckless, Thea. Acting first and thinking later. Did you really think I thought you believed me? Hrokr has been looking for me for centuries. Why didn't he storm the rune-gate? Why didn't he send Fallon through the gate for me? Or Maddie? Ciro, Haizea?

"Why did the Lord of the North not come for me himself, Thea?"

I jerked the knife away, slicing him thinly. He let it bleed.

"Because they knew what you were too foolish to consider. The runegate is gone. They knew they'd be walking into something they had no way of preparing for." His fingers reached up to cradle my cheek. "So kill me, darling. Cut my throat where I sleep."

His eyes took on a faraway look, and I swore he almost looked genuinely sad.

"What do you want?" I rasped.

"I want to finish what I started."

"Finish what?" I spat. "Why bother with the charade?"

He shrugged, somber lips melting into a grin. "Perhaps I enjoy playing with you."

"I am *not* playing," I snapped. "What do you want, Gar?"

He ignored my questions. "You'll play with Hrokr, but not with me?" He laid a dramatic hand across his chest. "I'm hurt."

Anger stained my cheeks. Even my chest and arms felt flushed. "What is your *obsession* with him? This has nothing to do with Hrokr."

"This has everything to do with him," he snapped. This game is mine and his. You are only a piece within it."

"I am no one's to wield," I hissed.

He cocked his head to one side. "But aren't you?"

Fire surged through my veins.

"I know you well. We're *mates*, after all," he chuckled, rolling his eyes at the obvious lie.

The words soured my stomach.

"What are you getting out of any of this?"

His eyes were deathly earnest when they met mine. "Everything I've ever wanted, Thea. I'm going to have it all."

"What is it that you want?" My voice was raspy, close to breaking.

"You will know," he said simply, "when I have it."

I opened my mouth to protest, but he waved me off. "Go back to sleep."

"And what makes you believe I won't slit your throat in your sleep, *Silas?*"

"Silas," he chuckled, rolling his eyes.

"That's your name, isn't it?" I snapped, shoving off of him to curl onto the farthest edge of the bed.

He considered that, propping onto an elbow to face me. "It's an alias, I suppose. I have many faces," he said with a wink. He lifted one arm, beckoning me back.

"No."

Why? he projected. There was a sharp and wicked glint to his thoughts. *You do not mind being cloaked in Hrokr's scent.*

"Your infatuation with him is very one-sided, I hope you know."

"So you really did tell him about me?" he asked, lips curving up slowly. "You risked little Sage's life to talk to him? Are you not scared he will hurt her?"

"You're the one making threats."

"Which is why you'll be playing along to save me the hassle of dealing with uncomfortable situations with Enzo and Roderick. It will be our little secret that you know, Thea." He had the gall to roll away, baring his back to me. "Go to sleep."

I curled against the edge of the bed, watching his body relax as warm tears collected on my lashes.

Finally, he drifted into a slumber.

I *wanted* to end it. But I wondered what other safe-guards he had that I'd not anticipated. I wanted him dead, but I would not kill him if I thought it would end Sage's life, too.

I slid farther away, putting as much distance between us as I could.

Thea.

My entire body stiffened as Hrokr's voice entered my mind.

He sounded worried, but not overtly panicked. *Did you take a walk down to the valley? I've looked all over Castle Habrem for you. We are having dinner in the Council Room. Come down.*

Tears beaded against my lashes.

Half an hour passed before he spoke again.

What have you done, Thea? Please tell me you did not go back to Oxcroft.

I could feel his exasperation as if he projected it along with his words. Exasperated, because he knew I could not respond.

Halls, Thea, he growled, and I had the vague sensation of him moving, of him throwing himself through the fabric of the world. *The runegate is gone.*

Was he in Oxcroft? And if he was, it meant Gar hadn't lied.

I could nearly see him, pinching the bridge of his nose between thumb and forefinger. *I don't know what version of Silas you know, but he is not to be underestimated. Get out of there, and get out now. Forget trying to kill him.*

Pacing, stressed. Angry. His emotions flowed into me like a stream I could not dam.

Find a way home.

Maybe it was luck. Or maybe it was some strange way my magic knew to cast its net out, to search for something my conscious mind had no way of attaining.

I must have fallen asleep because I opened my eyes to wind-swept ruins and a castle long demolished. The cold nipped at my flesh and tore my hair about my cheeks. Snow fell in heavy sheets, glimmering beneath the stars.

Letti stood in the middle of a pavilion, her tiny arms wrapped tight around her mushroom body. I rushed to her, scooping her into my arms. She clung to my thumb. "You called for me, lady. What is wrong?"

Tears were already brewing in my eyes, and I blinked against them furiously. My wounded pride ached, but it was a worthy price to pay to bring Sage to safety. "Can you get a message to Lord Hrokr?" I croaked. "Without him knowing who I am?"

Alarm flared in her eyes. "Without?"

"Please, Letti," I begged. I felt panicked and rushed. I knew how easily dreams could be shattered, how quickly she could be snatched from my arms. "I need him to know where I am, but he cannot know about Aphaedia. He cannot know who I am to you."

Her face was troubled, but she nodded. "Where are you, Lady Starsea?"

"I don't know," I admitted. "I can sketch the stars as I saw them."

Vague. So vague, but I had to trust that if anyone could read them—it was Hrokr.

"I can do this, lady. But I must tell you..." She trailed off, her eyes wide and troubled. "I cannot lie."

Folk cannot lie.

I nodded slowly, knowing I had no other options. "Then refer to me only as Thea—as your friend."

"And if he asks me why I am serving you?"

"You are not serving me," I told her gently. "You are helping your friend."

CHAPTER TWENTY

SEE THE HIDDEN

I woke after the dream and spent the night lying in strained silence. I wondered if Letti had trouble breaking into Hrokr's thoughts—or perhaps he'd not been sleeping when she attempted to find him.

But after long hours, I finally heard him.

I've received your message, Thea. I'll find you.

I felt weak and foolish at the relief washing over me.

Though my eyes were near to failing me when dawn finally began to break over the water, I leapt from the bed. With morning upon us, I felt I had fulfilled Gar's sadistic wishes enough for him to be appeased.

I was exhausted, enough so that my head swam. I battled not only a time difference, but long hours spent in the silent dark.

My eyes were strained and dry, and even my thoughts were hazy. I blinked past it and pushed to the bedroom door, eager to be out of Gar's presence.

Though I had risen with the dawn, the house was not asleep.

In fact, it looked like Gar and I would be the last ones downstairs. I could smell eggs and bread baking, and I was thankful someone had brought food from the mainland so I wouldn't have to eat fish for every meal.

It was only a sleepy thought—and one quickly discarded.

I couldn't eat this. I wouldn't put anything in my body that came from Gar.

"Good morning, Thea!" Sage beamed when I came down the steps. She was already seated at the breakfast table—Dorin, Lorenzo, and Roderick with her. As her eyes scoured my face, her grin faltered. "You look exhausted. Are you alright?"

"It was hard to sleep," I said as easily as I could. "It's not morning on my side of the world right now."

She flinched as if I'd struck her. "Your side of the world?" With the words, her jovial mood crumbled immediately.

Dorin watched me like a hawk.

My spine tightened. "Sage, I didn't mean it like that. I'm just not used to the new schedule, is all." I gave her an easy smile. The tension in my shoulders leaked out when she smiled back, appeased.

"Right. Sorry," she grinned.

As I moved closer, Roderick and Lorenzo studied me intently. I gave them both a saccharine smile.

As I slid into the same seat I'd taken yesterday, Sage again beamed at me. She was cheery as she began piling more food onto her chipped, orange plate.

Despite my general unease, it soothed something raw in me to see her alive and well. When she noticed me watching, she smiled. "Are you going to eat something?"

I shook my head, smiling back. "I'm not hungry."

She frowned, but took my words for what they were.

The meal continued on in mostly silence, with only a few comments between Sage and Dorin. When Sage's plate was nearly empty, Gar's footsteps sounded down the stairs.

"You started breakfast without me?"

"That's what you get for sleeping in!" Sage teased.

My stomach turned. Seeing them so comfortable with another was like a vice around my chest.

Would she believe me over him?

Of course she would. She was *Sage*. We had been as close as sisters for years.

But you've been gone, my own voice reminded me. *You've been gone, and he's been here, sowing her head full of lies. Telling her that you're wild and can't be trusted. That your mind is broken, that you've been sick.*

I shook the thoughts away, looking down at the woodgrain patterns in the table.

Gar slid into the seat beside me. "Are you alright, Little Shadow?"

I smiled up at him. "Just still a little sleepy."

He grinned back. I imagined ramming the jam knife into his chest.

Thank the Elders—Sage finished her meal and stood. Immediately, I rose with her.

"Woah, where are you going?" Gar asked, grabbing my arm. I wanted nothing more than to snatch it away, but I let him hold it.

"I was going to spend some time with Sage," I said innocently, eyes doe-wide. "Is that alright?"

He gripped me so hard it would have bruised a human, but his voice was smooth when he said, "Of course it is."

I turned away from him to find Dorin watching us carefully. I broke the gaze and followed a waiting Sage up the stairs to her room.

The second the door closed behind us, Sage whirled with rage-filled eyes. I stumbled at the sudden venom.

She hissed, "We are not leaving this room until you've eaten something and *slept*, Thea."

I should have known better than to think she was as cheerfully unaware of my mood as she'd pretended to be.

"Sage—"

"No."

I rolled my eyes, sighing harshly. "Why are you avoiding talking to me?"

"I'm not." But I heard the hitch in her voice, the evidence of her lie. "But I'm trying to take care of you. You won't sleep, you won't eat—"

"It's been one day," I interrupted. "Not even a day."

She took a step toward me, angry. "And the Thea I knew would have scarfed down two dinners, slept until noon, and drank three cups of coffee this morning." She shook her head. "Where have you gone, Thea?"

I frowned at her words. "I haven't had those kinds of luxuries in a long time. I've been up before the dawn and living off scraps since we left Ekin."

"But there is no reason to be like that anymore," she cried. "The hard times are over."

"The hard times are *not* over," I hissed.

"Don't," she sputtered, shaking her head. "I am not doing this with you until you act like a human being!"

I laughed harshly at the expression, an expression we had both been raised on. "I am not a human being, Sage. Neither are you."

Sage flinched.

"You always wanted to be human," she said in a small voice.

"If I had been born human, I would be long dead."

She stared.

"Are you going to listen to what I have to say?"

"No," she said obstinately. "I'm going to bring you some breakfast, and you're going to eat it. And then you're going to *sleep*. And *then* I will listen."

She turned toward the door, but I stepped with her. She spun around with a hissed, "*No*. You stay in this room, Thea."

I narrowed my eyes at her. "I need something out of my bedroom. I'll come right back."

I should be outfitted in full gear, not these flimsy summer clothes. I should have swiped Gar's dagger from his bedside table. I should be armed to my teeth, and suddenly cursed myself a fool for ever leaving Gar's room without it all.

But I noticed with a start the pale hand resting on the doorknob was shaking. "No, you don't. I don't know what your deal with Hrokr is, but it needs to end. You don't need to hold his things or wear his clothes or whatever else it is you think you need from him."

I flinched—but fury had hooked its claws deep in my chest. I felt it rise up in me, felt the flame inside of me beg to leap out. But now wasn't the time to let it show.

My voice was shaking with barely bridled rage when I said, "Fine."

Sage was gone and back in only a few moments. She ushered me to the bed where she placed food and water beside me. I ate in a strained silence while she watched me.

"Sage—"

"No."

I huffed a breath and just stared at her, finishing the food. I didn't taste the bitter oil of poison, and when I reached for the flame and healing inside of me, I felt them alive and well.

"Sleep," she commanded.

I slid into her bed, avoiding her gaze. When had life between us become this twisted thing? But she refused to speak, and despite my best efforts, my eyelids began to droop.

Sleep claimed me quickly.

I found myself floundering through the same half-sleep that often plagued me in situations of unrest. I felt all too aware even as I slept. Still, when my eyes finally opened, they were crusted with sleep and blurry.

I rose immediately, snapping straight up in the bed.

My heart faltered when I did not find Sage with me—but someone else.

Dorin sat in a chair across the room, watching me intently.

"Where's Sage?" I snapped.

"Gone," he said simply, his smooth voice low and calm. "Through a fresh runegate with Gar."

I threw myself to my feet, and he was quick to match me. "Why?" I cried. "Why are they leaving?"

"Relax, Thea," he said, raising his hands as if to ward me off. "It's routine."

"I don't care. I'm going after her."

I moved toward the door, but he blocked my path. His posture made it obvious he was trying to appear non-threatening, but that did nothing to sate the terror in my blood. I was here, and Sagira wasn't? What had she done?

"Talk to me," he said gently.

I shook my head. "I need to get to Sage."

"Sagira isn't going to listen to you," he said baldly. "But I will." His green eyes were wide, earnest. I wasn't sure I believed their sincerity.

"Why do you say Sage won't listen to me?"

"Haven't you seen her?" he asked, lowering his hands. "She's petrified. She's gone through too much too quickly. She wasn't built for a life like this one, Thea. She's coping the only way that she knows how to. She's clinging to what *feels* safe. You threaten to destroy that."

"*Excuse me?*"

"Stop," he sighed, falling into his seat. "I didn't mean it like that. I just mean that she is frightened, and she knows believing your truth will only terrify her more."

I said nothing, only staring him down.

"I do not trust Gar." His words were clipped, simple.

My eyes narrowed. "Why?"

He shrugged. "You can call it intuition if you'd like."

A crude snort ripped its way through me. "Where has that intuition been, Dorin? While you've been here, holed up with these people?"

Shadows crept into his eyes. "You believe me to be their ally."

I gestured a wild hand around the room, encompassing everything.

But he said, "You are not his mate."

I studied him for a long moment. "No."

151

He nodded. "He does not treat you as a mate treats his own. And you sure as all five Halls do not treat him as a woman treats her mate."

I plopped my hands on my hips, waiting.

I tried not to be aware of the fact he knew because of his own mate.

"I want to know your truth, Thea. I saw Gar running down the halls of the keep when he realized you were gone. And he was *enraged*. Not hurt or scared or hopeless. He was *furious*. I thought, even then, it didn't seem right."

"Yet you brought Sagira here?" I snarled.

He leaned forward, a buried rage flickering in his eyes. "What would you have had me do, Thea?"

I waited, but when he said nothing else, I realized he was truly asking.

"Anything but that! Take her away, put her somewhere safe!" I cried.

"I had only been with the Burning Arrow for a few months before you two arrived. I did only the work I was asked; Gar is not my friend. I know nothing of what he does. And so, while Gar was reacting strangely, I didn't know *why*. I didn't know he had nefarious intentions, only that something was wrong. And Sagira would have *never* left. She knew you would kill yourself trying to make your way back to her. Neither of us wanted you to make it back and find her gone. We had no reason to leave, not yet."

"And now you do?"

He looked me squarely in the eye. His gaze was heavy, all-seeing. "The Lord of the North did not taint your mind."

"No?"

He smiled, just a chip in his serious demeanor. "You are far too pig-headed to allow that."

I snorted against my will, and a little bit of the tension between us dissolved.

"I swear it on Sagira's life I am not double-crossing you. I know we need to leave, I just need you to tell me why."

With a deep breath—all too aware of the concession that I was making—I told him why. I left out a lot. I didn't tell him Hrokr was coming or about Gar's ties to the Cardinal Council.

Simply, I told him everything that happened in Balaca.

At the end, he looked more contemplative than angry. "So he has had a vision you will hold Valencia's Orb of Dolga, and he wants to take it from you?"

"I suppose."

He frowned. "He wants to bring his wife back."

I nodded, but his words reminded me of Gar's other close companions. I shot forward. "Where is The Nock?"

"Gar only said he is away, but I overheard him talking to Lorenzo about The Nock being in Jenmora."

I studied him for a moment. "You see more than you're supposed to, Dorin."

He smiled, baring white teeth as he shrugged. "Why do you ask after The Nock? Is he involved?"

"It's likely," I said. "Have you ever noticed the power dynamic between them is strange?"

He nodded. "It's like they can't decide which one of them is in charge."

"Exactly. The Nock leads the Guild, but if Gar is *Silas,* then—"

"Who commands who?" he finished.

The thought only left me with more questions.

"So what's your plan?" he asked.

"What do you mean?"

"Surely you're not just here to enjoy the beach. Why come through the runegate at all?"

I frowned, running my fingers through my hair. "I need to get you two out of here, but we have to be careful. Gar's wooden weapons neutralize magic. It would make things easier if I didn't have to take Sage forcefully."

I wondered if his eyes could see the thoughts spinning inside me. "But you would."

"Of course I would."

I couldn't leave her here to die.

"If Gar is Silas, and he's over a thousand years old, he doesn't need Sagira. He obviously has access to other healers. He keeps her here to bait you."

Even though I doubted he meant them to, the words caused a wave of guilt to break over me. It was my fault she was in this mess.

"So we go," I said abruptly. "We get her out immediately."

"I'll talk to her," he promised. "Maybe it will be easier coming from me. Gar has vilified you in your absence. He's cried—*lamented*—that his mate's mind has been warped by Hrokr's wiles. She hasn't had those defenses built up toward me. I can talk to her."

I sighed, nodding. "Alright. How fast can we get out of here?"

"Tomorrow at the latest, I'd say."

One more day. I could do one more day.

"Alright," I said, standing. "Can you do me a favor, Dorin?"

He eyed me warily. "What is it?"

"Warn Sage," I said calmly. "I'm going to gut him, and I don't want her to be surprised by it."

He huffed a breath.

CHAPTER TWENTY-ONE

REFLECTIONS AND TRUTH

Any comfort found in Dorin's presence dissolved immediately after I left their room. The house was full of people—at least twenty faces. The entrance room was full of blankets and bedrolls and pillows; they were here to stay.

I recognized most of them as *arrows* from Oxcroft, though I didn't know many of their names. Lorenzo and Roderick were present, crowded close to Gar, who grinned up at me with his victory.

Every eye in the room turned to look at me, and my stomach sunk. A figure broke through the crowd—*Sage*—and everyone quickly looked away from me. Sage met me halfway down the steps. "How'd you sleep?" she asked, and I hated that I could hear the other questions in her tone. *Are you done, Thea?*

"Like a babe," I replied, smiling at her. "Who are all of these people?" I asked, lowering my voice.

Though, in a room full of Fae, I should have known better. Gar grinned up at me. *Scared, Little Shadow?*

I met his hazel gaze, frowning and shaking my head in confusion.

Come, now, he continued. *I heard some really exciting news while I was out, mate. I hope you know I don't intend to let you go.*

Mate. The word grated against my ears.

"Thea, did you hear me?" Sage asked.

I dragged my eyes back to her. "No—what? I'm sorry."

"I was telling you they're just *arrows.* They come through every once in a while, but there aren't usually this many at once. Gar is probably just wanting to keep you safe now that you're home."

"Must be," I mumbled, half listening. "Listen, Sage. I'll be right back."

"I just got here," she frowned.

"I know," I said as reassuringly as I could. "I'll be just a second."

I turned to rush back to the bedroom, but she grabbed my arm. "Thea, wait." She glanced around the room covertly. "I want to talk to you. *Really* talk to you."

I tried to read the meaning behind her eyes. I was so jealous of everyone who could walk around projecting, speaking silently.

"Then let's talk, Sage. I need just a moment, but I'll meet you in your room, alright?"

She frowned, but mumbled, "Alright."

I walked back to the bedroom as calmly as I could.

Going to sulk, Little Shadow? Gar chuckled after me.

I grit my teeth, ignored him, and locked myself in his bedroom. For the first time since I'd left Valencia, I emptied my stomach into the toilet and dried my tears.

Once I was collected enough, I rushed to Sage's room. It felt wrong to leave my cloak and gear behind, but I didn't want to draw extra attention.

As soon as I opened the door, I wished I wouldn't have.

Sage was bawling.

"What did you do?" I hissed at Dorin.

He put a finger to his lips, pointing downstairs. But it was Sage who answered in an angry whisper. "What did *he* do? What have *you* done, Thea?"

I whirled on Dorin, but he was shaking his head. "Listen to me, Sagira," he pleaded.

"No!" she snapped. She turned terrified, cold blue eyes on me. Her voice was nearly inaudible when she asked, "You're going to kill Gar?"

"*That* was what you led with?"

He raised defensive hands. "You said—"

"Don't," I snapped. "Sage, I need you to calm down. We can't let them hear us."

"You don't think I know that? What is *wrong with you,* Thea?" She sniffled, wiping wildly at the tears rushing down her cheeks. "You're lucky all of these people are here so I can't tell him! Gar needs to know about this, but these people will tear you to shreds."

I cocked a brow at her, trying to let the anger roll off me before I said something I would regret. "You think me so weak?" I didn't say the other words I was thinking. *You would tell Gar?*

"You're so arrogant," she spat. I looked to Dorin for defense, but he avoided my gaze.

"Arrogant I may be," I said, stepping toward her. "But I *love* you, Sage. I am trying to keep you safe."

That was apparently the wrong thing to say, because her hysterics increased. "*Don't* take this away from me," she wailed.

Dorin and I exchanged a look. "Take what away from you?" I asked carefully.

"Life in Ekin was miserable!" she cried. "Oxcroft was the first place I was ever really, *truly* happy. Please don't take me away."

The anger in me burned away, leaving the only ashes of sorrow. "Sage," I murmured.

"You don't get it," she bawled. "You are perfect everywhere you go. I mean—look at you! You got kidnapped in *Valencia* and still managed to come out unscathed."

The words landed like a blow. "You think I'm *unscathed?*"

She shook her head. I wasn't sure if she was answering me or just trying to shake off the entire interaction. A long, terse silence stretched between the three of us.

"Sage," I pleaded. "I trust Dorin."

It was not enough. She turned her gaze on me, and I had never seen an emotion so strong on her face. "What is it that you want, Thea?" she snapped. "Do you want us to pack up and move—again—to go to Valencia? To go play with your new friends?"

I didn't even try to conceal the hurt on my face. My voice was small and brittle when my words finally came. "I *told* you to stay in Mortis Hollow. You wanted to come to Vanadey with me."

"Well, I didn't think it would be like this!" she snapped.

"And you think I did?"

She closed her eyes, trying to push the anger away from herself. "Thea, he poisoned you," she murmured. In my mind's eye, I saw Hrokr and knew what words she would speak next. "He *killed* Calix."

"And Gar killed my mother!" I hissed. I took a step toward her, and I could feel smoke swathing my arms. "I would watch Calix die a thousand times over if it could bring her back. I would kill Calix myself if it would spare her." I was feeling overly flushed now, and flames were near to bursting from my hands. The small, rational part of my brain urged me to keep my mouth shut, but the rest of me was large and angry and wanted to speak the words. "If Hrokr hadn't killed Calix, I probably would have ended up doing it myself. I threatened to kill him once, you know?"

"No," Dorin said, in time with Sage's, "You don't mean that."

"Yes, I do mean that. He was a liability and a coward, and he threatened to get us all killed on multiple occasions. Hrokr killed Calix for *a reason.* Do you want to know why Gar killed my mother? *Only to hurt me, Sage.* Do you see the difference?"

She saw something, but from the look in her eyes it was something different. "Are you defending him?" she breathed.

A wordless, broken sound cracked through my lips. "I tell you my mother is *dead,* and you're upset about Hrokr?"

But her voice was small, nearly broken. "He's a murderer."

I opened my mouth, and I wondered if the words were really written so clearly on my face. Dorin was shaking his head, and his eyes seemed to say, *You are not helping.*

But I was angry. "So am I, Sage. I've killed a lot of people, innocents even." I didn't know that for sure, but I could assume it was the truth at this point. I thought of Talon Fellsworn and the other Valencians I had slain. My breath came faster, my heart pounding harder. "Do you know *why* I killed innocent people? Because *Gar told me to.*"

"*Stop,*" she growled. "You're a mess, Thea! You want me to believe you, but do you even know what you believe? You didn't trust Dorin *at all* yesterday, and now look at you!"

She refused to look him in the eye.

He spoke to her anyway. "Thea was wary of me, as she should have been." His voice was soothing, calm.

Sage whirled on him. "As she should have been?" she repeated incredulously.

Dorin didn't waiver. "Sagira," he murmured. "How would you feel if you were in her shoes? How would you have felt toward Gar if I had betrayed you?"

She turned away from him, unsatisfied with his reply. "There is so much that doesn't make sense," she cried, burying her face in her hands. "It seems much more likely your mind has been tampered with."

"No," Dorin said softly. "That is not the likely option, only the easy one." He reached for her, and she ripped away from his grasp.

"Leave me alone," she spat. "I need some time."

She launched to her feet and bolted out the door while Dorin and I stared at one another in stunned silence.

After a moment to collect myself, I reached for the door. Dorin snagged me around the wrist, stopping me. "Don't go," he said. "She needs space."

I stared into his emerald eyes for a long moment. "No, she doesn't," I hissed, and raced out the door.

Night was in full swing, painting the world in the watery glimmer of silver moonlight.

Two moons made up the horizon. One was crystal-clear and cold—with hard, sharp lines, nestled far away in the night sky. The second was its reflection—closer, warmer, its lines undulated and blurred.

Beneath the glow of that cratered, rocky moon was Sage. She'd discarded her shoes and buried her toes in the warm sand, letting the current sweep toward her and wrap sea water around her ankles.

"I didn't want you to come," she said without turning to me.

I made for her anyway, wading out into the water. Still wearing my borrowed shorts, I let the sea come up to my knees. "Too bad."

She snorted, though there wasn't much humor in the sound. "If Gar is Silas," she whispered, "then I have spent the last season of my life calling a monster friend."

I waited, but she said nothing more. "How do you think I felt, Sage?" I asked quietly. "I loved him."

"What does he want with you?" she asked. Her voice was strong, but glittering tracks of tears stained her cheeks.

"I don't really know," I sighed. "It has something to do with Hrokr. His problem is more with him than me."

"Then let's go," she said, turning to me abruptly. "Let's go home and get as far away from both of them as we can."

"I'll go anywhere you want, but I have something to do first."

The remaining light in her eyes banked. "You're going to kill him."

I cracked a weak smile. "Of course I am. What else could I do?"

"You could walk away," she said more harshly than I expected. "If this is Hrokr's fight, then let him fight it."

"You don't want Gar to die? Do you not believe me that he is Silas?"

"I don't know what to believe. So we should just go. It doesn't matter if he is Silas or not if we never have to see him again."

I shook my head. "I can't let him live. What if he hurts other people?"

She looked away from me, wrapping her arms around her chest. The salty air whipped her lavender hair around her face, catching on the long points of her ears. "Let Hrokr kill him."

"Hrokr doesn't even know where we are."

"You don't know that."

"I do."

She blinked slowly, her eyes scouring my face. "You've been in contact with him." It wasn't a question.

"Sage—"

"Just tell me the truth, Thea."

"Why do you care?" I snapped suddenly. I balled my hands into fists so tight that crescent moons bloomed in my palms.

Her eyes were far from this little beach. "Hrokr is not good company to keep."

"You don't even know him," I said. I kept my voice calm and steady, but my body was so tense it felt like it could snap. "You only know what Gar has told you."

She seemed to come alive, like a statue melting her shell of stone and lifelessness and being reborn into a glory the world hadn't yet seen.

Sage was *angry*.

"I know enough of the truth, Thea!" she cried. "Hrokr is well known for his ruthlessness. What is this desire for destruction you have? It's like you want to be in the middle of it, like you *want* to die."

"I don't want to die."

"Then stop. If what you're saying is the truth, then Gar is the man in the mask. Dorin said he's over a thousand years old! He's a powerful, immortal *monster*. And Hrokr isn't much better!"

I flinched at the words, and I know she noticed.

"Hrokr is old and powerful and known for cruelty," she continued on, her cheeks reddening with her anger. "I've seen The Path of Blood, Thea. His power is unimaginable. You do not want to get caught up in this fight between them. Hrokr is the Lord of the North! *You can't keep up with him.* I don't know who you think you are, Thea, but you're just an assassin without a name."

I am Thea Starsea, the Lady of the South, the Lady of the Southern Hall of Aphaedia. I am the Heir of a ruined nation, the nation watched over by the Queen's Crown, the nation cloaked in stars. I am the Heir of Aphaedia and my people will rise beneath the blood of my line.

The words came to me, unbidden, but full of a ferocity that knocked the wind from my lungs. Sparks danced at my fingertips, and Sage's eyes blew wide.

"You have no idea what I am," I said through clenched teeth. There was a part of me, a hidden part, that was *aching* to be set free. I was Hrokr's equal, and Gar was very far beneath me. For the first time, I wanted to tear away my bonds and force the world to acknowledge me for what I was. I was much more than an assassin without a name. I wanted Gar to know who it was that was killing him, what exactly he had dared to cross.

My hands danced with blue fame.

"Thea," Sage murmured slowly. The glassy, wide look in her eyes was not surprise—but fear.

I opened my mouth—though to say what, I wasn't sure. But a rushed, silver voice entered my mind, stumbling my guard.

Thea. Thea!

Panic shot through me. My head flashed toward the house, but Hrokr's thoughts were inside of me only.

Thea, if you can, get out now.

I was already running, barking Sage's name over my shoulder.

Her feet splashed through the water to get to me. "What's wrong? What's happening?"

"We have to go," I called. The calm of battle slipped over me, a white noise that snuffed out anything that could distract me.

I'd never heard Hrokr panicked.

I felt for my weapons belt, only to realize what I was wearing. I looked down, noting my shirt and shorts, my lack of sufficient weapons, and my bare feet. I swore under my breath, spinning toward Sage.

I unsheathed my only dagger and turned back toward the house.

"Are you going to tell me what's going on?" she cried, rushing alongside me.

What could I tell her when I didn't know what was happening?

"We have to go now. Is the runegate back up?"

Her eyes were wide, swallowing half of her face. Both fear and determination raced across her features. "You stay here," she whispered. "Let me go get Dorin."

"*No,*" I hissed. "You are not going in there alone."

"Yes, I am," she said, planting her hands on her hips. "They have a problem with *you,* not with me. I will walk in there and walk right back out with Dorin. And then we can go."

I swallowed a breath before taking her hand and pressing the dagger into it. "Go."

She shoved the knife back. "You keep it."

"No." When it looked like she was going to protest, I added, "I'm a better fighter than you, and I have fire. You need it."

She looked down at the blade. "I love you, Thea. I'm not leaving you out here without a weapon."

"I'm not keeping it."

She took off suddenly, breaking into a sprint toward the house. "Then throw it in the ocean!" she called over her shoulder.

I scowled—and watched my precious friend disappear into the home of our enemies.

CHAPTER TWENTY-TWO
SIGNS AND SIGNALS

I waited countless, silent moments with my dagger clenched between my fingers. I watched the house, waiting for the bloodbath that was sure to come. But nothing ever did.

Sage appeared in the doorway, walking casually down the steps with Dorin in tow. It seemed too good to be true, that we could just waltz out of this island prison. But I wasn't going to complain.

I pounced as soon as Sage reached me. "What's going on in there?"

She shook her head, looking slightly dazed. "Nothing. I'd say everything is fine, but everyone seems strained. There is a lot of tension in there, but nobody seems to be angry."

I nodded, though I hardly enjoyed the words. If they weren't angry—had they expected this all along?

Why was Hrokr shouting at me?

We reached the door of the runegate shack, and I paused outside as Dorin shouldered it open. "I *do* trust Hrokr," I said, and their eyes swiveled back to me. "But I have kept a few secrets from him. I am asking that you keep them, too."

Dorin arched one brow.

"I told him I was born in the Hall of Flesh and Blood."

Sage's strain was momentarily wiped away by a look of confusion. "Why?"

I shrugged, finding it harder to meet her eyes than usual. Maybe it was because I was lying to both of *them* now, too. "I don't want him to know I was born on his Hall," I lied on a whisper.

Only Sage had seen my flame, only Sage would understand.

Sage shook her head. "I don't understand why it would matter."

"It's a long story, but—"

Dorin cast a glance toward the house. There was a flurry of movement inside, but no one was stepping out. "Perhaps we should discuss this another time. I will keep your secret, Thea." He glanced pointedly at Sage, and she nodded hesitantly.

Dorin stepped through the rune gate without another word. Sage gripped my hand tightly and we stepped through together.

Or tried to.

I closed my eyes preemptively against the flash of vertigo that accompanied voidstepping, but there was no spinning behind my eyelids. There was nothing—only darkness. My hand fell limp at my side, Sage's fingers gone from my grip.

She was gone. Dorin was gone. And I was standing alone *outside* the darkness of the shack.

I was warded from entrance.

Gar had—he had *trapped* me. Again.

I fell to my knees in a daze, burying my face in my hands.

Where are you? came Hrokr's voice, pounding with anger. *Your friends are here, and you're not? What are you doing, Thea?*

I wanted to laugh or cry; I wasn't sure which.

The door of the house blew open, and my fingers shook as I fisted them against my thighs. How could this even happen? I had passed through the ward before, no? I laughed a short, hysterical sound. It didn't matter how; it just *mattered*.

I drew myself up to my feet, still clutching my single weapon. I was barefoot and vulnerable.

But I was Thea Starsea.

I stalked out to see the amassed party of *arrows*. There were nearly forty now, geared up and grinning with their teeth.

Hrokr's voice came to me again, though it was cold with a steely determination. *I'm coming to find you.*

I didn't bother to let myself hope.

I repositioned the dagger in my hand as Gar parted the crowd and stalked down the steps. He moved with the slow, surefootedness of victory.

He looked every inch the resplendent vigilante of Alynthia that he truly was. He wore a navy tunic, the silver brocade at his chest nearly glowing beneath the moonlight.

"Put the knife down, Thea," he chuckled, hazel eyes crinkling at their edges.

I gripped it tighter. "What have you done?" I growled.

He smiled wide, baring gleaming, wet teeth.

"I let your friends go," he said simply. "You're welcome."

"Surely you do not think me so foolish as to believe you don't have eyes on them now."

He laughed again. "Then you know I can see them. What they're doing, who they're interacting with." He gave a look of faux mourning, blinking up the sky. "How tragic, for Hrokr to await you only to be dumped with those two instead."

Some of the amassed laughed with him, as if it were very funny indeed.

"Leave them out of this," I said. "Leave *everyone* out of this. This is between you and I."

His laughter was gone as quickly as it arrived. "This has *nothing* to do with you, Thea. This is about *him.*"

"Then why am I here?" I spat.

He shrugged his broad shoulders, smiling. "We kept Dorin to entice Sagira to stay. Kept her for you. Kept you for him." He shook his head. "You all have made this very, *very* tedious for me."

"If you want Hrokr so badly, just go ask for him. I'm sure he'd be *more than happy* to speak with you," I hissed.

Gar laughed. From their post behind him, Roderick and Lorenzo laughed. Soon the entire beach was full of chuckling Gentry Fae watching me as if I were endearingly ignorant.

"I'm not going to talk to him, Thea," he crooned. "I'm going to kill him."

I smirked, baring my teeth. "Good luck." I'd sparred with Gar, *fought* against Gar, heard the way his mind worked. And he was no match for Hrokr.

No match for me.

"Listen to you defending him," he chuckled. He said something else, something about Calix, but I didn't hear enough to understand because suddenly another voice was inside of my head.

Thea. Hrokr was strained, angry. *I think I'm close. Watch for our flares. If you see one and have the means, send some kind of signal to us.*

The first twinklings of hope began to bloom.

"You have nothing to say to that, do you?" Gar continued. "He killed your friend and still you'd defend him?"

Maybe it was worth stalling this fight long enough for Hrokr and the Council to arrive. Long enough to ensure we had the numbers to kill all the assembled. "Why do you hate him so much?" I asked Gar.

"For as much as you wonder how I could hate him," he mused, "I wonder how you can stand to be in his presence. And not just stand—but revel. I felt you in your sleep last night, Thea. Cold to the bone. Did you dream-walk? Did you go to him? Did he know you were in my bed?"

And—rejecting all caution—I sent my dagger careening right for him. He lunged to the side, but it still stuck him in the shoulder. He hissed, jerking in pain. I tensed for the chaos sure to break loose, but Gar only held up a hand.

He removed the dagger, wiped it clean, and reached into his cloak pocket. A man laid a hand against his skin, likely healing him. Gar drew out the iron mask, and even knowing him, knowing who he was—*what* he was—it still sent a chill down my spine. He secured it over his features.

His voice was muffled beneath it. "You will regret harming me, Thea."

"No," I said. "I don't think I will."

It was no grand gesture—just a small thing. But he waved his hand toward me, and with an excited cry, his people lunged for me.

I was unarmed, exposed, and bare-footed.

I held up my hands and sent a spray of flame toward the front line of warriors. They jerked back, stumbling into those behind them. I turned and ran. I hardly had anywhere to go, but maybe if I could get far enough away I could circle around and get to the house. Surely there were weapons lying around inside I could snatch up.

I ran, but it was hardly graceful. I couldn't gain any traction with the sand shifting beneath my feet and ocean air whipping my hair into my eyes. An arrow whistled past me. I ducked and rolled through the sand just as three more whizzed overhead.

I slid to my feet and reached down to snatch the arrows off the ground. With three in hand—one held as some weak, wooden knife—I spun on my heel. There were three closing in on me fast. One—a large, stocky woman with green hair—lunged for me. She was strong, but not at all fluid. I jammed the arrow into her throat, and she went down gurgling.

The other two shared a glance and took a step back before rounding on me. I dropped the arrows, fire shooting from my fingers. They screamed as the flames licked up their throats, kissing up their faces.

It was a sickening sight, but one that brought me a warped sense of joy. It didn't kill them, but they swatted against their faces, dropping their weapons and turning the other way. I scooped up their weapons, slinging a bow into position and shoving knives into the waistband of my pants.

I pulled the string back, and the faeries before me looked around in panic, trying to find cover. I nocked an arrow and—

A burst of light erupted far to the north. Barely a speck in the distance.

My heart leapt.

I cried out as a dagger landed squarely in my hip, cutting through bone. A large man grinned from ear to ear, a sadistic curl to his rosy lips. I ripped the dagger free, grunting through the pain. Blood poured readily down my bare legs.

I roared something wordless, throwing the knife back. It landed between his eyes, and I hardly saw him hit the sandy floor before another burst of light. Closer, brighter.

Thea, I just sent out my eighth signal. I don't know if you can't see me, or if you just can't respond. Please—please—send something if you can. The words on Hrokr's tongue were tight and angry. Impatient.

He probably wouldn't see it, but it was all I had. I shot an arrow into the sky, sending it as high as it would go.

"*Thea!*" Gar roared from across the tiny island. As my eyes flashed to his horrible, disfigured mask, the entire world slowed. Two men flanked him with their hoods drawn so far around their faces I could see nothing. But still—I knew those forms.

Roderick and Lorenzo.

They moved as a unit, striding toward me.

"Is that him?" Gar howled. "Is that *him?*"

He pointed an angry finger toward the last explosion of light. For all of Gar's desire to encounter Hrokr, he didn't seem to enjoy it coming to fruition.

Another burst of light, and my heart fell. Hrokr was going the wrong way.

I scrambled to nock another arrow, but I knew it was no use. I was running out of time.

With a hiss under my breath, I slung the bow around my back and put my hands up to the air.

"*No!*" Gar cried. "Stop her, stop her *now!*"

I shot forth a ribbon of flame that warmed my face and hands. Fire poured from my fingers in an arc that licked the sky. It was a short burst—only the quickest moment—before arrows slammed into me, ripping through my flesh and tearing through my clothes.

I screamed, falling to my knees. But I couldn't find it in myself to feel anything but dark joy as Hrokr's voice sighed right in my mental ear.

Halls, Thea.

I began ripping arrows from my flesh. They were in my thighs, my arms, my calves, my stomach. I grit my teeth and pulled, healing the damage along the way. I felt like some caricature of a newborn baby, covered in stringy flesh and hot blood.

All of Gar's men stepped back, wide-eyed.

The wind changed, and for a moment the scent of the sea was washed away. I smelled something of the night, something cold and refined. Something fresh and dark. I smelled rain in the air and silent thunder pounding against the shore. Silken petals and rain-drenched lavender.

Gar's men were not staring at me.

"Thea." Hrokr's voice was a caress, an anchor thrown into the ocean of this frenzy.

He was equal parts beauty and terror. Everything that made him polished and refined was gone tonight, replaced with a warrior that looked capable of leveling the entire Hall. His hair was already stuck to his temples with sweat as if he'd come from another killing field.

Black leather pants and a matching tunic showed off centuries of honing. The pale moonlight bleached the scars across his skin in stark white, bringing attention to the tiny knicks and cuts scattered across him. A cloak was draped around him, but it was pushed back, the hood drawn down.

He was here to fight.

He was a beacon of deliverance, bathed in the glow of the shattered reflection of the moon on the sea.

And there I sat in a pile of bloodied sand, smiling up at him.

The way he looked at me—it was like he'd never seen me before.

Vaguely, I registered Fallon and Maddox behind him. Hrokr reached a hand toward me. "Are you healed?"

I knew what he was asking. If there was rowan wood present on the island, if I was smiling at him like an idiot because I had lost too much blood. "I'm alright," I whispered.

I reached toward him, but a bellowed, "*No!*" from Gar had both our heads snapping toward the far end of the beach. The howl kicked the *arrows* into action.

The nearest one lunged for Hrokr. Hrokr's lips split open to reveal a wide, vibrantly white smile. His fangs brushed his lower lip as he readied his sword. In an arc that must have required a tremendous amount of strength, Hrokr drew a sword straight up between the man's legs.

He severed the man in two, half his body sliding to the sand. The other soon followed; blood spattered both of us.

"Sorry," Hrokr laughed, not sounding sorry at all.

"I don't suppose you have a knife you can spare," I said. climbing to my feet.

Impossibly, he smiled even wider. He reached around his waist and unlatched a weapons belt; he wore two. He handed me one stocked with throwing knives, and I quickly wrapped it around my waist.

Maddox was already engaged in combat with two large men, and Fallon was nowhere to be seen. I scoured the beach and finally spotted her—but only for a moment.

She voidstepped across the beach in short, unpredictable bursts. She was more smoke and night than corporeal body. Bodies fell in her path. And she was making her way toward Gar.

Gar, who was backing toward the runegate. I lunged into the fray, dancing around enemies and throwing knives on my way.

After what felt like only a blink, I had already killed six but was only halfway across the beach. Gar wrapped his hand around the handle of the door to the shack.

"Coward!" I screamed, pushing my legs harder than I ever had, trying to clear as much distance as I could.

His head snapped up.

We will meet again, Little Shadow.

He pushed the door open, and I howled a wordless cry at him, palming my daggers. Lorenzo and Roderick moved ahead of him, leaving Gar between us.

But before I had a chance to strike, Hrokr projected a quick, *Move.*

I fell to my knees just as an arrow soared over my head, sailing straight for Gar's heart. He forwent the runegate, instead voidstepping on his own. The arrow flew through the leftover smoke, landing squarely in Lorenzo's chest.

He stumbled, caught by Roderick, and they both disappeared.

I screamed my rage at the empty shed, curling my fingers into the warm sand in an attempt to anchor myself. I hung my head, trying to breathe, but my lungs felt hollow.

We'd been so close.

My mourning was cut short, as boots were immediately kicking up sand beside me. Another *arrow*.

I sent a dagger into his chest, knocking him back into the ground. I hardly had a chance to recover before someone knotted their fingers in my hair and ripped me backward.

Standing above me was a beautiful woman with eyes like a storm-tossed sea. Cold, platinum hair blew around her face. I was half-laying in the sand from the awkward grip she had on my hair, defenseless as her boot connected with my ribs.

I screamed as they shattered. She drew her free hand back, and in it was a shining, curved blade. I grappled for her but found no purchase. She slammed the blade into my thigh. I bit my lip, stifling my cries, as she drew it out and slammed it in again.

"This is for my sister," she said, spitting. "She found you in Valencia, and you—"

Her words were cut off abruptly. She was lifted clean off the shore, her throat in the hands of—

Hrokr.

She slumped—still held only by her neck—as her consciousness left her. Hrokr handed her off to a suddenly-present Maddox, and he scooped her into his arms before disappearing. Behind him, the beach was littered with bodies. Fallon was nowhere to be seen.

I twisted toward Hrokr and winced, the pain in my ribs flaring. Black spots danced across my vision.

He fell to his knees before me, hands instantly hovering over my body, his face drawn in concern. The high of battle still shone in his eyes, the blood spattered across his skin black beneath the moonlight.

"Oh, Thea," he murmured, gaze falling to the knife still buried in my flesh. I hadn't noticed it was still there; the pain in my ribs was far too great. I tried to focus my magic and heal them. But I had expelled more today than usual.

I wasn't as starved or sleep-deprived as I'd been in Balaca, but I also hadn't been burning through magic with the power of flame then, either.

"Let me do it," he whispered. Before I had a moment to react, he ripped the dagger from my thigh. I cried out, biting into my lip. He gave me an apologetic smile, though it didn't reach his eyes. "I thought it would be better if you didn't see it coming," he explained as he pressed lightly on my shoulder, lying me down in the blood-soaked sand.

His fingers brushed against my skin, and it knitted together beneath his touch. "I feel empty," I groaned.

He frowned. "I can see that; you're not healing yourself."

I tried to rise again and winced. "I think my ribs are broken," I explained on a panting, hiccuping breath. I sent the dregs of my magic toward the sight, feeling the tissue move in me slowly.

"Stop," he whispered. "Conserve what you can." His fingers ran across my stomach, up to my lower ribs. When his fingers moved again they were ghosts against my skin, featherlight and ephemeral.

My flesh stitched together, the shards of my bone reconnecting beneath his touch. I closed my eyes, and his fingers brushed my hair from my face. "Are you alright?"

His touch was warm and wet and sticky. I wondered whose blood coated his skin. "You came," I whispered.

"I told you I would," he said, dropping his eyes back to my flesh. "I'm sorry I took so long."

I was frowning and shaking my head before he finished speaking. I wanted to see him, but my eyelids were so heavy. "No one has ever rescued me before."

He chuckled lightly. "I don't think you're one that often needs rescuing."

"Everyone thinks that," I mumbled, "so they never come."

He was silent for a moment, and I found the strength to open my eyes. The stars were bright in his gaze, outshining even the night sky. I seemed to swim in them, the black hole of his pupil swallowing the light around us.

"You've lost too much blood," he murmured, dragging his eyes across my splattered and stricken body. "I can't believe you were on your feet at all, much less fighting." He frowned.

"I was beaten spectacularly," I grumbled, letting my eyes fall closed again.

When he spoke again, the words were near to my ear. "No," he whispered. "You would have taken her down."

"Then why?" I mumbled. *Why did you kill her for me?*

The dark was a calling, luring me down into its soft quiet. I was so tired.

I felt his arms beneath me, hauling me against his chest. I leaned into him, resting my head against his shoulder.

"I didn't like watching her hurt you," I thought he said. "I didn't like it all."

CHAPTER TWENTY-THREE

FAIRSHROUD

I woke to something warm pooling around my legs. I blinked against the darkness. I was still in Hrokr's arms, but he was setting me down against something.

"Hrokr?" I croaked, tilting my head back to see his face still splattered with blood.

"Hey there," he said softly.

I looked around the room, slightly dazed. We were in the bathing cave, and he was standing in the water, setting me on the ledge I usually perched on. Red fogged around us in the water.

"How are we here?" I asked.

He released me, standing to his full height. He was still wearing the cloak, and everything below his chest was soaked. Down beneath the surface of the water, I could see the faint shimmering of his boots.

"We voidstepped," he said simply. "I thought you'd enjoy a bath and a nap. You've been asleep for a few hours."

Gyda was present.

She ignored us, going through her usual motions, dumping oils into the water and readying her supplies. The warmth of the water and the lulling scents of lavender and sage pulled me back toward the comfort of sleep. I tried my best to keep my eyes open lest I fall forward and drown, but it was a losing battle.

Gyda helped me through the motions, stripping me and scrubbing away the blood, sweat, and sand of battle. I let her drape a robe around me and lead me to the dressing room in a sleepy daze. I changed into a set of black sleeping clothes before plopping onto the seat before the mirror.

Before she began drying my hair, she pressed a cool glass into my hand. "S' wine?" I slurred.

She smiled at me—endearingly, for once—and shook her head. "Just juice. Drink up, Hrokr will be here soon."

Had he left?

I took a small sip; it was good. It was the color of dark plums and tasted spiced and sweet. "Why is Hrokr coming back?" I asked, letting my eyes fall closed.

Her thin fingers moved through my hair, massaging my scalp. She was being extra nice today. I wondered why.

"To take you to your room."

I cocked a brow over closed eyes. "I think I can make it down the hall, Gyda."

She chuckled. "Well, Lady Thea, I hope you have not grown too fond of the cell because we moved you out, remember?"

I wondered if I fell asleep in Gyda's chair or if Hrokr just suddenly voidstepped into the room, because I blinked and he was present. With as exhausted as I was—and how likely he was to appear and vanish—I supposed either was likely.

He was looking at me, but his words were directed at Gyda. "You gave her something to drink?"

"Yes, my lord."

He nodded. "Thank you, Gyda. Have a good night." His dismissal of her was quick but kind. She curtseyed and disappeared out of my view.

I moved to stand, but Hrokr caught one of my arms to steady me. "I'm fine," I mumbled, stepping toward the door. He rolled his eyes and scooped me into his arms.

I was asleep before my head touched his chest.

Wrapped in the warm embrace of white silk sheets and pillows stuffed in down, I woke. A slight wind flitted through the room, smelling of cool rain and warm thunder. I was positive something had woken me, but I wasn't sure what.

I blinked against sleep and found I was nestled in the crisp sheets of my new, golden bed. I whirled around, as if I expected him to be beside me.

The room was empty.

A soft glow came from beneath the door of the bathing room, a soft warmth in the otherwise crisp, silver light of the moon. It was late, telling from the starlight outside. I needed to get up, find Hrokr, find out what happened. I needed to find out a lot of things.

I squeezed my eyes shut, stretching the remainder of sleep from my limbs. I arched my back, feeling the familiar snapping of my joints. When my eyes opened, the room was aglow with soft light leaking from the bathing room.

Hrokr stood silhouetted in the doorway, watching me openly. He wore fresh clothes, and the light coming from the balcony bleached him a bone white. His hair was wet, towel-dried and mussed around his face.

"You're awake," he said softly. "I'm sorry if I woke you."

"It's alright," I said, yawning. I scooted to the edge of the bed, moving to rise.

"Don't get up," he said as he waved a hand in my direction. "It's still late."

"You should go to sleep, then," I said.

He nodded. "I will soon." He walked to the marble fireplace across the bedroom and retrieved the poker, idly prodding at the burning wood.

I crawled out of the bed and padded toward him, stopping to fold myself into one of the leather armchairs before the fireplace.

He turned back toward me, worry and anger and a thousand other things etched on his face. "You should sleep," he murmured, leaning back against the wall.

"You can," I said, nestling into the seat. "I'm not tired anymore."

A deep inhale. "I'm not either."

"Liar," I quipped.

He smiled, pushing off of the wall and seating himself beside me.

A comfortable silence settled between us, and the air in the room chilled considerably. It was nice after the hot hours I had spent on that wretched island. I tucked my legs beneath me.

"Too cold?" he murmured.

I shook my head. "I like it."

The ghost of a smile passed across his lips.

"Where were we?" I asked softly, studying the flickering flames.

"The Hall of the Heavens," he said quietly, avoiding my eyes to watch the fire curl around blackened logs. "South. On an island off the west coast."

I said nothing.

After long moments, he asked, "How are you feeling?"

"All better," I said, glancing down at my skin. I was clean and free of blood, and the arrow wounds had healed quickly enough that I hadn't even scarred too badly.

"I'm serious, Thea."

My stomach turned in knots. "I'm alright. What about you?"

He chuckled darkly, glancing down at his hands. "What about me?" he repeated. His eyes flashed to mine, and they held a wealth of anger I had not suspected. But his voice was gentle when he said, "I'm not the one who took an island's worth of arrow volleys, broke six ribs, and took two gashes to the bone from a khopesh."

"I've had worse." I cracked a lopsided grin, but he did not return it.

"Have you?"

I shrugged, hoping to diffuse some of the darkness in his gaze.

"Thea."

My eyes flicked up. "I am not weak, Hrokr."

A rough exhale. "Do you honestly think I believe you are?"

"I'm not sure what you think of me."

"Why did you leave?" he asked me.

"I had to."

His fingers tightened against the armrests. "Did you not think I would have helped you?"

"This is my fight."

"If it was the killing blow you wanted, I would have gladly ceded it."

I summoned the courage to watch him before the flickering firelight. But it was a long moment before I found the strength to speak. "What did he do to you?"

He cast his gaze into the flames. "More than is easily recounted in a single night. I'm sure you can say the same."

I curled deeper into the seat. It was answer enough.

He turned to me fully, his eyes so black they no longer looked like stars. They only reflected the snapping flames. "Are you leaving?"

"I should," I said softly.

After a heavy moment, he said, "But?"

"Not yet," I conceded. "Not until he's dead."

Hrokr nodded slowly. "May I help you?"

It was childish that those words got my back up. I hated the need I felt to prove myself, to claim my own victory over Gar. "I could have made it out on my own."

He didn't laugh or sneer as I half-expected him to. Instead he said, "I know that, Thea. Believe me, I know that," he sighed. "Take lead on the job if you must. I needn't wet my own blade to sate my bloodlust. But let me help you, so he is dead for good."

I watched him carefully for a long moment, watched the flickering light dance across his black clothes and ivory skin. Finally, he raised to his full height, looking down at me. "I know you don't need my help. You will carve your own place in this world. We are all our own hero."

Any semblance of peace was immediately wiped from my face. I'd heard those words before. Those were Gar's—Silas's—words coming from Hrokr's lips. "What did you just say?" I whispered.

His head cocked to one side. "What's wrong?"

"He used to say that," I whispered.

His face was less surprised than troubled. He collected himself quickly, saying, "Get some sleep, Thea. Sage and Dorin are in guest quarters. You can see them in the morning over breakfast."

"Alright, but I have one more trip to make."

His eyes were guarded. "Where are you going?"

I don't know why I'd expected him to tell me I couldn't, why I expected a bargain or a sentence.

Perhaps I was free. Or, as free as I could be while still in this body.

"He had my family in holding," I explained. "Supposedly Calix sent my family home, but..."

"You have no way of knowing if he kept his word," he supplied.

I nodded. "Or knowing if they would have even made it to the border on their own."

He adjusted the cuff of his shirt, gaze trained on his wrist instead of my face. "Are you opposed to company?"

"Yes," I replied, though not unkindly. "Ekin is not kind to Gentry."

A soft, melancholy smile turned his lips. "I am not afraid of Ekin and their backward customs." Meeting my eyes, he added, "If you'd like to go alone, you're free to. But if Silas knows where you're going, I'd feel better if you took someone. Not to mention that any one of us could voidstep you and make the journey much easier."

I would have laughed if the situation weren't so dire. I couldn't imagine a single one of them in the humble, crumbling village of Mortis Hollow—let alone Hrokr himself. Even his face looked wealthy. He could wear rags and would still draw every eye we passed.

Voidstepping wasn't something I could pass up, though. "How soon?"

"As soon as you like," he answered promptly. "Sleep the rest of the night, as they are asleep as well. Talk with your friend in the morning, and then we will take you."

I nodded, thankful to finally go.

Afraid of what I might find.

When I woke, the night was still high.

As I waited for the dawn to finally break over the horizon, I crawled out of the chair and onto the balcony behind my bed. I folded myself on the floor and watched the sunrise over the city. Those awake before the sun were scuttling about, opening windows and curtains and preparing themselves for a day that would be no-doubt busy.

Valencia never stopped.

The dawn was beautiful and stained the city—and the snow beyond—shades of red and gold and burnt orange. The valley seemed to glow, as if an aura radiated from the cobblestone streets.

I leaned my head against the stone archway, its crisp bite comforting.

"It's beautiful, isn't it?" came a smooth, rich voice from behind me.

I turned my head, spying Hrokr leaning against the other side of the arch. He extended one of two mugs to me. "Coffee."

"Thank you," I murmured as he slid down next to me. "What's it called—the town?"

He smiled wistfully down at his city. "Fairshroud."

"Fitting."

He chuckled, drawing his mug to his lips. "It is."

We sat in silence for long moments as the dawn broke around us, and cool winter air brushed our skin. "How did Sage and Dorin get back here?" I asked.

He frowned down into his coffee, which did not bode well for how breakfast would go. "He came willingly, but..."

His silence said enough. "How bad was it?" I asked.

He cracked a half smile. "Ciro and Haiz were there with me, so I left them behind to attend to your friends. The man—Dorin—he was..." He cocked his head to one side. "He was trusting, but your Sage was very frightened."

I sighed, shaking my head. "I'm sorry. Convincing her was even worse than I had anticipated."

"It is not your fault," he said simply.

"It is." When his silence made it apparent he was waiting for me to elaborate, I admitted, "I allowed her to come with me into Vanadey from our human village. She acclimated well and made more friends than I did. She was finally free to use her magic. She found friends, found love." I sighed. "And now I'm taking that away."

Hrokr watched me carefully. "She wanted to leave Ekin with you, no?"

"Yes," I said, studying his eyes. "She did."

"Then it is not your fault," he repeated. "She is grown and therefore free to make her own decisions. You couldn't have known the outcome of your time in Vanadey." A thoughtful expression crossed his face. "She found him. I would think that would make the journey worth it."

I considered that. I'd had love, I supposed. Though I was happy to see it go.

But Hrokr and I had already had a conversation about loves and love lost, and I had no intention of revisiting it.

We sat in introspective silence for heavy minutes before he rose. "Your friends are awake."

CHAPTER TWENTY-FOUR

THE SAME

Hrokr instructed me to dress for outdoor traveling, so I dressed in a thick, brown sweater and padded leggings, stuffing the hems into long boots.

He gave me the space to prepare, waiting in the sitting room as I dressed and tied my laces.

As I finished tying off the tail of a loose braid, I stepped into the front room. He leaned against the mantle of the unlit fireplace, studying me with careful eyes.

I kept step with him as we left the room in silence, the only sound our footsteps against cold tile as we descended through the stairwell.

"They are welcome to stay in Castle Habrem," he said, breaking the silence with a quick flick of his eyes in my direction. "But I wasn't sure they'd want to. Perhaps they'd feel more comfortable with their own space."

The thought was strange, knowing Sage and I would be reunited but not beneath the same roof. But perhaps he was right. Especially considering I was leaving for Mortis Hollow to see Mellian and Alek, and when I returned, I would be devoting my time to hunting Gar.

I wasn't sure how either of them would take it.

Dorin was not a violent man, at least not the sides of him I had become familiar with over our months together.

And Sage was so much better at putting people back together than taking them apart.

I regretted that she had to come to Valencia on her own without me by her side. I knew she had Dorin, but I felt personally responsible for bringing her here.

I would remedy it now, and face whatever form of hurt or wrath may be on the other side of her door.

I realized suddenly that I'd not responded to Hrokr, but when I glanced up at him, he was only watching the hallway beyond, silent enough to give me space in my own thoughts.

Swallowing the remaining, melting chips of pride I still held, I whispered, "I appreciate this."

He nodded firmly—eyes ahead—as if he knew I did not want to meet his gaze in this moment. But he added, "It is truly no trouble, Thea, and I would hope you don't think it is. Fairshroud is quite large, and Castle Habrem's royal coffers quite full. It is not an imposition at all."

Something tight in me eased.

He led me through the grand doors of the castle, opened by waiting heralds dressed in black and glistening blue. The air beyond was chilled with the bite of ever-present winter, but not as cold as it should be this deep in the heart of the mountains. I was thankful for the warmth, even as the cold bit the tip of my nose.

The dip of Fairshroud was not far from the steps of the Castle. I'd had this view before, but suddenly the divide seemed less daunting now that I was able to view the capital city as Sagira's sanctuary and not a trap sprung and ready to catch me.

The sun had crested the mountains behind us and now bathed the face of the city—and the endless snow beyond—in a pink-tinged orange.

Hrokr walked close beside me, far enough to give me space, but near enough to tell the onlookers that I was a companion and not a threat.

And onlookers there were.

As we strolled down the bustling, cobblestone main street, we passed many faces. At the first pair of eyes that met my own, my back stiffened beneath my collar. I expected a sneer, an aghast look of surprise. Perhaps a look of distrust toward Hrokr beside me for walking someone who had been such a threat to their people right down the heart of their city.

But that first face—belonging to a plump, older-looking man—only smiled. He did not hold my eyes long, turning them to Hrokr with a low nod of respect.

Hrokr returned it with a soft smile of greeting.

I considered that perhaps he knew this man, or this interaction was a gentle hiccup in the otherwise crass morning we were about to share.

But every face we passed was smiling or waving. We even passed a small tavern window from which a small child on the second story leapt away, only to return with an even smaller child a moment later, peering at Hrokr with awe in their little, blue eyes.

You look surprised, he said softly, just as we made our way past a bursting flower shop full of paper parchment and drooping foxglove lattice.

"I am," I admitted quietly, reaching out to brush my fingers along the velvety petals as the shopkeeper's back was turned.

Hrokr's gentle chuckle drew my eye. "Is it so unbelievable that my own people would view me as kind?"

No, it wasn't unbelievable at all, and that was perhaps my most worrisome thought. "It isn't their kindness toward you that is surprising, Hrokr."

His eyes gentled. "You've done nothing to earn their wrath."

I cast my gaze away. That wasn't true, and we both knew it.

"I'm being honest," he said, as if he could hear my doubting thoughts. "Most of these people have lived a very long time. They know what true enemies look like, and you are not that. Not to them." There was a catch in his words, as if he wasn't sure if he should continue. But he did, saying, "Not to me."

My stomach tightened. I was unsure of what to say, how to respond at all. Thankfully, I was spared doing so by a sun-kissed woman waving her arms from a bakery a few shops down the path. While most of her skin was warm bronze, the tips of her ears—visible beneath her curly, brown hair—were tinged pink with the cold. "My lord!" she called, waving us over.

Hrokr glanced at me, nodding toward her. I followed as he moved more quickly down the path.

"You are not often out before the stars, my lord," she said, beaming at him before offering me a warm smile I did my best to return.

A grin turned his lips as he laughed softly. "No, I am not. But you are."

She laughed, a wild thing that tilted her head back and shook her chest. "Yes, I am." Reaching into the open shelving behind her, she produced a parchment bag. Glancing at me, she asked, "Two today?"

Hrokr replied for me. "Four, actually. Thank you very much, Griselga."

She filled the bag with four muffins, all larger than the size of both my fists together.

I was suddenly starving.

Hrokr slipped the bag over his arm, offering another polite thanks before we stepped onto the path.

I continued the way we'd come, but he guided me into a turn with a gentle hand at my lower back.

The hand fell away, accompanied with a larger breadth of distance between us.

There were a few more shops, but it was apparent we had entered a residential quarter of the city. We passed post boxes, windows open to cozy kitchens, and the sound of children playing inside.

An ache squeezed like a vice around my chest.

I had missed the sound of happy, playing children. Truthfully, this was likely the first time I'd ever heard happy *Fae* children free and open like this.

I did not have long to sit in my thoughts, as Hrokr's steps slowed when we neared the last house on the block. I felt a sudden trepidation as I looked at the cottage.

Perhaps it wasn't so strange to have her so far away. That's how it had been in Mortis Hollow, after all. Myself, in the heart of the village, and her in a flower-drowned cottage outside the magic-barring ward.

But guilt chased away any sense of familiarity.

This was not the home she'd shared with her mother and father before their untimely deaths. This was not even a home—as Oxcroft Keep had been—in which we built memories together.

This was somewhere she was alone. Somewhere I'd dragged her. Out of Ekin, out of Vanadey. Entirely off the Hall of the Elements.

I balled my fingers into fists, straightened my back, and tried to trick my body into believing everything was alright. Wearing all the false confidence I could muster, I strode up the perfectly polished, wooden steps.

Hrokr followed silently behind.

I tried to see a bit of Sage in the space, as if forcing myself to believe this place was good for her would somehow make it truer.

The walls were made of mudded cobblestone, and windows overgrown with drooping wisteria stared back at me like tired eyes. Dark terracotta shingles framed the house, making the grey stone look not so sad.

But I knew no matter how happy it looked on the outside, the girl within would mourn.

She'd mourn for what I'd done, mourn for what she'd lost—even if those now among the dead had never been her true friends at all.

I knew this, because in some dark corner of my mind, I still mourned for the Gar I thought there was.

I cast a look back at Hrokr—expecting what, I wasn't sure. He stood silently two steps below me on the porch stairs, face carefully painted into a gentle, inflectionless mask.

I watched him for a long moment. So long, he asked, "Would you like me to go?" in a voice that had far less bite than mine would have had.

"No," I said, and wondered why I hadn't said yes. Before I could think on it too long, I turned my face back to the door.

And didn't move.

Did I knock? Did I barge in?

As my heart hammered against the walls of my chest, I sucked in a shaking breath, trying to think, trying to tell myself it would be alright.

A warm, tentative hand laid against my lower back. Hrokr—with a gentle understanding in his eyes—guided me to the side and opened the door himself.

I dropped my eyes in shamed thanks and stepped into the front room of the cottage.

Inside, it was as richly furnished as I should have expected from Hrokr. Plants in both crystal and pots of baked clay adorned most surfaces, but the space was still open enough to carry that cold Valencian class I'd grown used to seeing within the castle.

But the plants didn't matter. Neither did the bleached wood underfoot or the smooth white walls.

What mattered was Sagira running full speed across the room—eyes swollen with tears she'd *already* been crying, I noted—and barreling into my chest. I caught her as we stumbled back a few steps, and Hrokr gracefully slipped to the side to avoid being a part of our collision.

"You're alright," she cried. "You're alright, you're alright, you're alright."

"I'm here, Sage," I croaked, holding her closer.

I met Hrokr's eyes over her shoulder. Briefly, for just a moment, before looking at Dorin standing at the far end of the room. He gave me a deep, solemn nod.

I returned it with a weak smile.

Sage extracted herself from my grasp and kissed both my cheeks, choking on a sob that turned into a broken giggle. "Halls, we have to stop doing this, Thea."

I laughed, too, even though it felt like a fragile thing. "Doing what?"

She looked at me knowingly as she took a step back. Some of the mirth drained from her face. "It kills me to know how much danger you're always in."

I wanted to assure her the danger was over, but we both knew I couldn't.

She barrelled on, as if she didn't want her comment to settle any more fully between us. "When can we go home?"

And, Halls, the way she asked it with a smile on her face.

Hrokr's mind leapt the same moment mine did, and he projected, *I'd advise against that.*

"We can't go home, Sage," I said, doing my best not to look at Hrokr, lest she think I looked to him for some kind of permission.

It would only put her at further unease.

Dorin made his way further into the room, standing just behind her as if he knew a storm was soon to come.

I prayed it didn't.

Sage's crystal blue eyes flicked to Hrokr at my side before returning to settle on me. "Please, Thea," she said, voice pitched low.

I begged with my eyes, pleading with her to understand. "It's not a good idea for us to be on our own right now, Sage."

Her voice was so soft—as if she wished the air between us would swallow the words before they reached me. But she spoke them anyway. "It's been a long time since we've been on our own."

I heard the words beneath them that she didn't speak. I could see them in her eyes.

We haven't been "on our own" in months, Thea. We haven't been on our own in months because you chose our last allies.

And you chose wrong.

My eyes flicked behind her to Dorin, finding him studying Hrokr at my side. But when my gaze slid to Hrokr, he was already watching me. I said nothing, but he nodded as if he heard my thoughts all the same.

He strolled through the room, past a frozen Sage. He gestured to Dorin, and they both disappeared around a corner in the kitchen.

I did not doubt they'd both be listening, anyway.

But Sage's shoulder fell with relief at their absence.

"We need to go home, Thea."

"We can't," I repeated.

She was already shaking her head. "We can't keep doing this. It's over. If Mellian and Alek are back in Mortis Hollow, let's go there. This fight is over."

My back immediately tightened. "It isn't over."

"It has to be," she pleaded, her face crumpling further. "I can't keep doing this. I can't keep knowing you're in danger."

I gentled my voice as much as I could, but even I could hear the rage simmering beneath it. "I cannot let him live, Sage."

She looked almost...disappointed. Fresh tears collected on her lashes as she asked, "Is your hatred for him stronger than your love for me? For Mellian? For Alek?" The tears spilled over. "For *yourself?*"

The words were a punch, and I did not want to think about the answer to them. "They're not mutually exclusive. We *can't* move on while he's still alive. He will find us. He will find *me,* find you, find my family. We can't go back to Mortis Hollow, not until he can never find us again."

She fidgeted with the sleeve of her white sweater. "I don't think this is healthy for you," she admitted, eyes on her hands. "I think as much as it hurts, there comes a point where it's time to let it go."

I flinched, my throat suddenly choking on the lump swelling inside it. "He killed my mother, Sage."

Her eyes flashed up to mine. "I know," she whispered. "Bad things happen. And sometimes the best thing to do is just keep going. Sometimes chasing retribution is giving the monster even more to take from you."

My chest was burning. With anger, hurt, betrayal—I wasn't sure. Unbidden, I was flooded with memories from years shrouded in darkness.

Bloated Fae corpses swinging in public gallows. Children from school that I called *friends* watching faeries be killed with no inch of remorse, only curiosity. The scent of waste and decay and burning flesh hanging thick in the village square. The pillars of smoke from crowded pyres chasing away the shine of the sun.

A young Sage crumpled with grief in my mother's arms. A young *me* standing beside Mellian and Alek, unsure how to comfort a small girl who had just had both her parents ripped from her and strung from creaking gallows.

If anyone knew the pain from a murdered parent, it was Sagira.

Knowing the only place my thoughts could have gone, Sage said, "I had to move on."

Tears stung my eyes. "I loved him, Sage. I *loved* him, and he did this to me."

Her lips pulled into a melancholy smile. "I loved them, too. The people who killed my parents were our neighbors, Thea. Our teachers, our friends."

I shut out her words. "I have to stop him."

"You've done enough. You killed everyone on that island."

"It's not enough," I croaked, my voice breaking with unshed tears.

"I love you," she said, offering me a wistful, disappointed smile. "I love you *so* much. But I can't continue to support this." She hesitated before adding, "It's selfish, Thea. And I know you don't mean it to be, but it is. You're risking so much—and for what? Gar is not the last monster on Alynthia. Killing him won't save the world. Killing him won't bring your mother back. It will only risk your life and impose grief on everyone you love."

I took a step away from her, begging my lungs to give me more air. She stepped with me, laying a cool hand on my arm.

"You're losing yourself, Thea," she said, softer now. "And I get it—I do. I can't even imagine what is going through your head on a daily basis, but look at what you've already done. You killed *everyone* on that island, Thea. *Everyone*. What if there were other people like Dorin there? People like me?"

A choked sound poured from my lips. "They were attacking me, Sagira."

"Would it have mattered if they weren't?"

My lips pressed together in a tight, trembling line.

"It's selfish," she repeated softly. "Just come home with me."

"*Everything* I did, I did for you. *Everything, Sagira.*" My voice broke, and hot tears beaded on my lashes.

"That isn't true," she whispered.

"How can you—How can you even say that? I was willing to let myself die here, Sage, if it kept you safe. I was willing to *let myself die,* do you even know what that means?"

But of course she didn't. She didn't know I was the Heir of Aphaedia. She didn't know it was my duty to my land—to my people—to stay alive. Yes, I was willing to lose my life for her. But more than that—I was willing to let the hope of my people die, my lineage be for naught. I had been willing to leave the Hall damned forever, all for her.

"Do I even know what that means?" she repeated, the first layer of her calm exterior beginning to crack. "You don't think I'd die for you?"

"Of course you would," I breathed. "It's just different, it's—"

"It's *different?*" she asked, cocking a brow. "You don't think me dying for you is the same?

Panic flooded me. "I didn't mean it like that, Sage."

She held up a hand, halting me. Her fingers were shaking when she lowered them. "Not everything you did was for me," she said, guiding us back to point.

But I said nothing, as I had nothing to say. She was wrong.

In a shaking voice, she continued. "I walked away from *everything* for you, Thea. My life was awful in Mortis Hollow, I'll admit that. But it wasn't *this*. We had to avoid the danger that came at us, but at least you weren't chasing it." She paused, taking a rattling breath. "But I followed you—because how could I not? I was there for you through so much, Thea, through so much." A tear streaked down her cheek. She did not wipe it away.

"You don't think it killed me?" she continued. "It was eating me alive to watch what you went through. I thought I was going to break after Talon, Thea. You were *dying*. If you had showed up a minute later you would have been *dead*. But you kept going, for your mother and Alek and Mel. I understood it, I really did." The tears poured readily.

"You would have done anything for your family, Thea. You let him turn you into a monster for them."

I flinched again. "Please stop, Sage," I whispered.

"Why?" she pushed. "It was *killing me,* Thea, to watch you go through that! And then—and then—" she hiccuped a great, gulping breath. "And then you came here. And even after everything, you still won't stop. I begged you—I *begged* you to let this go. But you did it anyway. You left me—again. And this time there was no reason to. But you've got some desire to die or something."

All the blood drained from my face, but she barrelled forward.

"I don't know why you feel like you need to save the world. I don't know who it is you think you are, or what responsibility you think you owe the universe. But you're wrong."

"It wasn't right," I whispered, "to let them live. I had to."

"No," she said. "You didn't."

Hrokr stepped around the corner, a cunning and dark spark in his eyes, a tightness to his jaw. My stomach immediately dropped as I recognized the hard slate of his shoulders, the gentle flaring of his nostrils telling of his anger.

But he said nothing to Sagira, only cutting straight through the room to stand at my side, Dorin following carefully behind. "Thea, love," he said, voice calmer than I'd expected. "You're welcome to return here after our trip, but we should be leaving soon."

Such a casual statement, accented by the fact he still carried the bag of muffins tucked beneath his arm.

Sage croaked, "Where are you going?"

He turned those eyes onto her, eyes I knew were far too heavy to stand beneath. I reached out, wrapping my fingers around his forearm to corral him, to stop him before he treated her with any kind of disrespect. He laid his fingers over my own, well aware of the threats I'd hurl his way if he stepped over any line with her.

Dorin and Sage's eyes both dropped to our hands.

Hrokr was well in control of his voice as he calmly said, "Thea is correct that her siblings are likely in danger staying in Mortis Hollow. We need to handle that."

"*Handle* that?" she squeaked.

Hrork's fingers flexed against my own.

I stepped forward, dropping his arm. "I only want to check on them, Sage."

She stared at me for a long moment, so long I was sure she did not believe me. Her eyes told me she'd only just realized there was a deadly side of me she'd never known. A side that thirsted for vengeance, that *would* slaughter an island of strangers if it meant it would protect her or Mel or Alek.

I only hoped she remembered all the soft pieces of me were just as real.

She nodded tightly.

I stepped forward tentatively, and she accepted the farewell hug I offered. "I'll come back," I whispered.

But she held me tighter, saying, "I don't want to know any of it, Thea. If I have to stay here... fine. But I don't want to be updated. I don't want to know the danger you're in."

I stiffened in her arms, but agreed with a soft, "Alright."

When I finally pulled away, Hrokr already had the front door propped open with his boot. He gestured me forward, pulling the door shut tight behind us.

He didn't speak—for which I was grateful—as we wound our way through the streets and back to the entrance steps of Castle Habrem. I caught him watching me a few times, but he never voiced the thoughts I knew had to be assaulting him.

I had no doubt he had an opinion about what had transpired, but I wasn't sure I wanted to hear it.

We moved in silence until we made it to the bottom of the stairwell that would lead us to our respective rooms. But the walk up the steps suddenly felt too far. Insurmountable.

Hrokr slowed with me, turning toward me at the base of the steps. "It won't hurt anything if we wait to travel," he said softly, eyes gentle as they bored into my own. "Ciro is already there, watching for any threat from Silas. If your family made it to Mortis Hollow safely, then they are still safe."

Tears threatened to bead against my lashes; I blinked against them. "How did you know what town I'm from?"

"Your friends told Ciro last night."

I folded my arms tight across my chest. "Why did you bring me back here if we don't need to leave?"

There was a bite in my voice, but from the softening of his eyes, I knew he didn't think my hurt was directed at him. Instead of answering my question, he said, "I appreciate her devotion to morality, to valuing health and closure over retribution."

I waited.

"But you are not wrong, Thea. He will come for you, come for her, come for them."

My skin felt too thin, as if it might snap or tear from where it stretched over my bones. I pressed a hand to my chest, as if I could force the sobs wanting to break free back inside.

His dark eyes, swirling with multicolored stars, scrolled across my face before he turned away, prepared to proceed up the steps. He lifted his boot to the first stair.

And I didn't know, really, why I said it. But I whispered, "And if I would hunt him even if he were no threat?"

After a long, weighted moment, he looked back at me over his shoulder.

"Then I would say we aren't as different as you wish we were."

CHAPTER TWENTY-FIVE
BLEEDING STONE HEART

I didn't want to follow him up the steps, not if there was a chance I'd catch him. I didn't want to be the same as him. I didn't want to find solidarity with him, not when I couldn't even find it with Sage.

I didn't want his kindness, knowing I had no idea why he extended it.

I let the darkness take me as I slipped down the hall and into the stairwell of the bathing chamber, thankful to find the cavern empty. I stared at the bubbles of glowing light, the dripping stalactites and stalagmites.

I sat on the edge of the natural tub and let my feet slip into the water.

How many people had to have a problem with me before I realized the problem was myself?

Things had been so heightened, so frantic, I hadn't given myself a moment to really evaluate things.

Hrokr had shown me kindness, something akin to friendship even, but why? He had said he simply believed me to be innocent, but was that enough? Hrokr was a very well-known man, and that reputation involved nothing of kindness. He was vicious, vile, brutal—but he'd never been to me. Except for that very first day when I found a blade healed into my femur. But even then, I had walked away with my life.

Why?

He couldn't know. There was no way he knew I was the Heir of Aphaedia, but what other reason was there? What else was it that could make me different from anyone else? Hrokr had told me himself he didn't like loose ends—and I was the loosest of them all.

I guessed it was possible the rumors were false, that he was truly just a kind man. But I didn't believe that, either. I'd seen the way he'd treated strangers, the way he'd treated his own men who'd hurt me.

I groaned, leaning back on the stone floor.

I patted the ink on my hip, reminding myself it was safely concealed.

Gar was out on the loose again. I wondered if Lorenzo survived the arrow he took to the chest. I hoped he hadn't.

I didn't want to think about Gar, but I knew I should. The fact he had access to rowan wood terrified me. I wondered why he didn't use it on me in Balaca or even on that summer island.

I supposed I wondered a lot of things about Gar.

I was living in the home—nearly the private chambers—of someone who was my greatest enemy only a few weeks ago. Gar was hunting us—or running from us, I wasn't quite sure. My little brother hated me, and my sister was taking his side. That is, if they'd even made it home safe. My closest friend thought me nothing more than a bloodthirsty killer.

What had I done wrong?

I didn't recognize that the low keening around me was actually coming from my own body until a ragged sob broke through my chest.

Alone, alone, alone.

Always alone.

I pulled my feet out of the water and curled into a tiny ball on the floor, letting the tears overtake me.

There was no enemy to kill, no creature to hunt, that would make them love me again. The only monster I had to contend with was myself.

I wasn't sure how long I lay there. Maybe minutes, maybe hours. If someone had told me it was days, I would have believed them.

I only moved when I heard a tiny gasp.

I shot up to a sitting position, my heart suddenly pounding.

A tiny, black-haired figure stood before me. Gyda.

I forced a smile, brushing the tears from my cheeks. "Hello, Gyda. I was just going."

She plopped her hands on her hips and frowned down at me. "If you intend to cry, it would be prudent of you to do it in your own room."

I scowled, ears twitching. Anger burned through the remaining fog of my sadness. "Well, if you must know, I hadn't *intended* on crying."

Her voice gentled. "I am not judging you for your emotion. It is something so endearingly human."

"We all have emotions," I shot back.

"Sure," she agreed. "But humans are raised to feel things so differently, are they not? They are bleeding hearts and empaths. Those of us raised with them bear the gift of their exceptional humanity."

"You were raised with humans?"

"Not I," she said with a soft smile. "Come."

An hour later, I was wearing the humblest of the clothes Hrokr had left me, sitting on the end of the bed as I twirled a dagger between my fingers.

Safe. At least she is safe.

It was a mantra I chanted over and over, anything to fight against the tears threatening to spill down my cheeks. When a soft knock came at the door, I called, "Come in."

I hated that my voice sounded as weak as I felt.

Hrokr strolled inside, his face overly guarded. "How are you feeling?"

"Fine," I said, shooting to my feet.

I thought he would push, but he didn't. He only eyed the one measly dagger strapped to my thigh. "Is that all you're taking?"

"I don't need more," I said, stepping around him.

He caught me by the wrist, but I promptly jerked my arm free.

"Thea."

"Don't," I said, meeting his eyes with all the venom I had left.

"Don't do this," he said, shaking his head. "Be angry. But please acknowledge it's not at me. I am not your enemy."

"Aren't you?" I snapped. It wasn't true, I knew.

His dark eyes narrowed. "Do you honestly believe my intentions to be nefarious?"

"I don't know what your intentions are."

I hissed the words like they burned coming up through my throat. Perhaps they burned because I knew Sage was safe on *his* land. I was clothed in *his* armor. I was armed with *his* weapons. I was fed with *his* food. I was traveling with *his* men.

I spit the words all the same.

"Have you asked me?" he challenged. His voice took on an angry, sharp edge. "Or have you just assumed the worst?"

"Do not presume to lecture me," I bit.

He leaned in, so close I could smell the night and jasmine leaking off his skin. "*Do not presume* to know my thoughts."

"Then what are they?" I asked tightly, tears collecting on my lashes.

Hrokr's eyes narrowed.

I knew I was just angry. *He* knew I was just angry. But it did not stop the harsh, flat look from settling on his features. "I can understand why you are wary of trusting again, but—"

"You've given me nothing."

A lie, a lie, a lie.

Incredulity flashed in his starry eyes. "Thea, I have given you *everything*."

"*Why?*"

His brows rose. "Is common kindness not enough of a reason?"

"No," I said baldly. "No, it is not."

Not after my own family had turned their kindness from me. Not after my closest friend had begun watching me through guarded eyes. Not after my own lover had become the greatest enemy I'd ever known.

No, I did not trust Hrokr's common decency. Not when he was infamous for his cruelty. Not when he stood to gain more from me than anyone else did. I was only a weapon to be wielded against Gar. And if he knew who I was to Aphaedia—then I was only a kingdom to be conquered.

"No," I repeated.

I waited. For what, I wasn't sure. But he searched my eyes until something of a cold haze settled over them. "Fine," he said darkly. "Do not trust me, Thea."

It was immediate, the ball of guilt that bloomed in my belly. "Hrokr—"

"Maddox will be downstairs for you. I'll follow after."

"I—"

Gone. Nothing more than a swirl of dark smoke, instantly smothered by the sun filtering in through the window.

CHAPTER TWENTY-SIX

SELFISH

It was either Maddox's standard state of being or he was just trying to diffuse my poor mood, but he greeted me with a wide grin.

"Ready?" he beamed.

I offered a half-hearted smile and a soft, "Sure."

While I began studying the signs above the rune-gates, he chuckled. "No runegates today. We are voidstepping right there."

I cocked a brow as he pulled out a slim knife and cut his palm. "Voidsteppers can transport inanimate objects through touch and living things through a blood connection." His fingers wiggled. "Let's go."

I eyed his hand speculatively. "Didn't you all just tell me that a mating bond was cemented through blood-sharing?"

He laughed—a rich sound that came from deep within his chest—so hard tears welled in his eyes. "Well, not to worry," he said, still dangling his bloody hand in my direction. "That only cements a bond that's already there. We—we are not in danger of mating."

More laughter.

I scowled and ripped the knife from his hand, nicking myself and pressing my palm to his.

"Mates," he chortled, shaking his head.

"Shut up," I hissed.

He grinned at me, those orange eyes bright. "Ready?"

"I—"

I didn't even get the words passed my lips before we were tumbling through space, slipping between cracks in the fabric of the world. When my vision settled, I pitched forward.

Thankfully, I caught myself on a headstone, as Maddox wasn't going to offer. He only grinned, ear to ear. He'd deposited us in the middle of a graveyard east of Mortis Hollow, if I recognized the space.

"Thank you," I said tersely, righting my tunic. "How will I let you know it's time to go back?"

"I'll be right beside you," he said. "Hrokr and the others are waiting for you, too."

"No," I said firmly. "You will not." They could be in Ekin, fine. But I had no intentions of camping out in a cramped inn with them or playing host in my own house.

He only smiled wider. "I don't take orders from you, little girl."

"And I don't take orders from Hrokr."

He smirked and crossed his arms across his chest. "Then disobey all the orders you like. I won't be."

"I hope you don't think you're coming inside."

"Why not?"

I leveled a flat look. "Go."

He lost some of his mirth, gentling. "Look, kid—"

"Don't. I do not need your protection."

I tried not to think of a bloody beach.

"We all protect each other. We—"

"Have your protection. I don't need it."

Maddox let loose a sharp breath. "Fine, come home when you want, I guess," he said, waving a sharp hand.

"Valencia isn't my home," I snapped.

He paused, casting a harsh look over his shoulder. "No, I'm sure the hovel you're returning to is much more welcoming."

I took a step forward. "Excuse me?"

He bared his teeth. "Hrokr might coddle you, but you don't want to pick a fight with me. I don't care about your feelings, kid. You're being reckless—stupid. You messed up and trusted someone you shouldn't have. Don't throw away a good thing because you're punishing yourself."

A choked noise came out of me. It was almost a laugh, however snide and disbelieving. *"Throw away a good thing?"*

He took a sharp step toward me, a step so hard that most people would have cowered back. I know because I considered it.

But I held my own, nose to nose with Valencia's Commander. "Silas?" he growled. "Killed Ciro's unborn child. His wife. Inina, her name was. I loved her like a sister."

I shriveled, shrinking back. He didn't dare touch me, but he crowded me closer, his orange eyes flaring. "Haizea's husband, Orion."

"Stop."

Another step closer. "And *my* Lord. *My* king. Cadmus Stormblood slain because *I couldn't get to him in time.* And you know who was next? His son. Hrokr. Who faced his own torment coming home to his mother gutted, strung across their kitchen floor."

I was going to be sick.

"So, yes. I think you're disgustingly selfish not to help us, to think you need to hold this all on your own. You think your thirst for vengeance is greater than mine?" He bit the words at me. *"It. is. not."*

We stood in a silent stalemate. One in which he seethed, and I fought the tears brewing behind my eyes. "Let us help you. Let *Hrokr* help you. It doesn't make you weak. It only makes you a little bit less of a fool."

I couldn't bring my lips to shape words. Or perhaps, I could not bring my mind to think them. But Maddox didn't give me the chance.

"The rumors you've heard are true. Hrokr's cruelty knows no limits, but his benevolence is just as vast."

Toward my stilted silence, he vanished.

It took far longer than I would have liked to tuck away Maddox's words and remember what I was in Ekin to do.

Hrokr's mother.

I felt sick.

But I needed to make sure Mellian and Alek were alright.

The night was cloaking. The heavy cover of overhead trees blocked out all but a small filtering of moonlight. It felt like stepping into the past, as everything was familiar. The cold earthy scent in the air, the crunch of old snow and frozen leaves beneath my feet. The moonlight was fractured around me, glancing off a thousand ice-crusted twigs and branches. It was a crystalline forest, silent and still.

I knew exactly where I was. Maddox had deposited me just outside of town, not even a fifteen-minute walk from the outskirts of the lower city, near Wyn's bar.

I expected it to bring me comfort. It didn't.

Now that I was away, I couldn't help but think over what I'd done. How I'd abandoned Hrokr and his people for no good reason other than wanting to feel sorry for myself. I couldn't help but realize I had pushed Hrokr away, not because of any crime he'd committed against me, but because of his kindness. I had punished him—all of them—because of their kindness.

I was also full of guilt-ridden anger toward Maddox for making me think such things.

I couldn't stop remembering that Gar was still out here, doing Halls only knew what. He still wanted to hurt me, to hurt Hrokr.

It bothered me that I cared.

I wondered what the people of Mortis Hollow had thought when Mellian and Alek had come home, and I had not. I wondered what Alek had told them.

I wondered what they'd say if they saw me now.

It was too much to think about. I tried to push the thoughts from my head as I started toward the border of the village. While I didn't exactly succeed in clearing my mind, the act of stepping over felled limbs and swatting icicle-dripping branches out of my face was enough to burn away some of my restlessness.

And restless I did feel. Something within me was ill and off-kilter. Missing and broken.

Something I'd left behind in the north.

I broke through the tree front and cobbled roads, and old, faded buildings sprung up before me. I could see Wyn's bar, Bolly Boor's butcher house, and Montegory's leather shop. I felt the smothering blanket of the ward wrap around me, snuffing out any connection to my magic.

The colors here were softened, painted on a palette of greys and tawny browns. The moonlight seemed to bleach the world, to suck away its vibrancy instead of laying a glittering sheen over it all.

I could smell sweet, aged decay, the saccharine glaze of mortality. There was death here. The soft, unavoidable death of humanity. Things here were a cross between the glaring impermanence of human life and the immortality of a society that would never change.

My ears were secured beneath my hood again, but I no longer found comfort in the bindings. It was necessary, I knew, but it no longer made me feel human. Home or not, I was uncomfortably aware of how suddenly distant I felt. There was history I could not wipe away, and blood I could not wash from my hands. I was different.

I was only a faerie in a mask.

How many secrets did I have to keep?

Fae ears, pointed teeth, a crest of ink that sometimes burned like poison. There was not a single person in Alynthia who knew all of me.

I pushed forward, boots thankfully holding enough traction to keep me from slipping on the thick sheen of ice. It was late, and the streets were bare.

No humans or carts or horses. No late-night dawdlers ambling about. No children packing balls of snow in their tiny fists or parents waving them back to the warmth of their hearths.

It was dead here.

I rushed through the town, shirking away from the buttery glow of firelight pouring out of tired homes and clipping through the shoddy, broken parts of the village toward the residential areas.

After long minutes, I finally came to a familiar, curving road. There were oil-burning lamps alight inside, spilling light out onto the lawn. The small front garden was dead, and the icicles in the dead bushes clinked in the soft wind.

I could have fallen to my knees. Someone was inside, and I had no reason to believe it wasn't them.

The two-story wood home looked so small now. Fragile, even. Much more breakable than it had looked when I left it. The front door was still painted that same bright teal—a splash of color Mellian and Momma had crowned our home with together.

My chest tightened.

I took a step—and paused.

I was no longer welcome in this home. I had sold my soul, dipped my hands in blood, and amassed a wealth of emotional scarring I doubted would ever heal, and still—

I was not welcome in this home.

Trying to brush aside the bitterness sinking sour talons in me, I moved up the steps to the house.

I wrapped my hand around the handle. But before I turned it, I pulled away and curled my fingers into a painful fist.

And knocked on the door like a proper stranger.

The seconds were long and strained as I waited.

The door unlatched, swinging open to reveal my sister.

My sister, warm and wrapped in sleeping clothes. A fat, brown sweater brought out the dark tint of her eyes, and thick black leggings bulged in strange places, suggesting their interior was lined with wool.

Her warm blonde hair had been cut shorter, but the layers were now even and smooth, swinging down to frame her face. She was thicker, fuller, less emaciated than I'd last seen her in Balaca. The coal dust had long been washed from her skin. Her body was healthier, the whites of her eyes bright and clear.

I could only imagine how I looked, cloaked in midnight and bearing the seal and gloved scent of a lord she considered an enemy. But it didn't appear to matter.

Not as Mellian made a choking sound and threw herself into my arms, careless of the sharp corner of the dagger strapped to my body. I held her tight as she clung to me, her fingers digging into my skin even through the layers of clothing.

"Hey, Mel," I croaked, my voice suddenly thick.

She squeezed me tighter. "Thank the Elders, Thea, you're alright. Oh Halls, you're alright."

Time stopped as I held my sister. We clutched one another, desperate to undo the year that had separated us. Long moments passed as we held on, so long my cold nose warmed in the crook of her neck. So long that my fingers wrapping around her back froze in the frigid air blowing in from the open door.

But the moment she let me go, I instantly missed the comfort of her touch.

I prayed the bitterness inside me could not be heard as I asked, "How is Alek?"

Mellian tried to smile, but it was a sad, splintered thing—as if she too were recalling the words he had spoken to me.

"He's not good, Thea," she croaked. "Not good at all."

The cold I felt had nothing to do with the snowstorm beyond. "What's going on, Mel?"

She wrung her hands, murmuring, "Come inside. We'll talk."

A smothering heaviness settled in my bones as I followed her over the threshold. The small, worn front room was just as I remembered, with its ragged throw pillows and threadbare blankets. Our sagging, tawny couch.

I looked away quickly, trying not to draw on the memory of Momma knitting there, elbow perched upon the arm of the sofa.

I followed Mel into the kitchen where she began heating a kettle for tea. "He joined the Guard," she said, not looking at me.

207

My stomach sank, even though it was nothing more than I had expected. "Is he happy?" I rasped.

She chuckled a hard, short sound. "He thinks he is." My sister turned toward me, blinking furiously against the tears pooling in her eyes. "He's a ghost."

I perched on my usual seat, the familiar movement somehow only heightening the feeling of how foreign this life now was. "He could quit," I offered.

She huffed something between a scoff and a sigh. "He won't quit. He's so different now, Thea. I don't even know that you'd recognize him—not on the inside. He's a monster bent on revenge."

The words pelted me like arrows, sliding down deep to the bones. But no healing magic could take away their sharp cut.

Would she feel that way about me?

"The Fae hurt him," I mumbled, surprised to hear myself attempting a weak defense of my brother.

Mellian was silent for a long moment as the fire beneath the kettle snapped and popped. "They hurt me, too," she whispered.

I'd thought I'd reached the bottom of the well of pain. I thought I had been so deeply pained these last few months that anything new wouldn't be noticeable. I was already in such internal agony that nothing could make it *worse*. But watching my sister stare at nothing, watching her retreat into some place inside of herself—it broke me in a way I could not have expected.

"Do you want to talk about it?" I whispered, nestling farther into my cloak as if the dark cloth could shield me from her words.

"I—" her mouth opened and closed. "I don't know."

My brow furrowed as she turned away from me and began assembling our tea. The mugs were old and chipped, and she filled my favorite with black leaves. Seeing it hurt me, though she no doubt meant it as a comfort.

With her back still to me, she whispered, "What happened to us, Thea?"

"I don't know," I grimaced, fingers tightening on the mug. "I don't even recognize my life anymore."

"I'll drink to that," Mel said drily. She saluted me with her mug before drinking deeply.

I was almost a year older than Mel, but considering the heartbreaking situation that had brought us together, I'd never felt like her older sister. Pure equals. Twins, if anything. With the way our birthdays fell, she and I were both nineteen. I'd missed her birthday; I didn't think bringing it up would be doing either of us any favors.

I had been struck by her transformation when she'd opened the door, but now that I had a chance to watch her, I could see the signs of her age. Perhaps they weren't signs of her age at all—only signs of her stress.

They had been easy to dismiss in Balaca when I was so overwhelmed with joy at just seeing her *alive.* They were things I thought would wash away with the coal dust, but they hadn't.

There were tight lines around her mouth, stress lines at her eyes. Small dark circles bloomed beneath her eyes, and her nails were bitten down to the quick.

"Are you alright, Mel?" I asked softly.

She shifted beneath my gaze. "I could ask you the same."

I huffed a small, humorless laugh. "I suppose you could. But I'm asking you."

A rough, snide sound. "I'm doing better than Alek, I suppose. But—" she struggled, frowning down at her hands. "But it bothers me more to see him like this. I didn't want him to be so full of anger, so full of hate."

Again her words cut at me. "If that's the life he's chosen—"

"No," she hissed. I recoiled from the sudden, shattered venom in her eyes. "This was not how he was supposed to come home. I did *everything* to protect him." She drew in a shallow, hiccuping breath that jerked against her shoulders. *"Everything."*

I knew the feeling.

"And he hates me," she whispered, curling her legs up in her chair to the safety of her chest. "He hates everyone. I was stupid to send you away, Thea, so stupid. I know our choice was taken away, but—"

"Mel," I consoled. "It's alright. We didn't know what was going to happen."

"We aren't Momma," she lamented. "We can't fix him."

Her words were final, decided. I wondered how bad he'd gotten in such a short time. It couldn't have been more than a few weeks, could it? I realized I didn't know how long it had been since Balanca, as I was unsure how long I was unconscious in Calix's care.

I didn't want to ask.

"Everything I did, I did for him," she continued, digging her nails into her legs. I wanted to go to her, but I wasn't sure it would help.

After a moment of silence, I asked in a small voice, "What did you do, Mel?"

She looked suddenly ashamed, dropping her eyes. Staring into her tea leaves she whispered, "Did any of the guards ever hurt you, Thea?"

Unbidden images of Jonik flashed through my mind. The taste of his lips, his tongue, his blood. The feel of his hands pawing at me. And then the feel of his throat beneath my fingers, the life being ripped out of him. But the images were gone in a flash as I realized what it was that Mellian was really asking. "Who hurt you?" My voice was all Fae. It was ageless, cold, and predatory as my fingers brushed against the hilts of my knife

"They didn't hurt me," she said quickly. "I mean—not really." I waited for her to elaborate, wishing against the past that I had taken longer ending the lives of those Gentry Fae in Balaca. "I—I let them." Her voice was choked with shame.

When it became apparent she wasn't going to say anything more, I asked, "Why?"

"For Alek," she whispered. "We were only gone a few months—and still, I saw so many people die, Thea. There were people who arrived after us and were already dying. I knew some of the girls sold their bodies for extra rations or baths or other things." She met my eyes, tears rolling down her cheeks. "I bargained instead for them to go easy on Alek, to do what they could to preserve his life."

"Melly," I choked.

"He's thankful," she sputtered, wiping away the tears. "He says he's thankful, but—He cares about nothing other than vengeance. He won't talk to me or look at me or eat with me. He hates me. I'm alone here," she rasped, waving a hand to encompass our childhood home.

"Oh Mel," I crooned, throwing myself around the counter to pull her into my arms. "He doesn't hate you."

"He does," she sobbed, leaning into me.

I didn't want to imagine the horrors she had endured for his sake. "I'll talk to him," I said, smoothing down her hair.

She pulled away suddenly, eyes bright. "No—no, you can't, Thea." She gripped my hands, squeezing me tight. "You have to promise me you won't."

"What? Why?"

"He's lost his mind. He has led more purges, he's—"

"He's *what?*"

Her eyes were wide and panicked, twinged with guilt. "He's hunting the Folk, Thea. He's hunting Gentry Fae and any other non-human he can get his hands on. For now, it's being classified as magic users only, but they're not really screening anyone. Being Fae is enough to get you hurt."

"He wouldn't kill me," I croaked.

"I'd like to think he wouldn't, but—" Her pitying eyes crawled over me, noting my foreign gear as she quietly said, "You look dangerous."

"But I'm not, not to you two."

A weak smile. "I know that. But he is drowning so deeply in his grief that he isn't thinking rationally."

I was lightheaded with relief from leaving Sage in Valencia.

"Where is he?"

She shrugged. "He wanted to stop by Wyn's tonight. You should probably make yourself scarce when he gets back," she hedged. "You can stay in my room with me if you want."

"He will not even welcome me in my own home?" I snapped.

Mellian's heartbreak was obvious in her eyes. She quickly brushed it away, shaking her head to push away the heaviness. "Enough with all this. I want to hear about your life. You've been away from me for so long," she said gently, eyes suddenly aglow. "Let's talk about happy things."

But there were no happy things to tell.

I realized Mellian knew absolutely nothing of the life I'd lived since the day Cole had died and our world had shattered. She knew nothing of the atrocities I'd faced, the love I'd given, or the betrayal I'd received in return.

How was I to tell her the man I'd loved was the one she watched slaughter her mother?

But looking into my sister's gentle eyes, I found courage.

We stayed awake for hours, snuggled together beneath our mother's patchwork quilts as we had done when we were children. I told her everything.

Well, almost everything. I left out any mention of Aphaedia, as even my sister did not know my heritage. But I was honest with her about my magic, my love, my heartache, and my hands long stained with blood.

I even told her the whole truth about Hrokr, how he had gone from someone who had killed my friend to someone who had helped me rescue Sage. Of course, that led to explaining the rift between me and my longest friend.

We laughed and we cried, and we reminisced about our parents.

She talked to me about The Meridian and its orchestra and the changes Mortis Hollow had seen since the Fae invasion.

She told me how a kind faerie had voidstepped them home and what it was like to be back. To be *free*. She spoke of Alek's anger, his cold aloofness. But despite Alek's ugliness, he seemed to be the sole provider of companionship in her life.

I fell asleep with tears in my eyes, laughter on my lips, and my sister in my arms.

CHAPTER TWENTY-SEVEN

GRAVESTONES

"I'm kicking you out," a voice whispered as cold feet were planted in my back, shoving me toward the edge of the bed.

I swatted blindly. "Shut up," I groaned, nestling farther into the quilt. I was exhausted. I had spent far too long on my feet yesterday, stayed up talking until nearly two, and now I was being woken up by what felt like only moments later. "What time is it?"

"It's six," Mellian whispered. "You have to go. Alek is home."

I mumbled something wordless, snuggling into her. She shoved me harder, laughing. "Thea, I'm serious."

"I'm tired," I grumbled.

"Me too," she laughed, "but you really have to go."

I sighed, peeling my eyes open to glare at her.

She smiled down at me. "Go see your friends at The Meridian or something. But get out," she said with a playful strictness. "Come back at noon, and Alek will be gone."

"I want to see him," I said, wiping the sleep from my eyes.

"You will," she said before planting a kiss on my forehead. "But not yet. Let me enjoy having my sister back for a little bit."

"Fine," I grumbled.

She smiled, triumphant, as she crawled out of bed. "Keep your cloak and dagger look, though. It won't be good for you to show off your ears."

It was eerie to be prowling through Mortis Hollow in my cloak and leathers. I'd spent my life traversing these roads in heels and dresses and headscarves.

I felt so far from that life.

I recognized most of the people on the streets, and seeing a young man with a string bass strapped to his back wrenched an ache from so deep inside of me I thought I would double over.

Perhaps it would be worth seeing if Hrokr had any orchestras in Valencia.

Hrokr.

The thought of his name sent something of a pang through me. It felt strange, somehow, to be so far away from him, unable to communicate.

Stranger still knowing he was likely at the one inn in town, doing Halls knew what.

Perhaps I should find him, only to apologize.

I shook the thought from my mind. What did I need to check in with him for? But suddenly my bones felt heavy, tired. Weary.

I ignored it as best I could as I meandered through the town. Coming into the square, The Meridian loomed up before me, its tall spires rising far higher than any of the other buildings nearby. I wanted to go inside, but there were too many members of the Guard nearby. It was normal to find guards in the street, but something about Mellian's words had me pulling my cloak tighter and scuttling past, pausing only to cast a wistful glance to my favorite place in Mortis Hollow.

I needed to be careful, if only for them.

Especially considering I was now deep inside the heart of Mortis Hollow's ward, unable to feel even a faded ember of magic within me.

I found myself walking toward Sage's house, kicking rocks across the winding path that led to the outskirts of the village.

The stifling of my magic fell away as I crossed the boundary of the ward.

Soon, her tiny cottage loomed before me. Her gardens were overgrown and dead from our time away, but the bones of the house had not changed. It was a tiny, stone cottage, and even so many years later, I had memories of little Sage and her parents playing in the front lawn.

I also remembered the last time I had been here after I had dragged myself—bloodied and mangled—through the forest after Gar severed a muscle in my calf. I tried not to glance down to where my blood stained the porch.

I wanted so badly to step inside and find her sprawled on the floor—all our troubles gone.

But I would only find a house full of ghosts, both of those dead and those still living.

When I finally accepted that I'd exhausted every idle thing to do in Mortis Hollow, I swallowed my pride and made my way back down the ice-crusted path toward the edge of town.

I hadn't wanted to interact with anyone. I thought perhaps it was better if anyone who'd mourned me last year continued to believe me dead or captured.

I returned to Mortis Hollow's cemetery, having things to take care of I couldn't have done in front of Maddox. The silence here was deafening—that dull, over-pressured silence that could only be found in winter. The snow swallowed the sound here from where it piled up atop headstones and coated the ground in thick, white carpet.

The sun had just finished its descent behind the horizon, and the world was still awash in the cold, blue hues of twilight.

Poppa's gravestone was so old now. Chipped and cracked from too many years of changing temperatures. I brushed the snow off his name, off the years etched in stone indicating a life cut far too short.

Nikolaus Hawthorne

Loving father

So much more than a loving father and a loving husband to Momma. But now he was nothing, only here beneath me in weather-eaten bones. My eyes were drawn to the empty plot beside him, knowing I'd never be able to find her body to lay her to rest beside him.

Silent tears warmed my cheeks.

And the plot to the left—filled with the only Fae family I had anywhere near me. Uncle Dain, slain for the crime of having magic running through his veins. Magic that burned through mine, too.

I wished I could go to the grave of his brother—my Fae father. But he and Mother were buried so far away, somewhere I'd not been in many long years.

I brushed the tears from my eyes, determined to visit one last grave.

Across the graveyard to the east was the freshest set of plots. Even after a long year, there were still an overwhelming amount of mementos here. Baubles and letters and flowers and stones—all blanketed by the thick snow and ice trying to freeze away our grief.

I found his, kneeling atop it and resting my cloaked forehead against the cold stone.

"I'm so sorry," I whispered.

Because he would not have been killed if he'd not been at the Meridian the night Gar had chosen to take my life away from me. He'd not have been out if not for his love for me, if not for the foolish affection I gave him.

Cole Hadleigh

Beloved son

I curled around the gravestone, finally ready to give him the proper goodbye I should have offered him so many months ago.

When the tears began to grow cold against my cheeks, I rose to my feet, dusted the snow off my knees, and made my way to the only warm place I might be welcome.

CHAPTER TWENTY-EIGHT
LINE IN THE SAND

The door to the bar opened with the same creaking I'd grown used to long ago. I didn't even want a drink. No, not after I remembered that I'd only grown close to Gar because of a charged, drunken moment on a rooftop. Not after I'd escaped Hrokr to a too-sunny island only because he'd been too deep in a bottle to want to follow me.

No, I just didn't want to be alone—to be hungry and cold.

None of the patrons glanced up at my entrance. Truthfully, the bar was so crowded tonight that most of them likely missed it. The smell of warm stew and yeast filled the space, and the sound of laughter and howling conversation covered up the embers popping from stone fireplaces.

"By the Halls..."

My eyes snapped up to the voice, locking immediately with Wyn's across the counter. Seeing him filled me with more emotion than I'd expected. Wyn and I had never been overly close, but he was still a friend, still a piece of the life I grieved.

A few patrons glanced back at me, but they were no one I knew.

Wyn ran a hand through his dirty blonde hair and vaulted over the stained counter. I was surprised to hear it pass my lips—but I couldn't help but laugh as he ran to me, dipping to grab me around the waist and lift me smooth off my feet, spinning me in a celebratory circle.

Even as I laughed, a hand shot up to make sure my cloak stayed in place over my ears. He dropped me to my feet, steadying me at the shoulders.

"Where have you been, Thea?" he asked, stepping back to study me. His eyes darkened a shade. "I thought—"

"I can imagine what you thought, Wyn," I said, cutting him off with a melancholy smile.

He wasn't offended, only nodding in understanding. "Come on. I'll find you a seat." Before he moved, he appraised me once more. "Halls, I can't believe it."

With a smile, I followed him through the crowded bar until he found me an empty table in the far corner beneath a frost-covered window. "How long have you been back?" he called over the din of the bar. "I've seen Mellian and Alek, but—"

"Just last night," I said, sliding into the creaking, wood seat. I didn't want to think about my siblings.

He nodded, staring down at me with that same mixture of awe and surprise. But there was something different about him, some weight of shadow that clung to his eyes and shoulders I hadn't remembered.

"What can I get you, Thea?" he asked. "It's on the house tonight."

"Thank you, Wyn. I'll take anything. I haven't eaten all day."

He nodded, flashing a bright white grin. I watched as he sifted through the throng of bodies, watched until he disappeared around the counter and out of sight.

I leaned my head against the cool wall, closing my eyes to the tavern beyond. It smelled and sounded so familiar, I could almost pretend the last year hadn't happened at all.

For long moments, I did. I was only a human girl in a rowdy tavern, free of the guilt and burden of the truth.

The bench flexed beneath fresh weight, and my head turned, expecting to find Wyn returning with warm dinner.

But it was not Wyn.

It was someone who suddenly had my stomach tightening.

Hrokr—with fresh snow dusting his broad, cloaked shoulders—slid beside me, so close that his thigh pressed against my own.

Forgoing greeting, he asked, "Why aren't you with your family?"

My spine instantly straightened in defense. "Well, hello to you too."

His lips curved into a sharp smile. "Hello, Thea."

I dropped my eyes, remembering just how ugly things had been left between us.

Against my silence, he asked, "Did everything go alright?"

"Do you care?" I asked, staring at the faded wood grain of the table.

He sighed, and I swore I could feel his breath on my cheek.

Feeling something that may have been guilt, I admitted, "I'm just hungry, Hrokr."

He reached into his cloak, producing a red apple that he placed directly in front of me. Tentatively, I pulled it into my hands.

My teeth cut through the flesh before I set it back on the table, twirling the stem between my fingers.

"Is there a reason you aren't eating at home?" he asked softly.

Maybe he was just curious, or maybe something within him drove him to really care. Maybe he just wanted to go home and stop leaving his life on hold for me.

My fingers curled around the apple. "I haven't seen my brother yet."

He leaned an elbow on the table, turning fully to face me. This close, I couldn't avoid his eyes. "Why aren't you having dinner with your sister?"

I chewed on the inside of my lip, fighting against the lump in my throat. "Because she's likely having dinner with him."

He nodded slowly, cogs beginning to turn within his mind. "Well," he finally said, leaning back against the faded booth seat. "I suppose I don't mind sharing dinner with you."

I cracked a weak smile, one I knew didn't reach my eyes. I took another slow bite of the apple before whispering, "Maybe Sagira is right."

"She isn't."

I shifted my weight. "Sage wants to come home. Mellian—my sister—she isn't going to want to leave. And Alek, he..." I trailed off, frowning.

"You said it yourself, Thea," he said softly. "They aren't safe here."

"I can protect them," I said quickly, a childlike adamance rearing up in me.

"I've no doubt you can," he said simply. "Why did you say what you did to Sage, then?"

I shrugged. "I just needed her to stay somewhere safe while I figured it out."

"And have you? Figured it out?"

I sighed, leaning my head against the booth. "I don't know where to put them."

"Your siblings?" he asked, brow furrowing.

I nodded, taking another bite.

"Thea, you—you can't honestly believe I am not willing to extend shelter to them."

A faint flush coated my cheeks. "I can't ask that of you."

"You're not asking. I am offering."

Picking at the hem of my cloak, I whispered, "They're human."

"That doesn't matter," he said without an inch of hesitation. "There are humans in Valencia. Not many, I'll admit. But your family will not be the first humans my people have met."

"I'm not sure how welcoming they will be to that idea." Forcing myself to speak the words again, I said, "Maybe I really should stay here, Hrokr."

"Is that what you want?" he asked, studying my face intently. "To live within the walls of the ward?"

My eyes instantly flashed around the space, but no one was listening to us. He tracked the movement and cocked a brow as if to say, *See? Always looking over your shoulder.*

Before I could respond, my eyes met Wyn's across the bar. He was standing frozen but began walking once I saw him.

Hrokr followed my gaze over his shoulder, and we were both silent as Wyn made his way toward us, offering Hrokr a strained, "Hello," as he sat down a tray of roux sauce and goza bread and a drink of amber liquor.

I could only imagine what Wyn saw.

Hrokr did not look like anything that had entered Mortis Hollow before. And only now—with someone else's eyes on him—did I become aware of how lethally honed he was, how dangerous he looked deep within his cloak, how many scars bleached his hands, how many blades were strapped to his body.

Halls, he was wearing an arsenal.

Suddenly, Hrokr was extending one of those scarred hands, smiling, though it was more of a brandishing of teeth.

Of very sharp fangs.

Wyn—slightly bewildered but ever-full of charisma—shook his hand. "Nice to meet you," he said. "I'm Wyn."

"Crow," Hrokr replied. "Wyn, are you busy?"

At that exact moment, Fallon and Maddox were striding for the table—from where, I had no idea. They slid into the seats across from us, also cloaked in ear-hiding cowls.

I felt a little bit ambushed, and I knew Wyn had to be feeling something of the same. I had no idea what Hrokr had planned for him, but I knew it wasn't a good idea and would most definitely out me. As inconspicuously as possible, I laid a hand on Hrokr's shoulder. Eyes still on Wyn, Hrokr's head turned just slightly in my direction.

Flashing that lethal smile once more, he lifted the glass of liquor Wyn had just delivered. "I was only hoping to trouble you for a few more of these."

Liar.

But Wyn nodded, casting me a strange glance before disappearing.

Hrokr and I turned to each other immediately.

"I just want to talk to talk to him—"

"No," I interrupted, shaking my head. "Not him, not someone who knows me."

I swore he looked disappointed. "Are you going to hide forever, Thea?"

And the way he looked at me... It was almost as if he could see down to the ink at my hip.

Irritated, I turned my head to the center of the table only to find Maddox picking up a piece of goza bread and eating it dry with a sour expression.

"You're supposed to dip it in the sauce," I said harshly. "You'd know that if you grew up here, south of the Ward. If you grew up outside of the safety of your castle walls. If you knew the risk you will subject both me and my family to if you tell him what I am."

Maddox's russet eyes flashed up to my own. "It's bitter, and I don't like it," he said. "You don't want to do this again with me, kid."

A snappy retort was quick to my tongue, but Hrokr stiffened beside me. "Again?" he asked, arching a dark brow.

I turned more fully to him, finding his fingers wrapped around my glass. Fingers that were stained red.

As if he'd gotten roux sauce on them.

And it was such an unlikely thought, one to appear right at this moment. But he followed my eyes and turned his palm away from me as if to hide it.

As if to hide he knew how to eat it.

As if the bittersweet taste wasn't unappealing to him, as if maybe it was a strange taste he'd acquired as most southerners had.

And he had lived so long, it was not a far-fetched thought to believe he'd just encountered human culture. But the way he shied away from it, the way he hid his hand spoke of more.

"It was nothing, Crow," Maddox said, waving off what had most definitely not been nothing between us in the graveyard yesterday.

A dark look flashed across Hrokr's face, but Fallon laughed. "It's so nice and quiet inside the ward without you badgering us endlessly. Hrokr finally having to use his voice instead of projecting every idle threat has been quite nice."

He scowled, knocking back half my glass in one swallow. His voice was rough with burn when he grumbled, "I feel far too trapped in my own skin." He shook out his hand as if he could jostle the feeling out of his body. He reached out, indeed dipping a piece of the bread in the rich sauce before turning back to me.

"I need someone to talk to, Thea. If you'd like to choose someone else, go right ahead."

My face fell as the first sparks of fear speared through me. "Not here, not when I've been seen with you."

Hurt flashed across his features. He worked his jaw and said, "Alright."

He moved to rise from the booth, but I reached out, gripping his hand between my own. Hrokr paused, glancing down at our hands. "Please," I whispered.

He pulled his hand free, and his face was deathly earnest when he said, "I understand it, Thea. Believe me, I understand. It is another long story for another long day, but I did not grow up in Valencia. I grew up here, a few miles south.

"I will keep you safe," he vowed. "And I know—*I know*—you don't need it, but I am telling you all the same. I will house Sage, house your brother and sister. House you, Thea."

He took a steady breath. "But I think it's worth realizing that whether we are here or not, Silas is going to come here." He paused. "We would do well to know what the state of affairs are. We would do well to know how diminished this place's defense is."

"All you need to know is that Mortis Hollow is the same as any other village in Ekin. Magic use is illegal."

His eyes narrowed into something harsh and mocking. "And you're alright with that, Thea?"

"It doesn't matter what I'm alright with," I hissed. "It's just the way it is."

It truly was disappointment in his eyes, disappointment to a degree of anger. He leaned in, so close I could smell the night coming off his skin, could nearly feel where his lips peeled back from his teeth. "Do you even know how many faeries have hung in the gallows in the town square?"

The words slammed like an arrow into the center of my chest. I leaned into him, baring my teeth. "I am intimately aware," I spat.

Sage's parents. Uncle Dain.

I knew well how final those gallows were.

His eyes dropped to my mouth, the lips peeled back from my teeth, before flashing back up to my own. "And yet you would sit here hidden in a cowl, at peace with whisking your family away to leave faeries to die. To be hanged in gallows, to live a smothered life cut off from their magic, to live a life cut off from the ability to heal into immortality."

You're selfish, was what he was saying.

A phrase many were throwing at me of late.

And I wanted to howl. To fight with him, to draw my blade, to whip him with words that would cut deeper than any weapon.

But instead, hot tears began collecting on my lashes. From hurt or anger, I wasn't sure. I instantly turned away, forgetting Fallon and Maddox were even present until I met their eyes.

They were both guarded, but watching us carefully.

And suddenly this booth was too tight, this bar too crowded, this ceiling too low.

Hrokr far too close.

To make this horrible moment far worse, Wyn appeared with a tray of drinks. His face was weary, his dark eyes concerned as they met mine. "Thea, are you alright?"

Hrokr—with all the bark of the weight of his title—snapped, "It doesn't concern you."

I didn't know how I knew, but something about those words changed the course of my life forever.

Hrokr laid claim on me. Laid claim on me to someone I'd known since I was a child. Hrokr drew a line in the sand of my life and firmly planted me on his side of it, Wyn and humanity on the other.

Wyn knew it.

Something shifted in his gaze, and I could almost see the thoughts connecting behind his eyes.

Headscarves and cowls. My closest friend being Fae. Blades strapped to my body. A caravan of Fae sacking the village months ago, Fae that no one could fight against.

No one but me.

Families shattered and shredded apart, lost to Gar's wiles forever, never to escape.

Except for my family.

And now here I sat with three hooded strangers who didn't look human at all. Strangers with scarred hands and bodies honed for hand-to-hand combat, something humanity did not see much of.

Wyn took a careful step back, eyes locked on my own.

If he did not know, he at least suspected what I was.

And even though my tear-blurred eyes were locked on Wyn's, my words were for Hrokr. "What can we do?" I whispered.

He turned to me, and even though we were in front of Wyn, in front of Maddox and Fallon, in front of the whole human world—his calloused thumb brushed my tear away.

His eyes were wholly gentle—perhaps sorry, even. Lost was the rage that had gripped him only moments ago.

Perhaps he'd realized what he'd done.

Hrokr slid out of the booth, and—Halls—Wyn flinched away. I swore I could hear Maddox chuckling under his breath even over the roar of the tavern.

Hrokr cast his starry night eyes on me. "Go home," he said gently. He offered a hand, and I hesitantly let him pull me to my feet. He leaned down into me, so close his nose brushed the curve of my ear. His words were only for me when he said, "Let me break the ward."

I pulled away, bewildered.

I wanted to tell him no, tell him to let life continue on as it always had here. But something had me wondering if perhaps he was right. If maybe—if someone long ago had had the means to change things—Uncle Dain could have lived.

Sagira's parents could have lived.

And so I straightened my spine and met his eyes as equally as I could from a foot below him. "I didn't know you knew how to ask for permission, Crow."

His eyes glittered.

I turned, face to face with an unsettled Wyn.

"I'm still the same me I've always been," I told him. And without further courage, I pushed past him to the door, willing to let Hrokr destroy what he needed to, but unable to watch it unfold.

And it was only once I'd gotten back to the steps of my childhood home that I realized my last words had been a lie.

CHAPTER TWENTY-NINE
RESTLESS HANDS

W hen I arrived, it was nearly one, and Alek was long gone. The house smelled strongly of awful cooking, but it brought a smile to my face anyway. Mellian had always been the worst cook in the family.

Still, I greeted her with a smile and crawled into my favorite seat at the counter. "What did you do today?" she chirped happily.

I smiled at my sister, at the messy knot of hair atop her head and the age-faded sleeping clothes she still wore. I tried so hard to see her and not the bar I'd left behind.

I told her about my day, about how I'd gotten a glimpse of The Meridian. I didn't tell her about my trip to the graveyard, nor any of the very illegal conversation I'd shared with Hrokr.

But as if she had some kind of sisterly sixth sense, she asked, "Have you spoken with your friend?"

"My friend?"

"Yes," she said with a smile. "Lord Hrokr."

Hearing his name aloud sent a jolt through my body, and I wondered if she noticed. "Um, yes, a little bit," I stammered.

"You could bring him here if you wanted." She smiled warmly at me, ladling soup into a bowl and sliding it to me. "I know that our home can't be half as opulent as his worst room, but he is welcome here, Thea."

I narrowed my eyes at her. "I have no desire to bring him here, Mel." At the flat look on her face, I added, "Thank you for the offer, though."

She made her own bowl and sat across from me. "I heard a little bit about him in Balaca, you know. Never much. People don't really know a lot about him."

I shrugged into my soup, growing a little bewildered at where this conversation was headed. "That sounds about right," I murmured noncommittally.

"They say he is vicious."

I said nothing, but I was watching her now. I didn't know what to make of that, what judgement I could find from her.

"But he has been kind to my sister."

"Yes," I drawled carefully.

She finally acknowledged the look on my face with a burst of laughter. "Five Halls, Thea."

"What?" I griped, dropping her eyes and spearing a piece of roast.

She was shaking her head when I again looked at her face. "You've always been something special, but I wouldn't have thought even you could wrap the Lord of the North around your finger."

I blushed crimson, which only made her laugh harder. "He isn't wrapped around my finger," I hissed. "He's just helping me on a job."

Her laughter faded, but no judgement entered her eyes. "He wants to help you kill Gar."

Silence blanketed the room.

"Does it bother you?" I asked. "That I am going to kill him?"

Rage flashed in her eyes. It was there but a moment before it vanished. "Why would it? He deserves to die."

I sagged in my seat from relief, releasing tension in my shoulders and jaw I hadn't even realized I'd been holding. I hadn't realized how much I feared Mellian would think of me as Sage did, as someone as warped by vengeance as my brother.

"Yes, Mel. He does."

After staying up far too late talking, Mellian and I retired to separate rooms. She told me Alek was away on some kind of training and wouldn't be returning home until late tomorrow.

It was strange to be back in the bed I had spent most of my nights in. My old nightgown looked strange on my body, and I felt almost naked knowing I was sleeping in a rickety house in Ekin, far from any true protections.

I snorted at myself. Was I going soft?

I curled into the bed, feeling anxious.

I could almost hear Alek and Mel bickering downstairs, smell Momma cooking an actually-edible dinner. I smiled to myself. If I pushed my memories back far enough, I could picture Uncle Dain coming to the front door. His rich skin and warm, green eyes. His hair that I pulled when I was little, a jet-black that fell in curling waves down to his waist.

I could even see Poppa, doting on Momma and ruffling my and Mellian's hair. Alek had been just a baby when Poppa died, but I remember how much they loved each other. Poppa hardly ever wanted to put him down, and Alek's tiny fingers were always grappling for him. My sweet, tender Alek.

I laid there, restless and wrapped in nostalgia, for long minutes.

Even before the words came, Hrokr's consciousness brushed up against my own. I sat up suddenly, heart racing in my chest.

The ward is gone, as I'm sure you've noticed.

My restlessness was gone, replaced by something else.

His voice was wry, rife with dry humor.

I see why you like the barkeep. He is... something.

I snorted aloud.

I expected more, but his presence dwindled into nothing more than a silent awareness.

There was a part of me—a feral, fitful part—that wanted to run through the snow and throw myself in Mortis Hollow's single inn. I wanted to be doing something, anything more than sitting here.

I didn't want to be alone, especially in a place where everything was the same, and I never would be again.

I locked my legs, forcing myself still. It would do me no good to think these thoughts. And still.

And still.

I dreamt of his hands.

They were restless. He chewed his nails or picked at his clothes, twisting his fingers in his sheets. I knew it was a dream because this Hrokr was far less refined than the one I knew while awake.

He finally gave up on the bed, tired but unable to sleep. After long moments—with a rough breath that hissed past his lips—he donned his cloak and slipped downstairs into the lobby, devoid of even a desk attendant.

It was dark, the sconces on the wall smothered completely. Only the moonlight reflecting off the snow and through the cloudy window gave any light.

He fell into a chair at one of the small, faded tables, running his fingers across the chipped rivulets on its surface.

He made it not even a full minute of still silence before Maddox strolled around the corner.

Hrokr was not polite, polished, or formal in any sense of the words with his commander. "What do you want?"

Maddox's brows rose, but he did not comment on his lord's sour mood. "I wanted to talk."

"Can it not wait until morning?"

Maddox's face gentled. He even cracked a lopsided smile. "You're both insufferable, you know."

Hrokr groaned, closing his eyes as his head fell backward. "Don't."

After a long moment, Maddox said, "She's only trying to figure things out. She—"

"You don't think I know that?" Hrokr snapped, eyes flashing open.

Another lopsided grin from Maddox. "In my eyes, you're just a kid figuring things out, too."

Silence descended between them, heavy and thick. A special kind of silence, reserved only for the anger between two souls that loved each other deeply. A rage that couldn't quite penetrate the tenderness. "I am no child," Hrokr said gently.

"Neither is she, Crow."

Hrokr was tense, agitated. Itching to break free from his own skin. To sprout wings and throw himself from the highest spire. To fall and fall and fall—

"What do you want?" he repeated, if only to pull himself out of his thoughts.

Maddox straightened his spine. "To apologize."

Hrokr tipped his head back against his chair again, trying hard to bury the rage riding his every nerve. It was irrational, he told himself. He drew in a deep breath and let it out slowly through his lips.

"Halls, Hrokr, look at you."

Hrokr's eyes snapped open. "You were apologizing? For how you spoke to her?"

Maddox's brows shot up his forehead. "You don't even know what I said to her."

I could feel it. I wasn't sure what *it* was, but it was old and lethal. Cold and feral. The wood of the desk groaned beneath Hrokr's hands. Whatever it was, Maddox saw it. Even as his closest friend, he had the good sense to take a step back. "Relax, Crow."

Hrokr tried. He pressed his fingers into his temples so hard they ached, as if he could physically push the thoughts from his mind. "What's wrong with me, Maddie?"

It was a smaller voice, one I would have never expected to hear from him. Vulnerable and *young*.

Hrokr hung his head, and Maddox's soft footsteps sounded across the room. A few soft clinks as Maddox helped himself behind the counter, filled two glasses, and pushed one toward Hrokr.

Clear liquor.

He downed it in one swig, the liquor burning as it slid down his throat.

Into the swollen silence, Hrokr spun the glass by its rim. "I can't—"

"You can," Maddox said, nodding encouragingly.

Hrokr only buried his face in his hands. Maddox rose and rested a firm hand on Hrokr's back.

They sat that way for a long time, the heavy touch conveying more than their words could.

Hrokr collapsed more fully against the table, crossing his arms to rest his head on them.

After a long moment, Maddox silently vanished.

A signature move for the two of them, it seemed.

Hrokr sighed. When he finally rose, he downed Maddox's drink before studying the discarded glasses before him. He fidgeted, bouncing his leg and drumming his fingers against the tabletop.

Finally, he pulled from his cloak a bruised apple, cut with my teeth.

I woke with a gasp, shivering as if the cold from the barren inn had been real. Gooseflesh peppered my arms and legs, and I rubbed my hands against them.

I felt a hard, red blush creep across my cheeks. Had I really been dreaming about Hrokr? As if I were him?

I shivered again, nestling down into the blankets. The panic in my blood cooled, replaced only with a hollow restlessness. I closed my eyes and begged a black sleep to claim me.

"Momma, Daddy, look!"

I ran through the field, letting my fingers brush against the chest-high flowers, swimming in an ocean of petals and pollen.

Momma laughed, looking down at me. "They're very pretty, Thea."

I ripped one from the dirt and ran toward her, offering it to her. Her full, rosy lips twisted into a smile as she tucked the flower behind her pointy ear. Loose strands of chocolate-colored hair blew around her face. She kept it cut short, to her chin, and I thought it helped her look like a grown-up. Momma always looked so young, what with her big yellow eyes and freckles.

Daddy wrapped an arm around her shoulder, pressing a kiss to her cheek. "Where's mine?" he asked me.

I giggled, ripping a peony from its home. In my haste, I knocked loose a few petals. "Oh no," I wailed.

"It's okay, baby," he said, kneeling down to be at eye level with me. His eyes were orange, like fire, and his hair was a rich, rich black, like the night-time. "Let me see it," he said, holding out his hand.

Lip trembling, I dropped the dead flower in his palm. He held it by the stalk, and I watched in wonder as fresh pollen burst at its center, and new petals unfurled. Eyes aglow, I leaned in closer. I loved when Daddy did his flower magic.

"Are you going to wear yours in your hair too?" I asked.

Momma laughed. "Yes, he is." She swiped the flower from his hand and began pushing it behind his ear. The light shone on the circular tattoo she had on her forearm. Daddy grinned at her before planting a kiss on her lips. I scrunched my nose and looked away.

They laughed together now. "Do you want to pick flowers for Amara? She can take them home to Mellian," Momma said.

I looked past my parents toward the house, noting my mother's handmaiden in the doorway. She smiled and waved at me, and I waved right back. Mellian wasn't here today, and I missed her terribly, but I bet she would like it if her mom brought her home flowers.

I began scooping up the ones I thought my friend would like best. When I had a fat bouquet clenched in my fist, Momma and Daddy led me up the stairs and into our house. As we passed Amara, she leaned down to ruffle my hair, and I smiled up at her.

Amara took me into the kitchen to find twine to bind the bouquet. When I complained that I missed Mellian, she promised she would bring her next time. Appeased, I helped her tie the stems of the flowers together.

When we were almost finished, a loud crash sounded in the front room of the house. I gasped, looking up into Amara's eyes. Hers were wide, and they looked scared. My stomach sunk down to my toes.

Before the tears rising in me could take over, she reached down to grip my hand tight. "Come on, baby."

I nodded even though she wasn't looking at me, and followed her across the marble floor. There were more loud noises, like people yelling and things breaking. I poked my head into the front room right as Amara gasped.

She pulled my arm hard, slamming my face into her stomach. She held me tight as she began backing away, but it was too late. I had seen it.

My daddy lying on the floor with red all around him.

We needed to help him, needed to see if he was okay. I pulled against Amara, but her grip was like iron. "Don't look," she whispered.

I ignored her, thrashing and pulling until I could see into the front room. There was a knife in his head, a knife—

A broken sob choked through me as I tried to run toward him. But Amara had her fingers wrapped so hard around my arms that she was hurting me. "We need to help him!" I shouted.

"Hush," she barked, but her voice wobbled. "We have to be quiet, okay, Thea?"

"No," I cried, tears blurring my vision. "We need to help him. We need to find Momma!"

As if summoned by my words, my mother sprinted through one of the doors into the foyer, and she had blood on her, too. She looked unharmed even though she held a dagger in each hand.

She met Amara's eyes instead of mine. "Please," was all she said.

There was a long pause between them, one full and heavy.

"With my life," Amara whispered.

She began pulling me away, tugging me harder. "Momma!" I screamed, trying to rip my arms free of Amara's grip.

Momma turned around, and big, fat tears rolled down her cheeks. "I love you, Thea Starsea. I love you more than there are stars in the sky." And then she turned away.

The entire house, and the world beyond, turned to black. As if all the light in Alynthia had been sucked away. I couldn't see anything, couldn't see a pinprick of brightness.

Amara began pulling me, but I fought her. I screamed aloud, trying to race toward my parents even though I couldn't see them. But Amara clamped a hand over my lips.

I didn't mean to burn her—I really didn't.

But she only tightened her hold over my mouth as thin strips of acrid smoke curled around us.

"You have to be quiet, alright?" she whispered, and I thought it sounded like she was crying. "Your momma needs you to be quiet, Thea."

I nodded through my tears, and her hand vanished from my lips.

Amara scooped me into her arms and ran.

But she didn't run fast enough. I saw the blade that shattered the darkness.

The blade that ran through my mother.

CHAPTER THIRTY

STORMS

T he dream set a bad stage for the day.

I was sad, missing both my human and Fae mother. I was reminded of all the family I had lost. Momma, Momma Amara, Daddy, Poppa, Dain.

Mellian was concerned about my mood, but she tried to act like she wasn't. I was also pretending this morning. Pretending that I was fine.

My thoughts had gotten away from me last night. I shouldn't be dreaming about Hrokr, especially in that capacity. And while I normally wouldn't mind seeing the faces of my loved ones, I surely did not want to relive their deaths.

I helped Mellian tidy the house, and I made lunch so I could be spared her cooking. We moved in a comfortable, companionable silence, one borne of many years spent sharing a home. And by the time the dishes had been washed and the table cleared, I'd eased enough to rest in the joy my sister offered.

The remainder of the time Mellian and I had together was easy. We didn't speak of lost parents or strained relationships or anything else too heavy for our shoulders. She had laundered my clothes from Valencia the night before, and I donned them, nothing they now smelled like Ekin's soaps.

I secured my hood and dagger holster before lacing up my boots.

"I wish you didn't have to go," Mellian said, perched on the arm of the sofa.

"Let me see Alek, then," I countered.

Her face soured. "Yeah, I wish. I'll try to talk to him tonight about what it would be like if you came back. If it goes well, then maybe tomorrow."

I looked up at her, frowning. "Can it honestly be that bad, Mel? He's my *brother.*"

She only shrugged, unwilling to give me a lie for an answer.

As I was preparing to tell her goodbye, a knock sounded at the front door. My eyes instantly locked with my sister's, and I watched the blood drain from her cheeks as surely as I knew it was draining from my own.

There was a pause of stilted panic, and then she was ushering me toward the kitchen and around the bend of the wall. My heart leapt into my throat, and I was preparing to crawl through the window when I heard a voice that slipped around my spine and held me in place.

All he said was, "Hello," but I heard it with every inch of my skin.

What reason could Hrokr possibly have for coming to my *house?*

There was more speaking, but I couldn't hear it over the pounding of blood in my ears. I felt suddenly bashful, recalling the dream I'd had about him. I took a steadying breath, and by the time I forced myself out into the front room, he was standing in it, and my sister was wearing a blushing grin.

Five Halls.

We only looked at one another across the expanse of my living room.

Mellian—while flushed—looked bewildered. I remembered it suddenly—that overwhelming aura that leaked off his skin and seemed to be sucked up by the wood and earth below.

I'd always wondered if humans could feel it, and I decided in this moment that they absolutely could.

"Why are you here?" I asked.

A choked sound ripped out of Mellian. "*Thea,*" she hissed.

Hrokr cocked a dark brow, a smooth smile curving his lips as my cheeks bloomed scarlet.

"Don't worry," Hrokr said, turning his head only slightly toward her as his eyes held my own. "I am quite used to her crass manners. Fond of them, even," he admitted, flicking his gaze to my sister.

I narrowed my eyes.

Now was far from the time, but I couldn't help but notice how out of place he looked here. He was polished to perfection, even his skin more illustrious than most Folk's.

But his too-perfect posture was at ease. He didn't blink an eye at the faded state of living, of the chips in the aged wooden floors, at holes worn into fabric by harsh elbows and heavy bodies.

"I came only to relay a message I thought you'd be more comfortable hearing in person."

I sighed sharply. "What do you want, Hrokr?"

Mellian looked like she was choking. "Well, I will invite you in if she won't," she sputtered, her manners absolutely shuddering through her skin.

Momma would have been proud.

"Can I get you anything?" she asked. "Tea, water?"

He smiled, a warm thing that made his eyes glitter. "Tea sounds lovely, thank you."

She turned toward me, mouthing a sharp, *What is wrong with you?* as she skittered past.

I practically ran to him. "Why are you here?" I hissed. "Alek will be home any minute, and—"

"The Guard isn't happy about the ward," he interrupted.

I paused.

To the widening of my eyes, he said, "I thought you'd panic if I projected that to you, and do something rash. It's alright, but I think you should stay here. I think most Fae should stay inside, in fact, but Ciro is working on that."

Halls.

Tackling one crisis at a time, I said, "I can't stay here. And neither can you."

239

"And why is that?"

I pleaded with my eyes. "My brother doesn't even know I'm here."

"I'm sure you planned on seeing him sooner or later."

I huffed a sharp breath. "Yes. *Alone.* Not with someone who looks like you," I said, frantically gesturing at him.

He paused—a little jerk into stillness. And then a long, slow grin turned his lips into an uneven smirk of a smile. "What does *that* mean, Thea?"

He practically purred the words.

I flushed, a blossoming of red across the apples of my cheeks. "You know *exactly* what that means, Hrokr." I pulled at the hem of the cloak at his chest, the backs of my knuckles brushing across the silver brocade of his breast beneath. "You look far too expensive to blend in Mortis Hollow."

He caught my wrist, eyes raking over the Valencian cloak I wore. "So do you."

I ripped my hand free. "But they know my face."

"Which is exactly why you should stay put."

I huffed a breath. "Fine. But you need to leave."

"No," Mellian barked from behind me, sliding into the room. "He does not." Having far more courage than any five-and-a-half foot human should have next to the most powerful faerie on Alynthia should have, she offered him a steaming, chipped mug. "You are more than welcome to stay."

Turning to me, she said, "Alek has no reason to go into your room. You two can go there when he gets home."

I scowled openly at her. "Then why have you been making me leave?"

She retreated to the sofa, sitting like a perfect lady. "Your absence would be ideal if you wish to avoid him, but we accommodate guests in this house, Thea."

The words settled into an empty room. From the look on Hrokr's face, he couldn't decide if this moment was endearing or amusing.

I loosed a long breath. "He is no guest, Mel." But even as I said the words, I moved a spare quilt from the armchair across from the sofa. "Here. Sit."

He chuckled, a low sound that wrapped around my bones. "Your hospitality overwhelms me, Thea."

"Much warmer than the hospitality you offered me," I quipped, plopping down beside my sister.

"That's not true," he said, affronted. "I have made it very clear how welcome you are in my home."

First with a dagger in the thigh and second with a prison cell.

He winked.

Mellian pitched forward in her seat. "I'm so sorry, my lord. This is a trying time for her. She is quite kind."

Halls.

But he waved her off. "Please. Call me Crow." With a quick perusal over my seated form, he said, "She is a kind woman, yes. Quite tenacious and carrying the burden of a large heart." He took a sip of tea. "Your parents must have been lovely to raise you both."

Mellian smiled, though it was edged with something melancholy. "They were, thank you."

Hrokr's mental voice slid to me across the space. *How much does she know?*

"All of it," I said aloud.

Mellian's face puckered in confusion, but Hrokr said, "I came to extend an offer."

"Alek won't go," I interrupted.

He needn't say his piece.

But he wanted to. "Then he won't," he countered smoothly. "The ward surrounding this town is gone, and I have no intentions of letting it be laid again. This is the best decision for long-term safety and peace between our respective peoples, but sometimes the transition is brutal."

"Sometimes?" I asked, cocking a brow.

His eyes swung toward me. "I told you I grew up near here, Thea. I have long lent my hand to humanity's reconciliation with the Fae."

My mind spun at the words. That explained the Valencian presence in the Hall of the Elements. The wagons, the resources stockpiled in the warehouse. Talon and the other victims. Old expanse and the warmth at which they received the Fae.

Guilt was a sour taste on the back of my tongue.

"You both have a home on my Hall if you'd wish it. Whether that be permanently or only while things are settled here, it is your decision. Sagira is there," he added for Mellian.

"She doesn't want to be," I interjected.

"And she will be safer when she returns because of what we've done," Hrokr said.

As if summoned by the words, or perhaps the Elders had a hand in this moment—the front door exploded.

Exploded.

Cracked down the middle, chips of wood flying throughout the front room. I dove in front of Mellian as she screamed, curling in on herself to protect her head.

I blinked, and Hrokr was standing at my side, Mellian behind us.

In walked Alek, his face looking older and harsher than it had even in Balaca. Filing in behind him were an assembly of five guards.

The Guard.

Five humans. Five weak, fragile humans poured through the hole in the wall.

In my flustered state, my brain was delayed in realizing Alek was *with* these men. I shoved around Hrokr, lunging for my baby brother to *protect* him.

But then he was pulling away, and a human soldier was ripping me backward against his chest.

I could get away. I had the speed, strength, and training I needed to escape.

But my mind was moving so slowly trying to catch up to what was happening. Maybe I had all the tools, but I couldn't seem to find the emotional wherewithal.

Human?

A *human* was hurting me—and in Mortis Hollow of all places?

My hands were nearly gentle as I laid them against the burly forearm pressing against my throat.

Thea, Hrokr said, frantically projecting to my mind.

I only blinked, trying to reconcile what was happening to the home I knew.

I thought Mellian was screaming, thought maybe Alek was trying to get to her.

But someone was between them. Or some*thing.* Something dark and cold.

My eyes—so slow—rolled over to face what was between them.

Hrokr.

Hrokr with shadows skittering off his skin. Hrokr, standing like an immovable, cold pillar between my brother and sister. His eyes were harsh with some mix of confusion and panic as he stared at me.

I only shook my head, but what I was shaking it about, I wasn't sure.

The arm at my throat moved, and then the cold bite of steel replaced it.

I didn't know what to do. I didn't want to hurt them, not when they were Alek's peers, and we were right in front of him.

I dug my nails into the guard's arm, only enough to draw blood. Only enough to make him *stop*.

But he shouted, gasping as he dropped his blade. It clattered against the wooden floor, the ringing the only sound more shrill than the shrieking the men were doing as they leapt away from me.

A heavy beat of stilted silence pulsed through the room.

All six of the guards—five strangers and my brother... *my brother*—drew their swords.

And immediately dropped them as confusion puckered their ruddy faces. And then they were falling to their knees, kneeling before me. Only Alek remained standing, where he stumbled backward, the murderous look on his face replaced only with fear. He moved until his back hit the wall.

I looked on at the guards, who were all kneeling, but with strain lining every inch of their bodies.

My eyes swung to Hrokr's.

His jaw was clenched so tightly it could have snapped, and I thought I could hear his teeth grinding.

Taking a visibly heavy breath, he shook out his shoulders and buttoned the cuff of his sleeve.

And I realized—albeit belatedly—he'd brought the men to their knees.

He looked at me, his starry eyes patiently waiting for my reaction to all that had passed.

But I wasn't yet sure what that reaction would be. I was still struggling to understand what had just happened—just how much of my future had been wiped away.

And why? Was it Alek? Wyn? Hrokr? A bystander at the bar last night?

Alek had enough gall to recover, pushing off from the wall while he looked at his friends kneeling in the center of our front room. His eyes flicked between me and the Fae lord at my side. "Who is this?"

Though his eyes were murderous, Hrokr's lips only twitched. "Who are *you?*"

Alek's nostrils flared. "I am Soldier Hawthorne of the High Guard."

Hrokr's lips split into a wide grin, though the glint in his multicolored eyes was ravenous. "It is a pleasure to meet you, Soldier." He gestured a lazy hand at Alek. "Would you like to be civil or should I also put you on your knees?"

A bolt of defensiveness shot through me, but a quick glance at Mellian had me holding my tongue.

Alek eyed Hrokr's ears as if the Fae essence of them could rub off and taint him. It did not escape Hrokr's notice.

He turned his back on Alek to stride down the hall. I remembered that move, that casual baring of his back to the enemy, as if not an ounce of fear or trepidation lived inside of his body. "I'm getting some more tea, if that is alright, ladies."

Alek glared behind Hrokr's back. "I asked you a question," he barked at Hrokr.

As Hrokr stilled, I saw red.

"*Alek,*" I snapped, baring my teeth.

"It's alright, love," Hrokr said, half turning his head back toward us. "What was your question?"

"Who are you? On what authority do you command me?" Alek growled.

Mellian whimpered, and the sound gutted me.

Hrokr grinned, feral firelight glinting in his eyes. "It doesn't quite matter who I am, does it, Alek?"

Alek lunged for him. But the movement only gained him a few inches before his knees were crashing into the wood floor.

I didn't understand the feelings swirling inside of my body.

"Let me go," Alek seethed.

I managed a shaking step forward. "What have you done, Alek?" I cried.

He looked incredulous, as if he couldn't believe that I was asking. "Look at what *you've* done, Thea."

Hrokr took a step forward, but I flung out a hand, laying it on his chest. He met my eyes as I slowly shook my head. I retreated to the far wall, wishing I could slip through the wood and plaster and be out of this suddenly cramped room.

I took a deep breath, begging the flames within my body to bank. When I had collected myself enough that I was only speaking with a shaking voice instead of screaming, I asked, "Alek, what are you angry at me for?"

I thought his brown eyes were going to bulge from their sockets. "This has always been about you, Thea. We were only at The Meridian because of you."

Of all things Alek could have said, I did not expect *that*.

Immediate tears blurred my vision.

"The Meridian was as busy as it was because *you* were playing. We were there *because of you*. We were taken *because of you*. Cole is dead *because of you*."

The tears spilled from their nest in my lashes, warming my cheeks in salty tracks.

Alek bared his teeth at me. Teeth that were so blunt, so human. "And I'm glad he's dead, Thea. Because he loved you so much. It would have killed him to learn who you ended up standing beside," he seethed, eyes swinging to Hrokr. "How can you stand to be in his presence?" he asked, sounding disgusted. "He is not a man."

For the first time, I could hear a note of fear in his voice. It was far overshadowed by the distaste. "Can you not feel the darkness inside of him? I'm a human, and I can feel it," he snapped.

I did feel it. I'd always felt it.

A vast, dark presence. It was something old and primal, a magical aura that I had no name for.

But was it any surprise that magic was dripping off his body when he was the most powerful Gentry Fae in all of Alynthia?

"It makes sense though," Alek continued with a sneer that soured his once-boyish features. "You're wicked, Thea. It is no wonder that your dark soul would find comfort near his. Like calls to like."

Though Hrokr was silent, I felt the cold slithering of his shadows as they spilled from his body, thrashing across the floor like severed tentacles. "It is your fault Mother is dead," he bit. "Your fault for associating with the man in the mask."

"I didn't," I pleaded, hating how much my voice sounded like a sob.

But I had. Oh, I had. I'd associated him more than Alek could even imagine.

He pulled against Hrokr's invisible bonds, straining his neck to scowl at me. "Or are you perhaps worse than him?" he asked, jerking his head in Hrokr's direction. "Perhaps worse than him *and* the masked man? Did you think we couldn't see from that tower in Balaca, Thea?"

Ice crusted around my heart.

"Did you think we couldn't see what you did?"

My feet carried me forward, fast with the pulse of fear burning through me.

Hrokr could never know what happened in Balaca, couldn't know I had the ability to wield flame.

"Stop."

But Alek continued, grinning like a madman at finally getting a more expressive reaction from me. "Does your new friend not know, Thea? Didn't you tell him how it rained blood? Didn't you tell him—"

"*Stop,*" I growled.

Alek grinned, and the sight curdled within me like soured milk. "How many people did you kill, Thea? How many people walked off a battlefield of hundreds? Only two. How many people did you b—"

I dug my fingers into his uniform, ripping him to his feet, past Hrokr's bonds, past my own knowledge that I needed to stop.

Alek's eyes widened.

Not at my display of rage.

No, not at me at all.

But at the scarred, porcelain hand that was clasping over my own.

Hrokr's fingers were gentle as he tugged my hand free of Alek's clothes. They were gentle as he released my hand altogether, capturing my chin in his hand and turning my face toward him.

He shook his head. Slowly, softly.

You will regret hurting him, he said.

Tears returned to my eyes in full force, blurring my vision. How could he think I'd ever hurt my baby brother?

But Hrokr only pulled me away with steady hands and deposited me into the arms of another.

I clung to my sister as Hrokr took a deep breath. His fingers moved slowly to the button at his breast, undoing his cloak and folding it neatly on the arm chair. Beneath it, he wore a crisp, black tunic and dark leather pants.

He picked up his mug of tea, drinking deeply from it.

The room was wholly silent as he set the mug back on the table.

He walked to the kneeling guards, standing behind a man with blonde hair and bloodshot blue eyes. Hrokr hauled him to his feet.

"Alek," he said. "I'm going to show you something."

I lunged forward, but Mellian corralled me. Her strength was no match for my own, but I yielded as she banded her frail, human arms around me and attempted to hold me in place.

"Do you even know how what you call *magic* works, Alek?" he asked, his voice deathly calm. "The ether? The arcane? The tides of unseen fibers? Do you know that the lifeblood of the entire world flows in our veins?"

I felt Hrokr. Not in my body or my mind, but somewhere deeper inside of me. I felt his power swell and wrap around me, licking at my skin.

And then I watched in awe-struck horror as night descended over Mortis Hollow. The late morning sunlight streaming through the windows around us was snuffed out as fat, black clouds rolled low across the sky, lightning flashing throughout their depths.

As if he had leaked away his own darkness, the stars in Hrokr's eyes were deathly bright. Stars ruptured into supernovas, swallowing each other whole only to be birthed again, happening all inside of the gaze pinning my feet to the floor.

I could smell the human fear in the room. It was a bitter, earthy smell full of rot and decay.

"Come here." His voice was thunder given tangible form, darkness personified.

Alek's eyes flashed to mine, and I held his gaze. Waiting.

He had the good sense to stumble forward.

The clouds outside broke free, rain slamming into the windows and the earth below. Wind whipped the trees of the courtyard, Hrokr unleashing his rage on the world.

I knew that he could control the weather, but I never could have imagined this. His power was staggering.

With only a whimpering human separating them, Alek turned from Hrokr to search out Mellian. She avoided his gaze.

"On your knees."

Those shadows I sometimes caught sight of were slipping across Hrokr's body now, coiling around his wrists and licking up his throat.

The storm outside rolled steadily, battering against the shutters and filling the quiet space with a dull roar.

Alek's eyes were wide, blossoming with all-encompassing fear.

Hrokr's hand laid gently against the guard's back.

"Close your eyes," I whispered to Mellian.

Because I knew those gentle hands. I knew that Hrokr's cruelty was best delivered when it was soft.

But Mel's eyes were wide open.

"Alek," Hrokr breathed. His voice was like the rain outside, low and raw, full of the promise of the storm. "Do you know how easy it is to die?"

As if the guard's body was made of nothing more than butter, Hrokr's hand pushed through his clothes, through his flesh, through his muscle and bone. His blood-soaked fingers came through his chest on the other side, gripping a still-beating heart.

No blood sprayed, no red pooled or shot. Because his magic was there to bend it to his will. The guard did not even scream. Or if he did, Hrokr's power over the air swallowed the sound before it reached my ears.

But then those fingers curled.

He crushed the heart in his hands, blood spattering Alek's cheeks.

The body of the guard collapsed, leaving only Hrokr with an arm gloved in red. He crouched down as if speaking to an errant child as he beheld my brother.

It wasn't his right to do this, wasn't his place to punish Alek. It was mine, and *Halls,* it should not be this severe. I lurched forward, but Mellian was there to hold me back.

The only thing that kept me from launching across the room was remembering that Mellian was just as much his sister as I was.

I watched in shaking silence as Hrokr bent down, eye level with Alek.

"I'm going to kill the rest of them," he said softly. "And it's not because I'm angry—though believe me, I am. It's because I need you to understand." And in only a blink—before I even had the chance to move—heads were sliding off of shoulders and tumbling to the floor.

My living room was a bloodbath. "I know you think your sister has done nothing for you," Hrokr said into Alek's bewildered face. "But she has. She saved your life today, Alek."

Hrokr leaned even closer. His eyes searched Alek's.

Alek flinched.

"Get out of my head," Alek hissed.

Hrokr was projecting.

"Hrokr," I mumbled.

My voice was soft, but his eyes lifted to mine from across the room. Only for a moment did he look at me, and then his dark eyes were sliding back to my brother. "Your sister may kill," he whispered, voice lethal. "But if she is a blade, then I am a *butcher.*"

He rose to his full height, looking down on him. "Do not ever disrespect her in my presence again."

Silence fell within the room.

It stretched so long that Mellian tumbled forward a step.

"I miss Momma, too," she said softly, her voice swallowed by the rain and thunder. "You aren't the only one hurting, Alek."

"This isn't about Mother."

"Of course it is," Mellian said. "And she wouldn't want this. She loved us, Alek. She loved Thea. She wouldn't want you out killing the Folk just because a few hurt us."

"A *few?*" Alek cried. He shook his head, cheeks flushing in rage. "You've changed, Mel. Both of you have," he said with a grim glare in my direction.

But how could he not see had warped he, too, had become?

"I had to," Mellian cried, thick tears rolling down her cheeks.

"I will remind you," Hrokr said in a cold, sour voice, "that you have suffered the least amount of loss. Your freedom was purchased by sacrifices not your own. You were protected by these two valiant women who you have done nothing but disrespect. What have you lost that they have not lost, too?"

Silence.

"You have nothing to say? You have nothing to say to the sister who sold her body to buy you ease? Or to the sister who sold her soul to drag you out of misery?"

My eyes whipped toward Mellian.

How did Hrokr know that?

"It's her fault," Alek croaked.

Grief washed over me in a powerful wave, threatening to pull me under.

"How?" Hrokr asked quietly, and the death in his voice frightened even me.

"Mother was killed simply for loving Thea," Alek rasped, his emotions threatening to consume him. "It's all been about Thea."

"Incorrect."

My eyes flitted to Hrokr.

"Your mother was killed to hurt Thea, sure," Hrokr replied. "But have you considered *why?*"

When Alek said nothing, Hrokr clenched his jaw. His head cocked to one side, watching Alek as a predator watches prey. "Thea was manipulated by a man named Silas, burnished into a weapon to be wielded against me. Your mother was killed to break Thea, to hurt her, to make her more easily moldable. Your mother was killed so that Thea could be sharpened in order to cut *me.*"

My chest ached. My eyes filled with tears.

"So you're saying it is your fault?" Alek asked. There was venom in his words, but it was subdued. Confused.

"Child," Hrokr breathed. "If you need someone to blame other than the man who wielded the blade that ended her life, then yes. It is my fault."

It made me sick to hear the words. It wasn't true, not in the slightest. Hrokr did not need to carry my weight on his shoulders. I prayed to the Elders he was lying for my benefit and did not truly feel that way.

I leaned forward, but his voice sliced into me.

Stay back, Thea, please.

I halted, watching the inky shadows ripple from his exposed skin.

"If it is any consolation," Hrokr continued, and there was a gentle undercurrent to the blade of his voice, now. "I found my mother slain, and her blood still colors the wood of my childhood home."

I thought my heart was actually cracking. Mellian looked horrified.

"It has been six centuries, and the stain of grief does not ever wash away."

Alek looked up, confusion covering all the anger on his features.

"But if you think for a moment that will persuade me to allow you to disrespect her ever again, you are gravely mistaken."

Hrokr's eyes touched on me for only a moment, and then he was striding for my front door, over blood and corpses, and out into the rain.

CHAPTER THIRTY-ONE

ANYONE ELSE

I was instantly on my feet.

I didn't know where to go first.

The bewildered Alek frozen on the floor, the half dozen corpses rapidly drenching the rug, or Hrokr charging out to wreak whatever other havoc he could find.

I made for Alek.

But Mellian caught me around the wrist. "You should follow him."

"Hrokr?" I cried.

"Yes," she said, some strange emotion turning her eyes. "I'll deal with—" a flick of her eyes to the mess behind us, "—that. He came by this morning, while you were still asleep."

"*Hrokr?*" I repeated.

"Yes," she said, nodding and beginning to push me toward the door. "I agree with what you two are doing, Thea."

"I'm not doing any—"

She gripped me by the shoulders. "He's leaving some of his people here. I will be safe, and I will help Alek acclimate. The Guard has been in the wrong for a long time. If we embraced our Fae, they may have protected us that night."

Something twisted inside my chest.

"Go. I will be safe, and you will have a home here. But you should go to him, Thea."

"No," I said harshly. "He doesn't need me. You do."

She smiled, though her eyes held only something soft. She brushed my hair back behind my pointed ear, looking at it with marvel for the first time in our lives.

"I think maybe he does."

Outside, Hrokr stood in the rain.

After a moment of hesitation, I followed him. I stepped through the door and out into the downpour muddying the dirt paths. It was ice-cold, chilling my ears and cheeks.

Hrokr had his back to me as he tilted his head up to the sky and let the rain wash over him.

The evidence of his magnificence was all around me, and it was slightly disorienting to be in the midst of a storm that had come from his own will.

It was easy to forget the cooling bodies staining my rugs red as I watched his back struggle through steadying breaths.

I wondered what that said about me.

He did not move as I strode toward him, stopping just at his back. I reached out with shaking fingers to lay my hand against him. He stiffened, spine tightening.

"You should go," he rasped, voice raw.

"Why?" My voice was small, swallowed by the rain bearing down on us.

His body burned beneath my palm, even between the cold rain and the fabric of his soaking clothes. He shuddered, whispering my name.

I tugged gently, and slowly he turned to me. His eyes were hot and clear as they bore into my own. "You should go," he repeated.

"Why?" I asked again, tilting my head back to meet his eyes. The rain pelted me, soaking me through.

He ran a hand through his wet hair. "I am feeling quite disconnected from myself at the moment," he said thickly.

My hand fell away as I blinked up at him. "In what way?"

His eyes darkened. "In every way." When I made no move to respond, his nostrils flared. "I hope you know that if he were anyone else I would have left his spine on the floor."

I shivered from the image, from the knowledge that he was deadly enough to do it. "I'm sorry," I whispered.

He took a step closer, his chest brushing against my own.

He was beautiful this way. Wet and raw and angry. Deadly.

I curled my fingers into fists so tight that the skin broke into half-moons beneath my nails.

"What," he snarled, "do you possibly have to apologize for?"

His anger was a kindling beneath me, something that set my heart beating fast, the muscles in my stomach clenching.

"I know he shouldn't have spoken to you like that—"

"You're out of your mind, Thea."

I started. "I—what?"

His lips pulled back from his teeth, and his eyes still glowed with deadly starfire. "I showed him mercy because that is what you wanted me to do. Do you understand that?"

"Yes," I croaked.

"Good." He leaned down close to me, his breath coasting across my skin. "Because if anyone—*anyone*—else had acted the way he did—"

He took a shuddering breath as if he was indeed struggling to calm himself.

I'd never seen him so undone

"I wouldn't have used magic, Thea," he said roughly. "I would have used my hands, and I would have savored each moment."

Silence bloomed as I studied him, as I felt his rage pulsing in my veins.

"If it were anyone else, Crow," I whispered, "I would have enjoyed watching you hurt them."

A figure materializing only a few feet from us caused our heads to whip away from each other.

Maddox, long hair coated in cold rain. His eyes flashed between the two of us, sodden and standing entirely too close.

Hrokr took a step away from me, frigid air rushing into the space between us. "Let's go home, Thea," he rasped, eyes on Maddox.

Maddox looked at me, ready to reprimand me if I once again said Valencia was not my home.

But I kept my mouth shut and offered my palm for whichever one would take it.

Maddox did.

We materialized in the center of the Portal Room in Castle Habrem, dripping onto the smooth floor.

Maddox immediately vanished again, leaving Hrokr and me alone.

The enormity of what had just happened began to settle around my shoulders.

"Are you alright?" he asked gently.

When I didn't respond, Hrokr reached out to tap my cheek. The touch was so small, yet so profoundly comforting. Instantly, I felt myself snapping mental walls into place, throwing bricks and stones between us.

"I need to go," I mumbled, turning away.

"Wait," he said, grabbing my arm and spinning me back. His face was shadowed and full of concern, his cold rage left behind in Ekin. "Where are you going?" The question was soft and quiet, full of the promise to come along.

Hating myself just a little more, I pulled out of his grasp. "I just need to go."

He didn't follow me. And though I knew I'd made my wishes clear, it still lodged something aching into my throat.

I practically ran from him, but once I was free, I felt a stinging tightness in my chest.

Resigned, I trudged up to my room, praying he wouldn't follow me.

Praying my prayers wouldn't be answered.

CHAPTER THIRTY-TWO

BROKEN BOTTLES

I t was cold on the balcony.

I'd donned a pair of burnt orange sleeping clothes and folded myself onto the stone floor. I stared out at the city, watching the bustle and light as it dimmed and night fell across the valley.

Hrokr never showed.

I knew it was my own fault. But still, I was left with the same oily feeling that always seemed to find me. Loneliness.

Alone, alone, alone.

Always alone.

Something was wrong with me—deeply wrong. I just wasn't entirely sure what it was.

I always found myself this way, alone with only the promise that someday my life would return to normal, and I'd go home to live a human life in Mortis Hollow.

Even that hope was now gone.

I wished Momma were here. She would croon Alek into submission and probably chastise Sagira, too. Everything would be fine if she were here.

Though, if she were here, then of course everything would be fine. Alek wouldn't have a death to blame me for, and I wouldn't have a murder to avenge. I'd be home, safe and sound, with Sage.

Though even as I thought the words, I thought the picture was somewhat dreary. Not my mother—no, I would do anything to have her back.

But life in Ekin.

Was it really a home to me? It was so freeing to watch the city and feel the wind in my hair and on my ears. I could smile openly here, bare my teeth—bare what I was.

Well, most of what I was.

Even Mellian approved of what Hrokr had done, the freedom he'd brought—albeit at a bloody price.

I sighed, wrapping my arms tighter around myself. This was all my fault. I should have never let Sage come with me into Vanadey. I'd known how dangerous it would be, and still, I'd let her come.

I shouldn't have brought her to the Guild, shouldn't have put her in a position to be subjected to any of these people.

Most importantly, I shouldn't have opened my heart. I should not have loved Gar. I shouldn't have let him in, let him know enough to hurt me.

And now I'd done it again.

I'd given these strangers—these most powerful Fae in Alynthia—every piece of myself. I'd left my family in their care.

Were my siblings staying at our house? Would whoever Hrokr left with them stay close? In my home?

Though my self-hatred spiraling was in full-swing, this thought did not fill me with panic. Hrokr wouldn't let anyone who would hurt them anywhere near.

I felt that truth somewhere deep inside of me, as surely as I knew I would not hurt them myself.

I sighed, rose to my feet, and dragged myself to bed, letting my melancholy thoughts rock me to a somber sleep.

Something woke me. Though—in the way that was often when something rips one from sleep—I didn't know what it was. A sound, a thought, a scent. I didn't know.

I cast my eyes toward the balcony, but night was still fully overhead. I didn't think I had been asleep that long, maybe only a few hours. It couldn't have been far past midnight.

I heard a rustling and the hard clink of glass against the countertop.

I should stay in bed. I had all but expressly told Hrokr to leave me alone, and he was doing it. He was listening. I was sure he hadn't meant to wake me, and honestly, he had every right to make as much noise as he liked.

It was I who was intruding on his life.

He was definitely awake, though. I could hear his footsteps now, walking across the floor of his front room in the hall over.

I squeezed my eyes shut, hoping to drown out the noise and thoughts enough to fall back into sleep.

But there was a small crashing noise followed by a rough grinding as if he had hit something, and it slid.

I sat up straight, and before I could give myself the option to lie back down, threw the blankets from my body. I made my way out of my rooms, across the hall, and through his door.

The door opened to a receiving area, similar to my own room. The color scheme was darker here, made up of ebony floors and slate, stone walls. Floor-to-ceiling windows took up the entire right wall, the view far different from my balcony facing the west.

The mountains were *so close,* as if we sat right on the edge of the world. Below us, a massive cove of water gone dark with the night undulated gently. The mountains came right up to the water, closing around the lake in a semi-circle that opened to allow the cove to lap at a shore right next to the castle.

My mind took it all in quickly.

A small sitting area with wing-backed, black chairs and glass tables. A large leather sofa as dark as the night. A clean, black fireplace. A small kitchenette in the same colors, complete with a granite island and barstools.

Barstools that Hrokr was stumbling into, knocking them into one another.

My eyes widened, but he sighed sharply, righting himself.

"Halls, Thea, you startled me."

"Sorry," I mumbled quickly, but there was something strange about his voice. Something off. And when did Hrokr stumble? When was he—

I exclaimed a wordless noise, rushing toward him. "What happened?"

Blood. There was blood all over him. Caked around one nostril and smeared down his lip. It pooled on his chest, soaking the white fabric.

"Nothing," he said harshly, turning away from me. But his movements were sharp, far less fluid than they normally were. "Go back to bed."

He stumbled again, losing his footing and catching himself on the ledge of the island counter.

I rushed across the room to him, hands hovering around him as if there was something I could do to help. If he was injured, why wouldn't he just heal himself?

"Hrokr, really, what's wrong?" I asked, and the panic in my voice was loud to even my own ears.

He turned to me, and something cold filled me when I met his eyes. Fear—it was definitely fear I was feeling.

His eyes were half-lidded and lazy, but his pupils were blown wide, their black hole having swallowed all of the stars around it.

I reached my hand toward his face. "What happ—"

He swatted me away. "Go to bed. I'm fine."

"You're not fine. What happened to you?"

He growled out something wordless and made to move past me, but he couldn't even walk. He lost his footing, but I caught and steadied him.

As I did, I took in the countertop and its contents.

Something inside of me sunk.

Liquor.

So much liquor.

Multiple spent bottles, one shattered against the floor.

"What is this?" I asked, voice small.

I reached to touch it, but he had enough dexterity to snatch my hand out of the way, his long fingers closing around my wrist. "Leave it alone," he said.

"Hrokr—"

"Do *not,*" he interrupted, dropping my hand. There were a wealth of emotions in his eyes, but anger sat front. "Do not presume to lecture me, Thea."

His voice...

Images of myself pelted me. Liquor in glass bottles, hazel eyes beneath the rain, the mistakes that came from chasing drunken solace.

My voice was a lot smaller, a lot weaker, when I asked, "Why are you bleeding?"

Something in his expression softened. "I'm alright."

We stared at each other in silence, the only illumination coming from the balls of lights floating in the corners. Moonlight reflected off the lake below his wall of windows, though it wasn't enough to seep into the room.

Slowly, he reached up and began brushing flakes of blood from his face. "Go back to bed, Thea," he repeated, though in a voice far gentled.

"Alright" I agreed quietly, heart swelling in my chest. "If you let me help you get cleaned up first."

This wasn't right. He was drowning himself with only the moon for company.

"Thea, I don't need help. I don't need—"

"Please," I blurted. "It will make me feel better."

Even in this state, he was beautiful. He looked raw and animal, as if he had locked the humanity—if I could call it that—away.

Hrokr sighed, long and drawn. "I suppose."

He started to move across the room, his steps sloppy and shuffled.

I grabbed ahold of his arm to steer him into the bathing room. As soon as we stepped over the threshold, little orbs of bobbing light warmed to a muted glow in the corners. They remained dim, as if they knew the full light would be too much for his eyes.

The room was ornate, as I'd expected. Black crystal, black herringbone tiles, and a massive clawfoot-tub—also black. Everything metal was a shining gold.

His brow was pinched, his lips thin. He looked like he was in pain, but fighting it.

"Are you hurting?" I asked quietly.

He opened his mouth. Closed it. Opened it again. "Kind of."

His gaze bore down into mine, looking pained and dark. "What hurts?" I asked.

I tried to steer him to sit on the edge of the tub, but he pulled out of my grasp, leaning against the counter near the sink. His fingers gripped the marble so hard I wondered if they'd crush through it.

He didn't answer my question.

I grabbed a washcloth and wet it with warm water before returning to him. His eyes were closed now, but the tendons in his forearms were nearly bursting from his skin with the grip he had on the counter.

I started to raise it to his face, but I paused when he spoke. "I shouldn't be here."

I frowned as his eyes fluttered open. "This is your room, Hrokr."

He sighed, his breath washing over me. There were only inches separating us, and I could smell the bite of spirits on him. "Then maybe you shouldn't be here."

I tried to keep the hurt off my face. "Do you want me to go?"

"I don't know," he whispered.

I took a breath, steeling myself. I deserved that; I'd been awful to him. He should hate me, just like everyone else I cared about did. I lifted the cloth to his face and gently wiped away the blood on his chin.

Hrokr sucked in a sharp breath, quivering slightly.

I stopped. "Am I hurting you?"

"No," he said, the breath barely audible.

I cleaned his face, careful to be gentle.

"Why?"

"Why what?" he asked, eyes still closed.

"Why are you doing this?"

He was quiet as I stepped away and rinsed the cloth, watching blood and water swirl down the drain.

When he finally answered, his voice was rougher, as if the words had to be dragged out of him. "I had a bad day."

Guilt flooded me. I wasn't sure if it was more arrogant to assume I was the cause or to assume I wasn't. Sure, he was angry at Alek, but...

It wasn't really about Alek, was it?

I returned to him, standing between his legs as I made one more pass over his chin and cheek. "Do you want to talk about it?"

His eyes opened, but he didn't meet my gaze. He roved over my face and hair before settling on my lips. His parted slightly, and I could feel his breath on my fingertips as I lowered the cloth.

"Not really," he whispered.

Without warning, his hand snaked out to wrap around my hip.

I sucked in a shrill breath as warmth sparked through me, beating fast and hard in my chest.

I made the mistake of looking up into his eyes just as his other hand made its way to my body. Hands on my hips, he pulled me into the cradle of his own.

"Hrokr," I whispered, cautioning him. Or maybe I was cautioning myself, trying to quiet the dull roaring taking up residence in my ears.

"What?" he drawled softly in a voice like rich silk. One hand left me only to pluck the cloth from my fingers and drop it on the floor before it returned.

I dropped my eyes, having nowhere to look but the pulse hammering in the hollow of his throat.

"You told me I shouldn't be here," I whispered.

"And I meant it."

"Why?"

"So we wouldn't find ourselves this way."

My heart skipped, but I forced the words past my lips. "Maybe you should let me go, Hrokr."

He smirked, leaning in. I stiffened as his nose skimmed the flesh of my neck. "Let me touch you, Thea," he pleaded, hands tightening on my hips. My eyes fluttered shut as he smiled into my skin.

I carefully pulled away, pressing against his chest to gain room. My head was spinning in a thousand directions.

"You're not sober, Hrokr," I croaked. *Not at all.*

"It doesn't matter," he breathed. "I want this. I want *you.*"

I was shaking my head, but he ignored it. He grabbed my hands and pressed them against his chest. "*Touch me,*" he pleaded.

Drunk and full of lust. It could have been any woman who heard him in his rooms.

"Come on," I said, extracting myself from his grasp. "Let's get you to bed." As I gripped his arm and led him from the bathing room, I tried to ignore the disappointed, shamed look in his eyes.

In his bedroom, the grey walls were carved from smooth stone, opening to a balcony that matched my own. His bed was enormous—low to the ground and adorned with rumpled, ebony sheets I knew would smell like fresh storms. It was crowned with a simple headboard fashioned from slats of dark-stained wood.

A massive crow in flight had been painted in glistening black directly onto the wall above it, embellished with thin strokes of rich green and deep purple.

I steered him past the black marble fireplace and leather chairs until we reached the edge of the bed. He frowned, and in what I suspected was a surprisingly rare show, a trace of pink touched his cheeks. "Do you hate me, Thea?"

My breath stuck in a painful lump in my throat. I understood why he would ask. He was forward tonight, but it was more than that. And I knew better than to think much of this day. He was drunk, and we were well into the early hours of the morning. There was a good chance he hadn't meant most of what he said. I wondered how often he did this. No wonder he always looked exhausted.

But it was more than just this day. I had been cold and aloof to him.

"No, Hrokr," I whispered. "I do not hate you."

I released my grip on him as he curled up on the bed. I gave him one last look before I turned to the door.

Once I reached it, I heard the bed rustling. "Thea?"

"Yes?" I called without looking back.

"Stay with me."

Something cracked just behind my ribs. "Goodnight, Crow," I whispered. The closed doors between us felt like more than just wood and hinges.

CHAPTER THIRTY-THREE

GOOD LIAR

I woke to a soft knock at my door.

I stirred, rubbing sleep from my eyes beneath the morning sunlight. My silence was taken as invitation enough—which I supposed was appropriate after how I'd barged in on him last night—because Hrokr gently pushed open the door to the living area.

Across the long space, he froze, and we regarded each other carefully for a stretching moment.

"Thea, I'm so sorry."

The sleep was burned from me instantly, leaving me unsteady and nauseous.

"Don't be sorry," I said softly. "It's alright."

He snorted self-derisively. "*It's alright.*" He avoided my gaze, staring down at his wringing hands and restless fingers. "I had absolutely no right to put you in the position that I did."

"No," I whispered. I reached my mental fingers toward the bricks to build up the wall between us. "It was my fault for barging in. You did nothing wrong."

"Nothing wrong?" he repeated. A slight look of panic entered in his eyes, and fear crested over me. "Thea, we can't—"

"Nothing at all," I assured, throwing the words down between us and forcing a smile I didn't feel. "I shouldn't have barged in," I said, pulling my blankets around myself like a shield. "I was only worried. I'm sorry."

He didn't look convinced, not as his brows drew together. He opened his mouth, but—I couldn't hear it. I couldn't hear him tell me what he was thinking.

He cast his eyes away from me.

I refused to have this moment between us on top of everything else. I padded over to the closet and started retrieving clothes for the day. "It's forgotten, Hrokr. What plans do we have for today?"

After an uncomfortably long pause, he said, "You're free to lounge."

I glanced over my shoulder to find him smirking. His easy attitude was likely just as fake as my own, but I'd take it. His arms were folded behind his head as he lay on the bed, the perfect picture of ease.

Hrokr was a good liar.

"Yeah? And what do you plan on doing?"

"I have lord-like duties to attend to."

I narrowed my eyes, but he laughed. "I really do have things to do today, Thea," he said. "How about you let Fallon take you into the valley?"

Frowning, I asked, "Shouldn't we talk about Silas or—"

He held up a scar-flecked hand. "We can have one day off. You've reported what you need to, and I'm working on it."

I chewed on my lower lip, clothes forgotten as I stood in the doorway of the closet. "Maybe I should go see Mel and Alek, then"

He grimaced. "Or *maybe* you should let Fallon take you into the valley."

I almost asked if I could just come with him, but after last night, that didn't seem like the most prudent idea.

"Are you trying to get rid of me?"

"Maybe."

I knew he was just playing with me, but worry wormed its way into my gut. "Is this about Alek's behavior? Because—"

"No," he interrupted. "Your family is yours to deal with how you choose."

I nodded slowly. "Any news about Sage?"

"I'm expecting there to be no news for as long as she stays here," he said. "She and Dorin are both fine, though keeping to themselves."

"Right," I said, nodding numbly. I loosed a breath and curled my fingers into tight fists. "Do you want me to stay there with them?"

"You're free to do as you wish, Thea."

Images from last night poured into me.

I want this. I want you.

Touch me.

Stay with me.

"Are you asking me to go?"

Confusion blanketed his features. "You're the one asking."

"No," I said. "If you want me to leave, Hrokr, just say so."

The bite in my voice—it was so childish. So afraid.

He smirked, and relief was a cool balm to my frayed nerves. "I suppose things are a little drab around here when you're gone."

Silence fell between us in a thick sheet.

"You spoke with my sister," I said softly. I'd meant it to sound like an accusation, but it didn't.

"I like her," he said. "She is a good sister to you, Thea. You deserve someone good in your life. Your other friends are wretched, if I may be so bold."

I wanted to laugh, but I couldn't quite reach it. "Thank you for this," I croaked. "I know it's been a pain. Especially Alek."

I couldn't stop hearing Maddox's words. Young Hrokr—facing the gruesome death of his mother.

"It hasn't," he said earnestly.

I leveled a flat look at him. "It has."

His smile was soft and full of knowing pity. "Family drama happens, love. The Elders know the Council can be rife with it. Just you wait," he winked.

I tried to offer a tentative smile back. "I can't imagine it's worse than my brother."

"Well, then you'd be wrong," he said as he rose from the bed. "I have to go. Maddox won't shut up, and his projecting is starting to give me a headache."

His headache was likely from his recent festivities, but there was no need to kick a man while he was down.

"What are you two doing today?"

"Training. Running formations and sparring with the Weathermen."

"The Weatherman?" I repeated, cocking a brow.

He chuckled. "The guard, our soldiers. It's a stupid name from an old stupid joke, but it has chosen to stick around for centuries."

"You are going to go spar, and you want me to go shopping?"

He rolled his eyes. "I would *much* rather go shopping in the valley than deal with this."

I snorted because I believed him. "Can I come?" I asked, pushing away my earlier reservations.

"No," he said, striding across the room and pushing past me into the closet.

"Why not?"

He pulled his cloak tighter around his shoulders. "Because it wouldn't be good for morale when you wiped them across the training floor."

I smirked and rolled my eyes even as the warmth of pride licked through me. "Not confident in your men?"

"It's not that. I'm just terrified of you."

I snorted, shaking my head.

"I've got to go," he said, and I moved to let him out through the doorway. "Go to the valley with Fallon today. You'll enjoy it."

I watched him as his long legs ate up the distance between me and the bedroom door. He turned back once he reached it, waiting.

"Alright," I said hesitantly.

CHAPTER THIRTY-FOUR

ALL THE STORIES

I paused outside the door to the Council Room. Only a few minutes after Hrokr left, he projected to me.

She's in the Council Room. She'll pay for anything you'd like, and I'll settle the tab with her when I get home. Have fun.

So here I was. I wore a floor-length, long-sleeved olive dress that would be thick against the winter chill, and polished black boots that laced up to my knees in case I had to trudge through any snow.

I straightened my shoulders and pushed into the room.

Fallon was inside, alone at the table. She hopped up immediately as I stepped across the threshold.

"There you are!" she chirped. "Are you ready to go?"

"Yes," I said, smiling hesitantly at her.

She smoothed her hands down a navy dress that was quite similar to my own. "I hope you haven't eaten," she said as she ushered me out of the room and shut the door behind us.

"Not yet," I said, falling into step beside her.

"Good. There is a little café that Haiz and I always go to. You're going to love it."

"Is she coming?"

"No," she said with a frown. "Everyone is working today. Ciro is in Ekin overseeing the small group we sent out there for your family."

I cringed at the lengths the Council was going to for me, but Fallon didn't sound upset in the slightest.

"He'll be home soon, as he's just getting them settled. And then Maddie and Crow are out with the Weatherman, and Haiz is in Halls-only-know-where."

"What is she doing?" I asked as we clipped across the grand entry hall of Castle Habrem. It was dead, of course, other than a few passing servants scuttling about.

"Looking for Silas. She's been voidstepping all over Alynthia, going to past Burning Arrow locations. No luck so far," she lamented, tossing me a frown. "He's disappeared."

"Should we help her?" I asked.

Fallon pushed open the grand doors, and bits of snow flitted inside, swirling around us. "No, we don't need to," she said. "She likes the space, honestly. And she makes the most meticulous notes you'll ever see. She'll be at it all day." She nudged me in the shoulder, grinning. "We'd get bored."

I liked Fallon. I liked her very much.

I let her lead me through the brisk morning air and down into the heart of the valley. Everyone looked on her with warmth, and I caught no glares despite being who I was. They were just as kind to me as they'd been when I had Hrokr at my side.

I wondered if any of the Valencians I'd killed walked this path.

Fallon pulled me into a tiny café with tables and chairs made of log barrels. It was very clean and kept inside, but decorated like a true tavern. She ordered for me, promising me it was the best they had.

With a mug of hot coffee and a slice of pumpkin bread, I followed her to a table beneath the front window. It was frosted over from the condensation of the heat inside, but I could still see the shopfronts outside and the groups of well-dressed Gentry Fae strolling down the streets.

Fallon was silent as she ate, and I used the moment to absorb the people here. Everyone seemed happy, laid back. These were not the vicious and blood-thirsty monsters I had first known them to be.

That piece of ruthlessness still lived in them, I knew. I remembered Hrokr hanging that man on the terrace of the castle, and the way his people treated the corpse like a centerpiece at a party.

I supposed that bits of both light and darkness swirled inside us all.

"How are you?" Fallon asked gently after a few minutes.

"I'm alright," I answered—an off-hand, automatic response.

"No. I'm really asking."

She brushed a lock of silver-blonde hair behind one ear, as if to more fully bare her golden eyes to me in earnest. Her lips were tilted in a slight frown. She looked somber.

"I'm as alright as I can be, I suppose," I admitted.

"Do you want to talk about it?"

I gave her a small smile. "I don't need to bore you with my family drama."

She thawed a little as she chuckled. "When you've lived as long as I have, you learn to enjoy all the stories."

"How old are you?" I asked, avoiding her question. I ate the last bit of my pumpkin bread, finding myself disappointed it was gone. The food here was good. *Really* good.

"It's almost my birthday," she chirped, which reminded me of my own nearing. "It's a big one this year. Twelve hundred."

I nearly choked. "*Twelve hundred?*"

She laughed a rich, earthy sound. "I know, I know. I'm older than dirt. I don't look it, though," she finished with a wink.

No, she really didn't. She was full and voluptuous, a type of beauty far different from my own. She definitely did not look like what I'd imagine someone her age to be. Magic at its finest.

"Is the rest of the Council your age?"

She smiled. "No." She drained the rest of her coffee before leaning back in her seat. "Maddox is the next oldest. He's been in Valencia the longest. He was Lord Cadmus's War Advisor and the only one left after Hrokr picked up the crown."

"What happened to the others?"

She smiled, but it was something wicked. "I should let him tell you. But they are no longer with us."

I shivered, wrapping my fingers tighter around the mug.

"Maddie is nearly nine-fifty. Perhaps it's why we are the funnest ones. Maybe you get so old you revert into something like a child," she chuckled.

I smiled along with her. It was nice to listen to her talk about them as friends. As people instead of titles.

"Ciro and Haiz are both in the early eights. Ciro was a grunt for a long time, but happened across Hrokr in a tavern. He liked Ciro's *tattoos,*" she teased. "They've been inseparable since."

"They're not tattoos?"

"Not at all. They're something like a burn. He channeled too much lightning, but the ice in his body froze it. It was a strange, strange thing, he says. But he's had them ever since."

"And Haizea?"

"A regular farm girl. She lived back west on a farm with her parents for a long time. She's always been ready to take on more, though," she said, smiling fondly. "With her help, her dad produced a bunch of rare crops—things Hrokr liked. They were invited to the castle for one of the balls, and I caught her snooping through the library. I reamed her and the little monster tried to ream me right back."

Fallon laughed to herself, eyes glossed over with memory. "I love her."

I smiled, taking a warm drag from my mug. "And you?"

A little bit of darkness entered her eyes. "Born in the Hall of Flesh and Blood. Momma and Papa got caught up in some bad debts. Gambling is common there." She was silent for a moment, and my gut twisted as I waited for her to continue. "They were killed when I was sixteen, and I was sold to a flesh trader to pay their debts."

Horror filled me, washing away the warmth of the café. "I—"

"Don't," she said, holding up a hand. "Long forgotten, and my captors long dead." The wicked twist of her lips told me she was probably the one to end them. Her next words confirmed it. "After a few years, I snapped. Killed the whole lot of them."

I didn't know how many *the whole lot* was, but I imagined it couldn't have been a small number.

"I was wanted by the Guard. I kept myself away from them for a long time, but I got caught eventually. A rowan wood arrow to the back doesn't do anyone any favors. I couldn't shift and hide."

"Shift?" I interrupted.

"My affinities are poison, healing, and shifting. My secondary form is a dragon," she said, as if it were no big deal. It definitely was a big deal. "But I can use extra magic to become whatever I want. I did whatever I had to to hide, but—none of us can stand against the rowan."

I didn't know what to say, so I waited for her to continue. I wanted to ask about her dragon, about the whole of a life that was over a millennium old, but now wasn't the time.

"I was sold again. It was that or death. They made it a big thing to try and auction me out of the Hall. They wanted to sell me to someone high-profile enough to pay off my 'debts.' Apparently killing a bunch of people is expensive."

I tried to hold back the pity in my eyes at the bitterness in her voice.

But now she was smiling. "I was bought by none other than Lord Cadmus and Lady Consort Araceli, Hrokr's parents."

She laughed at the horrified look on my face. "It was a ruse. They bought me out of kindness and let me free into the Hall. I lived here, actually," she said, waving a loose hand. "In Fairshroud.

"Once all three of my powers manifested, everyone thought I was some sort of *Chosen One*. I enlisted with the Weatherman, but I did all kinds of things over the years." She brushed her hair back behind her shoulder, grinning triumphantly at me now.

I smiled, honestly happy to see the darkness lifted out of her golden eyes. "Hrokr called me to the *Royal Service,*" she said with a smile. "It was only a few years after he got here."

"And you've been with him ever since."

"Ever since," she repeated with a grin. With a content sigh, she braced her elbows on the table. "And then Crow is the baby, of course. He tells everyone he's six hundred, but he hasn't even hit that milestone yet."

I chewed on that for a moment, digesting the centuries that had come before me. "And now you are happy?"

Her face softened. "Very. I loved Lord Cadmus and his wife very much and was so disheartened to see them go. But their son is a good man. They'd be proud of him."

Warmth suddenly filled me, closing my throat. It spurred my next words.

"I am sorry," I said slowly. "For the crimes I committed against your people."

It was the first time I had said it, just flat out like that.

"Don't be," she said, and her voice melted into that motherly croon I'd heard her use with Haizea. "You had no idea."

I shifted uncomfortably in my seat. "I should have thought harder about it instead of throwing myself blindly into the fray."

She shrugged, as if the death of her people were no big thing. Though we both knew it was. "Aren't we all willing to damn ourselves for those we love?"

I supposed we were. "Are any of you wed or mated?"

The shadows in her eyes returned. "That's another long story for another long day," she said with a long-suffering sigh. "But in short, yes. Our Council is three members short."

Maddox had spoken true, then.

"It wasn't me," she said softly. "Though watching that kind of grief shatter a person you love is something devastating on its own. I would gladly step into their shoes."

My heart suddenly felt too heavy for this quaint coffee shop. Too heavy for my tired body.

And though I knew that it was none of my business, I asked in a small voice, "And Hrokr?"

Her grief was a palpable thing. "No, it wasn't Crow either. He has long been a closed, hardened man. It would take a gift from the Elders to lift him out of his self-imposed loneliness." Her tone spoke of the anger she felt. I would wage every coin I owned that his friends had tried. "Hrokr's brand of darkness is something else entirely."

I said the only thing I could think of. "He doesn't seem to mind."

"We all wear masks, Thea."

The words settled between us.

Perhaps it was because I had kept asking, but she let loose a small sigh. "Don't ask them about it. It will only bring up things they still aren't ready to deal with. But Haizea's husband Orion was killed in the War of the Cleaving almost three centuries ago."

As if to paint the picture for me, she projected an image of a man holding Haizea. They were smiling at me, smiling at *Fallon*. His red hair was stark against his pale skin, hanging in long matted locks down his back. Gold piercings adorned his nose and ears.

"He was lovely," she said softly. "Ciro's wife died in the War of the Cleaving, too. The only consolation we all have is that they died together." The image she sent now was a crushingly beautiful woman with long, black hair. Her eyes were brilliant green, bright against her dark brown skin. In this picture, it glowed like bronze against the backdrop of firelight.

I watched in silent, borrowed grief as Ciro walked up behind her, smiling. I'd never seen him smile like that, so open and genuine. He wrapped his arms around her, placing reverent palms on her swollen stomach.

"Oh Halls," I whispered.

"Inina was pregnant," Fallon confirmed. And even though Maddox had already told me, it hurt in a different way to see it. The projection vanished into smoke.

"That's tragic," I whispered. "To lose their mates like that."

"They weren't mated," she said quickly, harshly.

"I'm sorry," I said immediately. "I just assumed—"

"It's alright," she said, though her frown remained. "Just—don't bring any of this up to them. It's still... touchy."

"I can imagine," I murmured. "Is it alright if I ask how? You said they died together."

I knew it was Gar, but the monster in me wanted to know *how*. I wanted to hurt him accordingly.

She frowned, one so deep and full of rage that it marred the beauty of her face. But when her gaze met mine, her eyes were full of guilt and trepidation.

She only nodded, as if she knew what Maddox had told me. She likely did.

"It's alright," she said, though I knew she didn't mean their deaths. That would never be alright. Neither would the death of my mother, the deaths of Hrokr's parents, the deaths that Gar had orchestrated at my hand. "We'll find him. And we will end him."

But guilt was already swirling thick inside of my chest, choking me. "I—"

"Didn't know what he was," she interrupted with a snap. "Don't you dare take one drop of weight off of his shoulders, Thea, you hear me?" she all but growled. But the words smoothed the ragged edge that had come loose inside me. "That monster deserves the weight of all he's done. You are not *allowed* to shoulder it."

I met her brilliant eyes, and she was suddenly blurry through the film of tears pooling in mine. I had held him, kissed him, confessed my love to him. Shared meals and a bed with him. And his evil had reached shores I could have never imagined. "I mean it, Thea. You did nothing wrong."

"I'm so sorry," I still whispered, because I didn't know what else to say.

She huffed a sigh, as if she were irritated with herself. "Enough of this. I shouldn't have dropped all of this on you the first day we had together. Haiz will find his trail, and then you and I can bathe in his blood together, yeah? Let's not give him another moment of our thoughts. Today is a good day."

She stood up, dropping a few coins on the table, and reached out a hand. "Let's have fun today. Crow will kill me if he thinks I made this day bad, especially after I begged him to let me play with you. I'll take you to the best bookstore you'll ever enter, and then we can pick out something cute to wear. You know. Regular things."

Despite the sorrow radiating through every bone in my body, burning my flesh to a crisp, I realized that she was right. Gar had already taken so much from us. I wouldn't allow him to have this day, too.

I took her hand and let her pull me to my feet.

CHAPTER THIRTY-FIVE
WEATHERMEN

"Just one more stop," Fallon promised.

I nodded, even though my legs felt like they were going to give out from beneath me.

I had marched across Halls, sailed to distant shores, fought on assassin's fields, and spent days on horseback.

And somehow shopping with Fallon Blightbringer had thoroughly exhausted me.

I could hardly feel the circulation in my arms beneath the weight of the shopping bags lobbed on them. My feet were even sore, which was honestly saying something.

"Relax," she chuckled, noting the sour expression on my face. "This stop is something you'll enjoy, I'm sure."

That made me wary, but I tried to smile as I followed her through Fairshroud.

Fallon stayed true to her word, and the rest of our day was light and easy. She talked about meaningless things, like her favorite pastries and the best material to make dresses out of. It was completely mindless, but comforting somehow. It also warmed a part of me to know that she could even care about such trivial things after such a long life.

I also decided that I really, *really* liked Fallon Blightbringer.

I wasn't sure that I was going to survive one more stop, though.

"Where are we going?" I asked, breathless.

She laughed again, grinning mischievously. "We are going to crash the boys' party."

"We—what?"

She shimmied her body in something akin to a victory dance. "We are going to the barracks."

"Hrokr said I can't go," I said, though she grinned at my tone of voice. I wasn't saying no.

"Alright? It'll be fun!" she grinned.

It would definitely be fun to give my arms and feet a break, but, "We aren't going to spar, are we?"

"Halls, no. I'm exhausted."

I breathed a sigh of relief and followed her up the path to the castle. She led me through the grand doors, and my shoulders sagged at being back in Castle Habrem. The sun was very near to disappearing behind the horizon, and while this day had been a good one, it had been *long*.

I followed Fallon up the stairs—calves screaming with every step—and down the hall into the Portal Room. She unceremoniously dumped her bags on the floor, and grinned at me to do the same. I followed suit, leaving a giant heap in the center of the floor.

She smiled down at it affectionately before gripping my hand and hauling me through the nearest portal. I hardly had a chance to catch my footing before I was staring straight into the setting sun as it sunk behind the mountains.

It was cold here. Like—*freezing* cold. Like—I'd never in my entire life felt temperatures like this.

Fallon still held onto my arm and began pulling me along an icy, slick pathway. I tried to take in my surroundings in the sudden, frostbitten twilight. We were close to the mountains, but they seemed to be both shorter and on the wrong side.

"Did we just voidstep all the way across the Hall?"

"Sure did. Castle Habrem in the east and the Cliffs of Chilital in the west."

Cliffs?

But as I looked around, I realized that where the mountains had appeared shorter before, we were actually just *in* them. No wonder it was so cold.

"Come on," she said, dragging me toward a large ivory building. It was crafted of the same stones as Castle Habrem, but it was obvious that this was a base of war. There were no pruned flowers or pretty grass. It was all harsh snow and blinding white. "If we don't go now, we are going to freeze our legs off."

I looked down at the legs I very much wanted to keep and let her drag me toward the entrance. No one was standing outside in this weather, but I suspected that we had eyes on us from the large watchtowers interspersed throughout the space. I could hear the clash of steel on steel and many voices coming from within the building.

The front doors were large and made of shining, dark wood. They swung open soundlessly, and I nearly melted from the delicious heat that rolled out of them.

We had to squeeze inside, though, as there was a throng of tightly-packed bodies that seemed to breathe collectively.

"What's going on?" I shouted over the clamor.

She only grinned.

I clung to her as she led me through the space, and even though their attention was obviously diverted, the bodies moved in deference to her. I even heard a few people whisper, "Blightbringer," reverently.

As we moved farther, I realized we were in a descending arena. The lower floor was made of packed dirt, and while the crowd continued to spill onto the space, they were giving a wide berth to—

"Oh Halls," I whispered.

I wasn't sure how Fallon heard me over the madness, but she turned to grin at me. "Fun, isn't it?"

In the center of the pit was Hrokr. Hrokr, face splattered in blood and grinning wickedly from ear to ear. He had a sword in hand, but it was pointed toward the earth as he spoke to Ciro.

"The blood isn't his," Fallon said softly.

I knew it wasn't.

Hrokr laughed at something and cocked his head to the side. A soldier standing before him yipped in glee and sprinted to the side of the room, where he was immediately embraced by other cheering soldiers.

"Domaldeur!" Maddox shouted, clapping his hands together. "You're up."

An olive-skinned man was pushed to the front of the crowd. He was tall and his entire form rippled with braided muscle, their curves illuminated by the blazing fire at the back of the room. He shook his head, sending the long, black braids down his back swinging.

I watched as Maddox's eyes briefly flitted to us, unsurprised of our presence. If Hrokr knew I was here, he made no effort to acknowledge it.

But Fallon was grinning with mischief, and Maddox's lips twitched.

"You're taking this one, too?" Maddox asked Hrokr.

Hrokr nodded sharply, smirking. From the look of it, he liked the fight *a lot*. He handed his sword off to Ciro.

Ciro was frowning, though.

They were all communicating with each other, I realized. About what, I had no clue.

Hrokr began unbuttoning his dark tunic, peeling it from his sweat-slick body. Just as it began to slide down his white undershirt, Fallon ushered me down the steps.

As soon as the crowd began to open for us, Hrokr glanced over his shoulder.

"Uh-oh," Fallon whispered under her breath, but she was smiling.

"Are you ready, my lord?" Maddox asked, grinning something fat and sarcastic. But Hrokr didn't turn. His eyes touched mine for the briefest moment, and I thought I saw something akin to panic inside of their midnight depths.

But before I could even begin to register the look, he turned his gaze on Fallon. And there was no mistaking the look in his eyes then. He was angry and freezing her with a glare that was more icy than the frozen cliffs outside.

She grinned and waved at him.

He huffed something that I couldn't hear from this distance, ripped his tunic the rest of the way off and shoved it at Maddox.

Fallon kept us near the stone wall and sat down on the first of the descending, wooden benches. We were only a few yards from the men now, but she seemed unruffled.

"Do you want to tell me what that was about?" I asked as I sat next to her.

"What was what about?" she asked, turning wide, faux-doe eyes on me.

I narrowed my eyes at her, but she grabbed my face and turned my gaze back to the other half of the Council. "Pay attention, it's about to start again. I don't need Hrokr sneaking out when he thinks you aren't looking."

I cocked a brow. "Sneaking out?"

"Hush," she chided playfully.

But a sour pit was blooming in my gut. "Fallon, if there is something he wishes to keep from me—"

"Hrokr keeps to himself, even from us sometimes. He's had a harder time doing that with you here, though."

That wasn't exactly addressing my concern.

"You know the rules, kid," Maddox said, interrupting my thoughts. He clapped the mammoth soldier on the back and stepped away. "State your chosen affinities."

"Chosen?" I whispered. We couldn't choose our magic.

He means Hrokr's, she projected to me. *In order to make it more of a fair fight, each fighter chooses the affinity he is allowed to use.*

"Light and shadow," the man said.

Hrokr took up stance, angling his blade.

Without any type of signal, the man—Domaldeur—lunged for Hrokr.

But the lord moved like lightning. Like the liquid of night, striking through the space like an asp. The loud clashing of steel rang through the air, sparks glinting from the force at which their blades met. Domaldeur receded a few steps, but was quick to steady himself.

He swung his sword in a high arc over Hrokr's head, and I winced.

As I knew he would, Hrokr took advantage of the opening. He landed a hard elbow to the man's gut, and Domaldeur grunted in pain.

Hrokr danced away before any harm could come to him. They circled around each other for a while, and I found myself wondering why Hrokr was dragging it out.

But suddenly, I realized.

"Hrokr is evaluating him," I whispered.

"Yes," Fallon replied.

A few more mishaps on Domaldeur's part, earning him a kick to the calf and a fist to the stomach, before Hrokr decidedly ended things. Hrokr cut through Domaldeur's guard and brought the blade to his neck.

I cringed as he cut through the skin and blood sprayed them both, but he halted the blade before it could do any real damage. Hrokr lowered his sword blade, and nodded his head to the left.

Domaldeur frowned, but lifted his head and walked past us to exit the pit. There were no cheers.

"He lost," I stated, though it was obvious. I was trying to understand.

"Yes."

"And the other one, the first man, he won?"

She snorted. "No one ever *wins*. Not when Crow is here to play, anyway."

"I'm confused," I admitted.

"They are seeking promotions, advancements to the next level of the guard. If we deem them skilled enough, they progress. Domaldeur did not."

I nodded. "He fights them all?"

A soft smile. "Or me or Haiz or the boys. We have four training camps, each dedicated to different terrain and seasons. I prefer to fight outside where it's warm."

I turned my eyes back to Hrokr, watching him plant his sword tip into the dirt. "That's enough for me," he said to Maddox.

But the crowd groaned in disappointment.

"Come on, Your Highness," Fallon called to him, and he turned a dark glare on her. "You never come to play anymore."

"I don't see you in the ring," he sniped back with more venom than seemed necessary for the situation.

A slow grin spread across her lips. "Are you frightened?"

She was allowed to speak to him this way, but the crowd did not dare laugh. In fact, they shifted nervously on their feet.

When he said nothing, she tilted her head in deference, but I knew it was a lie. "Forgive me, Lord Hrokr. I only tease."

"I tire of your jokes, Blightbringer," he snapped.

But at her answering smirk, he turned a sharp heel toward the next opponent. "My last fight," he hissed at Maddox who tried to swallow his smile. Tried and failed.

Ciro looked uncomfortable.

I spun on Fallon. "What are you all talking about?" I accused. They had to be projecting to one another.

"Hrokr is being a child. Me and Maddie think it's funny." Her words were short, simple.

"Why is he upset?" I asked. But as I asked it, I could feel his anger as if he were projecting it to the room. I wondered if he was.

She worried her lower lip between her teeth as if she weren't sure how to answer. "It's nothing. He just gets in moods sometimes."

She was lying.

But I moved on.

"What's wrong with Ciro, then?"

"Nothing," she answered too-quickly. But both our heads swiveled toward Ciro, who was very angrily not looking in our direction. He was watching Hrokr, concern written openly on his normally stoic features.

"Fallon," I began. "You've not done something bad, have you?"

"Me?" she shrieked. "Absolutely not." At my flat expression, she sighed. "Relax, Thea. I just wanted you to see what life is like here when we aren't out saving the world."

I sighed, settling against the wall. She wasn't going to tell me anything, and I knew better to believe it was as innocent as that.

I looked back at Hrokr just in time to see his next opponent stepping into the ring. He had the same frame and height as Hrokr, but where Hrokr was all tight, lean muscle, this man was corded to the point of bursting.

He was massive across the chest and arms and looked menacing even to me. The warm firelight gave his ebony skin an umber glow.

Hrokr wasn't smiling at the mock fight, but I didn't think that reflected on the man before him. I could feel his anger for Fallon simmering into me.

The man must have announced the magic he wished Hrokr to use while I wasn't watching, because he suddenly swung. Hrokr blocked, but—even from here—I could tell the difference in strength between this man and the first.

The fight was long.

They danced around one another for long minutes, though Hrokr was the only one landing body blows.

Despite that fact, the man was obviously skilled.

I watched as Hrokr's porcelain skin grew slick with sweat. I watched the muscles of his arms hold firm. The muscles of his back bunch and stretch.

And many times, I dropped my eyes to study my hands or the snow boots beneath me.

I'd always thought of his fight as something cold and sharp—cunning more than brutal.

I now saw it could be both.

When they reached something of a stalemate, the man lifted his hand, and water began to coalesce around it. I never got to see what he planned to do, because Hrokr vanished into a rift of smoke and appeared behind him, blade pressing in between his shoulder blades.

"Match," Maddox called, looking bored.

Hrokr dropped his blade to the floor unceremoniously and laid a hand on the man's shoulder.

Hrokr said something to him, so soft I couldn't hear, and the man made a choked noise of relief. The crowd cheered as he tore away from Hrokr and lunged to the victors' side of the room.

And there stood Hrokr.

Flushed and warm and *angry*. He was panting as he brushed his hair back from his forehead and looked up with dark eyes that bore directly into mine.

And then he was striding with purpose straight for us.

Fallon sat up straighter, smirking. "Did you have fun, Crow? We sure did."

"Your antagonizing isn't cute," he said baldly. "Save it for Maddie."

Her grin only widened. She said nothing aloud, but Hrokr's expression grew impossibly harsher.

And then they were talking with only their eyes in some sort of silent stand-off.

At least, it was silent to me.

"It's rude to keep secrets," I stated.

Fallon whirled on me, eyes bright. "Isn't it?" she exclaimed.

"Get out."

His words were flat, cold.

"Sure," Fallon replied breezily. "I have things to do today anyway."

He turned his gaze on me, and something softened in it minutely. "I am sorry you've had to put up with her all day. I'll see you for dinner."

I flinched internally at the dismissal, my back immediately up. "I don't know, Hrokr, her company has been much more pleasant than yours."

Fallon smirked, and—despite my rude words—Hrokr's shoulders sagged in something that looked like relief. "I apologize. Fallon is exceptional at getting under my skin," he said, throwing a quick glare in her direction.

And, suddenly, realization dawned on me.

A scalding flush burned me from head to toe. "Oh—I—" I frowned, sputtering as I tried to articulate my thoughts. "You don't want me here."

Maddie's head whipped in our direction.

Eavesdropping bastard.

Fallon chewed on her lip to hide what I suspected was another grin. But we'd had such a good day together—I couldn't think of a reason she'd want to upset me.

Hrokr let loose a breath, shaking his head. "No, no, Thea, it's alright that you're here. It's not that."

But I could see in his eyes that wasn't the truth. I just didn't know why. It couldn't be the fighting, as he knew I was just as deadly as he was.

"Is it—Is it because of *him*?" I asked in a voice gone weak. I dared not even speak Gar's name.

But I suddenly realized how much of Hrok's life I'd seen, how I had seen the layouts of his most secure locations, his home, his most vulnerable state. "I would never tell anyone what I've seen, Hrokr. You have to know—"

"Thea, no," he exclaimed, taking another step toward me. His hand shot toward me, but he hesitated, dropping it. He glared at Fallon again as if his rage could melt her into nothing. "I trust you, Thea, explicitly. Of course it's not that."

"Then...?" My voice trailed off into a question as my cheeks continued to burn.

"Halls, Fallon, was this really the time and place?" he snapped. He finally closed the distance between us, laying a warm palm on my shoulder. "You have nothing to be embarrassed about," he said. His gentle eyes told me he could feel the mortification leaking through my gown.

Fallon actually did look a little guilty now, her chin dipping in submission. "I didn't think—" she began.

"That's obvious," he interrupted. He squeezed me gently before releasing his grip. "I'm going to finish things up, Thea. I'll take you home in a moment."

"Home?" I squeaked. Did he mean to send me back to—

"Castle Habrem," he corrected stiffly. He leveled a cold glare at Fallon. "Get out."

And without another word, he spun on his heel and marched toward Maddox. Maddox, who was very intently studying the scabbard of his sword.

Eavesdropping bastard.

Fallon began slipping past me, but I dug my nails into her coat. "Where are you going?" I hissed.

"You heard him," she grumbled, pink tinging her cheeks. I wondered how rare it was for Fallon to be reprimanded, especially in such a public setting.

"So?" I snapped. "Don't leave me."

Apology flashed in her eyes, but she shook her head. "Sorry, Thea. I'd better go."

"It's not like he'll actually do anything to you," I pleaded.

"Sure, but I don't feel like dealing with him for the next six months if I don't listen." She hung her head, turning her eyes to the side. "I have to go."

She pulled herself gently from my grip and tore off into the crowd.

I sat in the uncomfortable clamor of the crowd as Hrokr talked to the males of the Council.

He had his tunic in hand now, and even from here I could see that he was gripping it so hard the tendons were popping out of his skin. He appeared to be giving Maddox the same reaming he gave Fallon, while Ciro stood by Hrokr's side. Ciro nodded sagely, agreeing with every word Hrokr said.

Maddox snapped something back so fierce that both of the other men flinched. And then tore into him together.

Maybe I should have snuck out.

But as soon as I twisted to look for an easy path to the exit, Hrokr's hand began swirling with smoke. His tunic caught flame and turned into nothing but ash that shifted through his fingers.

He shook his head angrily and spun on his heel, marching toward me.

I fidgeted beneath his glare, even though I didn't think the rage behind it was directed at me. "Let's go," he barked, not even stopping to see if I followed.

I scrambled to my feet and raced after him.

CHAPTER THIRTY-SIX

ENOUGH

Hrokr said nothing until we made it through the bodies and out into the snow. The cold immediately bit into my flesh, but he didn't seem to mind. In fact, he tilted his head back and basked in the drop in temperature.

No one was outside, and after the heat and shouting of the pit, the silent ice was jarring.

"Are you alright?" I asked softly.

A rough hand pushed through his hair, leaving the sable strands to blow in the frosted wind. "I'm upset."

"I can see that," I commented lightly, coming up to stand beside him. When he said nothing more, I tried for a smile. "It's a shame about the shirt. You didn't have to burn it to a crisp."

He didn't laugh.

"I'm sorry, I—"

"It feels good," he interrupted. "To let out magic in moments of strong emotion. Surely you've found that to be true."

I let his words settle into silence before I spoke. "I am not very connected to my magic."

"We can change that," he said, and some of his irritation ebbed out of the strong lines of his shoulders.

I'm sorry, he projected. *They've been grating on my nerves the past few weeks. I shouldn't have lost myself, especially in front of you.*

"It's alright," I said gently. "You don't ever have to apologize for that—not to me."

Because I understood it, having to put on a face around loved ones. It was tiring.

Something in my words seemed to upset him further, and the lines in his brow deepened as he stared out at the peaks.

Let's go.

He marched off into the snow toward the rune-gate.

I followed him in painful silence as he led us through the open gate, the castle, and up the stairs to his suite.

The walk only took a few minutes, but it felt like eons crawling by at a snail's pace in the thick silence between us.

I could smell him.

His sweat was rich and cold, like the jasmine and thunder I often scented on him.

He threw open the door to his room, and I followed him silently, pulling the door shut behind us. He immediately made for the counter, pouring a shot of amber liquid and downing it. I thought he'd pour another, but instead he took a long swig from the bottle itself.

"Should I go?" I asked quietly.

"No."

The mess of last night's escapade was still strewn across the counter, and we both pointedly ignored it.

I hung my coat slowly, trying to avoid the terse silence between us.

After being bundled all day, it was nice to let the cool air kiss my bare arms, my neck. When I glanced at Hrokr, he was studying me intently, though his eyes were not happy. He did not meet my gaze.

"Hrokr," I said gently. Unwillingly, he glanced up. "Do you want to talk about it?"

"We've not yet had this conversation because it is unnecessary to be had," he replied, tone clipped. He dropped the bottle on the counter, where it clinked loudly. "I apologize on Fallon's behalf. She had no right to drag you into my life, and she will be dealt with accordingly."

I tried not to bristle at the thought that he didn't want me *dragged into his life.* "Leave her alone," I snapped, perhaps a bit more harshly than necessary. "She was kind to me."

He ignored my words about Fallon, and instead heard my words unspoken. "I didn't mean it like that, Thea. I only meant it wasn't her place to burden you with my *shortcomings.*" He said the word with sour venom burning his tongue.

"What kind of shortcomings?" I asked softly, walking to lean on the counter closer to him. He stiffened, but did not move.

"My Council's opinions are forceful and childish. I'm not sure I wish to voice them." He was looking at his hands, studying them as if he'd never seen their scars before. "Maybe you *should* go."

"Tell me," I murmured. "Tell me what's wrong."

Instead, he asked, "Why didn't you give him all of yourself?"

My head whipped toward him so fast my neck twinged. "*What?*"

He picked a cigar up from the counter, lighting it taking a long drag. "You heard me," he murmured, voice thickened by the smoke. And the look in his eyes, the way his tongue shaped the words—I knew he meant my body.

My cheeks reddened—more from anger than shame. "How do you know I didn't?"

"You didn't," he said, so full of confidence that confusion rippled through me. "Tell me why."

"How is that—What does that have to do with you?"

He met my eyes, and the darkness in them was suddenly too vast, as if I could get lost in their space and never find my way back to Alynthia. "So you see."

Confused, my brows drew together. "Hrokr, if this is about last night—"

"It isn't," he snapped, resolve suddenly fractured.

"Then why would you ask me something like that?" I asked, voice breaking. *How could you ask me something like that? How could you ask me about the time I spent loving the man that shattered our families, who killed our friends?*

How could you know?

The gaze he turned on me was cold and distant. "You wish to ask about my life, but I cannot ask about yours?"

I huffed an angry breath, fingers curled into my palms so sharply they began to break the skin. "I didn't want to."

"Liar."

I blushed, slamming one fist down on the counter. He did not flinch, as if he had expected it. "We weren't very close," I lied through gritted teeth.

Another drag. "That's never stopped anyone else."

I blushed again, though whether from shame or anger, I wasn't sure. I didn't like hearing those words cross his lips.

I want this. I want you.

Touch me.

"Is that what you want?" I growled. "For me to be some nameless girl you can add to your long list?"

He titled his head toward me in acquiesce. "I deserved that."

"You sure as hell did," I snapped. My breath was coming faster, my heart pounding harder. "How could you ask me about *him?*" I cried, voice breaking on the name I could not speak.

Hrokr's eyes softened minutely, but he made no move to comfort me or take back his words. "Forgive me. I meant only to show you how unpleasant it is to have your personal matters dug into."

But there was something more, something his eyes were asking even if his lips could not.

I would not allow my own pride to be a shield he could hide behind. "There were pieces of myself I was not ready to give to him."

"And what are those pieces, Thea?" The gentle, dark way he said my name settled low in the pit of my stomach.

My breath and pulse got trapped together in my throat. But I admitted, "I have a secret. I would not know someone so intimately without being able to divulge it to them."

His smirk was more menacing than sultry. "And that secret is?"

"Planning on a repeat of last night, then?" I growled.

I nearly wept in relief when his lips twitched with a faint burst of humor. "I deserved that, too."

I sighed, letting some of the tension leak away. I couldn't tell anyone I was the Heir, but even admitting I was hiding something made the weight of an entire Hall feel not so heavy.

He felt the shift in me and sighed, too. "I apologize. The four of them make me go absolutely feral sometimes."

"Ciro seemed to be on your side."

He frowned. "Just because he wasn't on Maddox's side, doesn't mean he is on mine."

I waited, but was finally forced to admit, "I'm confused."

"I know," he sighed. He turned and reached into the wine rack against the wall, retrieving two glasses and a bottle of deep red. "Drink with me?"

I nodded numbly.

He did not meet my eyes as he let me toward the chairs before the fireplace. He lit it, even as the temperature dropped in the room, making the seat before the fire feel perfect.

He popped the cork on the bottle and poured us both a glass before making himself comfortable.

We settled into the silence, the only sound the crackling of the fire before us.

"I have a secret, too," he murmured. He met my eyes, their depths as alluring as they were haunting. "And it is so heavy."

I knew better than to ask if he wanted to share it; he didn't. "I know the feeling," I whispered instead.

"I pray to the Elders you do not," he replied, turning his gaze back to the open flame. The dancing firelight played across his features, making long shadows of his eyelashes and sharp bone structure. "I am celibate, Thea."

That was probably the last thing I expected him to say. But when he remained still and silent, I whispered, "What?"

"Celibate," he repeated. His lips twisted into a slow smirk. "So much for all your shameless insinuations, yeah?"

He took a long drag on the cigar, chuckling softly as he blew it into a sweet cloud above us.

I flushed. "Why are you telling me this?"

He chuckled at my red cheeks, but as his laughter faded, his smile went with it. His voice had no mirth when he spoke again. "My secret is a dangerous one."

I understood that, too.

"I had no interest in love, not after the heartache I'd seen it bring my mother. Love was a weakness, and my life was not stable enough to sustain it. And eventually my life was stable enough for it..." His voice grew softer with each word. "But then Orion and Inina died," he whispered, and his eyes were glassy with memory. "Orion and Inina were in the Cardinal Council," he croaked. "They—"

"I know who they are," I interrupted softly.

He sighed, closing his eyes. "The Cardinals have no sense of boundary."

"It's alright," I whispered, gently urging him back on track.

He sat his wine glass down, pulling hard on the cigar. I could almost feel it swelling his chest, sinking into his blood. "Losing two people I loved was hard," he said, voice thick with more than the smoke. "But watching Haiz and Ciro lose themselves is a hell I wouldn't wish on anyone."

His eyes were heavy and lined with silver when he glanced at me. The sight made my chest ache.

He cleared his throat. "They have gone through a great deal of healing in the last centuries. But they are not the people they used to be. None of us are."

I wanted to comfort him, to say that time would heal their wounds. But would it? They had already bore this grief for centuries.

"I've not touched a woman," he said finally. "What was once a lack of care has since become declaration."

In the silence that followed, I pulled a thread loose in my pristine dress. "Do you wish to?" I asked openly.

"No." He said firmly, shaking his head. "No, I do not."

He was afraid to love, afraid to put himself on the path of becoming like Haizea and Ciro. I suddenly remembered his old words to me.

You think it is a burden to be loved by them, I'd said.

A great one.

I felt much the same. I'd learned my lesson in love.

"Hrokr," I whispered, tasting his name on my tongue. His eyes shuddered, but he did not move. Still, I admitted, "My secret bars me from love, too."

His fingers dug into the armrest, but remained otherwise still.

I wondered if it was wrong—or if not wrong, at least uncalled for at present time—but I laid my fingers over his, squeezing gently.

He shifted his weight as if he were uncomfortable, but let his eyes fall closed. Suddenly unsure, I began to pull away until he murmured, "You don't have to go. Not unless you want to."

In the heavy silence that followed, he flipped his palm to twine his fingers with my own. After a long moment, I asked, "Why are you angry at Fallon?"

"She thinks you believe me to be a monster."

I waited.

"She thinks that if you saw me with you my people, if you saw me as a leader and not some detached dictator, that you would respect me." His body tightened, but he did not pull his fingers from my own. "She thinks you will love me if I know who I truly am."

I couldn't help it. I froze, my spine snapping to a straight point.

"Fallon is only worried. She's a mother hen, that one. I am happy in my solitude, Thea, but she doesn't understand that." His voice softened. "She never will. She hopes you're something that will lure me out. That's absolutely no excuse at all, of course. I'll be honest and admit I don't wish for you to hate her. Forget about it, she will tire of her games."

I pulled my fingers from his own, trying to fight the strange tightening in the pit of my stomach. "If you are lonely—"

"I am not," he said, shaking his head. But his eyes were dark, his starlight fled inward. His movements were slow and careful as he rose to his feet. I was as still as a feral animal as he studied my face, as he towered above me.

"My Council is enough. Friendship is enough." Silence swelled between us. He nodded once—to assure me or himself, I wasn't sure. "This is enough."

CHAPTER THIRTY-SEVEN

ORBS

I took the time to shower quickly, relishing in the hot water that washed away the emotions of the day.

I wasn't angry with Fallon.

I was hardly more than a stranger to her. It didn't bother me that she would wish for me to help her oldest friend out of his darkness. And—if I was willing to admit it—I was sure there was a part of her that believed she was doing me a favor by forcing me toward him.

I closed my eyes and let the thoughts ebb away.

If only she knew.

I dried my hair as much as I could with a towel and pulled on the black slip I'd decided on for the evening.

As I was combing through my hair, a soft knock preceded Hrokr stepping into my bedroom. He had scrubbed the remaining blood from his skin and was now wearing a golden sweater over black pants. His curls looked fresh.

"Is it bad form to go to dinner barefoot?" I asked. "My feet hurt."

Hrokr laughed, silently agreeing to ignore our prior interaction. "Go ahead. I assure you no one will notice your toes what with the rest of the conversation."

I narrowed my eyes and dropped the comb on the counter. "Why do you say that?"

He leaned against the wall, crossing his arms over his chest. With a smirk, he said, "You'll see."

"I don't like the sound of that," I admitted.

We made our way down to the Council Room in easy silence. Inside, half the Council was missing. Ciro and Haizea sat beside one another at the dining table, looking relaxed and easy. Still, it was hard not to picture their grief. I schooled my features into something blank.

I doubted they wanted a stranger's pitying eye.

"Welcome home," Hrokr said in greeting as he seated himself at the head of the table. I sat at his right, with Haizea and Ciro down on the other side of the table.

I noted, belatedly, the table was already set. The myriad of scents flowed up to me as Hrokr poured us both a glass of wine.

"Is it just us tonight?" Ciro asked archly.

Hrokr pursed his lips. "I do not know where the children are."

Haizea sighed loudly, propping her elbows on the table. "Don't be mean, Crow."

"You," he replied evenly, waving a fork in her direction, "were not present for today's festivities."

Haizea glanced nervously at Ciro. "What'd I miss?"

"Nothing," the men replied in unison.

Sparing them, the door creaked open, and in came Maddox and Fallon.

"So kind of you to join us," Hrokr hummed, leaning back in his seat.

Fallon pursed her lips as she made her way to stand between us. "My dearest apologies, my liege," she said, pulling a tiny box out from behind her back.

His eyes lit up like a child's on Winter Fete as she thrust it at him. "Ahh, Fallon, you didn't have to."

She rolled her eyes and plopped into the seat across from me as Hrokr opened the black velvet box.

Beautiful, glimmering diamond earrings set in gold. "I suppose I'll let you keep your seat on the Council," Hrokr said to her.

Fallon snorted as Hrokr pulled the earrings out of the box and set them in his ears. Thoroughly primped, he drained the rest of the wine from his glass, my glass, and poured us both more.

"You seem better," Maddox commented to Hrokr as he slid into the seat next to me. "Hey kid," he said to me.

"Five Halls, Maddox, you have no tact," Fallon grumbled.

Not deigning to respond, Hrokr filled a plate with rice, rare beef steak, squash, and a piece of bread the size of my fist. And sat it gently in front of me.

"Thank you," I said softly.

Once everyone gathered their meal and began eating, I glanced covertly—or so I thought—around the table, and everyone was stealing glances of us.

Halls.

Hrokr shattered the silence in the room with a flat, easy sentence. "Haiz found the Guild."

"*What?*" I shrieked, whipping my head toward him. Similar exclamations broke out down the table. Haizea sketched a seated bow and grinned triumphantly.

"Where?" Maddox asked.

"In the Hall of Flesh and Blood," Haizea announced proudly. "Camped out in some hovel like they always are."

I wanted to ask if Gar was there, but I couldn't bring myself to. Yes, I wanted vengeance, but I didn't want even his name souring the air.

Besides—if she had found him, she would have said something.

"So we have a little trip to take," Hrokr said, grinning.

"We're going to get them?" Maddox asked, bloodthirst in his eyes.

"Don't think so small, Maddie," Hrokr purred. "We are going to get the Orbs of Dolga."

Silence.

Silence and then a roar of voices, all disagreeing with him.

"Shouldn't we just kill him?" Maddox grunted.

"No. He deserves worse than death," Hrokr replied smoothly. "He wants the Orbs because his wife is dead, and I want her to stay that way. Haizea found their camp near Maedonia, so it's safe to assume Silas is continuing his mission to retrieve them."

"You know we can't take the Orbs, Crow," Ciro cautioned.

"Why not?" he challenged.

The Council shared looks of concern, but Hrokr looked unruffled.

"You know why," Haizea said. "They're split up for a reason. The other Halls will come for us if we take them."

"Let them."

Everyone shifted uncomfortably.

"Thea, love, what do you think?" he asked.

"She doesn't get it, Crow," Fallon began.

He moved only his eyes, but his glare cut through the room like lightning. "Excuse me?" The invisible darkness around him swelled, pressing up against my skin in a dark caress.

She dipped her head, not willing to go toe-to-toe with him for the second time in one day. "I swear it by the Elders, Hrokr, I did not mean that as an insult. I only meant there are domestic affairs she is unaware of."

"Maybe you'd wish to enlighten her then, instead of silencing her."

As he met my eyes, I willed him to hear the thoughts I couldn't project. *Easy.*

Completely out of place, I heard Maddox coughing to hide something that sounded an awful lot like laughter.

Fallon said nothing but again bowed her head in deference.

"We have a slight overpopulation issue," Hrokr said.

"*Slight,*" Haizea scoffed. "There are *birth bans,* Hrokr."

"Relax," he said calmly. "I have a plan for that, too."

She leveled him with a glare. "Do you wish to divulge said plan?"

"Not at the moment, no."

Haizea huffed an irritated breath and crossed her slim arms over her chest.

"It isn't going to go over well," Ciro said with quiet fervor. "The people are stressed out enough as it is. We've already cut them down from two births to one. They aren't going to take kindly to a war brought to their doorsteps."

"Births?" I interrupted.

Hrokr turned his easy eyes on me. "People don't often die here in Valencia. We are bound to run out of room eventually when people live forever. Birth restrictions were put into place under my father's reign, allowing each mated couple to have two children. We recently took it down to one."

"Oh," I whispered.

His eyes shuttered. "It's awful, I know, but we haven't had a choice. But worry not, my dear subjects," he intoned mockingly. "I will fix it."

"You going to pull an island out of thin air or something?" Maddox asked around a mouthful of rice.

Hrokr winked. "Maybe."

"The point is," Ciro continued, "we can't bring a war here."

"Then make sure your wards hold," Hrokr fired back. "They've yet to be breached."

"People still die," Haizea said, voice breaking, "when the wards stand."

At the swollen silence that engulfed the room, I knew she spoke of her late husband. Heartache battered against my ribs.

Ciro laid a gentle hand on Haizea's shoulder. "They weren't home, Haiz," he said softly. *When they died,* went unspoken.

"So it's us, then?" she snapped at the group at large. "We are going to go out into the world and risk our lives for this? I want him to suffer, of course, I do! But I don't wish for his death as much as I wish to keep the rest of you alive. We need to just find him, kill him, and be done with it. Isn't that why I've been searching for him?" she cried, tossing her hands up.

I could feel the love—strained as it may be in this moment—that flowed throughout the members of the Cardinal Council.

"It's not about revenge," Hrokr said gently. "While that is a nice treat, it's not the point. We have to assume Silas has a second. Even if we kill him, someone else is likely to take up the cause if only for their own fame, possibly to bring *him* back.

And while you found the Guild, we do not know where *he* is. So the only thing we can do is to make sure we have the Orbs."

"There's no need," Ciro pointed out. "They don't work unless all five are assembled, and no one knows where Aphaedia's is anyway."

My heart skipped a beat; my palms dampened.

"I do," Hrokr said, smirking. "We can get that one first."

Ice sloshed through my veins.

Hrokr, likely having no idea why he could suddenly scent fear on me, gripped my leg. His fingers gently stroked my bare skin. *It's alright. We'll figure it out.* Despite myself, I did feel my pulse slow.

Wait—was he slowing my pulse?

His lips twitched just a little. *You're welcome.*

"It doesn't matter if we have Aphaedia's," Ciro pushed. "There is no reason to risk ourselves to assemble all five here. If we just keep ours safe, he can't do anything with them."

"No, Crow's right," Fallon said. "Even if Silas gets the other four, he will still want ours, and he has to channel the ley lines to use them. He's coming for us whether we like it or not. We might as well draw him out on our time."

"Which is *why,*" Haizea interrupted sharply, "we should just kill him and be done with it."

"We don't know where he is," Hrokr said, exasperated. "We can't turn a blind eye on him, as he's obviously willing to be patient. He killed my parents six hundred years ago. Orion and Inina three hundred years ago. Thea's mother this year." The words were crass, but no one flinched. It was only the truth. "If we give him time to assemble them all, he could drag it out as long as he wants."

"So we do the grunt work for him?" Haizea growled, tiny hands balled into fists on the table. "We would be assembling them all here for what? He could still wait us out."

"He won't," Hrokr said baldly. "He wants his *wife* back, Haizea." He paused after he said the words, willing them to sink into her. "If we have all five, he knows we can bring back anyone we want. He'll act fast."

Ciro said, "It's unlikely he can get Aphaedia's."

"Unlikely but not impossible," Hrokr replied.

"It's a risk." Maddox, wise for once.

"Hrokr," I said gently, and he turned toward me immediately.

"Yes, love?"

"You said that there is only Orb still living. Why don't we just bring someone back so he can't use it?"

"No," Ciro and Haizea said in angered unison.

Long story, he said. *I'll explain later.*

"Sorry," I mumbled.

"No," Maddie said, bumping his shoulder into mine. "It was a good idea. It just—we can't."

Painful silence filled the room.

Ciro broke it. "You'll be calling down the wrath of all the other Halls."

"I don't care," Hrokr said haughtily. "I am not afraid of them, and you shouldn't be either."

"You'll anger Ivaylo," Fallon grumbled.

Hrokr only shrugged.

Overwhelmed with too many emotions, I reached for the wine. I downed the entire glass.

Hrokr chuckled and refilled it.

"So we agree?" he said.

"You haven't given us much of a choice, Crow," Haizea said.

"The facts haven't given us much of a choice," he countered.

Maddox sighed dramatically. "Fine. I'm in."

Hrokr tipped his head in respect. "Thank you, Maddie. You've always been my favorite."

"I bought you earrings," Fallon hissed.

He winked at her.

I inadvertently bristled at the gesture, and Maddox shook with silent laughter next to me.

"When do we go?" Fallon asked.

"First we need to get through the Annual Halls' meeting. I haven't seen the Orb in Maedonia in years," Hrokr said. "I say we book an official visit, scope it out covertly. And then we can sneak back in and take it once we've officially left."

"Cornelius is going to know it was us," Haiz said flatly.

Hrokr shrugged. "Maybe. But at least hiding it will keep us out of trouble for a while while he thinks it over. If we just take it outright, it will be war right then and there."

"Aphaedia's?" she asked. I willed myself to breathe steadily, not to react in any way.

"I'll get it," Hrokr said.

"Heaven's?"

Another shrug on Hrokr's part. "I could probably just ask Ciri for it."

Haizea snorted. "Yeah, right."

"She's a good woman," he said. "She'll understand."

"And Ivaylo's?" she pushed.

Hrokr shifted his weight, growing agitated. "We'll get them all. I'll reach out to Cornelius in the morning," he said. "With his obsession with his panel, he's bound to be slow in responding. In the meantime—Thea?"

"Hmm?"

"Would you like to train with us? Work on your magic use?"

I hadn't expected that.

"Oh *Halls*, yes," Maddox exclaimed, clapping me on the back. "I've been waiting my turn to spar with you."

"I won our last fight," I said baldly, recalling when I had accidentally stabbed him in the gut.

It was hardly the truth, but—

"And she broke my rib," Hrokr interjected, chuckling. "Don't look so eager."

"The knife fight didn't count," he insisted. "I wasn't allowed to hurt you, then."

"And now you are?" Hrokr asked.

It was such an out-of-place comment, cold and bristled.

But Maddox rolled his eyes. "Sparring isn't sparring if I'm not allowed to inflict damage."

"Her call," Hrokr said, topping off my wine glass.

Maddox grinned at me, begging with his eyes.

"Of course," I grinned, baring my teeth. He returned the gesture, clapping me once more on the back.

I turned back to Hrokr. "And for magic?"

"What about it?"

"What are you wanting to do? I know how to use my healing."

He smirked, drinking directly from the bottle of wine. "I'm going to help you find your second affinity."

All the air was immediately sucked out of the room. Cold blanketed me, and it was all I could do to keep my expression frozen.

"Relax," he chuckled, winking one glittering eye. "It'll be fun."

I nodded numbly, trying to keep my smile frozen in place. "If you say so."

All levity gone, the ink nestled on my hip suddenly felt far too heavy.

CHAPTER THIRTY-EIGHT

MONSTERS AND SWEET DREAMS

I couldn't bring myself to relax for the rest of the dinner.

Thankfully, it didn't last much longer, but every minute felt heavier. The Council chittered and teased one another, and all the day's tension evaporated for them.

I felt like I had spooled it all back up into myself.

Hrokr remained silent with me, even reaching out another hand and slowing my heart. It didn't help.

I kept the secret. It was what I had to do, what I'd always done. I was supposed to be frightened at the possibility of Hrokr finding out what I was.

But what had me sweating, shaking, and absolutely horrified was the relief I felt for a split second.

The relief that someone would finally find me out, and I wouldn't have to hide it anymore. The relief that I could be what I was, out in the open. Valencia had the walls to protect me. Hrokr had the kindness to lend me his aid.

I didn't even have to worry about having a child anytime soon, anymore. I could live forever.

The thought made me queasy, especially when I remembered Gar's vision that I would be here—in Castle Habrem—a century from now. It was selfish, too, to keep myself from having a child. My birth didn't heal the land, and I shouldn't be denying my people their right to return home if my child's could. But—I was nowhere near ready for that.

I had thoroughly worked myself up and was struggling just to breathe when Hrokr finally announced we would be retiring for the night.

The others made no move to go as I rose on shaking legs and followed him to the door. They bid us their goodbyes, and I had only enough mental clarity to smile back at them. If I spoke, my voice would betray me.

Hrokr held the door open for me, and his eyes were dark with worry as he ushered me through. As soon as it snicked shut behind us, he touched the bare skin of my upper back.

I could feel him more strongly out here, as if he were pouring far more magic into me. He murmured my name gently as he turned me to face him, continuing to beat my heart for me.

"Do you want to talk about it?" he murmured. "You've been a mess the last half of the night."

"I'm afraid," I whispered before I thought better of it. There was something about those dark eyes that pulled me in. I wanted to tell him everything, just so that I wouldn't have to carry it on my own anymore.

But I couldn't. I knew I couldn't.

"Why?" he whispered, stroking my skin carefully. Hrokr being in charge of my pulse was keeping it slow enough that I wasn't entering a full panic attack, but the fear was still present.

"I—" I shook my head, breaking off my words. "I just—I'm ready for bed, Hrokr."

He frowned, disappointed. His hand came up to cradle my face, and his thumb wiped away a tear I hadn't realized had fallen. My skin was cool as he spread the tear across my cheek. "You can tell me anything, Thea," he said softly, coaxingly. His voice was a lull, a tide I found myself desperate to be swept out into.

"I have not felt that kind of fear from you in a long time."

It made something ache desperately in my chest, but I lied. "There is too much happening at one time. I can barely keep up with Sage, Dorin and my siblings. Now Gar is missing, and I've not done *anything* to help. I feel sick to my stomach knowing he's the one who hurt Orion and Inina."

Maybe it wasn't much of a lie at all. I shuddered as I stepped out of his touch.

"I am a monster, Crow."

A monster for ever loving Gar. A monster for bringing Sage into this world. A monster for all of the things I'd done since then. A monster for abandoning the people of Aphaedia.

He moved immediately, bending down so that he was eye-level with me. He shook his head adamantly. "Don't you ever say that, Thea. You didn't know what he was."

"But I should have known something was *wrong,*" I cried, voice breaking. "I knew going into my work with the Guild that anything could happen. Yes, they turned out to be far worse than I could have ever imagined, but I would have done anything to get my family back.

"I killed innocents. And those innocents turned out to be your people, and it feels so much more real now. That makes me a monster, Hrokr."

"No," he whispered fervently. "It makes you someone who is willing to do anything to save the people you love."

"Is there a difference?" I croaked.

Not to mention the terrors I couldn't voice. That I risked the entire Starsea bloodline to save three people. They were my family, yes, but—

No wonder my birth had failed to revive Aphaedia.

I wasn't fit to be Lady of the Hall.

Hrokr pulled away, looking down into my eyes. "I'd like to think there is," he said, offering a pained smile. "I'm afraid to even confess the sins I have committed in the name of my loved ones. I can assure you, Thea, I am a far greater monster than you."

I only shook my head, beyond words.

He took my hand and pressed a soft kiss to the back of my knuckles.

The flesh down my spine prickled, a swift surge of something that felt like guilt sweeping through me. I pulled my shaking fingers away, fighting the warm tears brewing on my lashes. "I should go," I whispered.

He hesitated, his hand suspended as he studied me. He nodded slowly as he lowered his hand. "Alright. Goodnight, Thea."

I didn't get to rest.

Only an hour after dinner, Gyda summoned me to the bathing chamber, even though I had my own in my quarters now.

It was Fallon's request.

The water was hot as it soaked into my skin, and Gyda's fingers were firm as she scrubbed my scalp and rubbed my shoulders.

"You know you don't have to do this, Gyda," I said anyway.

But she hushed me just like she had the last three times. "Don't be absurd, lady Thea."

"I'm not being absurd. But you're very kind."

I let her work the knots out of my shoulders for a few more minutes before she stepped back and rinsed the soap from my hair. I was thankful Fallon had asked her to come find me.

In the same manner we'd used before, she turned her back as I slid into a robe and followed her into the dressing room.

"You can put me in anything," I told her as we walked across the stony floor. "I'm just going back to my room."

She sighed—everyone in this Hall always wanted to be thoroughly primped—but released me in nothing more than soft sleeping clothes.

When I made my way back to my room, I pushed the door open softly, and was met with a silent and dark room. I tiptoed through the space, creeping toward the bedroom door, which was slightly ajar.

I poked my head inside to find Hrokr fast asleep on his back. In my bed.

He looked so vulnerable in his sleep. Nothing at all like the destroyer of worlds I'd encountered in Ekin or the harsh politician I'd seen over dinner. His lips were parted gently, and his hair was already mussed with tossing and turning.

He slept peacefully through the storm that raged beyond the balcony. Rain fell in heavy sheets, but did not hit the floor of the balcony or splash into the room. Still, a cool wind whipped through the space.

Unsure if I should, I took a gentle step into the bedroom.

But as soon as I did, he mumbled my name.

I froze at the foot of the bed.

"You came," he mumbled, sounding not fully awake.

"I'm sorry I woke you."

"Don't be," he whispered, his eyes fluttering open. "Come here."

Warily, I sat beside him, careful to keep a healthy distance between us.

Healthy distance that he quickly closed. With languid fingers, he pulled me down beside him, caressing the side of my face. "Today was long."

I should have pushed him away. I should have sprinted from the room and found Gyda or one of the Cardinals to retrieve their wayward King. But I cracked a small, genuine smile. "I'm inclined to agree."

He smiled something faint, but it was gone almost as quickly as it had come. "Are you angry with me?"

"Why would I be?"

He just shook his head. He didn't answer the question, only let the sound of the rain bloom between us.

"I'm falling apart, Thea," he whispered on a wind, so soft the rain and thunder threatened to swallow the words whole.

"What happened, Hrokr?" I whispered.

He shuddered as his name crossed my lips, his throat working through a thick swallow. His voice was silk and water and thunder and something older than the world. "Do you know how crazy you make me?"

Ah.

Intoxicated by more than just sleep.

"Hrokr—"

"You're tearing me apart," he murmured, leaning down to skim his nose against my throat. He pressed his lips to its hollow, and I immediately leaned just far enough away that he was not touching me. "I need you."

"I can't let you," I croaked.

He was silent for a long moment. "I can't think straight when you're here, Thea. You've made a mess of me."

He lifted himself just enough to meet my eyes, and the wealth of adoration in them threatened to disarm me.

He was so different this way.

"I'm cracking, Thea," he confessed. "I'm making mistakes. I'm falling apart."

I held myself perfectly still as he brushed his eyes in phantom kisses across my skin. "What are you doing wrong, Crow?"

"Everything."

I thought if I asked, he'd probably tell me what *everything* was. But I couldn't stay here, not when any words that passed his lips were stained by amber liquor.

"I should go—"

"Don't," he rasped, tangling his fingers with my own.

"You're not sober."

"Why do you think that is?" he asked softly.

My voice was as silent as the ice hidden outside of Fairshroud. "I don't know."

He sighed, his breath washing over my parted lips so heavily that I could taste him on my tongue.

"I can't stand it," he lamented, eyes on my mouth. "I'm forgetting everything I've ever sworn to myself. That's not good, Thea, I can't. I *can't.*"

Daunting silence followed, filled only with nervous breath and pouring rain. "Why aren't you sober, Crow?"

"This darkness is suffocating. Sometimes I can't bear to be around you, but it doesn't hurt as much this way."

His words were something sharp and sour between us.

"What hurts?"

"Everything."

As the words settled, I hesitantly squeezed his fingers. "Your darkness does not frighten me, Hrokr."

Though his eyes remained glassy, his voice was deathly clear when he said, "It should."

I watched him for a long time, and he was content to let me.

These moments felt stolen, plucked out of time only for me to hold. He would not remember, at least not in the way that I would. Perhaps it was wrong of me to hold them, as stolen as they were. The thought pushed me to whisper, "I should go."

He was so gentle—so hesitant—as he nestled his head against my arm and curled around me. "Do not leave me alone," he whispered, pleading with lovelorn eyes. "Not yet."

Tears collected on my lashes as I beheld his naked vulnerability. I nodded, letting him lie against me with only the sounds of the storm and our soft breathing to fill the moments of the night.

When I woke, he was gone.

I wasn't surprised, not really.

I lay there as grey, cloud-blanketed light permeated the room, and tried to orient myself for the day to come. When I finally found the strength to crawl out of bed, I shuffled to the bathing room.

Inside, I saw something that cracked my remaining resolve.

A bleached wicker basket was filled with fresh-cut flowers and tiny chocolate treats. There was a book inside, bound in rich leather and golden seam. And a note penned in a perfect, elegant hand.

I'm sorry.

I dropped the note back into the basket and sat on the floor in a daze.

And cried.

And cried.

I wasn't sure why.

CHAPTER THIRTY-NINE

DARE

I felt better after a bath.

I was here for a job. I only needed to find Gar, kill him, and go home. I was not meant for anything more than a soft, human life, and that was enough for me. I didn't need friends or stolen moments in the dark.

It was with my head held high that I strode downstairs to the Council Room for breakfast. I didn't knock before pushing the door open, finding a room that was peacefully bathed in silver, cloud-choked sun.

As expected, every set of eyes flashed to mine.

All but one. Hrokr—who studied only the mug before him.

And from the stilted, concerned faces of the rest of the Council, his mood was not hidden. At least Maddox attempted warmth, booming, "Thea!" with a little too much excitement.

But I was thankful for the rope thrown and made my way across the room to sit at the table between him and Hrokr. "I'm sorry for running late," I said.

Fallon waved me off, taking a deep drag from a glass of champagne before her. She looked like she'd just rolled out of bed herself. "Breakfast?" she chirped.

As she began pushing a gold plate toward me, Hrokr projected, *Thea, we should talk before—*

"No," I said sharply. Fallon's eyes snapped to mine, her fingers stilling against the plate she offered. "Um, no, no thank you," I tried.

She was unfooled, her cool golden eyes touching on Hrokr for the briefest moment. The silence was deafening and uncomfortable, prodding at every inch of my skin. I could practically feel the darkness roiling off the lord beside me.

Ciro sighed loudly, leaning back in his seat. "Out with it, Crow."

Hrokr shifted in his seat, the rustle of his clothes the only sound in the room. "Thea."

I forced myself to look at him, but the second I met his colorful, black gaze, I regretted it.

I saw his night-drunk eyes as he'd held me, saw the broken gaze of a man devoured who'd crawled into my bed instead of his own. I felt his breath across my lips, his body nestled against my own.

He paused for just a moment, a catch in the mask. Guilt, regret, or simply shame, I wasn't sure. But something cold hardened the skies in his eyes. "If you're up for it today, I hoped we could go over what traveling will entail for you."

"Of course," I said instantly, relief flooding me.

He broke eye contact, instead choosing to study his untouched meal. "Good. I hope to organize things before we leave for the Annual Halls' meeting."

"When do we leave?" I asked.

The silence was like a blanket—suffocating and tight around the throat. "You're not going," he said. His hands were braced together, and I swore I saw his tendons jump as they strained against his skin.

"I'd assumed I would."

"You assumed wrong."

A slap, those words. One public and right across my cheek, leaving my skin pinked with embarrassment.

I grit my teeth, fighting to keep my words civil. "I'd like to go."

His eyes slid to mine, and there was nothing of the man of yesterday within them. "No."

My hand dropped to the table in a thick thud. "Why?"

"It's unnecessary. You'll stay back here with Maddox and Fallon. You—"

"I do not need a keeper," I hissed. "Tell me why you're not taking me, Hrokr."

"No."

My spine snapped straight. My lips curled back from my teeth as a helplessness settled alongside my bones. "Is this about—"

"*No,*" he growled.

From the harsh look in his eyes, he knew I referenced last night.

It was uncomfortable, the amount of silent gazes upon us. But still I whispered, deathly cold, "Liar."

I shoved against the table, leaping to my feet. Quick as an asp, his fingers reached out to trap my wrist.

I ripped free, glaring down at him. "Do *not* touch me."

His fingers fled me, but not before I saw the flash of hurt within his eyes.

Fallon pitched forward. "Thea—"

"Don't," I interrupted.

A room of the most powerful Gentry Fae in Alynthia, and they all dropped their eyes.

My cheeks burned and my spine ached from its rigid line.

"Do you—" My voice broke, emotion choking me. "Do any of you care at all what it has cost me to get here?"

Hrokr frowned. "I—"

"Do *not* speak to me," I growled. "Not you."

The room was silent as I mastered myself, as I tried to remember I was angry for reasons that had *nothing* to do with stolen moments in a night-dark room. "This is my fight," I finally said. "And maybe it is yours too, but it is *mine.* I will not be locked away or wait for someone else to do this for me."

My fingers shook as I marched toward the door. "You can take me and treat me as your equal," I said, eyes boring into Hrokr's. "Or I will give you nothing at all."

It took hours for anything to change. No one dared speak to me, even from their minds. I wondered if they truly had nothing to say, or if Hrokr had commanded them not to.

I knew I was being selfish—but so was he. He could not be so afraid of his emotions as to cut me out or force me to sit aside.

I deserved to be a part of bringing Gar down.

Finally, after long moments sat curled in the chair beside the fire, a soft knock came at the door. My eyes fluttered shut before I took a steadying breath and forced myself to answer it.

Hrokr stood outside, a covered dish in his hands. "You haven't eaten," he said by way of greeting.

I studied him for a long moment—the navy sweater pushed up his forearms, the loose brushing of his curls—before I finally stepped aside and let him pass. We were silent as he set the dish down on the small wooden table.

His fingers toyed with the handle of the dish cover, his eyes trained on the shimmering silver instead of my face. "You have every right to be angry with me."

I met him with silence.

"I only think that perhaps we could use some distance. I wouldn't want you to have the wrong idea, and—"

I laughed. In a garish disbelief that made my chest feel like it was splitting open down the sternum, *I laughed.*

"The wrong idea?"

He turned to me, his back braced against the table's edge. "I fear my words are not coming out the way I intend."

"You fear correctly."

He sighed sharply. "You can't go, Thea. It isn't some picnic, it's the Annual Halls' meeting."

I wanted to tell him who I was and just how much I deserved a seat at that table—if only to spite him. But instead I buried what little pride I had left, and said, "I deserve to be there. It is *my* information that will help you find them. You could get me in, and you know it."

His fingers worried his jaw. "It's more than that, Thea."

"Then explain it to me," I cried, throwing my hands up.

He shoved off of the table with something dark in his eyes. I refused to cower even as his six-foot-something body crowded me. "People *will* have an opinion about you and I, Thea, and it will not be a friendly one. I do not open my borders, nor do I invite people into my life. My Council has not added a member in *centuries.*"

He leaned with his words, eye-level and nearly nose to nose with me. "They will assume you are my lover, especially with how closely I will command my Council to hover. They'll need to make sure you don't run off or get swiped up and carted to another island—" His words faded away as he registered the look on my face.

Cheeks red and spine tingling, I stepped into him.

He stumbled back a step.

"You won't let me go because you're afraid someone will think I'm your lover?" I scoffed, choking on a snort stuck in my throat. "You are *ridiculous,* you—"

He recovered, swiping up my wrist between his fingers and squeezing gently. "*Listen to me.*"

I paused, chest flushed and fluttering in rapid pants.

"You have no idea what they will do to you if they think it will hurt me," he said, voice deathly cold. "And if I claim you're not? If I claim you are only an informant? They will not believe me."

His eyes grew wilder. "If they think you are my secret, they will do anything to uncover you. They will shred you apart." His eyes shuddered as he took a step back, as he took a full breath.

Stilled, I whispered, "Do you not think me capable of handling myself?"

"I think I have seen people hunted across the Halls for the sole purpose of hurting their mate. I think I have seen kings and lords bury their wives because someone disagreed with their policies, Thea. The only thing I can do to keep you properly hidden is keep you *here.*"

I searched his eyes.

"I know you think me wretched. Continue to believe it if you choose," he said, waiving a loose hand. "But I will not have your blood on my hands. Not yours."

His pulse hammered away in the hollow of his throat.

"It is one meeting, Thea. Let it go."

"It's not just one," I whispered. "You'll have to travel to every Hall to secure the Orbs. Will I be locked here during that, too?"

Silent, his eyes pleaded with me to understand.

I said nothing.

"I care for you," he said baldly, his throat working as he swallowed. "It has been a very long time since I have had a new friend. They will smell it, Thea, they will know. They will assume, they—" He broke off, closing his eyes as he ran his fingers through his hair.

"Would they really cross you?" I whispered.

His starry eyes bored into mine. "If they thought me weak enough to hide you."

I swallowed the thought, drinking in a deep breath. I refused to stay here while they hunted him. I refused to sit pampered while Gar terrorized the world beyond.

"Then hide me in plain sight, Hrokr. Claim me, if you'd be willing to do so. Let them believe what they want." I lifted my head to meet his eyes more fully. "Dare them to hurt your mate, if you must."

All the colors of starlight ruptured in his eyes as he processed my offer. It was just like him, really. I could not imagine him not showing off his new mate, brandishing her as the newest medallion pinned to his cloak.

He was not wrong to think the other leaders would believe him losing an edge to hide her away in an ivory castle.

"So you would accompany me," he said carefully, "Not as my informant, but as my mate."

I shrugged gently. "If they are to assume anyway, I suppose I could enjoy the perks of a royal title."

He laughed, and I could have wept at the sound of such a glass moment shattering. I smiled, letting loose a heavy breath. But his voice was sober as he said, "It is still a risk, Thea."

I knew that. But he didn't know I'd already spent the entirety of my life knowing the others wanted me dead. For whatever the true reason was, Aphaedians had long been hunted—and I was not an exception.

Now it would be not only my name they hunted, but my face.

It was a risk I was willing to take. I could not be sidelined in this.

"I'll be alright."

Hrokr studied me for a long moment, a strange glint in his eyes. Finally, he said. "Very well."

Tacked on as an afterthought, he murmured, "*Mate.*"

CHAPTER FORTY

OLD FRIEND

I stood in the center of the Portal Room, outfitted in Valencia's highest glory. It was a little much, but I supposed such affairs were in order.

The dress was cleanest silk—black that clung to my waist and poured down my legs like water. My hair was straight and down my back, unadorned. Thin straps with no jewelry, not even shoes.

You are wild in the most glorious way, Gyda had said. *Embrace it.*

Still, my nails were black, and my eyes lined just as dark.

Hrokr was resplendent beside me, sparing no extravagance. Rings and jewelry decorate his skin, and he would not truly be dressed without the spiked, polished boots I was sure could smash a grown man's skull. Everything was black and form-fitting, showing off the true flaunt that was his physique.

He'd filled in the rest of the Council after our agreement, and the morning had come more quickly than I anticipated.

Fallon was in a waterfall dress of purest gold, thoroughly primped back into the terrifying, ageless woman I'd first met. Maddox, dressed similarly to Hrokr, looked infinitely more raw and barbaric.

Haizea and Ciro would stay behind to oversee Castle Habrem, including my siblings and the efforts in Ekin.

Hrokr's fingers gently brushed my arm. "Are you ready?" he murmured.

I nodded. Today would be better when we could expose Gar to the other royals. He deserved to be hunted by every Hall.

"Fallon, would you do the honors?" he asked.

"Of course."

There was no portal to the Annual Hall's Meeting, as it changed locations every year. This year it was being hosted in the Hall of the Elements on the coast of Jenmora. While there were only four—five, if I could count myself—greater lords and ladies, they each had many political leaders eager to show off their own work and lordships.

We would be traveling to Jenmora's capital, Asena.

With nothing more than those parting words, Maddox and Hrokr both void-stepped away. Fallon grinned at me. "Are you sure about this?"

"Yes," I said, offering my palm. She nicked me carefully, pressed her own bloody palm against mine, and sent us sailing through the world.

We were deposited on a stone terrace looking out across the water.

The scent of cold sea spray tickled my nose as I righted myself.

Winter was in full swing, and heavy snow drifts could be seen to the west where the gentle hills rolled into the heart of the country.

But to the east, the sea went on forever, the cold water lapping against stone and cliff. The water was a burning gold beneath the red, setting sun. Lamps and bonfires—and likely magic—kept the space warm enough, even with the wind from both the snowscape and the ocean.

Hrokr stepped before me, gilded by the backdrop of the burning sea. He licked his thumb and gently wiped the pinprick of blood from my palm. I stiffened only a little as his arm slid around my back, his hand gentle and warm at my waist.

He leaned down to whisper, his breath warm against my ear. "Cold feet?"

"Quite warm," I whispered back.

He chuckled, squeezing me gently. I turned my face up to his, finding him smiling softly down at me. He'd slipped into his role easily.

Eyes—both curious and cautious—found us immediately. In my quick perusal of the grounds, the most common reaction I found was shock.

Hrokr was quick to meet it.

"There'll be dancing and all kinds of catching up for a while," he said. "Would you like something to drink?"

He wanted to step away from me already, to dangle me before the others. He must have taken my words to heart.

Dare them to hurt your mate.

I offered my warmest smile, and something shifted in his eyes at it. His hand skimmed across my back as he pulled away, and I fought the gooseflesh that chased his fingers.

With one final, lingering look, he strolled away toward the tawny stone veranda. I turned to Fallon and Maddox who had embraced wholly their grinning, irreverent personas.

I supposed for them it wasn't really much of a persona.

Fallon wagged her dark brows at me. "Excited to be Lady Consort?"

Maddox rolled his eyes, elbowing her.

"I suppose," I said, just to say something. But my thoughts were far from the two of them.

I couldn't help my eyes tracking Hrokr across the stone expanse, Gentry Fae, Folk, and curious glances filling the space between us. The capital castle of the city of Asena featured a different kind of opulence than I'd grown used to in Valencia.

The stones were tan and crumbling, filled in by twirling vines and overgrown wisteria. They were a vibrant green despite the silent winter around us.

The sounds of glasses clinking and the roar of idle chatter floated around me as I took a few, hesitant steps away from my guardians. I walked to the edge of the terrace, bracing my arms on the rough, crumbling stone railing. Sea-brined wind flowed through its pillars, rustling the silk about my legs.

I'll be just a moment, love, he projected to me, warmth and mirth in his voice, two things I was quite unused to hearing. *I ran into old company. I'll introduce you, if you'd like.*

I smiled, turning to brace my back against the railing.

Across a sea of people, Hrokr stood with the rim of a whiskey glass held loosely between long fingers. He was smiling—something I'd dare call genuine. A man stood beside him in equally lazy finery. This entire party was the kind that viewed the laziest shows of wealth as the most scintillating.

A small crowd had amassed themselves around the dark-clad duo, eager to listen but not forward enough to intrude. They stood beneath a ceiling of stone, vines and fragile leaves creating something of a curtain.

It was beautiful, something as equally refined as it was wild.

Perfect for the lord standing beneath it.

The dark-haired man squeezed Hrokr affectionately on the shoulder, leaning in to say something that set them both laughing. And during that laughter, I caught the man's side profile.

Everything inside of me turned to glass, turned to *ice,* and shattered with the choked sound that came out of me.

Gar.

I knew that face. And maybe it was set beneath darker hair and adorned with brighter eyes, but—

That was Gar.

Gar in indolent elegance, hand on Hrokr's shoulder as if they were the closest friends in the world. In a—likely failed—attempt to school my features, I spun toward the sea, clutching the balcony as if it were the only thing that kept me on my feet.

He *did* look different. Darker hair, clean-shaven face. But I'd know him anywhere. I would not be fooled by hair dye and a shave.

A cool set of fingers were instantly at my back, blonde hair sweeping into my vision. "Thea, what's wrong?" Fallon asked, her pale face ashen. "Hrokr said you were worried, that—"

I raised panicked eyes to hers. "The man he's with, he—"

"Garbhan?" she asked, looking back over her shoulder toward them. Hrokr was trying to keep easy conversation, but his eyes kept flicking toward us, concern written openly in them. "Thea, look at me."

Dazed, I complied.

"Garbhan Silsto?" she clarified. "What's wrong? Do you know him?"

"Silas," I whispered.

Hrokr's head snapped up, and Gar began to turn.

Quick as lightning, a slash was cut in my arm, and Fallon was ripping me through the fabric of the world.

We landed in an opulent suite, one that looked out across the open expanse of the ocean. Maddox appeared a moment later.

"Thea, are you *sure?* Are you—"

"Yes, I'm sure!" I cried. "He—"

"Is anyone going to tell me what just happened?" Maddox interrupted.

Fallon glared up at him. "Get back out there. Now."

He looked appalled, confused, and quickly barreling toward angry. "Um, may I know what happened first?"

"Thea says Garbhan Silsto is Silas," she said baldly. "Do *not* leave Hrokr alone with him."

She'd hardly finished the words before Maddox was gone, a curl of smoke the only thing left behind. Fallon turned her golden eyes on me, eyes that were equal parts fury and fear. She shook her head gently. "You were far away from them, Thea, you—"

"It's him," I hissed. "He told me his name was Gar."

If it were only the looks, I could believe other options. Maybe they were only family to one another. But knowing his name was *Garbhan.*

It was him. It had to be.

The name was too close, the looks too similar.

Fallon took a few steps away, running a hand through her hair. "This is bad, Thea."

"Take me back," I said, thrusting my hand at her. "Hrokr is up there."

"Absolutely not. He can take care of himself."

I flinched. "Are you *out of your mind?*"

"Maddox is with him, Thea, relax. And there's a possibility that Garbhan didn't see you. It's safer if he doesn't."

"So we just *leave him?*" I cried. "No." I made for the door to the left, but Fallon voidstepped to block my path.

"Sit down."

"Get out of my way," I snarled.

Her arms shot out in a pleading gesture. "Please. I understand, alright? I don't want them anywhere near Silas either, but if you make a scene, it could get bloody *now.*"

"Perhaps it should."

She placed her hands on my shoulders and took a deep breath as if to guide me into my own. "He is a powerful man, Thea. *He will be alright.*"

As if on cue, the ivory door to the suite burst open. I yelped, but it was only Hrokr, striding with dark shadows leaking off of his skin, which were left in quickly evaporating puddles about his boots. The green carpet underfoot swallowed the magic.

He came to me instantly, fingers plunging into my hair and holding me tight against his chest. "Halls, Thea, you scared the hell out of me."

"Silas—"

"I know," he murmured, laying his cheek atop my head.

I could smell the rage—and perhaps fear—coming off his skin, mixed with the sweet perfume of night-flowers and cool lilac.

"I came as soon as I could," he continued, releasing me. His eyes were bright again, as if the dark magic that leaked off him was drained right from his eyes. "I can't stay long."

I nodded. "We can go, I just—"

"No," he interrupted. "You need to stay here."

My heart leapt into my throat. "But you said—"

He leaned in. "I know what I said," he murmured gently. "I will take you to the Hall of the Heavens, I will take you to Flesh and Blood. Halls, Thea, I will take you to the Aphaedian Orb. But I *refuse* to sit you beside Garbhan."

I studied his eyes.

He will not take you away from me, too, he whispered for only me.

My lips parted with the ghosts of words I could not catch.

"Just let me get through this with as little fanfare as possible, alright?" he whispered, brushing a stray lock of hair behind my hair. "Please, Thea. Let me hide you, just this once."

A moment of silence bloomed between us.

"I'm afraid," I whispered.

He gathered me into his arms, my ear pressed against his rapidly beating heart. "You don't need to be scared."

I tentatively pressed my shaking fists against his chest. I wished this weren't happening. I wished Gar wasn't here. I wished I didn't have an audience. But I whispered, "I'm afraid he will hurt you, and I will be too far away if I stay here."

He stiffened against me before pulling away, his eyes full of centuries of troubles. He cupped my chin with gentle fingers. "Silas has tried to kill me for a *very* long time, Thea. But Garbhan has some kind of plan, and being hostile while under this name has never been in it." His fingers slipped away only to brush a tear I hadn't realized had spilled over. "I will be alright," he said, voice thick.

He seemed to suddenly remember Fallon and Maddox in the room and straightened his posture. "Fallon will be here with you." At my open mouth, he added, "You do *not* need a keeper, but he is no fool. If he has seen you and plans to do something about it, you would do better with a teammate, yeah?"

"Yes," I whispered.

"Good," he said softly. "Maddox, we'd better go."

"How will I know if something is wrong?" I blurted.

Fallon waved from behind Hrokr, concern written across her elegant features. "I will tell you, Thea. I swear."

But that wasn't enough. How was I supposed to know if things were turning south? I wanted to see for myself, watch it unfold with my own eyes. "I want to see, Hrokr," I whispered. "Please."

He took a deep breath that expanded his flushed chest. He worried his lower lip between his teeth, casting heavy glances at Maddox and Fallon. I wondered if I imagined it, but I thought Fallon nodded softly.

"Alright," Hrokr said. "Come here."

He led me to the silver and forest bed and gestured for me to sit. Back propped against the twining gold headboard, he sat beside me. "Close your eyes," he murmured. He gathered my hands in his own, and a small gasp escaped me as I instantly felt his power flood my system. "It's alright," he said softly.

Everything was Hrokr. He was all I could smell, all I could hear, all I could see, even with my eyes closed. "It's a little disorienting at first," he whispered.

"That's alright," I whispered back.

Slowly, he released my fingers, and I saw.

My eyes were still closed, but I saw myself. I sat on the bed with hands in my laps, the kohl around my eyes smudged from my tears.

I won't be able to hear you, but you can still speak aloud to Fallon, he said to me. *She can get me a message if you need to.*

I *was* him. I could feel his thoughts, his fingers in the duvet as he pushed to his feet. I saw what his eyes caught on, the smudged kohl around my eyes, the piece of loose hair he'd tucked behind my ear. The glance he stole around the tan walls, catching on the balcony behind us, searching for anything lurking.

Stranger still, I knew things I wondered if he was even aware of.

Hrokr stepped across the room, purposefully ignoring the concerned glances from Fallon and Maddox. "Let's go," he said.

Do not *leave her,* he projected to Fallon.

I know, Crow, she replied softly.

He let himself out of the suite, Maddox in step beside him. The hallway was beautiful—ivories and gold and greens.

They didn't speak, even mind to mind. But Hrokr attempted to school his features, even bloodbending within himself to calm his racing heart.

He was worried, but wanted to hide that from me. He gave it as little thought as possible, deliberately working his thoughts around it.

They reached a massive outdoor stairwell, one thick with the salty brine of ocean air. In the time since we'd come inside, the sun had tucked itself fully beyond the horizon, and stars glittered against the choppy reflection of the ocean.

Maddox's voice entered our head. *I assume we pretend we know nothing.*

A tight nod from Hrokr as they cleared the staircase and entered an ornate meeting room, one complete with a gold chandelier falling from the vaulted ceiling. Around the massive table, the executives were already seated, Hrokr and Maddox being the last to arrive. The lords and ladies looked resplendent and lazy where they lounged in their dark, wooden thrones. The ebony table between them was full of food and wine and haphazard stacks of papers.

Every eye swiveled to the Lord of the North and his commander.

Through his eyes and thoughts, I knew them all.

Ciri—The Lady of the Hall of the Heavens—gave him a wide grin, one that was gloriously bright against her rich, sun-darkened skin.

He winked.

I scowled.

She sat between two women, both as beautiful but not quite as glorious as her. She looked loose and free, with her black hair braided down her back and a teal two-piece dress of easy, gauzy material that drew out bright flecks in her wide, olive eyes.

"Kind of you to join us, young one," an *ancient* man said, gesturing Hrokr and Maddox to their seats. Pure white hair was pushed back from his forehead, matching the age-bleached beard that covered his chin. While he sported none of the age spots common in humans, his dark skin did wear a few deep wrinkles.

Cornelius—Lord of the Hall of Flesh and Blood—looking on with night-dark eyes.

"Be quiet," Maddox chuckled, swaggering to his seat. "I'm older than you. I don't know why you still insist on wearing that haggard skin."

He only heals away his age every so many decades. He wants to age, Hrokr explained to me. *I don't understand it.*

Cornelius sat alone—absent of his Council as usual—Hrokr noted as he slid into his seat directly across from none other than Gar—*and The Nock.*

He was in a simple, navy suit that was dark against his sun-tanned skin. Brown-blond hair was pushed back from his forehead. He had not altered his face the way Gar had. His light brown eyes—set beneath a strong, smooth brow—looked on with disinterest.

"Fallon," I said aloud, feeling strange to use my own lips even as I could feel Hrokr's.

Through the sea of noises within the meeting chambers, I heard Fallon reply, "What is it?"

"The man to Gar's left was known as The Nock. He's the leader of the Guild."

Hrokr, Fallon's voice instantly came to his mind.

I felt the need within him to jump, to voidstep out of this room at the slightest worry. But his body was loose—unconcerned—as he poured himself a glass of champagne.

But his mental voice was rushed and strained. *What is it?*

Thea says the man on Gar's left is the leader of the Burning Arrow. Went by the name The Nock.

His eyes flashed up to The Nock's. Or, as I now knew him to be through Hrokr—King Jaeger. King, but not lord.

Greater lords and ladies ruled over Halls. Kings and queens beneath them ruled over their respective countries, and any smaller provinces could be assigned the local governing of a lesser lord or lady.

That was the standard idea in the Hall of the Elements, anyway. I didn't know how strictly the others adhered to it.

Halls, how did Hrokr keep up with it all?

King Jaeger sat between Gar and a polished, blonde man. Lord Ivaylo. In their group was also a ruddy-cheeked, black-haired King of Vanadey.

The long table held two empty chairs. One for the human leader of Ekin that Hrokr was unsurprised to find empty.

And one for the missing Heir of Aphaedia.

His eyes skipped over it quickly.

Hrokr couldn't help but study Gar, a raw and primal protectiveness swelling within his chest. When Gar caught his eye, Hrokr offered a half-grin.

One they'd shared many times as friends.

It was definitely Gar, but he *was* different. His eyes—they weren't hazel at all. If Hrokr's eyes were the night sky, Gar wore their earthly equivalent. They were the richest green, inlaid with stars of burnished gold.

Gar smiled back. *Everything alright?*

Yes, Hrokr said easily. *Court drama.*

Another grin. *Anything fun?*

Hardly, Hrokr said on a laugh. *Fallon and Maddie are in another of their tiffs.*

Gar's eyes slipped quickly to Maddox. *I was wondering why you'd not brought her.*

Hrokr downed the rest of his champagne.

With a pang, I realized they were *friends. Really friends.*

You know how she gets, Hrokr said loosely.

That I do, Gar chuckled.

Even though the room was relatively silent—save for the clinking of glasses and rustling of papers—Ivaylo said, "Alright, everyone. Settle down, let's get started."

I supposed it wasn't a stretch to assume that likely everyone in the room was tangled in projected conversation.

Gar ignored the command. *How was your Fete this year?*

Drab, Hrokr replied, even though his thoughts suddenly summoned me. He remembered how I was that night, the black gown that clung to my skin, the guarded hatred in my golden eyes. *You should have come, had a little fun. There's always something that goes wrong,* he said, grinning.

Gar smiled, shaking his head as he refilled his own wine glass. *Wouldn't be a party without a little chaos, I suppose.*

Ivaylo, still prattling in the background, said, "And you, Hrokr?"

"Nothing to report," Hrokr replied, voice clipped.

It hurt to hear. This would have been our moment to out Gar, to explain to the others the things we'd learned about him and hatch a unified plan to bring him down.

But seeing him here in the most elite meeting room in Alynthia—now wasn't the place.

Hrokr studied Gar, the loose body language and easy grin. He struggled to digest the thought that one of his only—and *oldest*—friends could truly be Silas. But he grinned and bore it.

Hrokr's normally still fingers worried a loose threat in his pants as he pretended to study Element's reports before him. It didn't make sense. Silas was *Silas*, but Jaeger was overwhelmingly Garbhan's superior. But the way Thea had explained it...

I found myself hearing my own name, swimming through his thoughts.

Silas had always been in charge. And even from his own dealings, Hrokr knew Silas answered to no one. Unless he did?

Hrokr's eyes flicked up to study Jaeger. Of course he knew of Garbhan's betrayal of the Halls, but how far did it extend? Did Ivaylo know? What about the other kings, the lesser lords and ladies?

Hrokr filled another glass of champagne, if only to have something to do with his hands.

Drinking the table dry, old friend? Gar laughed.

I hate these things, Garbhan, Hrokr bit back with a bit more force than necessary. *Sober is a hell of a way to get through them.*

Hrokr met his eyes, and Garbhan's were easy and full of mirth.

Hrokr was sick to his stomach, knowing what Garbhan had done to his family. What he had done to Inina and Orion. What he had done to *Thea.*

He wanted to leap across the table, to throttle him until he snapped, to tear his head from his shoulders. He reveled in Thea's bloodlust in a way he hadn't before. He—

He cut off his thoughts, as if he remembered I could hear them.

To Gar, he offered only a bored roll of the eyes.

Come out with us tonight, Garbhan said. *Jay is trying to bring Cornelius, too.*

Let me know if Cornelius comes, Hrokr replied smoothly, his mental voice belying none of the rage riding his every nerve. *So I can know to avoid it.*

Gar projected a laugh, even grinning openly across the table.

In the background, Ivaylo prattled on with his reports that no one cared about.

These meetings should really be moved to once per decade, Hrokr thought. Or perhaps century.

CHAPTER FORTY-ONE

LITTLE SHADOW

A ll evening. It was perhaps the longest night of both our lives, but conversation between Hrokr and Garbhan eventually quieted as the meeting continued meaninglessly.

Ivaylo called a short intermission for everyone to group with their respective parties before the closing statements. Hrokr had only a few minutes, but he made his way as leisurely as he could stand it down the stairwell and back to my room.

It was a strange thing, to watch him walk inside and spy *me* sitting on the bed. As soon as I came into his field of vision, he broke the connection, leaving me blinking and floundering as I found myself in my own skin.

He perched on the bed beside me, worry etched across his features.

"You lived," I said lightly, offering a half-smile.

"As did you," he murmured. "That was wretched."

I said nothing as he buried his face in tired hands.

Maddox burst in only a moment later, groaning. "Awful," he spit.

Hrokr lifted his head, studying my face. "It's customary to stay for the night, but I won't risk it. We leave as soon as closing remarks are finished."

I nodded my agreement. I didn't want to be beneath the same roof as Gar any longer than was absolutely necessary.

"Are you alright?" he asked softly.

"Are you?"

He shrugged, tapping the side of his head. "I suppose you know exactly how I feel."

I tried to smile, though it didn't feel quite right. But it was almost over; we could get through a few more moments.

"Are you going to say anything?" Maddox asked, leaning against the wall. "You could out him now if that's what you wanted."

Hrokr shook his head. "Not like this. We have no idea who knows or who has been working with him."

"You think Ivaylo would do that?"

"I don't know what I think," Hrokr admitted. "But I'm not willing to risk it without the entire Council together and none of the Weatherman nearby. Not while we are separated, not when I'm downstairs and Thea is stuck up here"

We entered a thick batch of silence before Fallon said, "Maybe you should talk to Ciri."

"I don't know," he whispered.

"Who is Ciri?" I asked. I knew her to be the beautiful, dark-skinned Lady of the Heavens, but I knew nothing else.

"Dromnael Ciresu," Maddox said, rapping his knuckles against the wall. "Ciri, for short. She's a good woman."

Hrokr shifted, his eyes suddenly far away. "I thought Garbhan was a good man," he murmured.

I laid a hand on his forearm, drawing his troubled eyes. "So did I," I whispered.

He covered his fingers with his own before rising to his feet, leaving me to pace across the room.

"We don't have much time," he said. "Walk me through it all, Thea."

So I did. The abduction of my family, the way Gar had seen *something* of a vision and taken an immediate interest in me. How I'd been crafted to be nothing more than Valencia's destruction. About how no one seemed to understand the power dynamic between Gar and The Nock. He'd heard most of it already, but I answered his new, niche questions as best I could.

In the end all he murmured was, "Alright." Hrokr let me back through the door of his thoughts and left me to finish the last moments of the Annual Halls' meeting.

Maddox grabbed Hrokr by the shoulder in the silence of the empty stairway, stopping him. "Crow."

"What."

Maddox gestured to Hrokr's hands. "You're shaking, man. Get it together."

Hrokr snatched himself away, stuffing one hand in his pocket. "I'm angry."

"So am I." Maddox searched his face, pleading silently with Hrokr to control himself.

Finally, Hrokr sighed and said, "Let's go."

Once inside the meeting room, things were far more laid back than the first half. People chatted and clinked glasses, tired and ready to retire to their festivities for the night.

Gar smiled at Hrokr, asking, *Are you coming for drinks?*

Hrokr's fingers did indeed shake with fury as he pulled his seat out and reclined leisurely. He fought to keep his voice steady as he said, *I think I'm ready to go home, Garbhan. You know how much I hate these things.*

Ivaylo called the closing to attention as Garbhan's lips twisted into a cruel smirk.

You know, old friend, I really thought you'd have the balls to call me out.

Hrokr's nerves turned cold. It wasn't fear—not how I knew fear to be at least. It was a frigid rage, an ancient roaring in his blood.

Garbhan tilted his head to the side. *Do you think I cannot scent her on you? That I couldn't the moment I saw you?*

Hrokr, ever in control of his body, raised a lazy brow. He deigned not respond until he'd poured a fresh glass of champagne.

If there is something you'd like to say to me, Garbhan, just say it.

Is it eating you alive? Gar purred.

Impossibly, even amidst the rage, a flash of hurt speared through him. *Why?*

Garbhan leaned back, easily reclined in his seat. *An age-old question.*

You were foolish to give her your name, Hrokr said.

Not foolish, Gar replied quickly. *Only tired of waiting.*

Maddox's voice slipped into the fold of Hrokr's thoughts. *Does he know?*

Yes, Hrokr replied curtly. To Garbhan, he said, *What do you want?*

Gar grinned, a soft chuckle projected to Hrokr. *You're so much like her, Crow.*

Every inch of his body was screaming at him, howling for him to leap across the table and shred him apart. It wouldn't begin to repay the crimes he'd committed. But peeling his skin from his bones would be a nice start.

Was it all you? Hrokr asked, though it was more of a growl than a real question. *Cadmus? Araceli? Inina and Orion?*

Gar smiled. *Those hurt you, I know. But don't pretend it's not all about* her.

There was no reason to bring her into it, Hrokr snarled. He knew he was rising to the bait, but he couldn't help it. His field of vision was blurring, shadows slithering like cool snakes between his fingers.

Killing her mother was nasty, I'll admit, he said, not at all repentant. *I only wanted you two to match, give you something to bond over in those early days. Tell Thea to be proud. Her mother stared her death in the eyes, confident her daughter could bear it.*

Tears welled in my eyes.

Unlike Araceli, he chuckled. *Your mother knew her death would break you. And she was not wrong.*

Old wounds became fresh within the Lord of the North. He saw a kitchen—not at all like the one I'd expect. It was humble and small, cramped full with warm love. Creaking floorboards and walls with peeling paint. It was the home of a poor, little boy who loved his mother—not the opulent castle of a lord.

And then there was a head on the floor, unseeing eyes at the end of his scuffed boots. Blood puddles sinking into the faded wood below.

Why? he asked again.

You have taken so much from me, Crow. And you're far too self-absorbed to even see it. You are a child, The Boy King, indeed. My anger goes back far longer than you, but you—*you have made it infinitely worse. I am prepared to repay you in kind.*

Suddenly, Gar was projecting images. He showed a beautiful woman, slender with up-turned eyes and creamy, porcelain skin. Hair of purest silver fell down her back. Her eyes were the same color, like moonlight given flesh. The images moved in rapid succession. Her, standing within an orchard, her head tilted back to watch the petals fall. Her toes in the sand, the starlit ocean reaching the fingers of the tide up around her legs.

New images. Hrokr's cold, rigid body turning away from her. Hrokr studying her with open speculation in his eyes. Hrokr leaving her locked in the ivory tower *of my bedroom.* Hrokr hovering above her, dragging an ebony dagger across her slim throat and her last projected memory, *Garbhan I will always love you.*

It was a strange thing—to experience this without word or explanation. There were things revealed to me through feeling alone, discovered in this complex headspace I now occupied with both Hrokr and Gar.

The wife Hrokr had almost taken—the fiance he had slain—was the beautiful, silver girl. And that same girl was Gar's dead wife—his dead *mate*—that he had never stopped mourning.

The images faded, and Gar and Hrokr stared at one another across the table. Gar asked, *Do you know what it feels like to have a dead mate?*

But there was not an inch of remorse inside Hrokr, only a sick, twisted kind of glee. He set his glass down gently, leaning forward to pitch his elbows atop the polished table. He garnered a few surprised glances from the other leaders.

He did not care.

You were a fool, Garbhan, and your lover died for it. I did kill her, and I would do it again. If you raise her, I will do it again. Is the Hall what you want? You sent her—a foolish, meddling girl—to attempt to share my bed? Did you think I would love her? he mocked. *Did you think I would crown her my equal? Did you honestly believe she would sit my throne and you would be my replacement?*

Gar was silent, but Hrokr and I both recognized the tells of rage bracketed around his lips, the tightness of tendons within his clenched fists.

She was a fool, Hrokr pressed on. *Always lurking somewhere she wasn't meant to be. Too forward with advances you should have known I would not want. I smelled her coup from a mile away, and I put her down for it. I do hope her sacrifice has served you well.*

Garbhan leaned back, crossing one leg over the other. *Taunt me all you like, Crow. In truth, should you not be thanking me? I deposed your parents. I put you on that throne.*

Should I thank you for half of my dead Council? Hrokr asked calmly.

Gar only grinned. *Say it, Hrokr. Say who it is you're really angry about.*

Something snapped within him, became untethered from a body he normally had expert control over. He said nothing. He was unsure if he could speak—even mentally—without shattering something. Without calling down hail and thunder and plunging this entire hall into infinite darkness.

What is it that bothers you the most? Gar pushed. *Is it that she was a blade in my hands? A body beneath my palms? Or is it knowing she was the one who killed your friends? Is it knowing her mother is dead because I wanted just another nail in your coffin?*

Silence.

How much did she tell you, Crow? he asked, pitching forward. *How much do you really know? Did she tell you Jay had her on her knees scrubbing floors for three months? Did she tell you about the comfort she found in the bottom of a bottle? Did she tell you how I tasted, Hrokr?*

A glass candle shattered across the room. The entire table flinched, and Gar chuckled softly beneath his breath.

Ivaylo groaned, barking something neither of us heard.

Hrokr had eyes only for Gar.

Did she tell you the best part, Crow? Did she tell you I saw something when I first met her?

Stop.

Gar grinned. *Did she tell you she can't quite figure out what it is? I bet you know what I saw. I bet you know she—*

Stop, Hrokr growled, louder this time. I felt it, his attempt to shield away Garbhan's words. His thoughts were moving too quickly, a jumble of madness I couldn't follow. Fires and ice and empty bottles and snow-heavy trees.

But Garbhan's brow furrowed for only the shortest moment until realization dawned in his eyes. He looked right at Hrokr's forehead, as if he could see the mind beneath. *Is she in there?* he asked in wonder. *Naughty, Crow, you know the Annual Halls' meetings are not to be projected to anyone.*

Hrokr hands burned with unspent flame, his shadows cold as they attempted to smother the heat.

Hi, Little Shadow.

I felt ill.

There was a break in the conversation of the meeting—only a short pause. But Hrokr took the moment—lazy and leisurely as ever—to groan softly. "Ivaylo, do you plan on wrapping this up any time soon?"

Ciri stretched her body, arching like a cat. "Thank you for saying what we were all thinking, Hrokr."

Ivaylo scowled.

Growing antsy? Gar taunted.

"Fine," Ivaylo grumbled. "Any closing remarks?"

He was met with weary silence.

He dropped a stack of papers. "Alright. Get out." Everyone chuckled and drew to their feet, tired and unaware of the strife in their midst.

It took everything inside of Hrokr not to choke Garbhan until he cracked, not to rip his entrails out with his nails, to snap his neck and send him straight to Mavka if that was what he wanted so badly.

But death would be too kind.

Not to mention impractical at present time.

So, fury like a blast powder within him, he rose to his feet and strolled lazily into the hall. He'd barely made it to the stairwell when a smooth hand slid across his shoulder. Maddox, to his left, stiffened.

Hrokr could feel Garbhan's breath on his ear as he whispered, "Do tell our girl how much I've missed her."

Hrokr turned into him, their eyes locking. Nose to nose, I felt sick to my stomach being this close to his face again—even experienced through Hrokr's head.

We could smell him, sunshine and baked leaves. Choking.

Hrokr tried to push me out. I felt it—a struggle against the connection binding us together. This bond should have been one-sided—I'd assumed at least—but I was inside every piece of him. He could not push me out if I did not wish to go.

Resigned, he let me stay and leaned even farther into a Gar that did not back down.

"Hurt her, Garbhan," he began slowly. A muscle feathered in Hrokr's jaw, and Gar must have heard his teeth grinding. But his voice was as smooth as silk when he said, "Displace a single hair on her head, and I will pull your spine through your throat."

Gar grinned, a lopsided smirk.

Hrokr grabbed him by the chest, his fingers curling into Gar's dark shirt. He pulled him closer, moving his lips to his ear. "If you hurt my Thea, I will raise Mavka myself. And I will make her beg death to return."

Hrokr pulled away, and Gar had the good nature to at least look angry.

Hrokr's fingers uncurled from the cloth of Gar's chest, and they shared one last heady moment of threatening silence.

And then Hrokr turned his back on his enemy and took the stairs two at a time.

I let him release his projection bond as soon as he stepped through the door of the suite. "Let's go," he barked.

I scrambled to my feet. "Hrokr—"

"We are *leaving*," he said as Maddox pulled the suite door shut.

"Maybe we should trail him," I offered. "If we lose him—"

"Thea," he interrupted, whirling on me. "If I stay under this roof for one more minute I am going to *gut him.*" A heavy breath sawed through his chest. "And that is going to make our lives *very* complicated." He waved an impatient hand in the air. "Fallon, come on. Let's go."

Fallon scurried to my side, cutting open her own palm and holding it out to me. I narrowed my eyes at Hrokr. "What are you doing? Why can't you take me?"

"Just go," he said, eyes darkening. "I will leave when I know you're safely gone."

"And if you get trapped here?"

"I'd rather me than you."

"What is that supposed to mean?"

"Thea," Fallon said gently, nudging me. "He has connections that you don't. Come on, let's go."

I frowned as I held Hrokr's eyes, but offered my palm to Fallon.

In only a blink, I found myself in the open breeze of the terrace outside the throne room. Before I had a moment to panic, Hrokr materialized beside me.

"Hrokr—"

But he was gone, stepping up the edge of the railing and throwing himself from its heights. A crow rose in his place, flying into the heart of the night.

I took a step toward the edge, as if there were anything I could do. Fallon laid a cool hand on my arm. "Let him go, Thea. He's alright."

But he wasn't, I didn't think.

I didn't think any of us were.

CHAPTER FORTY-TWO

HIDE

I fled to my room, not having the energy to put on a face for Fallon or Maddox.

Gyda delivered me a sad, private dinner I ate alone in the bathtub.

I ran my fingertips through the water, watching the ripples over my tattoo. I kept thinking about that empty seat at the Halls' meeting table. How I should have been in it, a political ally Hrokr knew would support him leading a movement against Gar.

I thought of many things and finally settled on the uncomfortable truth that the tattoo didn't do anything magical.

It just was.

Any Gentry Fae could plant the Aphaedian crest on their body and claim to be the Heir. And—truth be told—many likely had. But there were no imposters sitting in my seat at the Halls' meeting—because it was more than the ink. The lords and ladies—*my* equals—would not be fooled.

Not by anyone but me.

I wondered how I felt about my secret now—now that I could see the hole it had created.

Drawing my eyes away from the ink, I laid my dinner tray on the floor, refilled my wine, and opened my book. I read until my eyes could no longer hold themselves open, and crawled to bed.

My lungs were going to burst inside my chest, but I kept running. My feet pounded against the stone, sending sharp stabs of pain up through my heels.

I thought I was putting some distance between us, but as I rounded a corner, I realized I'd made no progress at all.

I screamed, falling to my knees before the dead end.

An ugly stone wall rose up before me, so high it blocked out the shine of the sun. I stared in horror at the bodies mounted there.

They were infinite, crawling up toward the sky in a gruesome display of my sins.

Momma, dead because I'd loved her.

My Gentry Fae parents, brutalized and broken, nailed to the wall just out of reach of the other's outstretched palm.

Talon, because I'd killed him.

Calix, because Hrokr had.

Sagira, because I'd brought her into the world of the Fae.

Mellian, because I'd left her.

Alek, still wearing hate in his unseeing eyes.

Wyn, because he knew what I was.

All my friends from The Meridian.

And beneath them, at eye level—

Haizea. Ciro. Maddox. Fallon. Gyda.

Rough hands were suddenly in my hair, ripping me backward into a hard chest that smelled strongly of fall leaves and choking sunshine.

"Garbhan," I seethed. Gar. Silas. The man in the iron mask.

"Don't be angry at me," he replied, chuckling. "I didn't do this. You did."

Horror racked me as I looked up at the bodies. There were thousands of them. Some I couldn't remember their names, but I knew I loved them. I knew I'd caused their deaths.

"The eclipse is soon," he crooned in my ear, breath hot and vile against my cheek. "You've been here for a century, now, Thea. Look at all the evil you've done. Look at all the lives you've taken."

"I didn't kill them," I croaked.

"Some you did," he said, smiling as he pointed to Talon's rotting form. "But they are all your fault, Thea. It's all your fault."

"Stop," I rasped, struggling to break free.

He leaned in, nuzzling against my neck. I fought him, but it was no use. My limbs were far too heavy. "There's one more."

Ice filled me, ripping away all the warmth of life.

"You're destroying him, Thea. You're killing him. You've not tried to help him at all."

My panicked eyes shot back to the wall to see a broken form lying at its base.

"No," I croaked, lunging toward him. Gar's hold tightened.

Hrokr.

As he looked up at me, the life rapidly drained from his eyes. "Thea," he rasped.

"Hrokr," I pleaded, pulling against Gar with everything I had. But it wasn't enough.

"Thea," Hrokr pleaded again, reaching a hand for me.

But then a blade was suddenly—from nowhere—shoved through his chest. Blood sprayed as his eyes went dark.

I screamed. I screamed and screamed and couldn't seem to catch my breath to stop. My throat ached, and the taste of blood was in my mouth, but I couldn't stop screaming, I couldn't stop—

"*Thea.*"

I lunged again, and Gar released me. I pitched forward, still screaming,

And—

The world shifted its axis. Light turned to dark, and day turned to night. I blinked against the new surroundings, but my throat was still aching. I was still screaming, he was still dead, he was still—

"*Thea!*"

Hands were gripping my shoulders hard enough to bruise.

"Stop screaming, Thea, it's alright. I'm here, it's okay, you're okay."

The hands were rubbing me now, trying to rouse me.

"It's just a dream," he continued. "It's just a dream, Thea."

My screams tapered off into a rough sob.

Just a dream.

Hrokr came into my focus—whole and breathing—with eyes wide with panic. "Oh Halls," I rasped, choking on my tears.

He let loose a shaking breath, relaxing against me. We were sitting in my bed, safe in the tower of Castle Habrem, and—

I ripped away from him, stumbling over myself to crawl out of the bed. He called after me, but I didn't stop. I hurtled into the bathing room, slamming the door shut behind me.

My knees ached as they hit the tile floor, and I barely made it to the toilet before vomit was spewing from me. The images came rolling back into me as my body convulsed.

All my fault, all my fault, all my fault.

I cringed as the door swung open, and I tried to angle my body to hide my flushed face. I was still heaving as he crossed the room and crouched behind me. I tried to shove him away, but he captured my hand and placed it on my leg.

His fingers were slow and gentle as he gathered my hair and tied it back. His hand felt like it touched every inch of my back as it slid beneath my shirt and pressed up against my spine. I felt my pulse slowly rapidly, felt the tremors in my body ease.

I clung with shaking fingers to the toilet. I thought I saw a wisp of smoke twirling around my fingers, and my panic tripled.

"Easy," he whispered, stroking my skin. His magic grew stronger, bending my blood to his slow, steady will.

I willed my own magic away, praying he wouldn't notice my slip, praying I hadn't outed myself.

Back bowed, I rested my head against the porcelain, struggling to slow my breathing. But his work on my heart helped, and—after long, swollen moments—my breathing evened out.

"I'm sorry," I croaked.

"For what?" he asked gently.

I sniffled, wiping my mouth on the back of my hand. "I didn't mean to wake you."

His touch faltered before he resumed his light stroking. "Do you dream often?"

"Sometimes," I admitted, my voice a rough scratch. "Usually only when things are bad."

A long pause as tears pooled in my eyes and dripped down my cheeks.

He moved to sit beside me, and I missed his touch immediately. He seemed to sense it and reached out to hold my hand. "Talk to me," he murmured.

I shook my head.

He reached out to tuck a stray lock behind my ear before pressing the back of his hand to my sweat-slick forehead, frowning. "You're burning up, Thea."

Panic pulsed through my veins, hard and fast. I moved to pull away, but he held me tight. "Talk to me. Are you ill?"

"No—I—Just flushed," I sputtered. If my fire magic was making me hot, he was going to notice. He was going to know I'd lied about where I was born. He was going to know who I was, he was—

"Thea," he murmured, stroking the inside of my wrists. Again, I felt my pulse slowing.

"Thank you," I rasped.

He frowned. "What happened?"

I tried to breathe deeply, to will the magic away from me. But it didn't want to go. It needed a way out, it needed—

"Look at you," he said gently, solemnly. "Your magic is upset, Thea."

Panic was a live, writhing thing inside of my chest. "No, it's—"

But my words broke away as he released me and used his nail to cut a long line down his forearm. Blood flowed readily, and I cried out. "Hrokr! What are you doing?"

He grabbed my hand and laid it against his forearm. "Let it out," he said softly.

Less out of obedience and more out of an unwillingness for him to bleed out all over the floor, I sent my magic spearing into him. My relief was small but immediate, and I felt the sharp edge inside of me smooth as his skin closed together, no trace of a scar beneath.

"Why would you do that?" I breathed, looking for something to wipe away the blood with.

He captured my hands, stopping me. "Calm down, Thea. I'm alright."

"But you're all bloody, now, and—"

"Calm," he repeated, taking in a deep breath as if to guide me into my own. "You feel a little better now, yeah?"

"Yes, but—"

"It's alright," he interrupted. "We need to find your other affinity so you can release magic a little easier."

"You shouldn't have hurt yourself, Hrokr. Halls, especially after that dream—"

His eyes flashed to mine. "The dream? What happened?"

I was almost embarrassed to admit it, but this man had just tied my hair while I vomited. And then he had bled all over us both, so I supposed a bad dream would be the least of the intimacy we shared tonight.

But as I looked at him, I remembered his prone and ragged form. My pulse kicked up, and his touch immediately worked to slow it.

"Gar was chasing me," I admitted in a rush. "And I got away only to find all of these bodies. It was everyone, Hrokr. Everyone I knew and loved. Mel and Alek and Sage, and Halls, even the Council, and—" I looked him in the eye as tears spilled down my cheeks. "And you were dead."

He stiffened.

"I know it was just a dream," I pressed on, swiping roughly at the tears. "But I knew you were hurting, and you kept saying my name, and—"

I didn't get a chance to finish, because he was suddenly pulling me hard against him, cradling my face against my chest. Beneath my ear, his heart was pounding.

"Hrokr."

"Shh," he crooned, holding me tighter. "Just—let me hold you."

The words tripped me for a moment, but I chose to take them as the comfort they presented. He was here. He was alive and holding me.

We sat in silence for long minutes until the tension slowly eased out of us both.

"How did I die?" he asked in a small voice.

I whirled, twisting up to face him. "What kind of morbid question is that?" I hissed.

He shrugged, cracking a weak grin. "Sorry," he murmured as his fingers slowly traced the side of my face.

In the silence that followed, he repositioned me on his lap so we were both more comfortable. He tucked my head back against his chest. "What else happened?" he asked softly, rubbing my back, beating my heart.

I leaned more fully into him. "It was all my fault that everyone was dying."

He stiffened, looking into my eyes. "It is *not* your fault," he said vehemently. "Not the deaths that have passed, not any that may come. None of it is your fault, Thea."

"I know it was just a dream," I rasped, "but I can't stop hearing it."

A frightening sort of calm settled over him. The dark aura that always swam around him swelled further, pressing up against my skin. It smelled old and cold, and full of wicked promises that a mortal mind couldn't comprehend.

"I'm going to hurt him, Thea," he said softly.

My heart seized in my chest, and I knew he felt it. "It was just a dream, Crow."

His eyes were dark and full of swirling madness, full of the time before time, the time before life, the time after death. His rage was depthless and eternal, honed sharp. "Your mind assigned his face to those words for a reason."

But I didn't want to think about Gar.

He offered nothing more, so I nestled back into his chest, and he held me tighter. "Do you want to go back to sleep?" he asked softly.

"I don't know," I admitted.

"Are you tired?"

As the fog of sleep and the terror of nightmares ebbed away, clarity forced the rest of my day onto me. Instead of answering, I ducked my head farther, as if I could hide a face he already couldn't see. "Are you mad at me?"

"What?" he asked, sounding genuinely bemused. "Why would you ask me that?"

"Just tell me."

"No, Thea," he said strongly, brushing his fingers through my hair. "Of course not."

I twisted to look up at him, frowning. "Then why?" I asked in a small voice.

Why did he run? Why did he hide from me and his Council? Why did he choose to fly away instead of staying with me?

I tried to chase the thoughts I saw behind his eyes, but they moved so quickly I was unable to latch onto even one. He sighed, his breath a balm against me. "I just needed space."

The words came so quickly to my lips that I could not stop them. "From me?"

He shuddered delicately. "I don't know how to be what you need." His voice was smaller and more defeated than I'd ever heard it.

I reached out with a steady finger, tapping his cheek. Silver lined his eyes, but did not spill over.

I wrapped my arms around his neck, pulling him into an embrace that—after a heavy moment—he returned, banding his arms around my waist. "Don't hide from me," I whispered to him. "I am the same as you, Crow."

His voice was cracked and broken when he croaked, "I can't, Thea."

"Why?" I asked gently.

He held me tighter, crushing me against him. "I don't keep friends well. I—I tend to push them away once they come too close."

"And do they?" I asked. "Do they come too close? Do they come this close?"

Silence.

And then, "No. Never this close."

Warmth swelled inside of me, chasing away the darkness of this night as I clung to his shoulders. Still embraced, I asked, "Can I ask you something, Hrokr?"

"What is it?"

"Do all seer's visions come true?"

He stiffened against me, and I felt something old and dark leaking through the room. He was silent for a long moment before he answered, "Yes and no. Not always in the capacity we expect, but—yes."

I squeezed him a little tighter. "Then you know you'll have me for another hundred years."

Gar had seen me holding the Orb in Valencia beneath the centenary eclipse. If visions had to come true...

"I know you'll still be here in a hundred years, yes," he said.

"Don't say it like that," I said, pulling away to look at him. "*You* will have me."

The thought of an eternal life had always felt so terrifying, so alien and daunting. But after coming here, I had come to know that I could find a place in the world of forever.

He shuddered, smiling even as silver lined his eyes.

I cradled his cheek in my palm. "You care for me, Hrokr."

He started, lips parting. "I—"

"Yes or no."

He let loose a warm breath that tickled my face. "Yes."

"Then don't hide," I whispered. "No matter what happens in the night, know that I will still be there in the morning. Don't shut me out the way you did today."

He chewed his lower lip, chest rising and falling with heavy breaths. "I don't want to hurt you, Thea."

"Then don't," I replied simply, giving a soft smile. "Be my friend, Hrokr."

He searched my eyes, looking back and forth between them as if he could read the thoughts I didn't give voice.

Finally, he whispered, "Alright."

CHAPTER FORTY-THREE

BEWITCH

When I woke for the morning, a part of me wondered if *all* of it had been a dream. But a small note was left on my bedside table, penned in immaculate scrawl.

Sleep well. I'll be in the Council Room.

I smiled, setting it back down. I took a fresh bath, towel-drying my hair before slipping into a warm sweater and leggings, and bounding down the steps.

Inside the Council Room, all of them were present. Haizea and Fallon played chess on the floor, and the boys were crowded around something on the table.

Hrokr met my eyes as I entered, smiling gently.

Warm relief filled me.

I was thankful to see him back with the others, to have left the silence that yesterday brought. Hrokr vanished, only to reappear at my side with a covered dish in his hands. I stumbled a little, and he chuckled.

He led me to the table, uncovering it.

"Is no one else eating?" I asked, sliding into my usual seat.

"Thea, it's ten thirty," Fallon chirped from the floor. "You slept *forever.*"

I blushed as I brought a warm mug into my hands.

"It's fine," Hrokr said. "You didn't miss anything."

As I dug into a breakfast of rice and eggs, I leaned over to see they were all pouring over a map. "What's this?"

"Maedonia," he said. "The capital of the Hall of Flesh and Blood."

"For the Orb?"

He nodded. "I sent word to Cornelius yesterday that we'd like to visit. It will take him a while to mull it over with his board, but at least the request is in."

"And until then?"

"We take a friendly trip to Heavens," he said, sliding into the seat beside me.

Ciro shook his head, eyeing Hrokr. "I still don't know if that's the best course of action. What makes you think Ciri will just hand it over?"

"I think she will," Haizea called from her place on the floor.

"And if she doesn't?" Ciro pushed.

Hrokr took a deep breath, spinning a pen between his fingers. "It doesn't really matter. I'd like her to give it to me, but we'll get it one way or another."

"I still think it's a bad idea that we are gathering them at all," Ciro frowned. "We are doing his legwork."

"Maybe," Hrokr mused. "But we will draw him out. We will end it. He can't voidstep onto the Hall, so we will see him coming."

"It's going to be a war, Hrokr."

Hrokr's eyes met Ciro's. A long, unspoken conversation flowed between them. Ciro's eyes flicked to me before he frowned and turned back to his map.

I opened my mouth to speak, but Hrokr projected, *Don't worry, Thea.*

I frowned.

"War it will likely be," Hrokr said aloud. "Let's get through this trip with Ciri, and then I will address the people."

Maddox groaned, dropping a fist against the table. "I can't believe we are back here. Again."

"It won't end the same," Ciro said sharply.

Hrokr eyes were far away, likely wading through grief of the past.

"When do we leave?" I asked. "To Heavens."

His lashes fluttered as he brought himself out of his thoughts. "Anytime. We don't need an invitation to go see Ciri."

"We ought to go soon," Fallon chimed in. "She seemed stressed during the meeting. She knows something is wrong, Crow."

Hrokr cocked a brow at Maddox. "Were you projecting the meeting?"

Maddox shrugged.

None of the Cardinals cared much for the global rules, it seemed.

Hrokr sighed.

It was only that evening we stood together in the Portal Room. I was primped to the same dark, glorying degree as I had been for the Annual Halls' meeting, though I hoped the outcome of this trip would be different. Hrokr was looser, wearing only his boots, dark leather pants, and a flowing button-down in midnight black.

Fallon and Maddox would accompany us again, and Ciro and Haizea would stay behind to watch over Castle Habrem.

I didn't need to share blood with anyone, as the Portal Room held a runegate directly to Gloriala, the capital of the Hall of the Heavens.

Hrokr took my arm like a perfect gentleman as he led me over the threshold.

I wondered if I'd ever get used to the strange feeling of slipping through the fabric of space. As soon as my feet were steady beneath me, they felt suddenly unstable for other reasons.

"Wow," I breathed.

"Isn't it?" Hrokr murmured.

We landed beneath an endless canopy of stars, their shimmering reflections painted across the ocean. We stood on a stone veranda, overlooking a beach filled with pyres and laughing, dancing bodies. Hrokr's arm slid around my waist, tugging me close to his side.

He turned me toward the rest of the room, which was an opulent suite filled with navy couches and polished, dark wood tables. The walls were white stucco, adorned with intricate art framed in gold. It was an open studio, a four-poster bed of dark wood and ivory gossamer separating us from the open, gilded door of the bathing room.

Fallon and Maddox had hardly solidified before a sharp rapping came onto the receiving doors.

"Come in," Hrokr called.

I gave him a puzzled look that he met with a smile. *We have long had our own quarters in Ciri's kingdom.*

"You're close?" I whispered.

Maddox snorted.

Old friends, Hrokr explained as the doors opened and in swept two male guards.

I flushed.

"Lord Hrokr," they intoned together, bowing low at the waist. "Lady Ciresu will be able to greet you momentarily."

Hrokr nodded sagely, and the guards—wearing white gear with crisp, teal brocade—turned away, leaving the door open.

It was only a moment before the woman—gloriously bathed in lilac gossamer—appeared on a wind in the center of the doorway.

"Friends!" she beamed. But her olive eyes immediately snagged on me. "My—who is this?"

Hrokr's fingers tightened on my hip. "My mate, Thea. I thought it prudent that I introduce you."

Her face lit up, and she immediately rushed into the space. "Mate." Ciri stood before us, scouring me from head to toe. She murmured something in a tongue I did not know.

Hrokr's eyes softened. He whispered, "Indeed she is."

"Beautiful," she said for my ears. I held myself perfectly still as she kissed both of my cheeks. I smiled, flushing at her display of affection.

She turned her eyes to Hrokr. "Happiness suits you well, old friend."

He smiled, tugging me closer to his side. "Thank you, Ciri."

She stepped away from us, turning to our friends. "Maddox, Fallon. Lovely to see you both."

They each offered her warm greetings.

Turning back to us, she asked, "Is this what had you so stressed at the Annual? Restless, away from your darling bride?"

He looked down to me, smiling something bittersweet. "Not quite," he admitted. "I hate to bring bad news to your doorstep, Ciri."

She frowned before plopping unceremoniously onto the navy sofa. "I would be more upset if you did not share it at all."

Hrokr's brow furrowed, his fingers warm where they dug into my flesh. It was a concession, we all knew. While it was one that Hrokr believed was slim, there was still a possibility that Ciri was involved with Gar.

And if so, we could be entering a world of danger.

But perhaps the greater danger was fighting him alone.

Ciri's eyes grew troubled as she watched him cling to me. "My friends," she murmured, gesturing to the sofa across from her. "Sit, sit."

After a stilted pause, Hrokr dragged me forward and sat us down side by side. His thigh brushed against my own, and he did not remove the arm that held me close to him. His warmth flowed into me, his muscles taught with strain where I could feel them. Maddox perched on the arm of my seat, and Fallon stood behind me.

"You worry me, Crow," Ciri said softly. "Please tell me what is wrong."

"It's Silas," he said.

Her eyes filled with a bitter knowing. "He cannot bring himself to leave your family alone," she said, her voice sounding like a true lament. "What crime has he committed now?"

"He hurt my mate," Hrokr said, and though his words may have been a lie, the fury riding his voice was not.

"Oh, my dear," she said, frowning as she scoured my body with her eyes as if she could see physical manifestations of the hurt he had put me through.

"Ciri, he..." Hrokr's voice trailed away. He was not one to struggle stringing words together, and I could only view his raw vulnerability as either a plea for her mercy or perhaps his friendship with her truly extended far enough back to lend him candor. "It's Garbhan."

She flinched as if struck. "Silas?"

"Yes," he said.

Her mind spun. I could see it in the unfocusing of her eyes, the frozen posture of her body. "How can you be sure?"

Hrokr nudged me gently. I met his eyes, and he nodded, stroking a gentle thumb at my side. "I knew him maskless. He went by the name Gar. I recognized him at the Annual meeting."

Ciri looked to Hrokr as if to check the validity of my statement. He stiffened, but nodded. "She speaks true, Dromnael."

She nodded slowly, reeling. Finally she said, "I assume he knows you're aware? It would explain your silent stand-off in Asena."

Hrokr gave one short, hard nod. "Yes."

Siri brought her hand to her mouth, worrying her lower lip between her fingers. "What can I do, Crow?"

I felt him relax as surely as if he had projected it to me. His body stayed just as still, his breathing just as steady. But I felt something within him ease.

"He wishes to bring back his dead mate from the Far Away."

Her eyes flashed up, hard and shrewd. "Hrokr."

"I know they are not to be used," he said. "But I fear we may lose the option of choice if we do not move proactively. I would appreciate your discretion in the matter," he said carefully.

"Have you spoken to Ivaylo? Garbhan answers to the Lord of the Center after all."

"No. Not yet."

She took a deep breath, blowing it out through her lips as she glanced out over the railing, watching her people and the sea lapping at her shores. "What do you plan to do?"

"Protect the Orbs from him. He will not raise her, Ciri."

A pause. "Perhaps you should let him," she murmured.

A muscle in his jaw feathered. "Pardon?"

Her eyes swiveled back to his, full of a mercy I could not understand. "His actions are reprehensible and without excuse. I am sorry for his crimes against you," she added to me. "But the death of one's mate is no easy matter. In fact, I am thankful to be un-mated for that very reason. Physical distance is said to be quite painful. Surely you have known this to be true, Hrokr?"

His eyes flicked to me. "Yes," he murmured.

"Give him the Orb. Let us end this stalemate."

It was Fallon who said from behind me, "No, Ciri."

"It's complicated," Hrokr tacked on.

"Explain it, then," she said, though not unkindly.

"You remember Mavka," he hedged.

She cocked a dark brow. "Yes?"

"And her... *unfortunate* death?"

"I do."

"She is his mate."

Ciri's brows show up. "That *does* complicate things."

"It's more than her," Hrokr continued. "She was sent to Valencia to unravel me. I'm not sure what it is he wants, but it predates her."

She nodded slowly. "Mavka's passing was very long ago, Hrokr. Perhaps returning her to him will restore things."

Fallon spoke again, "We will not restore him his mate when two of our Council are dead, Lady Ciri."

"Sometimes you must let the dead lie," Ciri said. Again, her voice was kind. "And while Inina and Orion's untimely passing was very unfortunate, they did not leave mates behind. In fact, perhaps some heartache was avoided in allowing Ciro and Haizea to explore their mating bond."

I jerked. Hrokr held me closer. *It's very complicated, Thea.*

But for Ciri, he leaned forward, his arm sliding out from behind my back. Elbows braced on his knees, shadows coiled at his knuckles. "I assure you no heartache was spurned when I buried my brother. My sister."

She bowed her head in deference—a show of kindness to her political equal. "Forgive me, Crow. I am your friend, and I do not take the loss lightly. Perhaps I spoke poorly. I hope you know my intentions were not to hurt or offend."

He said nothing, allowing the silence to speak for him.

"Forgive me," she repeated. "And tell me what I can do to help your problem with Garbhan."

He laid a hand on my leg as if to anchor himself. "I would like your Orb. I wish to hold them in Valencia, as it is warded wholly against outside sources."

"My capital is warded."

"Your entire Hall is not."

She studied us both. "And if this is what he intends? For you to gather them for him?"

"Perhaps it is," Hrokr conceded. "But he cannot voidstep onto the Hall. I will see him coming, and he will be dead before he is close enough. I want the Orbs to lure him, draw him in. He will not wait if he believes I have them all. This can be over quickly."

She nodded slowly. "And will you offer our fellow lords the same kindness you offer me?"

His voice was hard and unrepentant. "No."

She nodded again.

"He will come if he does not find them with me," Hrokr said. "He will raid you and take it for himself."

She laughed. It was warm like the sand beneath the sun, not a hint of cruelty behind it. "A way with words, you are."

He grinned. "I speak only the truth."

She sighed, though her smile remained. "I know you do. Very well. Stay with us for the night, and allow my guests to socialize with you and your new mate. We will discuss it in the morning."

We will have it, Hrokr projected to me. *She just wants to play with you.*

"I'd love to," Hrokr said.

"Lovely," she chirped, grinning at me. She rose to her feet, clapping her hands together. "Mingle as you wish, but do come splash about for just a while. You lot are always so snow-kissed. I'll make sure my staff has a dinner out by the end of the hour."

Hrokr bowed his head. "Your hospitality is always noted."

She grinned before offering me a tiny wave goodbye and voidstepping into nothing.

Hrokr let loose a breath, sagging against me. "Thank the Elders."

"Do you think she'll say something to Ivaylo or Cornelius?" Maddox asked.

"I don't know. I suppose it doesn't matter. It will come out eventually."

I frowned, drawing his eyes. "Is this dangerous for your people?"

His face gentled. "Valencia has already lost many people to Garbhan and his wiles. At least this has the potential to be the end."

As I digested that, he rose to his feet. "I suppose we should go out," he said, casting his eyes over the beach beyond.

"I'm so far ahead of you," Fallon laughed, shucking her pants off and kicking them into the corner. Maddox stripped beside her.

My eyes flashed to Hrokr's but he only laughed. "Children, they are."

Fallon—stripped down to a pair of bright white shorts and her simple, black shirt—chased a shirtless Maddox out onto the veranda. They both voidstepped only to reappear running out on the beach.

I turned to Hrokr, finding that he was watching me instead. "What?" I asked, a nervous laugh bubbling through my lips.

"Nothing," he murmured, smiling softly. He stepped out onto the veranda himself. When I stayed behind, he nodded me over.

Standing together in the doorway, we watched Maddox sling Fallon over his shoulder and launch her into the tide.

I could hear her laughter from here.

"They're so happy," I whispered.

"I know," he whispered back.

I met his eyes. "Are you not?"

He studied my gaze. I wondered if he would open up, if he would answer honestly. But he only said, "You sure won't catch me splashing like a goose."

I laughed, turning my eyes back toward the starry beach.

"Do you want to go down?" he asked, voice softening.

"Shouldn't we?"

"We can do whatever we want. We are Lord and Lady of the Hall."

I cocked a dark brow. "Lady?"

"My mate, remember?" he said softly, but there was something earnest in his eyes. "It comes with the territory."

"Right," I breathed, choking on a relieved laugh.

He rested his back against the post, facing me fully as he crossed his arms. "Does the thought of a crown scare you, Thea?" he asked. His voice was a dark lull, begging me to be honest.

I straightened my spine. "Not at all."

There was a long break of silence before he laughed, his eyes twinkling with mischief. "Come on," he said, offering his hand to me. "Let me show off my bride. We'll take the scenic route."

I appreciated him. I knew this was something we had to do to explain my presence, to keep me safe in at least some way. But still, I appreciated that he treated it like something light and easy. Like a game we could both enjoy playing.

I laced my fingers in his and let him pull me through the suite. His fingers were warm, his callouses scraping against my own in a way that felt more real than the refined, smooth skin I'd expected.

Our room wasn't attached to the main palace, I discovered, but a small spire off the main building. He led me through a hallway made of glass walls and ivory latticework, a view of the lapping water extending forever to our right.

Once we stepped outside, I reveled in my bare toes slipping through the sand. We must have been on the tip of the coast—or perhaps some kind of island—with the way the water surrounded us. Once we headed toward the beach—and I could see the lights from our suite shining down on us—I found the ocean extended as far as I could see. It was too dark to see if water bordered us to the south, but north, east, and west were all an undulating, endless sea.

As we entered the throng of beach-goers, many of them recognized Hrokr. Bows of deference, warm waves. And an infinite number of curious glances at me, the woman with her fingers wound in his.

We slowly gathered more eyes, but Hrokr seemed at ease with the attention. I supposed it was no more than he experienced daily.

Are you alright?

"Just strange, I suppose."

He chuckled. *They're just curious.* Aloud, he asked, "Do you want to swim?"

"We are both a tad overdressed, don't you think?"

"Easily rectified."

I flushed even as an accelerated drumbeat in my chest told me to worry. I couldn't bear my skin to all of these people. The last thing I needed was to be outed as the Heir, here of all places.

Though for a moment, I saw how easy it could be. I'd painted a target on my back already. And even if I hadn't, Gar had done it for me.

But all I said was, "I thought you didn't want to splash like a goose."

He laughed—a loud, boisterous thing, warm as it wrapped around me. He stopped walking and turned to grin at me, eyes glittering like the stars around us. "Thea."

"Hrokr."

"Do you want to swim?"

I answered honestly. Semi-honestly. "I do not want to be as nude as Fallon on a beach in front of a thousand strangers."

I heard that, she projected. *And there aren't a thousand people here. You're more dramatic than Crow.*

"Please tell her to stop eavesdropping on me," I said primly.

Hrokr chuckled, and even above the soft roar of people and ocean, I could hear Maddox and Fallon laughing too.

Something inside me eased.

Hrokr's eyes studied me from head to toe, a slow perusal with mischief brewing in his eyes. His fingers came to the throat of his evening shirt, deftly unclasping buttons.

"Hrokr," I cautioned.

But he only grinned. Before I knew it, he was standing before me with his bare feet in the sand, pants rolled to his knees, and bare-chested. I wanted to shove him or maybe run in the other direction.

But on his shoulder, front-faced, was his crest inked upon his flesh. Reservations—and perhaps all propriety—forgotten, I stepped up to him. He must have sensed the shift in me, because his body went entirely still.

"It's beautiful," I murmured.

He stiffened as my fingers met his flesh, sucking in a sharp breath. I paused, but he whispered, "Go ahead."

I leaned farther into him, tracing the edge with my fingertip. Beautiful. It looked so similar to mine, as if they were meant to be inked in a certain style. Thin lines were made in a perfect, crisp black. Mountains and a river in the sky.

But his chest was moving heavily beneath my palm. My eyes flicked up to find him studying me, his lips parted. I suddenly remembered how his entire court parted around him like water, how much he disliked being touched by *anyone*.

I suddenly remembered this was all a game. "I—" I began as I retracted my touch. But then I was yelping—yelping because he had bent and scooped me into his arms, throwing me over his shoulder. My fists thudded into the muscle of his back, warm beneath my hands. "What are you doing?" I hissed.

"Swimming."

My lips parted around a choked cry. "In my *dress?*"

He shrugged, a feat with me on his shoulder. Water splashed about his ankles.

"Hrokr, I'm serious."

"Thea, I am serious, too."

He began to shift me, to slide me down into the water, but my nails dug into him for purchase.

He laughed, the sound rumbling against me. "Can you not swim?"

"I can *swim*, I—"

He dropped me into the water. Admittedly, it was not a full drop, as his arm stayed tight around my waist. But I still glared at him, mouth open and aghast. Thankfully the dress was light and gossamer, flowing around me instead of clinging like silk to my legs.

"I cannot *believe* you."

He grinned, wading out into the water with his fingers twined with mine. "I think we make a fun lord and lady, don't you?"

"I think that just because Valencia doesn't have any beaches doesn't mean you need to force me into your desire to play in the water."

"Valencia has beaches," he said, chuckling. "There's a still pool right to the north of Castle Habrem."

A wave crashed over us both, sending me careening into his chest. It soaked my hair, leaving it plastered to my face. He steadied me, smiling. "Isn't it better this way?" he asked. *When you need only worry about me, and not the masses watching you?*

"They are watching me," I hissed.

He smiled, his cheekbones and wet curls gilded by the moonlight. "But you forgot," he whispered.

I searched his eyes, the rich starlight that rivaled even the bare sky above us. Dragging my eyes away, I flushed and marched up onto the beach.

Out of the water the dress clung to me, slick across my body. I leaned to the side, wringing my hair out if only to avoid thinking about how close we'd just been.

"Would you like some help, love?"

His eyes were open and earnest. Ornery. "No," I said.

He laughed, something he'd done a lot of tonight. *Thea, there's no need to be flustered. I—*

"I am flustered because my hair probably has seaweed in it, and—" my fingers touched my cheeks, coming away black with kohl. I huffed a wordless sound.

"When did you get so vain?" he asked, but there no was no bite behind the words. In fact, he sounded entirely amused.

"Maybe I thought being your mate would entail less frolicking."

"Have you met me?"

I laughed. I couldn't help it, the small sound that bubbled past my lips. He used the moment to capture me around the waist, his hand warm against my bare skin. "Are you mad?" he whispered, lips twitching as he used his magic to pull the bulk of the water out of my hair.

"Not mad," I admitted. "You're the one that has to be seen with me and my half-drowned glory."

He snorted, capturing my chin in his hands and tilting my head back. His thumb brushed about my eyes, smoothing me back into clean lines. "You're still beautiful, Thea," he murmured.

The words gave me pause. They gave him pause, too. And suddenly—bargains or not—the grounds felt entirely too small, his skin entirely too warm where it rested against my own.

I could feel his breath against my lips, nearly taste him on my tongue. A glorious show, put on by the set of skilled puppeteers we were. A drama to bewitch the masses, and pray we did not bewitch ourselves.

He glanced at my lips.

I thought he might really do it, and I thought I might really let him.

He straightened suddenly. "Come on," he said, voice rough.

As if summoned—and perhaps they were—Maddox and Fallon bounded over to us, dripping and disheveled themselves. "Hrokr," Fallon chastised. "You did *not* take that poor girl into the water." Like a true mother, Fallon huffed and marched over to me, pulling me out of his grasp. "Let's get you out of the dress at least."

My panicked eyes flashed to Hrokr's. Sure, he thought me only too prude to be stripped in front of strangers, but he protected my tattoo nonetheless. He shoved her off playfully. "She's fine, Fallon."

Fallon gave me a look, but I only flushed and nodded.

She groaned. "Fine. I'm going to get us food."

Maddox plopped into the warm sand, stretching out on his back. Someone had taken Hrokr's shirt and boots from where he'd haphazardly discarded them, and I wondered if he'd get them back.

He too laid on the sand, beckoning me down. Hesitantly, I followed, stealing a glance at Maddox beside us.

He looked unconcerned, only star-gazing and whistling some tune I'd never heard.

As Hrokr pulled me back against his chest—his arms loose and comfortable around me—I couldn't help but think perhaps swimming was the better choice.

Company came. I sat between Hrokr's knees, reclined against him. There were only a brave few who dared approach us at first, but throughout the night, many came by just to say hello, to get their look at the novelty that was the Lord of the North's mate.

It was awkward at first, sitting stiffly against him, all too aware of the almost-moment we'd shared earlier. It was made easier when Fallon returned with a tray of salt-dried fish and wine.

I wrinkled my nose.

"Try it, you *baby*," Fallon jeered. "You'll like it."

I did. It was good, but I wouldn't admit that.

Unsurprisingly, I recognized none of the Gentry Fae that stalked over to offer bows and well-wishes. I doubted I'd ever see any of them again. As the moon made its way across the sky, and too much wine settled in my belly, I found my eyes drooping.

Hrokr shifted behind me, his voice at my ear. "Are you tired?" His gentle thumb stroked a long line down my arm.

I shrugged—even as a stripe of gooseflesh painted my skin—eliciting a soft chuckle that reverberated against my back. Fallon and Maddox eventually gave up with sitting still and were now dancing in a big group closer to the suite. But there were still plenty of people milling about, feasting their eyes on us.

Ciri even made an appearance, though she did not speak to us.

I let my eyes fall closed and reclined fully into his chest. Hrokr's arms were warm around me, stroking me gently.

Luring me into a balmy sleep.

CHAPTER FORTY-FOUR

HEAVENS

T he next morning, the four of us made our way through the royal palace
toward Ciri's receiving quarters.

Our private breakfast had been quiet and easy despite the start I'd woken with.
I woke in a warm bed with a swath of pale blonde hair in my mouth, but it was
only Fallon, snuggled up against me after Hrokr carried my sleeping body in from
the beach the night before.

She and I wore matching dresses of easy, gauzy white as we strolled between the
towering sandstone pillars toward Ciri's dais. Maddox wore a loose linen shirt,
unbuttoned to soak in the warmth of Gloriala.

Hrokr looked the same as he always did, happy to find that last night's boots
had been returned to our room.

He walked beside me now, setting a brisk pace past the ivory metal-clad guards.

Ciri's dais was smooth, white stone, and the throne atop it was a sharp slab of
marble. Breezy curtains of teal and vibrant orange hung between the final pillars,
bringing warmth to the immediate space around her.

She leapt from her seat, beaming a greeting in her native tongue as she strode for us. But as she stepped up to Hrokr and I, her troubled eyes belied her warm greeting.

"Old friend," she said.

Hrokr reached out, grabbing my hand and pulling me to his side. "Yes?"

She noted the movement. "Have you consulted the Elders about your endeavors?"

His starry gaze narrowed. "You know they do not speak with me freely, Dromnael."

That was news to me, but I tried to keep the surprise off my face.

"They've always spoken."

"And have they spoken to you?" he challenged.

I squeezed his fingers gently.

"They have been silent of late," she said softly. "Which is worrisome. After I retired last night, I consulted them once more. I have heard nothing."

He straightened his spine, every inch the dark leader of the north. "Keep the Orb if you wish, Ciri."

"I fear I am being cruel," she admitted, eyes flicking between my face and Hrokr's. "I believe your threats, Crow, and I should not wish war on my doorstep."

"War is coming to mine anyway," he said darkly. "It is no burden. In fact, it will ease my own mind."

She nodded slowly, murmuring, "Very well."

She led us forward through a teal curtain and deeper into her throne room. We emerged into a small lounge of sorts, filled with more relaxed furniture and signs of use. A runegate sat in the corner. "Spelled with blood," she said. "I'll be back."

She stepped over the gate and returned just as fast.

It was anticlimactic.

The Orb was just a small gold ball, not even the size of her head. She held it unceremoniously in one hand. "A little thing," she chirped. "Strange that the world has been torn apart for it."

"It's always the little things we'll burn the world for," Hrokr said softly.

Ciri's olive eyes rested on me. "That they are." She took a deep breath and marveled at the Orb. "And you wish only to hold it, Crow? Or should I expect a visit from a ghost?"

He stiffened nearly imperceptibly—something I felt more than saw. But he said, "Worry not, it is only the bait I wish to lure Garbhan with. I prefer to let the dead lie."

She nodded and held the Orb out to Hrokr.

He released me to hold it, staring at it as if it held all the world's secrets.

Perhaps it did.

"I'd ask that you voidstep straight from here," she said. "So as not to catch any eyes."

"Of course." He offered a solemn bowing of the head, saying, "Thank you again." His gaze touched mine for the briefest moment. I felt Fallon's cool fingers wrap around my arm as Hrokr disappeared.

Ciri's eyes narrowed at the smoke he left behind, something puzzled shifting in her expression. "Thank you again, Lady Ciri," Fallon said, bowing low at the waist.

I swallowed my yelp as Fallon's nail pricked my skin before she sent us careening through space.

We landed together in the Portal Room, Hrokr standing in the doorway, already Orb-less. Maddox materialized quickly.

"Another easy victory," Hrokr said. Though his tone was blase, there was something rigid in his body that undermined it. "We can convene tomorrow regarding how to address the people. For now, I'd like a bath and some rest without listening to Fallon's snoring."

He left without another word—without meeting our eyes—and while Fallon laughed, and Maddox joined in with teasing, I couldn't help but feel like something was wrong.

CHAPTER FORTY-FIVE

TAKE IT

I currently felt like I was intruding, but I forced my feet to carry me to the Council Room. It had only been a few moments, but I suddenly was reminded of my outsider status and feeling incredibly distant from the others in the room. This was such a far cry from the last day we spent together.

The Cardinal Council was painfully silent as Gyda and a few other staff flitted about the room, setting the table.

Gyda offered me a warm smile that I did my best to return.

When the room was cleared but for us, Hrokr sat at his place at the head of the table. "So that was a success," he said gently.

"Then what's wrong with you?" I bit.

No one laughed—no one chided me.

He studied his steak and red wine, toying with the stem of his glass. "While we always have fun in Gloriala, we now have some unfortunate business to attend to."

Everyone nodded silently, as if they knew what was to come. Perhaps they did. When no one thought to clue me in, I said, "And that is?"

"Address the people. Tell them war is imminent."

I flinched, even my flesh recoiling from the thought. It was such whiplash to go from our cheery time last night to this.

Haizea shifted in her seat, drawing her hood up around her ears as if she could hide within it. "The people are going to riot, Crow."

"No, they won't," he said openly.

"They love you," Ciro pushed. "But good times make for weak men. Such is the price to pay for being the benevolent ruler you've been."

"Why would they riot?" I asked softly.

Ciro nodded tightly. "The birth bans have them angry. Afraid. They're terrified of Silas. They remember Cadmus and Araceli, Hrokr."

His eyes were cold. "Do you think I don't know that?"

Silence.

"It's fine," he continued. "I have a plan."

"Do we get to know it?" Fallon lightly teased, offering a half-smile that no one bothered to return.

"I'm going to offer them the option of going home."

It was a strange thing, the silence that deepened the room. Three thick heartbeats of pure silence, silence so thick that I felt it lifting the hair on my arms.

It was Maddox who said, "That's suicide."

"Not to mention impossible," Fallon chimed in.

"Not impossible," Hrokr said, which had me definitely concerned about the suicide comment.

"You don't even know where the Heir of Aphaedia is," Haizea pointed out.

Everything inside of me went so, so quiet.

It was a long, terrifying moment before Hrokr spoke gently. "I will find them."

I prayed to the Elders that no one could hear my heart, hear it threatening to burst through my chest or rupture the veins in my throat and wrists.

"And if you can't?" Ciro challenged.

"I will," Hrokr nearly growled. "How can you all possibly think he wouldn't want this? He will have his Hall. He will rule."

Wrong.

Wrong, wrong, wrong.

The prophecy had not been fulfilled. I didn't know what Hrokr thought he was going to do, but it wasn't going to work. And it would be ceding *everything* to tell him.

"And if he doesn't want to share his Hall?" Haizea snapped. "If he doesn't want to take the Aphaedians back?"

"Valencia has done *everything* for Aphaedia," Hrokr said harshly. "And now we need the Heir's help."

Silence.

"And if he doesn't want to give it?" Haizea asked.

The stem of Hrokr's glass shattered beneath his hands, toppling the wine and sending it pooling across the table. No one dared move to right it. He leaned forward, shadows coiling around his throat, leaking from his fingertips. "Perhaps I will take it from him."

I was going to be sick.

Vomit. I was going to actually vomit across the table.

I tried to breathe.

You made a mistake, my soul screamed at me. *You let someone else in, another someone who just wants to use you to cut someone else.*

Gar wants you to cut Hrokr.

Hrokr wants you to cut Gar.

Perhaps I will take it from him.

Smoke began to burn my palms. I shot to my feet, suddenly commanding every eye in the room. "Thea?" Fallon rasped.

I shot from the room.

I knew it brought attention, but there was nothing else I could do. If I lit the table on fire... Well, there would be no talking myself out of that one.

I ran down the hall and up the stairs, taking them two at a time. My hands were still burning, I—

I threw myself into my room, slamming the door shut behind me. I rushed to the bathtub, running my fingers beneath cold water. It was only then that I realized I was crying, fat tears rolling down my cheeks and dripping down into the water.

Had I done it again?

Had I truly let in another monster?

"No," I whispered aloud, but I wasn't sure who, exactly, I was pleading to.

I couldn't accept that Hrokr was the same. Hrokr *wasn't* the same. But he was still something happy to use me.

I wondered if he'd still be content to tear my Hall from my hands if he knew it was *mine*. If he knew that my face was the one that he was wronging.

Refusing to let myself think about it, I turned the water off. I dried my shaking hands, thankful when they did not burn the towel into smoking embers.

Right on time, Fallon materialized in front of me.

"Thea, what is wrong with you?"

I covered my tear-stricken face, curling away from her. "Get out," I snapped.

"No," she said firmly. She knelt down, jerking my arms away from my cheeks. "What is wrong?"

I did my best to control my breathing and not lose myself to a fit that would leave her burned.

And so I lied, with a sour, oily feeling in my stomach.

"What he said is *wrong*, Fallon."

"*What?*"

"I grew up in south Ekin, you know," I told her, hoping I could dig myself out of this lie in the end. "We heard stories about the Heir. He does not deserve to have it *ripped away* just because Hrokr values his own people more."

She reeled back, her eyes flicking back and forth between my own.

Oh, Halls, I felt sick.

"How are we supposed to hate Garbhan for the crimes he's committed in the name of his own mate and dreams if we are to do the same?"

She flinched.

"I will not stand for it."

"You do not have a choice," she spat, recovering herself. "He is the High King, the Lord of the Hall."

"He is not my lord," I snapped, rising to my feet to tower over her. "And I will not commit atrocities beneath his name."

Her lips parted on unspoken words. For the first time since I'd known her, Fallon Blightbringer did not know what to say.

"Get out," I hissed.

To my astonishment—and if I was willing to admit it, dismay—she did.

CHAPTER FORTY-SIX

THREE

G yda brought me dinner, a smoked salmon on a bed of rice pilaf. Likely instructed not to, she didn't pry.

I took my dinner on the balcony off the bedroom, watching the city of Fairshroud move beneath me. Once or twice I thought I saw a crow, and wondered if it was him.

It didn't matter if it was.

I studied the archway of the balcony, trying to imagine her here.

Mavka.

Gar's mate, Hrokr's slaughtered betrothed.

But she only led to thoughts of Gar, reminding me I would not be the first woman in Valencia's bridal quarters sacrificed to Hrokr's glory.

Do you want to come over and talk? Hrokr projected softly, as if he knew my thoughts had circled back to him.

I didn't.

Enough time passed that I found myself inside, curled into an armchair before a low-burning fire.

Thea. I spoke with Fallon. Let me explain.

I wished he could hear me when I whispered, "No."

Three days passed.

Three days of complete silence. Three days that Gyda brought me meals I took alone. Three days I saw no life but her and the far-away bustle of the valley city. I missed my family. I missed Sage.

I missed her fussy crooning, her child-like fingers soothing my hair.

But I found myself all alone, unable to find the will to seek them out.

Always alone.

But on the eve of the third day, Hrokr's voice reached me. Tentative, this time.

Cornelius accepted our invitation. We will be traveling to the Hall of Flesh and Blood soon. Before that, I must make for the Isle of the Elders, where Aphaedia's Orb is stowed.

You are welcome to come with me.

I frowned at nothing.

Swallowing my pride, or perhaps donning it, I changed and made my way downstairs.

I didn't allow myself a moment to pause outside the Council Room door. I thought if I did, I might lose my nerve. So I burst inside.

Fallon did not meet my eyes—whether out of anger or shame, I wasn't sure. Haizea didn't turn either, and Ciro kept his eyes trained on the meal before him.

Only Maddox offered me a weary grin.

"Where is he," I said flatly.

One of them must have summoned him, because he appeared beside me. He looked wretched, his dark eyes resting in a bed of bruised plum. His cheeks were gaunt, his eyes far away as if he hadn't slept.

I told myself not to notice.

"When do we leave?" I asked.

"Thea—"

"When."

He searched my eyes, his hard to read. He somehow looked equal parts guilty and angry as his throat worked through a swallow. "It will be an intrusion any time we go," he said. "So whenever you'd like."

My nostrils flared. I did not want his kindness. I knew the answer should be *now*—but suddenly, I couldn't face him. "I'll meet you here in the morning."

Silence.

Long, thick beats of silence.

"Alright."

I spun on my heel and marched out.

Later, I told myself that it was tears of anger that wet my pillow.

CHAPTER FORTY-SEVEN

MUSIC

O utfitted with a belt of throwing knives and a long dagger at my thigh, I stood outside the Council Room door. I was in dark gear, sporting a drawn cloak and boots to my knees. It felt almost strange to again be dressed for war, but I did not know what to expect on the Isle of the Elders.

When I finally found the courage to step inside, Hrokr was dressed similarly, his cowl down around his neck. His restlessness was even more pronounced today, and he offered me only a silent nod.

We did not speak as he led me out of the Council Room and down the hall to the portals. There was a new one, fresh runes at the back of the room. We stopped before it, and he offered me his hand, ready to cross over together.

I ignored it, stepping unafraid into the unknown.

I was met immediately with watery sunlight filtering into a cracked, stone structure. We were on top of a large spire, an ocean on all directions but one. A steep hike and an entire forest away, lay a crumbling castle of moss-blanketed stone.

When he appeared, I said, "You couldn't have set the runes closer?"

"No," he said solemnly. "I could not."

I huffed, holding out my palm. "Fine, let's get it over with."

"I cannot voidstep with you," he said. "The grounds are warded. This is as close as we get."

I stared out across the expanse, my stomach sinking. I'd hurt after, but I could handle the physical toll. It was the emotional toll of spending however many hours alone with Hrokr that I did not want.

"Is no one else coming?" I asked.

"Are you so afraid to be alone with me?" he snapped back.

We held each other's eyes for a long moment. With a huff, I started down the crumbling stairs.

A long trip it would be.

A long trip it was.

We walked in a painful silence for hours, until I was sweating even though the grounds were chilled with winter.

We trekked down to the lowest part of the island, stepping over fallen logs and storm-split boulders. Though swatting heavy branches and dancing around rocks helped keep my body busy, my mind could not help but suffer the pressure of silence between us.

It was hours before that silence was broken.

"We should take a break," he said softly.

"I don't need a break," I snapped. "Do you?"

He stopped walking anyway, holding my eyes for long moments. "Thea, please."

"I have nothing to say to you," I said baldly.

"I know you think what I said was monstrous—"

"It *was* monstrous," I hissed.

He took a deep breath, eyes flaring. He resumed his path.

The forest was even larger than I'd thought, and we were still walking when the sun began to sink behind us, bathing the world in oranges and purples. The only thing I'd eaten had been a few strips of dried beef that Hrokr had offered, and I'd grudgingly accepted.

He ate nothing.

We reached another drop in the terrain, and if I accurately gauged the distance, we'd be at the castle by the end of the hour.

I was not looking forward to the walk back.

I started down, and Hrokr started with me. Traipsing side by side, he said, "You shouldn't presume to know my intentions, you know."

I whipped my head toward him. "Excuse me?"

"You think you know everything," he said plainly, swiping limbs out of his way as his boots crunched over dried leaves. "You don't."

Bait. He was baiting me, trying to make me angry enough to engage him. I hated that it worked.

"I heard what you said," I said sharply. "It wasn't really open for interpretation."

"Perhaps I lied."

A crude snort tore past my lips. "Perhaps."

He stepped atop a log, hopping down playfully as if he had not a care in the world. It was a new tactic, I could admit.

"She loves music."

My footing stumbled.

"I think the Heir is a woman, to be honest. It's quite sexist to assume it's a man," he continued cheerily. "Most everyone does."

I said nothing, using all my focus to keep pace with him.

"She loves music passionately—*desperately*," he continued, still swatting limbs.

"What?" I asked, breathless.

"The first time she killed someone she cried. Assassins were after her, and she had no choice. But still, she mourned them. Cried all night long. I learned that one through a dream."

Everything inside of me turned cold. "What are you saying?"

He ignored engaging me, speaking only as if he had an audience to deliver to. "She takes away bits of my darkness," he said. "I wonder if she even knows it. I keep it at bay as best I can, but sometimes I feel myself slipping. I feel myself letting the weight go when I cannot hold it alone any longer. I hope she knows I don't mean to send it to her."

My steps slowed, but he kept going. I rushed to keep up.

Finally, he turned his eyes to me. "The Triplet Halls share a strange bond, you know? A kind of kinship. It is a massive concession that Ciri would place her allegiances to us above it.

"I assumed the Twin Halls—Valencia and Aphaedia—did not share such a bond, because I've never felt it before. But then one day—I did. For five years, I did. It was just a small thrumming, a strange awareness that someone else in this world was tethered to me.

"I looked everywhere," he continued. "Trying to find her, trying to understand what it was that I felt.

"But then the strangest thing happened. It became nearly painful to bear, and I knew something was wrong. There was so much rage and fear inside of her."

Oh, Halls. *Five years.* Was he describing the death of my parents?

"I tried so hard to find her," he said, eyes flicking to mine. "It spiked on that worst day of her life—and then it vanished. I searched for it, searching for it for so long I thought I'd drive myself mad."

There was something in his eyes, something he was begging me to recognize. Silence.

"And then what?" I asked in a small voice.

"I gave up."

My brow furrowed. "Why?"

"Because I had no desire to be a burden on her life."

My throat was thick, my heart cracking within my chest.

"But after long, painful years—it came back. And I realized then that I had no idea how old she was or where she'd been. She was hidden from me behind a ward, and was only slipping out of it intermittently."

My chest ached.

"I lied, Thea." He stopped walking, turning his body toward mine. "I will take nothing from her. But if she wished to have her Hall returned to her, I would restore it."

"How?" I rasped.

He waved a hand, as if the information were nonconsequential. "Long prophe-cy, longer story. But my family took in her people when Aphaedia fell. Some of them *want* to go home. Perhaps she wants a Hall, perhaps she doesn't. But I owe it to my own people to try. I owe it to her to offer her her birthright."

I was reeling.

My lips parted. Closed.

He took a shuddering breath. "Her soul is pure. I would hope that when we find her she would recognize my soul enough to trust it."

I fought the tears collecting on my lashes. "Why haven't you told your Coun-cil?" I whispered.

"They wouldn't understand," he said softly.

"I—"

I didn't know.

As if he sensed it, he held his palm out to me. I laid my shaking fingers in his grasp and let him pull me against his chest. He held me tight, his fingers smoothing my hair, his chin resting atop my head. He whispered nothing but my name.

I felt ill with guilt, but only clung to him tighter. When we finally pulled away, he brushed away my tears with his thumbs. And even though there were no prying eyes or eager courts, he held my hand the rest of the way.

When we finally reached the grand, wooden doors of the crumbling castle, Hrokr released my fingers. He took a deep breath and rapped the knocker against the wood. The door was unlatched, only resting against the frame, and he was careful not to push it open any further.

"What are you doing?"

He gave me a quizzical look. "Well, I'm not just going to barge in."

My stomach sank. "Is there someone inside?" I whisper-shrieked.

His eyes widened. "Isle of the Elders, Thea, what did you think? I—"

"You may enter."

The smooth voice came from within, carrying an authoritative edge that seemed to thicken the air around us.

Throwing me a strained glance, Hrokr pushed against the door with a steady hand. I was still reeling as the hinges creaked, the door swinging open to reveal an aged, dark-haired man with a groomed beard.

Hrokr—to my immeasurable surprise—dropped into a steep bow that nearly had his nose touching the floor.

But all I could see was the man. A man I had seen before. He was dressed the same way today that he had been that fateful day in Wyn's bar, his fingers still wrapped around the head of his clear-gold cane, his dark eyes still watching me with a preternatural understanding.

I could feel the power roiling off of him, just the same as I had then. But all I could hear was the blood pounding in my ears. "You," I hissed. "You were the—"

Hrokr immediately leaned up, grabbing me by the back of the cloak and ripping me down to my knees beside him. "Apologies, my lord," he said, nose at the floor.

Thea, what the entire hell is wrong with you? he practically screamed in my head.

But the man chuckled, causing Hrokr's entire body to freeze up. "Let her speak, child. I think I'm interested to hear it."

Hrokr's eyes flicked up, bewildered. It was a strange look on him.

I rose to my feet, staring the man—the Elder—down. "Why?" I cried.

"Why are you angry?" he asked instead, leaning on his cane.

"You *know* why I'm angry!" I cried, fat tears brewing in my eyes. "You could have sent me anywhere, and you sent me to *him.*"

"Perhaps I sent you here," he offered.

"No," I rasped, backing a step away. No, this man was an *Elder,* and he had sent me to my doom in Vanadey. He had sent me to find Gar, to be brutalized and heartbroken, to be imprisoned. To suffer the loss of my mother and the emotional crippling of my siblings.

"You knew," I accused.

He nodded sagely. "Yes."

"Then how could you?" I sobbed, tears pouring readily down my cheeks.

"You found your family," he said. "You found your *true* family, and you kept your life. I told you that I did not wish to see the St—"

"Stop," I blurted.

The Elder chuckled, and Hrokr looked like he was ready to murder me.

But I remembered the words he'd spoken that day.

I do not wish to see the Starsea lineage ended before your Hall has its chance at rebirth.

Hrokr couldn't hear those words.

"Both of you," he said as he studied us, chuckling. "Full of so many secrets."

Hrokr and I eyed each other warily.

Hrokr stepped forward, angling me behind him slightly. It did not escape the Elder's notice, but he did not appear offended. In fact, now that the adrenaline was fading away, I couldn't believe I'd just lived through this encounter. This one or the first in Wyn's bar.

"Lord Dolga," he intoned, and my stomach nearly fell out of my back. "We come for a favor."

"I know why you're here, Stormblood," he said. "Take it."

Hrokr rose to his full height stiffly, reaching back to hold my hand. He carted me inside, past *Dolga* who only grinned. Inside was only the shell of a room, a space of open nothingness and grey stone. Barren, except for another gold Orb that said on a table.

It had been waiting for us.

Hrokr plucked it up, shoving it inside his cloak. Turning back to Dolga, he dropped again into a bow. Rigidly, I followed.

"Thank you," he said. "We apologize for our crass intrusion."

Dolga laughed. "So respectful you've always been, Lord Stormblood. You have your hands full with this one."

My head snapped up, but I found that I was not looking at an Elder, but only the far wall of the Portal Room in Valencia. Hrokr rose slowly, taking in the space around us.

"At least we didn't have to hike back," I said.

"What is wrong with you?" he hissed, wide eyes boring into my own. "Do you even know who that was?"

"Well, I do now!"

"Why would you speak to him like that?"

"Why wouldn't you *tell me* that we were on an Elder's front porch?"

"You are unbelievable, Thea. You—"

A voice sounded from the hall. "Lovebirds are home early!" Fallon, grinning like a cat.

Hrokr voidstepped away. Only to reappear a second later with the bulge of the Orb gone from his pocket. "I'm surprised we are back at all," he quipped without missing a beat. "Thea verbally accosted Dolga on his own doorstep."

"Ha!" Fallon barked. "And I thought she had balls for standing up to *you.*"

He stared.

And then laughed. It was something wild and feral, a relief from the danger of the last few moments. It had me laughing. It had me saying, "I'm sorry. I met him the day Gar attacked me in Ekin. He sent me to the Guild. He could have saved me a lot of heartache."

But perhaps Dolga was right. In the end, he'd sent me here.

Hrokr's face only gentled, and he pulled me into a loose embrace.

CHAPTER FORTY-EIGHT

PIANO

I was too tired for real company. Too retroactively afraid of how I'd treat-ed Dolga this afternoon. But I was at peace after hearing Hrokr's story about—well, me.

There was something within me, something that I tried not to think about, but knew was coming.

I took a long bath and combed through my hair, content to flit about my room and drink wine in the peace of an orange silk robe—until I heard soft music coming from the hall.

It was piano-forte, a sound I'd not heard in long months. Barefoot, I slipped out into the cold, drafty hall. The door to Hrokr's quarters was shut tight, but the music wasn't coming from his room. It came from farther down the hall. I'd never been that way, but I made my way across the cold, stone floor and silently up the short steps into the tower.

There he was.

It was an open spire, all three exterior walls exposed to the night beyond.

He didn't notice me.

He wore loose dress pants over bare feet, and a black evening shirt that appeared to be unbuttoned with how it lay. His back was to me, bent over the keys as he played a most heartbreaking melody.

I could hear his breathing between notes, hear how much of himself he gave to it. I stayed for long moments, head resting against the stone pillar to my right, listening to him play for himself and only himself.

Tears wet my cheeks.

When his playing finally paused, I took a step into the space. He turned instantly, quite surprised to find me from the look in his eyes. The silver moonlight painted his flesh, turning him into something equal parts eternal and ephemeral.

"Thea."

"You're wonderful," I said, smiling as I wiped my tears. "I haven't heard piano in so long."

He studied me from head to toe, his starry eyes taking on a faraway look. "Do you play?"

"Cello."

He spoke as he rose, closing the cover over the keys. "It suits you." He turned, resting his back against the piano, studying me.

Gone was the kind friend of today. In his place stood someone I almost didn't recognize. Wintry moonlight gilded his flesh, running unfiltered down the open expanse of his chest. His breathing was calm, even. Hrokr often went through mood swings; I wasn't sure why I expected his good mood to last after we'd returned to Castle Habrem.

He was quite obviously upset.

The harsh, sharp line of his jaw was telling, as was the tightness limning his shoulders.

But I deserved his anger, I knew.

"I wanted to talk to you," I said softly.

His eyes were knowing—cold—as they studied my face, boring into my own gaze. He took a breath, gripping the wood of the piano behind him. "About what?"

"About storming out of the Council Room."

He only stared, his face devoid of any of the kindness or forgiveness I'd expected after this morning. When it was apparent he wasn't going to respond, I said, "I am—"

"Do you think I don't know who you are?"

His words—they took a moment to process. They settled deep in the pit of my stomach like jagged rocks, heavy and sinking. The frigid air from the open tower was suddenly too cold, pebbling gooseflesh across my skin.

"What?"

His eyes danced with a wicked kind of starlight—hurt, but cold with triumph. "I know exactly who you are, Thea Starsea. I have for a long while."

"But you said—"

"I know what I said," he interrupted sharply, nostrils flaring.

I searched his eyes, studying the hurt, guard, and accusation etched across his features. "I don't—I don't know what to say."

"You had plenty to say earlier."

Amidst the cold, mind-numbing shock was a lick of hot anger. "You said you'd take my Hall from me."

"As if you even care about that, Thea."

The words were a slap—sharp and stinging. "What?"

He shoved off from the piano, towering over me even from feet away as he straightened to his full height. "I shouldn't have said what I did in the Council Room," he said, though his tone was far from repentant. "But all I wanted was to push you—to get you to admit it."

My mind was reeling. I felt too small as he took one, single step toward me, and the wind began to whip around the tower. His eyes were too bright, as if there were freshly born stars rupturing within them. As if the darkness now leaking off his skin in inky tendrils had drained straight from his eyes.

And even though I'd come to tell him just this, I felt the high of anger taking over me. "You wanted to *push* me? By threatening me?"

"Threaten," he scoffed darkly, shaking his head. "Look me in the eyes and tell me you honestly believe I'd hurt you, Thea." Without even giving me a moment to do so, he stepped farther into me, forcing my head back as I held his angry stare. "Say it. Tell me that after all I've done, you *truly* believe I'd rip your Hall out from beneath your feet. Tell me you honestly believe you're only a means to an end, Thea. Say it."

"Hrokr—"

"Because you had no problem," he seethed, "comparing me to the man who murdered your mother. You were so wholly dedicated to your own cowardice as to compare *me* to the man who held you captive. Who imprisoned you, lied to you, held your family in chains."

"I—"

"You had no problem," he said, lips peeling back from his teeth, "comparing me to the man who killed Orion. Inina. Ciro's child. My father. The man who hunted me across Halls and tore my mother's head from her shoulders."

I threw up mental bricks between us, fighting to seal him away from myself. "Then why say what you said on the Isle of the Elders? Why show me the kindness at all?"

He was heaving, his breath coming in great, heated pants. "Because I truly believed that if I gave you my *honesty,* you would return the favor."

"I came here to do that," I cried.

A muscle feathered in his jaw. It was anger he tried to project, but I could see the pain etched on his features.

Betrayal.

And truly, had I not betrayed him?

I took a wobbling breath, tears brewing in my eyes. "This isn't fair," I whispered.

"I don't want to hear about fair," he said.

The tears broke free, warming my cheeks. His expression softened for only a moment, but I could see him fighting it.

As if he wished to cling to the anger.

"I was scared," I admitted, my voice cracking through the jagged tears sawing through me. "I saw my birth parents murdered. That *spike* you felt fifteen years ago, Hrokr?" I snapped, watching his eyes grow wide. "That was my mother hunted for being the Heir."

He gentled further, something like shame flaring in his eyes. "Thea—"

"They killed my father first. Ran a blade through my mother's chest. Mellian's mother was my handmaiden, and had sworn her human life to my mother's rule."

Silence fell between us as I hiccuped a sob and wiped tears from my eyes.

"The crest is inked on my hip, Hrokr. A crest that got both my parents killed. A crest that has made countless ghosts of my loved ones." I took a shaking breath. "My siblings don't know."

He shook his head, processing.

I dared a step closer to him, so close I could smell the storm on his skin. "I never told him," I whispered.

Hrokr's eyes widened.

"You asked me what reason I could have had to hide my body from him? I've never told *anyone*, Hrokr." I raised a shaking fist and planted a finger in his chest. "And I came here to tell *you.*"

"Thea."

"Can you imagine what he would have done to me if he knew, Hrokr?" I cried, dropping my hand. "I should never have compared you to him, and for that, *I am sorry.* But I loved him, Crow. I loved him, and he tore everything from me. Can you even imagine what it did to me to hear *you* say you wanted to *rip away my Hall?*"

The slimmest line of silver collected on his lashes. His voice was thick with unshed tears when he rasped, "I'd never hurt you, Thea."

Unsure if I was angry, heartbroken, or terrified, I grabbed his hand and squeezed it against my chest. "I know," I whispered, searching his eyes.

His free hand cupped my face, brushing away my tears.

My eyes fell closed as I took a step away from him, dropping his hand and fleeing his touch. Trying to steady my racing heart, I said, "No one left alive has seen it."

My fingers trembled as I gripped the hem of my robe. My eyes fluttered open as he sucked in a sharp breath. Gingerly, I pulled the robe above my hip, bearing the soft, black underwear I wore.

And my crest, proudly inked upon my flesh.

I held up my other hand, allowing a ball of flame to grow and flicker within my suddenly-steady palm.

And though we knew, I said the words aloud for us both to hear. "My name is Thea Starsea, and I am the Heir of Aphaedia."

He fell to his knees.

"This is it, Hrokr," I said, softer now. I let the fire die in my palm and lowered my hand to my side. "This is what I've spent my life trying to outrun."

His fingers were slow—giving me ample time to pull away—as he reached for my skin. I remained still, allowing his fingers to brush what no other had.

He traced the Queen's Crown constellation inked within the crest, and my heart thundered in my chest—loud enough for us both to hear.

Fresh tears warmed my cheeks.

His calloused fingers slid reverently down my thigh and curved around the back of my knee. He lowered his head in something like reverence, resting his forehead against my skin.

I released my robe, letting it fall softly back into place.

With his head resting against my thigh—with his body on its knees—he whispered, "You don't have to try and outrun it." He leaned back to behold me, silver in his eyes. "Not anymore."

My face crumpled further as the moment crashed over me. I began to lower myself to him, but he rose to his full height and wrapped his arms around me, lifting me off my feet and crushing me against his chest.

I clung to him, crying into the crook of his neck as he held me aloft. "I wanted to tell you," I whispered into his skin. "If there was anyone I trusted enough to tell, it was you, Hrokr."

He held me tighter, setting me gently on my feet. "I know, Thea," he murmured.

We both began to pull away at the same moment, twisting into one another. We paused with our noses nearly touching, sharing a moment of warm, tentative breath.

His hands were shaking as one slid to my lower back and tugged me closer, the other moving to cradle my face. His fingers tangled in my hair as he held me.

Breast to breast, bodies intertwined with limbs and breath and fear, his nose touched my own.

This moment was a feral animal between us—something we both wanted desperately to tame and not to be mangled in the process.

My eyes lifted to his, finding him staring with half-lidded starlight. His lips parted on a soft breath that coasted along my own.

My entire being narrowed to the feeling.

Hrokr tilted his head, and pressed a lingering kiss to my cheek. Soft eyelashes—both his and my own—fluttered against my cheeks.

When he pulled back, my skin was flushed and my lips parted, but a soft smile turned his mouth.

It was slight—so subtle I wondered if it was truly there.

"Goodnight, Thea," he murmured, voice thick.

"Goodnight, Hrokr," I whispered.

He didn't voidstep.

I listened to his steps as he made his way down the hall.

As he hesitated just outside his door.

And only once the door latched behind him did I raise my fingers and brush where his lips had just been.

CHAPTER FORTY-NINE

CROWDED

I t took long hours for my body to drift into sleep, but finally, the soft black found me. When a gentle knock sounded at my door, I lurched out of bed with my heart in my throat.

But it was only Gyda, arriving to prepare me for the day's festivities.

I now stood in the Council Room, my palms sweating. Gold pins held the fabric at my shoulders. I was wrapped up in the black fabric like a little present, everything black panels, black gossamer, and golden cinching at my waist and shoulders.

Every muscle in my body clenched to the point of snapping when Hrokr pushed open the Council Room door. All I could see were his half-lidded, starlight eyes; all I could feel were his fingers on my skin and his lips on my cheek.

But he appeared to be content and well, striding right to me with a soft tilt of his warm lips.

"Hello," he said, ignoring the rest of the Cardinal Council who stood silently in the room.

He was resplendent beside me, though a bit more wild than he'd been on our trip to the Heavens. He wore a navy button-down open to nearly his navel, and his sleeves were pushed up to his forearms. Rings and dark polish adorned every finger, and his boots shined bright over his dark leather pants.

"Why am I always dressed so plainly next to you?" I teased.

He smiled—a brilliant thing that displayed his fangs. "Because my power is in my might—and yours in your ferocity."

Before I could question what—exactly—that meant, Fallon bounded over to us with a wide grin on her face. "Are you two ready?" she chirped, adjusting the off-shoulder sleeve of her navy and gold gown.

In response, Hrokr offered me his arm. I laced my own through it, and let him lead us to the Portal Room. Maddox—in a garish, red suit—followed along.

Haizea and Ciro remained.

"Are they staying here?" I asked.

"No," Hrokr replied. "They are going to get the Hall of the Elements' Orb."

I cocked a brow as we crossed the arching entrance of the Portal Room. "Forcefully?"

"If need be," he replied smoothly. Flashing another bright grin, he gestured to the runegate. "Ready?"

Maedonia was something far different than anything I'd ever seen.

It was beautiful in a grim, dark way. Stilted, leaning buildings crawled high toward a foggy, overcast sky. Everything was cast in varying shades of grey—either from the cloudy evening, age wearing away the colors of paint, or a combination of the two.

Crowded was an understatement. It was packed, people shoving up against us all, unconcerned by our bodies being in the way of where they were going. The people were too close and the buildings built too tight together. Even the sky was thick and pressing.

There was no room to breathe here.

I spied every manner of creature. Goblins, grigs, nixies, sprites, Fae, and a whole slew of people that I had no idea *what* to categorize them as. Scales for skin, lizard eyes, thick fluffy tails, antennae.

No one looked a day over twenty-five.

It didn't smell bad, exactly. Folk didn't give off the same earthy, decayed scent as humans. But I could smell many bodies, tangling into a perfume that was hardly breathable.

The cobble roads were cracked and busted, the buildings broken and repaired with sloppy patchwork. It was a mess.

"This is the capital?" I asked.

It was Maddox who said, "You wouldn't guess it, would you?" He shivered. "I hate this place."

I could imagine.

"Don't worry, we are going underground," Hrokr said. "Cornelius enjoys things nice and neat. The city itself is only hard to maintain because of the overpopulation. The palace—Wyndmere—is quite nice.."

"Overpopulation?" I repeated, even though it was evident with the packed bodies.

"No birth bans," he said. "And Flesh and Blood is the home of the healers. There is only so much he can do to stay on top of ever-multiplying, never-dying people."

"They die," Fallon said darkly.

Maddox laid a comforting hand on her shoulder.

"Why didn't we voidstep straight there?" I asked.

"What is an entrance if not grand?" Hrokr purred.

Fallon laughed at that, tearing off to lead the way down the crowded road. Maddox caught up to her quickly, and none of the passing Folk seemed to care at all that Valencian royalty was in their midst.

They likely had no idea.

"Did you tell anyone?" I asked softly.

Hrokr's fingers found mine, winding together gently. *No. You are only my Thea for tonight,* he said. *Your crown is your own to wield as you see fit, but I would suggest making your announcement after we have retrieved the Orbs.*

I squeezed his fingers in agreement.

We finally came to a stop before a large mausoleum-looking building. It was a closed gazebo of grey stone, nearly swallowed by the moss encapsulating it. Hrokr slipped inside unceremoniously, pulling me along with him. We entered into a narrow, damp stairwell of crumbling cobblestone bricks.

"I assume this isn't the commoner's entrance?" I asked, trailing my fingers against the slimy rock wall.

Hrokr snorted beside me. "Wyndmere has a grand entrance, but I'd prefer to avoid the crowd."

As we winded down the spiral path, voices began to carry from the bottom. Once we reached the lowest landing and stood before a polished, ebony door, Hrokr turned his head toward me, smiling down his nose.

"Ready?"

I nodded, straightening my spine. It would be both better and worse than visiting Ciri in the Hall of the Heavens. Here, Cornelius's opinion of me didn't really matter at all.

We weren't giving him a choice.

Tonight would be easy. But tomorrow—tomorrow we would heap a weight of danger upon our heads.

Even if we were able to fool Cornelius—which was doubtful—Gar would know exactly where the missing Orb had gone.

Hrokr pushed open the door, and dull, flickering light washed his alabaster skin into shades of gold. He pulled me through, and we entered immediately into a throng of well-dressed, easily chattering citizens. Same as the streets above, there were more than just Gentry Fae here.

Antennae, tails, slit-pupiled eyes, and webbed fingers.

"Lord Stormblood!" a young—or looked to be—girl exclaimed, dropping into a hasty curtsy. She bowed so low that the furry, white antenna atop her head swept the ebony marble floor.

There was a catch in the conversation, a low pulse of silence as the other attendees dropped into respectful bows—though none quite as low as the girl before us.

As she lifted her head, she offered a shaking grin from behind black bangs. "Welcome, my lord. I hope your travels fared well. Fallon," she said, nodding behind me. "Commander Maddox." But when her eyes finally made their way to me, only a confused puckering of her dark brows.

"Thea," Hrokr supplied for her.

Her eyes went as wide as the wrought iron chandeliers above us when he slid his arm around my waist, tugging me to his side.

She dropped into another quick bow. "Lady Thea. Right this way."

She rose and took off through the throng of attendees. When I looked up at Hrokr, he was smiling ahead, confident and easy in his stride. "Lady?" I whispered.

His grin grew wider.

I've not yet informed them of our matrimony. It is only what she assumed you to be.

Without another word, our party of four followed her past dark paneled walls and flickering sconces until we reached a massive arched door as tall as Castle Habrem's. It was black wood, carved with grim scenes and the faces of monsters. Two knockers of burnished bronze crafted into leering gargoyles stared at us with beady eyes.

The doors were propped open, leading into a dining hall with a comically long table dressed with a scarlet runner.

There was no attention for the heads of the table, as it seemed that all the action was in the center.

I recognized Cornelius from my time in Hrokr's head in Asena. Seated on the left side of the center of the table, he immediately turned toward us. "Friends!" he exclaimed, waiving us over. "Come. Come sit."

He was far from me, at least twenty spaces, but I heard him as surely as if he stood beside me. Hrokr's fingers trailed across my back as he gently nudged me forward.

We made our way across the fray, and Fallon and Maddox peeled off to whatever wayward plans they had for the evening.

But as soon as I had the thought, Fallon's voice entered my head. *I won't be there to save you tonight. But I wanted to let you know I love you, just in case you die.*

A bolt of fear raced down my spine, and Hrokr's eyes shot to me immediately, even though his movements were still fluid and graceful.

Almost as if he'd felt that lick of fear burn through me.

Fallon's throaty chuckle filled my mind. *Look at you two. Relax. Dying is a real possibility, though. I know I'd be at risk of dying if I had to endure a night of conversation with Cornelius of all people.*

As the panic leaked out of me—and Hrokr projected a lazy eye-roll—I realized there was one word of her teasing that I wasn't able to tuck away as I stood before the ancient eyes of the Lord of the Hall of Flesh and Blood.

Love, she'd said.

My chest felt suddenly tight.

"Friends," Cornelius repeated, spreading his arms wide. "Hrokr. Who have you brought to my home?"

"This is Thea," Hrokr said, pulling out an ornately carved chair for me.

I sat as gracefully as possible in such an uncomfortable situation as Hrokr stood behind me.

"And she is your—"

"Mate."

And—ruse or not—there was a bite of thinly veiled aggression behind the word, a bite that said more than his words needed to. A bite that said what his centuries of actions had already shown.

Hurt her and you will not live to regret it, the bite said.

Nervous glances flitted down the lavishly filled table, made only tighter by Hrokr's easy and loose movements. He sat in the chair beside me, a picture of perfectly irreverent grace.

Legs folded, chin propped on a disgustingly ornate fist.

"I thought after all this time perhaps you would not find your mate," Cornelius ventured, eyeing me carefully.

"Good things come to those who wait," Hrokr said.

After a heavy moment of stilted silence, Cornelius laughed. It was an aged, wheezing thing. "Yes, they do." He snapped his fingers in the air, gesturing over his staff. "Please. A new bottle for my old friend and his new bride."

I eased as the staff rushed away. Even as all of Cornelius's assembled stole open-faced glances at me and Hrokr over the spread of meats, sauces, wines, and bread.

"Is this where you chose to debut her?" Cornelius asked, smiling. "I am honored."

Hrokr offered a warm smile in my direction. "She was the one who wished to visit. Thank her."

His dark, beady eyes turned toward me. "Well thank you, my dear. It is a pleasure."

"The pleasure is mine, my lord," I said gently.

He beamed.

But there was something heavy beneath that shine. Something that spoke of mischief. Or perhaps malevolence. "Will you have a public ceremony?" he asked.

Hrokr shrugged—a lazy lifting of his broad shoulders. "Perhaps at home."

"I'd love to see your home," Cornelius said.

I was unsure what to say. And Hrokr did not seem to feel the pangs of social discomfort. He was content in his raw silence.

But down the table, Maddox dropped a heavy elbow on the table, clattering forks and dishes. "Will you wear a new sack of skin if we invite you?"

I giggled.

It was there and gone in only a moment, followed by an immediate schooling of my features. But Hrokr's lips turned into an easy smirk.

Sorry, Maddox projected happily, winking at me from down the line of guests.

"Spritely, she is," Cornelius said, and I could have sworn he sounded impressed.

But Hrokr's eyes narrowed. It was hardly a disrespect—and I did not take it as such. But he glared all the same.

And I realized it was because they would not talk to *him* this way. So why would they to his mate?

"Whatever you decide," Cornelius said in the soft din of the dinner roar, "I would love to attend."

"Your kindness is noted," Hrokr said smoothly.

"Speaking of our long friendship," Cornelius hedged, leaning over onto the table. "I have lost contact with some of my old friends in your court."

Hrokr did not miss a beat. "I have closed my borders."

"Your borders are always closed," a woman with flowing golden hair said from Cornelius's side.

I fought the urge to stiffen. I was not sure who she could be to speak to Hrokr so baldly. He must have noticed, because he projected, *A member of his Council. He treats them as equals.*

Aloud, he said, "A full seal, for now."

"Is there trouble on the horizon?" she asked, the tan brow between her blue eyes furrowing.

But Cornelius laughed. "Do not fret, my dear. I've no doubt he only intends to hide his bride away for a while."

Old words rang new in my head.

They will tear you apart if they think it will hurt me.

Would they cross you?

If they thought me weak enough to hide you.

Perhaps it was brash—foolish—but a lie tumbled easily from my lips. "Not for me, lord. I won't be there."

A flicker of surprise—of interest and approval—speared from Hrokr.

Cornelius's eyes flicked between Hrokr and me. "No?"

"No," I said, delicately crossing my legs. "I have matters to attend to outside of the Hall."

His eyes narrowed with a mixture of surprise and confusion. "You would leave your Hall unguarded while you are gone?" he asked Hrokr.

Hrokr chuckled—a smooth, frigid sound that skated along my bones. "I think you and I both know that my Council is more than enough to guard my home."

A beat of silence passed between them—a beat of scarred history.

"But no, my people will not be without their lord. I'll be home."

HALL OF THE BETRAYED

"You would separate from your mate?"

"When duty calls for it, if I must," Hrokr replied, letting his eyes rake over me with leisure.

With claim.

Cornelius nodded in acquiescence, holding his hand out to retrieve the bottle of wine his servant returned with. He opened it, pouring the three of us each a glass.

"A frightening thought," Cornelius muttered, tipping his glass back to stain his lips.

"A lonely thought, I suppose," Hrokr said, unfolding himself to serve both me and himself from the mounds of food between us. "But frightening not. She is more formidable than I."

The old man chuckled. "No need to be humble in my company, friend."

Hrokr's body did not so much as feather a muscle, but I felt the shift in him. I laughed, laying a proprietary hand on his thigh. "Have you ever known him to be?"

Cornelius's feathery brows shot up. But a rough laugh escaped him. "Perhaps she is more formidable than one would think."

Hrokr's eyes flicked quickly to the hand on his leg before settling back on Cornelius. "Perhaps she is."

I pulled my fingers back into my own lap, but they felt warm from where they'd touched him. I fought against the blush that raced to my cheeks, but they both noted it.

Cornelius chuckled. "Formidable *and* bashful."

Hrokr's lips twitched into an easy smile, but his eyes were heavy. They tracked my flush carefully, a thousand thoughts spinning behind the stars in his eyes.

I wondered what they were.

I wondered if I knew.

CHAPTER FIFTY

HONEST

D inner crawled by at a snail's pace. Chatter devolved into talk of old memories and vague questions about my history that I danced around. As the night prowled forward—as I slipped around more questions and did my best to match the easy arrogance of Hrokr beside me—I felt something shift within him.

He thawed beside me, leaning more heavily into my space, not backing away from letting his skin brush my own. But something coiled tighter within him.

Restlessness.

He was tired of being here.

As was I.

As if he read the thoughts from my mind, he again rested his chin atop a lazy fist. "Cornelius."

The name cut through the center of conversion without regard for social propriety.

Hrokr did not care.

Cornelius paused his discussion with his advisors, turning his head toward Hrokr. "Yes?"

"Forgive me for retiring early, but I fear that Thea and I are reaching the end of our night."

Cornelius placed a weathered hand atop his dark-clad chest, positively affronted. "So quickly? Come. Let us at least retire to the lounge for a while."

Hrokr glanced at me, letting me decide.

"Perhaps I have a bit of night left in me," I said with a smile.

Cornelius clapped his palms against the table, pushing to his feet. "Lovely. Let's go!"

As if the entire table was waiting on Cornelius to wrap it up, everyone immediately leapt to their feet. People filed into a thin door behind us, disappearing quickly. Hrokr rose to his feet, offering me his hand. His palm was warm against my own. On our feet, he wrapped that hand around my waist, skimming bare skin and lodging my heart in the hollow of my throat.

Are you going to dance with me? he asked, leading me leisurely into the dark den.

"Maybe," I whispered.

His thumb rubbed a small circle into my waist. *I won't bite.*

A heady flush bloomed beneath his palm, speering to my cheeks.

I wasn't sure what I had imagined inside, but it wasn't this.

A string quartet took up notes as soon as we entered, the music gentle and soft. The floor underfoot was black marble, the walls a dark wood paneling. It was dim within, the only light granted by flickering candlelight in wrought iron chandeliers and burning sconces.

But I needed no other light than what was burning within his eyes as Hrokr suddenly turned us, clutching me to his chest.

A faint gasp escaped me, and he chuckled softly.

"Surely you are familiar with how dancing works, no?"

Some of his first words ever spoken to me—a lifetime ago.

His eyes glimmered beneath the firelight, his lips turning into a soft smile as he remembered, too. I thawed into his embrace, laying my head on his chest as his arms came around me.

He laid his cheek atop my head, more holding me than any type of dancing. Long moments passed, other dancers sweeping their partners onto the floor. An entire number passed before he spoke.

"You're doing better than you think, you know."

My chest tightened. "I'm only following your lead."

His fingers combed through the ends of my hair. "I don't mean the dancing."

"Neither do I."

We didn't share more words—as none needed to be spoken. But he held me, swaying softly with me through the dark night. Multiple songs passed, but I did not grow tired of the circle of his arms. Perhaps I'd spend the entire night this way, wrapped in the envelope of his warmth.

When another number ended, his fingertips skimmed against my spine, eliciting a soft shiver. "Would you like something to drink?" he murmured.

"Sure," I said just as softly.

As I pulled away to see him, his hands kept me close. He studied me, drinking me in as if he were cataloging every freckle—every errant hair. And when his eyes dropped to my lips, they parted for him.

He met my eyes for only the shortest moment.

Asking.

I was preternaturally still, as if even a breath would shatter the moment.

He leaned—so slowly—bending his head until his nose brushed my own. I could taste his breath—as sweet and dark as the eternal night that bloomed around him—on my tongue.

I wondered if it would be just like last night, another gentle press to my flushed cheek.

But last night had been true and unguarded. The mask holding me tonight—it did not need hesitation.

He closed the distance. His lips were full and soft, warm with unspoken whispers, tender as they moved against my own. His kiss was gentle and full of an eternity of trepidation.

And when I kissed him back, he pulled me even closer. My fingers coasted up his chest, finding his hair and tugging him farther into me. And when my lips parted—desperate to taste him just once before our game was over forever—he took my offer greedily.

So soft.

As if I were made of dreams and freshly blown glass, as if this moment were a flower between us—desperate to be watered and terrified of drowning.

He paused. A heady moment in which I drank down his ragged breath. My lashes fluttered open to find him studying me with half-lidded eyes the color of rupturing stars. And then his palm was sliding up my spine and plunging into my hair as his mouth slanted over my own.

Hungry and raw, as if his desperation were not a show—as if it were as real as my own. He kissed me hard, tangling long fingers in my hair and making a sound low in his throat that had me choking on my own heart.

I was drowning in him, eager to be swept away by his tide—never to be reclaimed again. His free hand covered the entire expanse of my back, clutching me desperately as if we could melt into one right here.

I'm not sure how we would have stopped—how I ever would have wanted to—but the decision was made for us. An aged laugh reached our ears, and Hrokr's fingers curled into me so hard I wondered if he would break my skin.

He pulled away, tucking me against him as he faced Cornelius. There was something wild and archaic in Hrokr's eyes, something *angry*—as if he wished to draw fight on the man in the center of the lounge.

Cornelius chuckled, taking a step back as I clung to Hrokr's chest. "Forgive me, lord," he said, bowing his head. "It is so rare that new pairings are conjoined, I forget how heightened your sense of propriety becomes." He made a show of taking a second step away.

Hrokr's eyes narrowed.

"I came only to tell you your room is ready if you still wished to retire."

Hrokr blinked as if coming out of a daze before plastering on his usual lazy grin. "Thank you, Cornelius. It is getting late." His arm loosened around my waist.

Cornelius smiled. "I'll have someone escort you."

Hrokr nodded his thanks, his breath still coming too quickly for his naturally unfazed demeanor. "And we will see you in the morning?"

"I wouldn't miss it."

Hrokr's touch was violently possessive as he held me to himself, following the dark-haired, antennaed faerie that had first greeted us. The other dancers gave us a wide berth, and I was sure I saw tendrils of inky darkness peeling off his skin, only to be swallowed by the dark corners of the room.

On the way out we passed Maddox and Fallon—

Grinning like a pair of fools.

Our walk was stilted. Once we left the tight enclosure of the den, Hrokr released me only far enough to lace his fingers with my own, and I thought I could feel his pulse within them. Our guide said not a word, but her gait was rushed and off-kilter.

We made her nervous.

We walked down a long, silent hallway and up a long flight of dark, stone stairs. Once in the residential wing, we passed many closed doors. Of course, we were afforded the one at the end, behind massive, arching doors locked tight. The faerie turned, dropping into a quick bow to us both before offering her key to him.

I took it from her fingers.

Hrokr's eyes cataloged the movement.

"Goodnight, my lord and lady," she said, and walked so quickly she might as well have run down the hall.

Hrokr took a deep breath, releasing my hand to run his fingers through his curls. When he held his palm out for the key, I handed it over and watched in careful silence as he unlocked the door.

We stepped inside, finding nothing more than what we could have expected. The room was grand, soft in the colors of Castle Habrem—an ode to our visit. Slate-grey walls and intricately carved wooden floors paired gently with the wall of windows extending onto the ceiling and offering us a view of the sprawl of Maedonia beyond. A massive bed sat against the glass, its wrought iron frame twisted into a labyrinth of latticework. Between the bed and an ebony-shelved wet bar stood a polished wooden table set, adorned with only a cut crystal decanter of whiskey and its matching glasses.

We stood there, the moment still and thick and heavy between us.

A large door of ebony wood was propped open to a lavish bathing room. Hrokr ran another hand through his hair.

"I'll run you a bath," he said and disappeared inside, shutting the door behind himself.

I used the moment to fight my racing heart. I pulled the door shut behind me and stood in the center of the room, wondering what exactly it was that was coursing through my veins.

In a daze, I removed my shoes, finding the polished mahogany cool underfoot. The sound of running water carried to me, loud enough to cover the rapid beating of my heart. Barefoot and alone, I stepped up the window, pressing my fingers against the cool glass.

Hrokr was gone far longer than he should have been. I spent the time watching the flurry of Gentry Fae and winged creatures flitting through the streets.

I didn't hear him—didn't even hear the creak of the bathroom door opening—but I felt Hrokr's presence behind me.

"Fairshroud is a much better view," I said gently.

He stood close, his breath coasting along my neck as he let out the first note of a breathless laugh. "It is."

Only as I turned did he take a step back from me.

We stood in a silent stalemate, gauging each other's reactions.

"I hope it's alright," he said softly, voice roughened. "That I kissed you."

Warmth slipped down my spine. "Of course," I said, albeit a bit breathlessly.

"It's better," he said, "the more real it looks."

"Right," I whispered.

"Right."

Silence.

It wasn't uncomfortable. No, it was charged and painful.

Hungry and afraid.

But not uncomfortable.

He leaned in suddenly, and I froze, my breath catching. So close that I could smell him, that I could taste him again if I dared. But then I heard the rough scratch of him sliding a glass toward him across the table.

"I'd like a drink," he said, never pulling his eyes from my own. "Perhaps you'll join me for one after your bath."

"Alright," I said softly.

It was a dismissal—and one I knew I should head. He needed space, and perhaps I did too.

It smelled like him.

Dark floral notes, accented by the petals floating around me. I tipped my head back, staring at the dark marble room, the flickering candles mounted to the wall beside me. I closed my eyes, trying to let the warm water seep down to my bones.

It was only a kiss.

A fake one at that.

But I couldn't help brushing my fingers against my lips, couldn't help but knowing I'd spend the night sleeping beside him.

When I finally found the courage to dry myself and step out in the soft, grey sleeping clothes left on the counter for me, I found him standing against the window, watching the city below with a glass of whiskey held by his fingers.

He didn't tear his eyes from the glass, but his free hand pulled out the chair. For me.

With a racing heart, I crossed the space, sitting with him at my back. In silence, he reached over me, pouring me a knuckle of golden liquor. The gentle drop of his glass against the dark table was loud in the roaring silence of the room.

I stiffened as his fingers were suddenly skimming across my neck, brushing my hair away.

"Do you want me to dry your hair?" he asked, voice thick.

"Alright," I whispered.

My fingers shook as I reached for the whiskey. But his fingers were steady as he combed through my hair, twisting it into easy curls the way Gyda often did. But his fingers were warmer, softer.

I drained my glass by the time he was near to finishing. As my glass settled against the smooth tabletop, he paused. "Are you upset?" he asked.

"Why would I be?"

Another curl between his fingers. "I didn't ask your permission."

"Did you think you didn't have it?"

He was still and silent for a long moment before he resumed his work. It was answer enough.

He knew.

He cleared his throat gently. "I can have Cornelius get me a separate room, and—"

"Are *you* upset?" I interrupted, twisting to face him.

He studied my face, his cheeks flushed, but eyes dark. I saw it the moment his guard snapped into place. The moment he hid once again—though this time not behind a wall of liquor and shattered bottles, but instead behind adamant will and cruel arrogance.

"It was just a kiss, Thea."

I narrowed my eyes, trying to ignore the sting his words slapped against me. "A fake one at that," I said curtly, turning my back to him.

I felt his regret as surely as if he had projected it. "Thea—"

"What."

"Don't be angry—"

"I have every right to be!" I snapped, whirling back around. I spoke far more harshly than the situation called for, but his eyes were not surprised.

He waited, but I held my tongue, trying to breathe through the tears I could feel closing my throat.

After a long moment, he finally asked, "Why?"

"Because you *do this*, Hrokr."

He took a slow breath. "Because I do what?"

"You open yourself up and then you regret it and you lash out. Treat your Council however you see fit, but you will *not* treat me that way." I stood, my chest rising and falling in heavy, rapid breaths.

He cocked a dark brow. "Because you decree it so?"

"Because I *see you*, Hrokr. I see what you have not allowed them to."

His nostrils flared as he took a step closer. "And what is that, Thea?"

I flushed, straightening my spine. "That you are *afraid*. Of love, of companionship. But you want it so desperately. *I will give it to you.*"

Wrong words to speak. He shoved his vulnerability away, but I could see it writhing from within, fighting like some archaic beast itching to burst forth.

I wanted it to tear free.

"I will give you friendship, Hrokr," I said, trying to control my wild breathing. "*Real* friendship, not something that you have to hide from."

"We *are* friends," he said, curling his fingers into fists. "I don't know what you want from me, Thea."

Yes, you do.

But I tilted my head back, glaring. "I want you to calm down."

"I don't know why you think something is wrong."

"Look at you," I said, waving a hand in his direction. "It was a *kiss*, Hrokr, it—"

"And it meant nothing," he snapped.

I paused, fighting the emotion swimming inside of me, surging through my veins. "Of course it meant nothing," I said icily. "None of it means anything, right?"

His nostrils flared again, the only physical flick of the anger rolling off him.

"But I think it's you who doesn't know that," I pushed.

His eyes narrowed. "Thea—"

"No," I said airily, waving another angry hand at nothing. "You're the one with the masks, Hrokr. You're the one who has spent the last five centuries *pretending.*"

"You know nothing of who I've been," he growled.

"Don't I? I think you're a liar. I think you know what you want, but you're too afraid to take it."

"And what is it that I want, Thea?"

"Truth," I said baldly. "To be honest enough with yourself that you don't believe your own lies."

He searched my eyes, his chest falling erratically beneath his broken breath. "I know who I am. I know what it is that I want. And I know that it meant nothing."

"Prove it."

He paused, a hitch rupturing his breath.

"Kiss me," I said harshly. "If it really means nothing, why not do it again? Why not let *anyone* in your Hall so much as brush your shoulder? Why not—"

His mouth was hard and claiming against my own—hot and angry—a blade his emotion had whetted.

His arm reached behind me, knocking glasses and whiskey bottles to the floor where they shattered against the marble, spraying us in shards and liquor.

His arms came around me, holding me close to his chest as his boot kicked both the table and the chair out of the way. And then my back was slammed against the glass wall, his fingers in my hair, protecting my head. His mouth never left my own.

He didn't wait for me this time. His lips forced mine open, his tongue sweeping inside and tasting of golden liquor and pitch-dark secrets. His hands were everywhere.

My hair, my back, my hips.

And I was kissing him back, whether I'd made the conscious decision to or not. I was clay in his hands, molded to whatever he asked me to be. He pulled away only to meet my eyes for a heavy, charged moment. His were dark and glittering—endless with the urge he'd given himself over to.

I said nothing, only dropping my eyes back to his lips.

But those lips...

They curved into a cruel smirk. He took a sudden step away, leaving me on unsteady feet.

Even though he was flushed and fighting for breath, he still appeared far more composed than I felt.

"And you say it is *I* who does not know how to be honest." He leaned forward, gently pressing a chaste kiss to my still lips. "Do not hide behind your assumptions of my desire to justify something *you* are asking for."

I flushed, pressing my back into the glass wall.

I knew he saw the hurt flash across my face, I felt it within him. But his face recovered its composure, not belying the angst and pressure I could feel building within him.

"Do *not*, " he said haughtily, "speak to *me* about lies."

And then he was gone. Spinning on his heel and marching through the heavy room, slamming the door behind him.

CHAPTER FIFTY-ONE

ALIVE

I didn't cry, though part of me wanted to.

I wasn't even sure why.

I knew it was fake, and knew I had pushed him into doing it. I waited at the table for half an hour for his return—but he never came.

I finally crawled to the bed, curling beneath the black silk sheets.

I didn't want to think about my lies, or about the words he'd thrown like stones. I embraced the dark that pulled me under.

Good, he thought. *She's finally asleep.*

He leaned his head back against the rough brick wall, listening to the patter of the rain beyond. He was just under an awning, the splashing rain still wetting his boots.

He'd only narrowly avoided Fallon and Maddox, who always seemed to smell when he was in a bad mood. They'd seen him, but he'd lost them now.

Fallon burst through the front door of Wyndmere. From the street, the door looked just like the other dingy building fronts of this overly crowded street.

Fallon looked right at him, but she didn't see Hrokr. She saw only a tired man in faded roughspun.

Exactly as he wanted to be seen.

Fallon huffed a breath, turning back inside, presumably to look for him.

"He's not out here," he heard her say.

Maddox grumbled something unintelligible, and then the door was shut.

Hrokr let the glamour fall away.

He groaned aloud, studying his hands.

He could still feel her beneath them.

Foolish, he knew it.

To let her get beneath his skin, to let her push so much farther than she should.

But that had always been Thea's way, hadn't it? To push him into something that he hardly recognized anymore. He knew it was wrong to be as cold to her as he'd been, but what was he to do?

He didn't want to think about her flushed and arched against him, or the way she was so warm but tasted like the first light of dawn beneath the winter. Tasted like the earthy grounds of raw desperation—and it was so sweet.

My friend, he told himself. It was all she wanted—and all that he wanted her to be.

He hung his head, burying his face in his hands.

Perhaps he should have let Fallon and Maddox find him.

But he knew what they would say—what they'd said for nearly six hundred years. He didn't want to hear it.

He didn't want to hear the sickly sweet lies he knew they believed were truth.

Hrokr ran a hand over his face and drew himself to his feet. He could feel Thea, her even breathing.

He could even feel her hurt, though she was unconscious. He knew he deserved to bear it.

He pushed open the door, hoping to slip back into their room as unceremoniously as possible.

He knew he deserved to hear her words, but that didn't make them any more palatable. It was wrong to bring her here, to bring her into any of this.

To take any part of her at all.

Fake or not, it didn't matter how he felt.

It was too late, and this job was going to hurt her. He knew it as surely as he knew each intake of her breath, three stories above his head.

But when he finally slipped inside, she at least looked peaceful in her sleep. Her lips were pursed just so, still swollen from the assault he'd waged on them nearly an hour ago. A delicate flush coated her cheeks, not yet swallowed by her sleep.

He should sleep in the tub or even on the floor, but he didn't want to. Not tonight, not when he'd have to hold her and parade her as his wife in the morning. He should drink the rest of the wet bar dry to try and smooth the sharp, aching pieces inside himself. But he didn't want to do that, either. Not now—not when he knew how it would end.

He laughed softly—at himself, at the world, at the deck of broken cards he'd been dealt. He kicked his boots off and unbuttoned his shirt, tossing them recklessly on the floor.

After changing quietly in the bathing room, he sat gingerly on the bed beside her.

I jerked awake.

"I didn't mean to wake you," Hrokr said softly, perching on the edge of the bed.

Gone was the heat of our last moments shared, and now he only studied me with a melancholy look in his starlight eyes.

I'd had the strangest dream, I'd—

My eyes flitted past him, landing on the pile of discarded clothes by the bathroom door.

Not a dream at all. But our bond truly had allowed me to slip inside his mind. I wondered if he knew. Surely not—or he would have thought it while I was within.

"You didn't," I lied, turning my eyes back to him and trying not to study the moonlight bleaching his bare chest.

He cracked a half smile. "You don't have to lie."

"Why did you hide from Fallon?"

His brow puckered. "Did she come find you?"

I blinked, looking down at myself. "I—no."

Shock flitted across his features, but it was gone much more quickly than I would have expected. "Did you come to me in your sleep?" He asked the words easily, as if they were not a surprise at all.

"Is it me who came to you?"

He shrugged. "I suppose it does not matter."

"Has this—have you slipped into *my* head before?"

Hrokr turned his head from side to side. "Kind of."

It didn't terrify me the way it should have. "A Hall's bond is that strong?" I asked.

He sighed, pulling a pillow into his lap. "We could talk about magic all night. You should get some sleep, Thea. I'm sorry I woke you."

"Don't you need sleep?"

"I will."

I took a breath, trying to still my racing heart. Perhaps I was pushing him again, but this time it was genuine. Honest.

I pulled the blankets back, opening them for him. "Stay," I said. I even scooted away, giving him the room that I could. "Don't be tired tomorrow. And... I'm sorry."

His face gentled, a look that had everything within me turning warm. He reached out hesitantly, brushing a lock of hair back from my face. "Don't be sorry," he murmured. "I'm thankful you want to be my friend, Thea, thankful you want to be... honest."

He gentled himself down beside me, leaving a healthy distance but lying on his side to study me. "*I* am sorry, Thea. I didn't mean... " He paused, trying again. "I shouldn't have been so cold."

I offered a half smile. "Don't worry, Hrokr. As long as you're honest with yourself, I'll be honest with myself too."

His expression turned troubled at that. Troubled, but not angry.

But it was enough for tonight, what I'd already said.

I let my eyes flutter shut, taking the scent of him deep into my lungs as I drifted back into sleep.

I woke in a room aglow with the gold of fresh dawn.

I couldn't even be surprised that our sleeping bodies had reached for one another.

Hrokr still slept, breathing low and even. His head was pillowed on my chest, one arm wrapped beneath me, the other lying on my stomach, rising and falling with each of my breaths.

I knew I should wake him, and should move before I did. But for now, I studied his face, so much less troubled in his sleep. The sunlight—pouring in from both behind us and above us—burnished his chest and reflected every tiny dust mote in the room.

It was only so peaceful because of who my legs were tangled with.

But this was not Castle Habrem.

A mass of bustling could be heard from every direction. There was scuttling in the halls—shouting, whooping, and calling in the streets behind and below me. This city was alive in a different way than Fairshroud.

Hrokr stirred against me, stretching. I released my hold, letting him blink up at me.

When he met my eyes, neither of us moved. It was silent and soft, peaceful in a way that didn't have to be shattered. I thought he'd speak, but he didn't. He only gentled himself down beside me, studying every inch of me beneath the morning sun.

I thought maybe I'd like to stay this way forever.

And he seemed content to do so as well. He even reached out tired fingers, paused, and let them continue on their way to pick up a strand of wayward hair. He rubbed it between two fingers, watching the sunlight bring out the hidden tones of red and gold in what normally was dark brown.

He finally broke the silence in a voice thick and rough with sleep. "We're probably late, you know."

I smiled, and he studied it.

"Good morning, Hrokr," I said.

He cocked a half-smile, but his eyes were bright. "Good morning, Thea."

"Why do you think we're late?" I asked.

"Well I'm usually up before this," he said, his eyes flicking up to see the position of the sun in the sky. "Normally for something like this I'd be up before dawn. And then there is the other matter."

I grinned again—something I couldn't seem to stop doing with him still playing in my hair. "The other matter?"

"Maddox is screaming in my ear."

I laughed—a tired, happy sound that flitted throughout the room and seemed to wend into the easy sunlight.

Hrokr's eyes glittered. "I'm more than happy for an opportunity to tell him to leave us alone, but perhaps we should go."

"Perhaps," I whispered.

Readying was an easy, quiet thing, a comfort between us that was hard to explain. Perhaps last night was good for us. Maybe there were things that needed to be said, walls that needed to be crumbled.

When Hrokr and I stepped out into the ground-level receiving area of the Palace, Maddox sighed sharply. "It took you two long enough."

Fallon only smiled at us both.

"Where's Cornelius?" Hrokr asked, ignoring Maddox's tone.

"I've been keeping him at bay so he doesn't think you've lost your sharp, punctual edge."

Hrokr rolled his eyes, straightening the cuffs on his coat. "I'm sure he just thinks my mate was commanding my attentions. It's no matter."

I flushed, Fallon tracking the gesture, but Maddox was not appeased. "Just be careful," he said in a tone more sobered. "Don't show her to be a weakness she is not."

I am sure he will not think any of us weak when his Orb is gone, Hrokr projected, likely to all of us.

Maddox glared, but Fallon only nodded in approval.

"Come on," Maddox said. "He wants to meet outside of Wyndmere."

Hrokr reached back to hold my hand as we stepped out into the city. The cold wind was biting, and I was thankful for the thick leggings and long-sleeved, white coat that clung to me. My white boots splashed through deep puddles from last night's rain.

We took the walk in easy silence, though in the morning light, we garnered much more attention than we had before.

No one bowed or tilted their heads in reverence, though we garnered many glances. This city was poor—impoverished—from the looks of it.

I could only assume the open stares were because of the clean-cut, expensive nature of our attire. A part of me felt guilty.

Get that look off your face, Fallon projected.

My head whipped toward her, but she only continued facing ahead.

Don't feel bad for these people. They gamble themselves into nothing.

I knew her history, knew she probably did not enjoy being back here. There *were* monsters here—but there were monsters everywhere. And she had not been a monster when she wore rags and the shame of her parents' mistakes. "Not all of them," I whispered.

Though Hrokr and Maddox heard me, they said nothing.

We stepped around a corner into an even rougher street with buildings that reached up to scrape against the open sky. Everything was varying shades of grey, the paint of years past long muted. Except for one door, painted a vibrant canary yellow.

It was—of course—the one we made toward.

The windows were cleaner than the others, but still carrying age-telling fog. A little sign hung upon the door, moving gently in the cold morning breeze. *Alf's.*

When Maddox pushed the door open, a twittering bell announced our presence. Immediately, tiny hands were on me, causing my heart to leap into my throat. But they were only some kind of pixie or sprite, peeling my coat from my skin.

Hrokr slipped out of his easily, and I followed suit, watching the little multi-hued, sharp-faced creatures carry my clothes to a rusted brass rack by the door.

Hrokr slipped an arm around my waist, tugging me in my olive sweater closer to his side.

Inside it was all creaking floorboards and scuffed, aged paneling. But the sunlight pouring in through the foggy windows was bright. It felt cozy within.

Stepping out from behind the receiving counter was a tall, thick woman, with dark skin and darker hair fanning around her face in a luscious halo.

"Alfretta," Hrokr said, even bowing his head in deference.

"My lord," she crooned, beaming at him. "Have you come again to visit Lord Cornelius?"

"I've come to visit you," he said, winking.

My spine tightened.

But she only laughed, her head tipped back and a hand on her belly. "You old cad," she teased. Her eyes were warm as she beheld me. "What is this beautiful creature you have dangling from your arm?"

And all of my tightness and reservations were washed away as he beamed, grinning ear to ear and showing teeth. "This is my Thea," he said, gently tugging me forward toward her.

Her eyes met his, a mischievous question behind them. "Your?"

"Mate."

The word was proudly spoken from his lips—a marvelous actor indeed.

It was Fallon who stepped forward, too beaming over me as if I were a fresh toy—a grand prize. "You'll love her, Alfie. She keeps us all on our toes."

Alfretta laughed again, her emerald eyes twinkling as she studied me. "Well, this is a happy morning if we have such wonderful news to celebrate."

Happiness is a good look on him, she projected to me, startling me. *It is a look we have long missed, and never one seen in such depth.*

My throat tightened as I bowed my head.

"Come," Alfretta said, clapping her hands together. "I'm sure Cornelius will be jealous to miss the fun."

Hrokr squeezed me, following her up the stairs in the back and up a narrow, spiral staircase into an open veranda above. Cornelius sat alone, sipping from a glass of bright orange. Not truly alone, as two guards were posted by the door.

"Your guests arrive, my lord," Alfretta called, sending me another warm smile as she ushered us inside.

The veranda was likely spelled—as the air was cool, but not cold—where it filtered in from the open wall leading onto the balcony.

"Friends!" Cornelius beamed, gesturing us over.

No one apologized for our tardiness—and he did not ask us about it.

I'd expected something of a repeat of yesterday, but I did not find it. As I slid into my seat next to Hrokr—our conjoined fingers clasped in his lap—I found nothing of the charged energy of last night's dinner.

Breakfast—or nearly lunch at this time—was a light, easy thing. The table talked in circles of idle nothingness, and I was content to listen. Nothing of substance was spoken, and while Hrokr, Maddox, and Fallon were at ease enough to be relaxed, they did not appear truly comfortable.

Not cheerful, at least.

But a heavy job lay ahead of us, and I'd learned very quickly that Cornelius was not their favorite company to keep. He seemed endearing enough to me, though.

He wants you to find him endearing, Hrokr projected as the staff appeared, setting down plates and bowls of steaming eggs, fresh meats, glistening fruits, and hot bread.

I cocked a brow at Hrokr as he heaped a pile of eggs onto a plate before me.

He shrugged. *Your thoughts sometimes carry to me.*

Was I projecting now?

I waited, but he said nothing more, only pouring me a glass of juice. After long moments, I poked him in the side. He smiled as he buttered bread for us both. *If you're trying to talk to me, I can't hear you. It doesn't exactly work like that.*

But if you're curious about Cornelius—I long knew him this way.

He projected an image of a beautiful man with long, dark ringlets. His eyes were smooth and vibrant brown, nothing at all like the beady, cloudy glaze of the Cornelius before me. *You can imagine the cute-old-man-look is less endearing when he wears this face.*

I stared up at Hrokr, and he flashed me an ornery smile.

Eat, Thea, he said, pushing my juice toward me. *I'm ready to be over with this already. Besides, if you have questions about Cornelius, they are better directed to Fallon.*

That only gave me more questions, but there was no way to ask them. So I ate and listened to their easy chatter. Hrokr—as if all of the heady strain of last night had evaporated in the morning sun—slipped easily back into his role. He picked at my meal, laid a warm hand across my back, and held my fingers in his lap.

And when we finally found ourselves back on the street—his fingers laced with my own—he seemed just as easy. He even put my coat on for me—to the chagrin of the café sprites—and pressed a soft kiss to my cheek.

Let me know if you see anything of concern, Hrokr projected to me, squeezing my hand as we wound through Maedonia. *This trip is just to get our eyes on it, but if anything looks worrisome, tell me, alright?*

I squeezed his hand back.

We walked through the streets of Maedonia, Cornelius and his guards in front of us and Fallon and Maddox behind us. Our walk took us out of the heavy bustle of the city and through a labyrinth of twining, gnarled oaks. It was cooler within the cover of the trees, the light not able to reach the ground to heat it. Everything was green and alive, and I could feel a wealth of power deep within.

Hrokr straightened beside me, and I knew he felt it too. Cornelius clapped his gloved hands together, rubbing them vigorously.

It will be different this time, Hrokr said softly. *This one is alive.*

I glanced up at him, my question written openly in my eyes.

The Orbs you've seen before—they are used. This one is not.

He said nothing more as we passed stoic sentries with their eyes trained on nothing. And when we finally made it through the break in the trees, my breath left me in a rush as I saw it.

It was like a star.

Like the noonday sun burning only feet from where I stood. It wasn't hot, but it was bright and overwhelming. It was massive, shooting off arcs of pure light and the essence of life and magic. The grass beneath it was greener, the trees nearby healthier.

"Is it bigger?" I whispered as softly as I could.

No, Hrokr said solemnly, his eyes too studying the spectacle. *That's just the ether, it's just as small as the others.*

"How?" I whispered.

It can be snuffed, believe it or not. It isn't true light, only essence. As long as we have it closed within something—which we will—it will not give its light. We won't be able to sneak past anyone with it, though. They'll feel it from a mile away.

"Glorious, is it not?" Cornelius asked, stepping into the blue-green grass.

"Breathtaking," I whispered.

He winked.

"Maybe you should touch it," Fallon crooned. "Perhaps it will turn you pretty again."

He turned a passionate grin on her. "My lovely Fallon. Won't you ever put me out of my misery and come home to this Hall?"

She snorted—and I saw it for the distraction it was. Hrokr was scanning, looking at guards, paths in the bushes, heights of trees, the slant of the sun.

"Cornelius, Valencia has been my home for centuries. And I'm a Cardinal. I very nearly outrank you," she said playfully.

He smiled, and the sultry curve of his lips had no place on his withered face. "Perhaps you could teach me a thing or two."

She returned the smile. "Shed the sagging bones, and I'll consider it."

Ever vain, ever flippant. It endeared him if the look in his eyes was any indication.

"What do you think, Thea?" Hrokr asked aloud. "Was it all you expected?"

He opened his arms, and I leaned fully into him. "Even more," I said.

"Enjoy the park," Cornelius said, studying us with a smile. "But afterward, I do hope you'll join me again for dinner?"

Hrokr smiled, curving a hand around my hip. "We'll be departing this afternoon. As you know, I must return home, and I still need to introduce Thea to Ivaylo and Dromnael," he lied smoothly.

"Ahh, well I do hope you don't stay away for so long again."

I heard the quick pause in Hrokr's breathing and braced myself for his next words. "I'll try not to. It's regrettable that I had to miss drinks in Asena with Jaeger and Garbhan."

But there was no flash of surprise in the old man's eyes. He could be a skilled liar—or perhaps he truly knew nothing of Gar and The Nock's lies.

"It's no trouble," he said. "You know how those two get—it was a short evening."

"Yes," Hrokr murmured. "I do."

CHAPTER FIFTY-TWO

SORRY

We didn't stay.

After walking around the Orb for a few minutes and making small talk with Cornelius, Hrokr announced our imminent departure, and he and I walked back to our room together.

As soon as the door clicked shut behind us, he said, "It's less guarded than it used to be."

"Isn't that a good thing?" I asked.

His brow furrowed as he ran a hand through his hair. "I'm not sure. He's always been friendly with Garbhan and Jaeger both."

"Sure, but aren't you all relatively close?"

His eyes were far from this little room. "He could be suspecting us, especially considering that Ciro and Haizea are in the Hall of the Elements right now."

He paced. Stressed.

"Hey," I said gently, stopping him with a hand on his forearm. "He's going to know it was us anyway, Hrokr."

He delicately removed himself from my touch. "That won't matter if he stops us. Speculation—even strong speculation—is a lot better than him catching us. It would shatter my allegiance with Ivaylo." A pause. "That is if he hasn't already chosen Garbhan over us."

I stalked across the floor to the wet bar in the corner. Hrokr paused his pacing only long enough to flash me a puzzled glance before returning to his self-soothing movement. "You could always lie to Ivaylo," I said, pouring a knuckle of golden liquor.

"No," he murmured. "Not if Cornelius has seen it. The Hall's bond will be enough for Cornelius to show Ivaylo he's telling the truth."

I walked over to him, standing directly in his path. He paused as I pressed the glass into his hands. "Like our bond?" I asked archly.

He muttered something noncommittal before downing the glass and handing it back to me. His voice was rough with burn when he said, "Thank you."

At that moment the door burst open, but it was only Fallon and Maddox strolling in.

They immediately stopped—Fallon exclaiming, "What *happened* in here?"

I followed her line of sight, seeing the table and chairs still knocked to the floor, and the shattered glasses and broken bottle of whiskey that had formed a sticky puddle around them.

"Nothing," he and I said together. When our eyes met, it was like every heated memory from last night was suddenly shoved between us. He turned away.

"As I was saying," he said, clearing his throat pointedly, "I expected a much greater guard detail. It's almost like he knows what we are here for. I think it could be a test."

"Doesn't matter if it is," Fallon said, plopping onto the bed. "He's going to know it was us anyway."

Hrokr sighed sharply, pinching the bridge of his nose. "Thea said the same thing, but—"

"It matters if he stops us," Maddox supplied.

"Thank you," Hrokr hummed.

Fallon rolled her eyes.

"It would get violent quickly," Maddox said. Ice wormed its way into my veins even before he continued. "We don't have the Weathermen here. Halls, we don't even have the entire Council. I know *we* are deadly, but..." His voice fell away, a grim despondency settling on his chiseled face. "Cornelius is still a lord, still a *warrior*. We are in his capital, surrounded by his armed Guard. It's entirely possible it could devolve into a battle neither of you walk away from."

I shifted on my feet. "Then what if we just... didn't?"

Everyone turned their eyes to me. I flushed beneath their gazes, but lifted my head. "Perhaps Ciro is right. Maybe we shouldn't do the leg work for him."

Hrokr cocked a dark brow. "What happened to your retribution?"

"My retribution had a bit more stealth," I said. "If it's an even larger risk than we'd already anticipated..." My words trailed away.

Hrokr sighed heavily. "It's quite unfortunate that things are likely to escalate faster than we'd originally intended. But we don't have another option if we want to leave with the Orb."

I suddenly wished Fallon and Maddox weren't here as I whispered, "It's not worth it."

He was already shaking his head, but I pushed on.

"Not worth risking your Hall or your connections. It's not worth it if we are risking your *life*."

But my words brought his shields back into place, his eyes hardening. "The risk is worth it to me," he said sharply.

Fallon stirred on the bed. "Crow—"

"Do *not*," he spit, voice suddenly full of venom.

"How is judgement worth the risk?" I croaked.

"He has to die, Thea," he said in a voice distinctly piercing. "There is no way around it. And this is the only way to lure him out."

"Is it worth *my* life?" I challenged.

His nostrils flared. "You can't die here, Thea, you know that," he said flatly. "You still have a centennial eclipse to attend."

He turned toward the door, but I leapt, grabbing him by the arm. He froze, looking down his nose at me from behind cold eyes.

"He's not worth it. Not worth you." I hated the salty tears falling down my cheeks in warm tracks. "Not worth any of you. We will find another way."

"He's not going to stop, Thea," Maddox said gently from his post by the door.

"Well we don't need to rush into it! I want him dead as much as you do, but... not if this is a test, not if this is a *trap.*"

"We don't know that it is," Hrokr said hotly.

"We don't know that it's *not.*"

I released my grip on his arm, but he stayed close and fuming.

"It's not worth risking your life," I repeated softly.

He leaned down, eye-level with me. "It is."

I couldn't seem to pull down enough breath. Fallon spoke from the bed, a cold anger in her voice. "Tell her why that is, Crow."

"*No,*" he growled, ripping away from me.

I was frozen as he marched toward the door. He paused, fingers on the handle, eyes cast aside. "Take her home, Fallon."

My entire body tightened. "What—"

"*No,*" she said.

He turned slowly, his rage leaking off of him in inky tendrils that slithered like snakes across the dark floor. "Fallon—"

"Take her yourself."

He was angrier than I'd ever seen him, but there was something else. Something underneath it, something I could *feel.*

Fear.

Regret.

Guilt.

It was only for a moment that his features broke, but break they did. Tears welled in his eyes as his brow furrowed—

And he was gone.

To where, none could know.

There was only soft smoke left where he stood.

I didn't cry. I wouldn't let myself.

I didn't help much, either. I let Maddox and Fallon—who were conveniently in contact with Hrokr—work out the rest of the plan. When the time came that I had to leave Wyndmere to protect our alibi, Fallon voidstepped me to a seedy inn on the other side of town, straight to our room.

It was dark and grimy, carrying a myriad of scents that were hard to place. Every manner of Folk had been in and out of here. "Put this on," she said, shoving true gear, fresh boots, and a bandolier of throwing knives at me.

I did as I was told without complaint, quickly finding myself standing before her fully outfitted and with my black cloak drawn up. "I'm going back to Wyndmere. I'll tell Cornelius you left, and that I stayed around to reminisce about my old Hall."

"Alright."

There was pity in her eyes, but she didn't bother to voice it. I was grateful.

"Maddox will come with me, lurking around in case things go south on my end."

"Take me," I said softly.

The pity swelled. "I can't," she said gently, reaching out with motherly fingers to brush back a strand of my hair. "It wouldn't make sense when Hrokr already told him he was eager to show you off to Ivaylo and Ciri."

"Fallon." My voice broke.

"I know," she whispered. "And it will be better for you two to do it together. I think you'll both be distracted if you're apart."

She looked at me, waiting for me to deny it.

I didn't.

"There's still the possibility that nothing will happen," she said.

I whispered, "Something already did happen."

We both knew I wasn't talking about the heist to come.

She cracked a sad, melancholy smile. "Just get through this one day, Thea. You can do it."

Tears beaded in my eyes, but I nodded. "Alright."

"Alright," she repeated, stepping away and straightening my cloak.

The three of us descended into thick, painful silence as we waited for him.

It wasn't long before Hrokr shoved open the creaking, oak door. He was dressed the same as I was, his cloak pulled up over his head and keeping his face in shadow. Two swords were crossed across his back, shining as brightly as the buckles on his boots.

"Ready?" He asked, voice curt.

I rose on shaking legs, daring not to even look him in the eyes. We didn't speak, and neither did Maddox or Fallon as we left them behind. Not as we slipped out into the frigid evening. Not as we started on the cobbled road toward the Orb.

Our weapons and cloaks didn't stand out amongst the night crowd. We passed several men and women who looked like they were up to as much trouble as we were.

It wasn't until the forest path became visible at the end of the long road that he spoke. "Killing them all would make this easier."

His voice was harsh and crass—as if he wanted to upset me.

"Over a *maybe?*" I challenged.

He shrugged, his broad shoulders moving tightly beneath his cloak. "We'll see what happens."

I gripped his cloak and ripped him back to face me. There was no shock in his eyes, only anger—as if he had expected. "I don't know what is wrong with you," I hissed. "But you are not killing *anyone.*" I took a deep breath, trying to bury my fear.

My hurt.

"Unless it's necessary," I amended. "But... not for nothing. You can't be that person."

"You don't know who I am, Thea."

My heart picked up a fast beat, panic—less at the situation and more at his reaction to it—settling into me. "Please, Hrokr. No death, not if it can be avoided."

He searched my eyes, his nostrils flaring. Finally, "Fine."

I let him go, and he tore off down the path. I followed in silence.

We slowed when we reached the opening in the trees. *You have a plan to get around these guards, then?* he asked haughtily.

I choked. "Do you—do you *not?*" I hissed beneath my breath.

They were posted at the end of the clearing, backs toward us. I moved to slip into the trees, but his fingers wound in my cloak, hauling me back to his side. *Relax. I have you cloaked in shadow.*

The tension leaked away from my shoulders.

He was being cryptic for nothing.

He paused. And faster than I could think to stop him, he'd pulled two daggers from his cloak and sent them flying. The guards were dead before I could blink.

A choked noise broke out of me as I stumbled forward. "You—you said we wouldn't kill!"

He stepped around me, unconcerned. "I lied."

Rage burned in me. "*Crow,*" I hissed.

He stopped, only half turning to listen. "Are you going to mourn them, Thea?" he crooned.

"You're being reckless and ignorant," I snapped. "You just made a problem where there didn't need to be one."

He had the audacity to roll his eyes and step farther into the clearing. A loose wave of his hand had the *ground opening* and swallowing the bodies whole. "Did you think they were going to live?" he called back, sauntering easily through the break in the trees and into the heart of the park.

I pushed in after him, my irritation nipping at me. "They could have."

The Orb was not alight, not how it had been during the day. Hrokr was right that it wasn't true light, only a display of magic. It now looked like the night itself had wound around it and was pulsing from within. Even with its massive shape, I could make out the Orb itself sitting within on a small pedestal.

Hrokr spun on me, sudden rage in his eyes. "How can you not understand how much I've already risked, Thea? I've shown the world your face. I have hung you like a target before the archers. *I have thrown you out with the wolves.*" He took a deep breath, fighting to steady himself. "I have already heaped enough sorrow onto your shoulders. I will *not* put you in more danger."

"Hrokr, what are you talking about?" I rasped, stepping into him.

He backed away. "I killed them, and I will kill more if that's what it takes. If I am implicated in my crimes, then so be it. But you will not be caught."

"Why does it matter?" I asked softly.

"I think you are in this mess because of me, and I just want you out of it."

I shook my head, even though he wasn't looking at me. He was studying the Orb. "It's not your fault," I said firmly. "I'm here because of Gar, because—"

"And why do you think that is?" he cried suddenly, spinning toward me. "Why *you*, Thea? Because he saw—" He broke off, heaving a breath. "Garbhan saw that you'd be here. He saw that you could be used to reach *me*. You are here *because of me.*"

"What does this have to do with *anything*, Hrokr?"

He shook his head, mumbling, "I shouldn't have let you come." And then he was plunging into the corona of the Orb.

I felt it the moment the magic met him, a blast of power to my senses. It hurt him, in a way. I could feel his strain—his entire being overwhelmed—as he walked through the power of the Elders. But he had the power to march straight through, rip the stone off the pedestal, and shove it in a bag beneath his cloak.

He was right. I couldn't see it, but I could feel an unimaginable force rippling off him.

A panicked voice entered my mind. *Get out!* Fallon.

Hrokr spun, meeting my eyes. *Why?*

He knows. Or—he knows something.

Hrokr hissed under his breath. *Get here,* he said. *Get here now and get her out.*

We can't, Fallon said.

Hrokr began scanning the skies, the trees beyond. He looked... *terrified.*

So much more afraid than I'd ever seen him.

"Hrokr, what's wrong?" I asked in a small voice.

It couldn't be Cornelius that had him so afraid, could it?

Why not? he growled at Fallon.

Because Cornelius is standing two feet from us, Hrokr, she hissed. *You said it yourself—speculation is speculation. But we cannot call down immediate war. We cannot fight a war on two fronts. Go home.*

"*I can't,*" he bellowed, both aloud and in projection.

It was Maddox who spoke gently, soothingly. I'd slipped into Hrokr's mind once before, long ago, when Maddox spoke to him as a father—as a piece of comfort. He used that same voice now. *Take her home, Hrokr.*

Something rustled in the trees.

"Hrokr," I whispered, palming my knives.

But he made no move for me. He unsheathed his swords. Power swarmed around him, the night sky darkening above. His eyes glowed with that silver fire of unspent stars, and darkness dripped from his skin. "Are you armed?" he growled, not even looking at me.

"*Hrokr,*" I hissed again. "Get me out of here."

"You can fight," he said. "You know Garbhan's vision. You'll live through this, and you'll be in Valencia at the next centennial eclipse."

"Then what are you so afraid of?" I cried.

He lunged passed me, angling the sharp edge of his blade. But—caution be damned—I wound my fingers in his cloak and ripped him back toward me. His eyes were wide.

"Voidstep me out of here. Now."

"Thea, no," he barked, ripping out of my grip.

"*Please,*" I begged. "What are you going to do—kill them all?"

Darkness swathed him like a midnight storm. It leaked from him in lethal ribbons, and sparks of electricity glinted within its depths. "If I have to, yes."

"You don't have to!" I cried. "You're only drawing unnecessary attention."

But I could see it in his eyes: the rising of those shields, the hardening of his heart. "Don't leave my sight," he said, his voice dipping into something heady and deadly. "It's suspicious they haven't voidstepped in, and I don't know what's coming. Because you can't project you—"

His words broke off into a surprised gasp as I drew a gash down his forearm. Panic—unlike any I'd ever seen—filled his bright eyes as blood poured down his

433

fingers. A choked, broken sound poured from his lips. I didn't give myself time to think before I slit my own palm.

He recovered only enough to whisper, "I'm sorry," before my bloodied palm gripped him tight.

CHAPTER FIFTY-THREE

INSIDE

Power engulfed me, surged through my veins, and ruptured inside of my chest. I was sucked out of the park, hurled through more than just space. Hurled through time.

Hrokr was everything. Inside every piece of me, his heart beating in tandem with my own. I could feel his skin as surely as I felt my own, feel his soul carving open and crawling into mine.

That first overwhelming, knee-bending aura I'd felt in Castle Habrem right before I met him—it was nothing compared to this. That aura was inside of me now—pulsing through my veins, spiking my blood.

My breath came from his lips, his heart beat inside of my chest.

And I saw... *I saw so much of him.*

He was a blast to my senses as I was thrown down the long, scarred corridor of his soul. All the way back to the beginning, when he was only a child.

When he was only a dark-eyed little boy with chubby fingers and unruly curls running across the sand. A woman with long black hair and full lips curved into a rosy smile laughed from the porch of a crumbling home. He loved her.

He loved her so much.

She called him to dinner, waving slim arms.

He tripped in the shifting sand as he ran to her. But he made it to her eventually, laughing wildly as she swung him up into her warm arms. As she pressed a smacking kiss to his cheek, the world faded into a myriad of colors, as if water had been splashed across a wet canvas.

He was older now, his mother reading behind him at his shoulder. Grasped in his fingers were letters from a father he'd never know, but still found room in his heart to love. His hands looked like a man's now, nicked with scars from training.

That training had been delivered to him by the only father figure he'd ever known. Valencia's War Advisor, Maddox Lamont.

Hrokr was older still. Fresh battle found its way to Valencia. He wanted to go home—to a home he'd not yet seen—but his mother wouldn't let him. He knew how severe things had become when Maddox was summoned back to the north to aid Lord Cadmus in the war.

Hrokr sat on the floor outside of his mother's bedroom, listening to her cry for the husband she feared she'd lose.

And then she did lose him.

He'd never forget the news—brought by a face he didn't recognize. Not only did he lose his father, but he was unsure if even Maddox lived. His mother did not sleep, did not eat. Hrokr thought it had broken him. It hadn't.

But something else had.

Only weeks later, he heard his mother's voice in his head. *I love you. Don't come home.*

Those words would never leave him—no matter how long he lived. Of course he'd gone home. Voidstepped right there.

And there she was.

The last place she would ever be.

Her head shorn from her shoulders, her unseeing eyes staring at the ceiling of their kitchen. The noise that came out of him—he sometimes thought he could hear it. As if it had come out of someone else and not his own body.

He fell to his knees, the decaying board groaning beneath him. But he heard nothing over the silence ringing in his ears.

Blood poured from her, the floor greedily drinking it down, her life staining this world forever.

He knew it was useless, knew she was long dead. But he couldn't help but crying the only name he'd ever had for her, from letting his lips shape, "*Momma,*" as he tried to put her back together.

But not even ether could help him now.

That's how he was found, cradling her shattered body.

A man in an iron mask stepped out from the hall, his blade still wet with her blood. "Get up," the man said.

Unarmed and marked in his mother's blood, Hrokr blinked up at him. The moment felt somehow illusory, as if nothing so cruel could truly be real.

The man flicked his blade, and scarlet drops of blood splattered against the white cabinet doors. They were heavy, marring the paint in crimson rivulets as they dripped toward the floor.

The sight burned through him, overtaking him in a blind rage that had him shooting to his feet and charging.

The man was quite obviously surprised, not expecting Hrokr to carry the strength that he did at only seventeen.

But fury was a mighty sword.

Hrokr's shaking fingers swiped a knife from the kitchen counter before plunging it into the man's eye. The metal ground against iron, scarring the mask forever. The man did not die, but blood poured readily from the thick gash Hrokr cut.

As he readied to take his final blow, the man voidstepped.

Disappeared into nothing.

Hours later, he buried his mother and started his charge for Valencia. He dared not voidstep, not when he did not know what he would be walking into. The masked man did not return, but he sent his warriors.

Hrokr slew them all on a long march through the Hall of the Elements. As if his grief fed the earth below, flowers and fields and trees turned the color of blood as he passed.

He reached the shores of his nation eventually. His mother had told him stories of a beautiful, snowy land. But he saw only devastation. Fighting in the streets, limbs and bloodied corpses.

But he righted his city, his Hall. He drove out the monsters, Maddox at his side.

But he was young and unguided. Names floated throughout the city, sometimes even on the lips of the Royal Council.

The Boy King.

He stomached the snide remarks, the resentment they felt for him that he was not his father, Cadmus. He stomached it all. Until they said, "Lady Araceli was a fool, and she died for it."

They died for it, too.

Things were better when they were gone. He forged his own path, made his own Council. Cardinals, he called them. Red, because they had been forged in blood.

He became a lord that his people loved and feared in equal measure.

He even made friends outside of his Hall.

Garbhan Silsto, Jenmora's Captain of the Guard. A kind seer who could pull genuine laughter out of him when no one else could. He became a friendly face at repetitive meetings, a man who would take him into the cities instead of leaving him cooped in the Halls' meetings.

Garbhan saw plenty of the future, many of the Elders conversing freely with him. Hrokr was a seer himself, but perhaps in name only. The Elders hardly ever spoke to him. But Garbhan would tell him what he saw sometimes.

One night, they shared a drink of dark liquor on a rooftop beneath a clear sky of stars. The Halls' meeting had raged on, but Hrokr was thankful at least for this stolen moment of silence.

Garbhan leaned against the railing, his long, dark hair blowing in the easy wind behind him. With a thick voice that sounded an awful lot like heartbreak, Garbhan told him a story of something that hadn't yet come.

It stayed with him for a long time. It stayed with him now.

Years later—centuries later—war was once again waged by the masked man. It did not breach his shores, but they battled for twenty long years in the heart of Eirlys. This war claimed Orion and Inina.

Hrokr could still hear Ciro and Haizea's screams. They were screams that sounded so much like the one he'd emitted in a cramped, cozy kitchen.

Centuries of a numb blankness. Howling silence in his mind, liquor on his tongue. Any blind numbing that could take away the horrors of the past and those still yet to come. He felt himself withdrawing from his Council.

He couldn't reach deep enough inside to care. He couldn't stop, couldn't face his own life.

His duty did not lapse. His house was in order, his people fed and warm in their beds, never to fear the monstrosities that haunted every breath he took. So many ghosts after so many long, lonely years.

Drowning in a mess of nights that blended into days, and days that blended into years, he felt something shoot through him, rip him from sleep. A thrumming, deep in his chest.

It took him years, but he learned that it was *her*. The Heir of Aphaedia. He could always feel her, beating just beside his own heart. A pull, a lure, cast out across the expanse of Alynthia, binding her to him. She was a ray of hope, of something resembling meaning.

She disappeared only to reappear, and he realized that perhaps she was not his mate as he'd once thought. It was only a Hall's bond. The Elders only knew how many different people he would have felt, but it was obvious the Aphaedians had hidden themselves behind wards. But still, he wanted to find her.

He looked.

He searched for so long, until he decided that maybe he wasn't *meant* to be searching. What could he offer her, anyway? A Hall in order, but a man in ruin?

He quit looking.

His lonely days became somehow lonelier. His frigid cold was a vast tundra of silence and thick ice underfoot. Fallon was worried. Maddox was worried, which hurt most of all. But he wouldn't face it. *Couldn't* face it.

Stories again made it to him from across the Eirlyn channel. The Hall of the Elements, rampaged by a girl solely targeting *his* people.

The Shadow of Judgement, she called herself.

Fury burned in him, burning away that ashen tundra of cold nothing. Talon Fellsworn was the first dead, but he was not the last.

So many more ghosts and unfinished lives.

Hrokr paraded his Eclipse Fete, sending out loose invitations, daring her to step foot on his Hall.

She did.

Hrokr had sentries posted throughout the entire Hall, guards dressed as attendees, Haizea and Ciro holed up in Eirlys, watching for her.

And when he finally found her standing in the heart of his throne room, her back was to him. Her dress was exquisite, a perfect black that lay against tan skin that looked as smooth as silk.

She turned—away from what, he wasn't sure—only to collide directly with his chest. "I'm so sorry," she'd said, perfect manners. Her hand shot out, as if to steady either him or herself.

He hated her, of course. Hated everything she stood for, everything she'd done. Every inch of burning heartache she'd wrought for him.

But Halls, he could have fallen to his knees before her.

He'd never seen anything so beautiful, so perfectly crafted. And set above her freckle-dusted cheekbones were not the shrewd, broken eyes of the monster he'd expected. They were gold and tired, nervous as they ticked around the room.

He pulled her into a dance, flush against his chest. He'd come here to kill her, to maim her, to tear her apart. He wondered what it said about himself that she felt so good—so warm and alive—in his arms.

He pushed it away as best he could. He broke her, cut her, forced himself to remember what she was. But once he realized whoever she served had lied to her, he felt his hate melt out of his skin and onto the floor beneath him.

She'd only been sent here by someone else. By the Burning Arrow—a guild of no ones—if her rat partner, Calix, spoke true. Perhaps she was evil, wretched, cold and malevolent.

But in this moment, he saw only a woman with burning, sunrise eyes.

He wanted to help her.

He had to let her go, of course. Had to cast her out into the wilds of Alynthia and pray her dedication would be enough to reel her back to him once she learned the truth.

His Council didn't know what to think. He couldn't sit still while she was gone. Couldn't eat, couldn't sleep. He wandered the halls at night, listening, watching, *waiting*.

Always waiting for her.

And when she returned—even though she was broken and malnourished, poison eating her bones from within—he could have wept.

Thea, her name was.

Just a part of his duty, a way to find his enemy. But he couldn't stop himself from staying by her cell, from feeling like his heart was eating through his chest every time he heard her crying, every time he realized just how quickly she was withering away.

Time passed, and she thawed. He felt a different kind of madness now. He'd tasted her blood, he knew what she was. *Who* she was to him. He told himself he'd been wrong before. He told himself he thought the Heir of Aphaedia was his mate, and he'd been wrong about that too.

He could be wrong about Thea.

But he couldn't stay away from her.

And then she was ripped away to a foreign island, and he felt like his heart had been ripped along with her.

A toad came to him in the night, telling of where Thea was.

A toad.

And he knew exactly who she was, exactly what she was to the people of Aphaedia to command their most treasured peoples.

Guilt and fear and terror ate him alive every time she smiled at him, every time she flushed within his arms. But she was a drug—and he could not quit her. He'd drink enough to kill a human, trying, *trying so hard* to numb what he felt. But he'd only wake up with half a sober mind, drowning in her scent in her bed, in the hall outside her rooms—as close as he could get.

His life became a crescendo of madness he could not contain.

He saw that he'd never been wrong. The Heir of Aphaedia was his mate after all. And it had been Thea's soul tied to his during all those empty years.

He stood in Wyndmere, deep in a palace he hated. But he found that he could stomach it because she was here. Thea wrapped in his arms, his body carrying her scent as she'd pressed herself against him. He leaned his face against her hair, breathing her in for long minutes. They weren't even really dancing, he just held her against him as they moved.

He couldn't help it.

He couldn't help—just this once—kissing her. She melted in his arms. He knew he'd made a mistake when she parted her lips, hungry to taste him.

But he did not deny her.

He'd never felt something like her. And when Cornelius spoke to them, he thought he'd lose his composure right then. For daring to address him while he held his mate, he thought he'd shred the man apart, outing every secret he'd ever kept. But by some brush of luck, he kept himself as leashed as he could.

But now, *now,* all those warm feelings were gone. His Thea still stood before him, but her eyes were bloodshot with tears. A war stood at his back, a crisis ready to open its maw and swallow them both whole. He had never known silence as he did when he felt her cut him, saw his crimson blood dripping to the earth beneath them.

Too late, he knew. She'd catch him even if he ran, and he couldn't voidstep without leaving her alone. So he whispered the only thing he could.

"I'm sorry," he'd said right before she pressed her blood into him, and he felt himself sucked not only through the world as he threw them out of danger, but into *her,* into every bit of her mind and memory.

CHAPTER FIFTY-FOUR

DECIDED

We landed in the center of the Council Room in Castle Habrem, both flushed and panting, even though we'd only been standing still. We stared at each other, centuries of life flowing between us.

He swallowed—choking, fighting to catch his breath—as he stumbled away from me. He shook his head vigorously as if he could undo it all.

I didn't understand.

Ciro and Haizea were out of their seats in an instant. "What happened?"

But Hrokr and I only stared at one another, a chasm between us, even though I could now feel this bond pulsing in me like it's own heart.

"Hrokr—"

"No," he said, silver lining his eyes. "*No.*"

"*Why?*" I cried.

His lips peeled back from his teeth as he panted, his hand on his chest—right where I knew he could feel *me.*

"Anyone but you," he choked.

I flinched as if struck.

"I would rather," he breathed, still moving away from me, "*anyone* but you."

Tears welled in my eyes, quick to spill down my cheeks. "You don't mean that," I croaked.

"I do," he said. "Halls, Thea, I do."

It *couldn't* be real, couldn't be wholly true. Not when I felt him, not when I—at the burst of his blood against mine—*became* him. "I felt—"

"You felt the bond," he interrupted. "You felt what my blood told me to feel."

"Hrokr—"

"You do not know what *I* choose, what *I* have decided." But his voice broke, tears welling and spilling down his cheeks. He shook his head again, backing toward the door to the courtyard. "And I don't choose this, Thea."

He pushed open the glass door into the cool night. I smelled a storm on the horizon, one that undoubtedly came from his power. The blood within me—his blood—called out to it.

"Wait!"

He paused, one foot in the night, one inside with me. I knew we had an audience, knew he'd made his position clear. But I also knew what I felt. "Don't leave me," I begged, voice wretched and pitiful. "I can't lose you, too."

His whole body shuddered, a gesture I felt deep within myself. But he gathered himself. "I am not yours to lose," he croaked before pushing into the night.

I rushed after him, but he shifted, flying away on the wings of a crow.

I fell to my knees as the sky broke, the rain of his emotion washing over me. I laid my face against the grass floor, sobbing into the open earth.

I realized how much I'd always been able to feel him, how much he'd *always* been a constant weight against me. I remembered the dreams that had torn me from sleep in a bed I shared with Gar, the conscious presence that seemed to cling to me everywhere I went. It was so much more now. I could feel everything inside of him, I just didn't understand any of it.

Grief, regret, fear, sorrow, panic, rage, terror, hopelessness.

Pushing up from the rain-sodden ground, I wiped my tears and marched back into the Council Room. Haizea and Ciro watched me with sorrow etched on their faces.

When I made it to the door, Haizea said, "Thea," but I was already slamming the door behind me. I ran through the castle, throwing myself up the stairs to his rooms.

Locked.

Not only locked, but I could feel magic pulsing through the door. *He'd warded me away, he—*

And, Halls, I could feel him on the other side, feel his aching heartbeat in my own chest. I slid to the floor, resting my head on the wood.

As close as I could get.

Not close enough.

CHAPTER FIFTY-FIVE
EVERYTHING THAT'S LEFT

I wasn't sure how long I laid there, crying silently and feeling him hurting on the other side—and not understanding why.

I finally slipped into a grief-ravaged sleep, but when my eyes opened, I was tucked into my own bed, a body stretched out beside me, brushing gentle fingers through my hair.

Fallon.

My heart swelled as she smiled something lop-sided at me. "How are you feeling?" she asked.

"How did I get here?" I rasped, my throat raw from a night of tears. The room was dark, night still overhead. I mustn't have slept long.

"Maddox carried you," she said gently. "It's hardly been an hour. You haven't missed anything."

I looked into her golden eyes, feeling my own fill with fresh tears. "What did I do wrong, Fallon?"

She clutched me to her chest like a warm mother. "Nothing, Thea. You didn't do anything wrong."

I cried into her chest, trying to melt into the feeling of her arms, trying not to feel so alone. "Why doesn't he want me?"

She kissed the top of my head. "He wants you so badly, Thea. He's always wanted you."

I shook my head into her chest, clinging to her.

"Can't you feel it?" she asked. "This pain—it is not only yours." She pulled away, gentling us down into the pillows to be facing one another. Her fingers reached out to wipe my tears. "He is avoiding you because he thinks he's dying, Thea."

"What?"

She smiled again—a sad, melancholy thing. "A seer told him long ago that his life would be taken from him in the presence of the ley lines beneath Castle Habrem," she said.

I could no longer feel the bed beneath me.

"When?" I croaked.

She shrugged. "No idea. I'm not even so sure the prophecy is to be believed. Garbhan is the one who told him."

Rage burned through me, turning my stomach into sick knots.

Gar had taken so much from him.

His mother, his father, his safety, multiple lifetimes of peace.

"It's been centuries since he heard, Thea," she said gently. "He was a little shaken at first, but he was alright. But once Orion and Inina died..." Old shadows filled her eyes. "He couldn't bear watching Ciro and Haizea having lost them. He didn't need to say it—we all knew he'd sworn to himself he'd never love. He did everything in his power to make himself smaller, to diminish the mark he would leave on this world when he left it.

"He did not want to be grieved—so he did not want to be loved."

My chest was going to split down the middle.

"We all suspected what you were," she continued softly. "It's been eating him alive, Thea."

I shook my head numbly.

447

"Maybe Garbhan lied," she said. "Or maybe he didn't. But this death could be millennia away. Should he suffer until then?"

I didn't want to think about it. Even millennia. I could not face the thought of a world without him.

But all I whispered was, "I can't get inside. He's warded the door."

She smiled something sad. "Do you want to be in there?"

"Yes."

She pressed one last kiss to my hair and rose from the bed. "I'll get Ciro. He can destroy the ward."

"Even Hrokr's?" I asked.

She laughed softly. "Yes, even Hrokr's."

And then she was gone. I pulled myself to my feet, slipping out of my cloak. Fallon—or Maddox—had already removed my bandolier. The clothes were still wet with rain, so I changed into soft leggings and a thin, black sweater.

And waited.

I curled into the chair before the fireplace, staring at the unlit logs.

I didn't want to cry again, but I couldn't help it. Gar was a monster—I knew that. But I didn't think I'd truly seen the depth of all he'd done until now. Lady Araceli, Lord Cadmus, my mother, Inina and her baby, Orion. All of the slaves in Balaca, Lonnie, Ellie. The pregnant woman in Old Expanse, her mate. All the centuries of those who came before them.

And all of us who he had broken beyond repair, but left breathing.

Hrokr.

My siblings, the Cardinal Council, Sage, and Dorin.

Me.

Knowing that Hrokr had spent so many years alone and afraid... I didn't have the words for it—the judgement that Garbhan deserved.

But all thoughts of Gar were wiped from my mind when a soft knock came at my door. Ciro gently pushed inside.

I thought it was the first time we'd ever been alone together, and I could have thrown myself at his feet.

"It's open," he said in his shifting, gravelly voice.

"Thank you," I rasped.

He nodded sagely. "You are welcome."

And then he was gone, and I was rising on shaking legs.

Standing before Hrokr's door, I fought to calm my racing heart. I finally found the courage to push inside, finding him leaning against the mantle of his fireplace, whiskey glass in hand.

His eyes widened at my entrance, but he did not run. He only studied me from beneath long lashes. "Was it Ciro?"

"Yes," I said, pulling the door shut behind me.

He released a long, tired sigh. "What do you want, Thea?"

I crossed as close as I dared, still leaving feet between us. "I want to talk."

"There's nothing to say."

"There's quite a lot to say, actually."

Silence.

Into that silence, I said, "You knew."

He took a long breath, pulling his glass to his lips. "Yes."

"For how long?"

His face hardened. "Don't you know, now?"

I tried not to feel the bolt of hurt his hardness summoned. "Does it bother you that I do?"

His eyes went faraway. "I suppose I saw more of you than you likely intended."

"See all of me, Hrokr," I said softly. "I want you to."

He refocused on me. "Thea, please—"

"Fallon told me," I said quickly. "About Gar's vision."

He took another long breath, collecting his thoughts. "It was never my intention for it to come to this."

"I know that."

"I'm sorry that it did," he said with a finality that split my chest. "We can't—"

"Do you want to?" I asked baldly, swallowing my fear and shame.

He rubbed his jaw, working it beneath his fingers. "I don't think I should answer that."

I studied his body, rigid and tight and as far from me as he could get while staying in the room. "Why pretend to be mates if you knew what we were?" I asked. "It would only force us closer."

His eyes flicked to mine. "I wanted you to stay home, but you refused."

"Why mates?"

I knew what he'd said before—that the people would not believe he'd taken an errant lover.

"I did say that, yes," he said. At my wide eyes, he added, "Things are very fresh right now. I'm feeling... a lot of you."

"Was it true?" I asked.

"Yes," he said simply, placing his glass atop the mantel where it clinked softly. "That and I knew there was a possibility they'd scent the bond on us, or—"

His words cut off abruptly. He made no effort to finish them.

"Or?"

His chest worked beneath his tunic. "I was afraid something would happen, and I'd show my hand being too territorial of you. And then you'd know, and..." He tapered off again, sighing. "You were feeling it too, whether you noticed or not. I felt it in you in Maedonia when you took the key from the guide faerie. You wouldn't even let her touch my hand."

I flushed.

"Don't," he said quietly. "There's no reason to be ashamed. It's—normal." After a long moment, he said, "I was wrong to let you get so close, and for that, I am sorry. I should have kept you home—kept you away. Better yet, I should have sent you back to Ekin."

My chest ached.

"It was selfish," he continued. "Selfish and reckless and a plethora of other things if I'm willing to admit them."

"How?" I croaked.

His eyes shuddered at my tone, but he continued. "As soon as I knew what you were, I should have sent you away. It was playing with fire to let you stay. And I burned us both."

"How could sending me away have helped anything?" I rasped. "It wouldn't make you something different to me."

"It would have," he said sagely. "A mating bond is so much heavier after cementing it, Thea. I'm sure you can feel the difference."

His words fell into the thick silence between us.

"You likely would have always wondered," he said, melancholy thick on his tongue. "I would have been something you couldn't *fully* escape. But I wouldn't have been *this.*"

He pressed his hand over his heart, where I knew he could feel mine beating.

"And when I died," he went on, "it would not have been what it will be now."

"Don't say that," I said sharply, tears warming my cheeks.

"And I will still do what I can to lessen it. You cannot stay, Thea. Not here, not with me." He laughed harshly, without humor, gesturing toward Fairshroud behind him. "Truthfully, you have just as much claim to these people as I do. Half of them are yours. If you want to stay until Aphaedia is restored, I can go, I—"

"Are you out of your mind?" I whispered. "And how do you expect me to fulfill that prophecy and bring a child into the world? With you? With someone else while you feel it?"

Something dark flashed in his eyes. I could feel it—envy, sorrow, anger. But his tongue was leashed when he said, "The prophecy says nothing about a babe. We could restore the Hall today. Perhaps we should."

"It says—"

"I know what it says."

My fingers curled into tight fists. "What does it mean?"

"It doesn't matter," he said. "What matters is that you have to go now, Thea. It will be better for both of us."

Silence thickened the space between us for so long that I dared whisper, "Because you think you're going to die?"

He stepped forward, lips peeling back from his teeth. "Because I *know* I'm going to die."

"Because *Gar* said so?" I cried. "He *lies,* Hrokr."

He only shook his head.

But as the tears poured hot and fast down my cheeks, I forced my chin up. "Then let it kill you," I said, hating the way the words tasted on my tongue. "We're assembling the Orbs anyway—"

"No."

The word was fast and hard. Final.

"Why not?" I choked.

"Is my life more important than anyone else's? Than Inina's? Orion's?"

"It is," I whispered.

His eyes shuddered. "It's not the safety net you think it is. Not for me, Thea. Never for me."

That dark, shadowy aura that always followed him seemed to pulse, perking up its ears. Darkness coiled around his wrists, thickening the midnight shadows of the room.

"No," I said.

"Do not use it on me, Thea. You have to swear, you—"

"I won't swear," I snapped. "And how can you even ask me to?"

I felt it in him, ready to give in to the fight. But he was afraid. Afraid that letting slip the beast of his emotions would lead to something he could not turn back from. So he only bloodbent his own heart into something slower, and said, "It's no matter. I'll instruct the Council."

I took a step forward, shaking. "Do you think I cannot overcome them?"

He studied me, the vehemence with which I spoke. "And this is exactly why you should go. Perhaps when I finally pass, enough time and space will be between us that you can let me go and enjoy your own life with whoever you choose."

"You're delusional if you think any amount of time will be enough for me to wish you *dead.*"

He took a step closer, looking down his nose at me. "It would be a waste. It won't work."

My brow burrowed. "Why?"

His voice was low and full of darkness when he said, "I'm already dead, Thea."

"You—what?"

"Coming back from the Far Away, it leaves a mark on a person. A mark of darkness. The Far Away will not release them a second time."

"What are you saying?" I whispered.

"Did you know most of the world believes there are two Orbs left to be used? Can you imagine how it felt for Orion and Inina to die, and my Council rejoice that they could bring them both back, when I alone knew they couldn't? How it felt for me to lie to them and explain that the Orb had already been used on some nameless face, and we only had one person to ever bring back again?

"How it felt," he continued, "to lie so that they could retain their hope that they could just bring *me* back? So that they did not have to live with the shadow of death over my life the way that I did? None of them take it seriously. Because they all think that they can just gather the Orbs and bring me back.

"How do you think it felt," he pushed, silver lining his eyes, "to listen to Haizea and Ciro decay with grief knowing that it was all so that I could be here—and for what? Only to die when Garbhan's prophecy came to pass?"

"When did you die?" I whispered.

"I was stillborn," he said. "My parents didn't even want a child. But my mother conceived accidentally. It was a time of war, and raising a child would make everyone vulnerable. And hiding me away would take her from her mate. But she could not bear to leave me dead once she'd held me.

"So she sacrificed everything—and for what?"

"Hrokr—"

"The Unborn, they call me. Those few who know."

These lands have tasted death, have come to ruin from a single shared birth.
And only from a special birth will they be healed.
Only when the unborn and the heir together touch the soil
Only when death has been gifted life, as our life was gifted death
Will the Heir be crowned.

"Your child is not the True Heir," he said. "You are."

But how did he expect me to care about that at all when he was saying his death would be final and irreversible?

"And that's why you should go," he murmured.

"Why?" I said, wiping away my tears. "Because you think it will make me not care about you?"

"In time, yes."

"You told me that prophecies don't always come true the way we'd think they would," I said. "And that is *quite* evidenced by centuries of Starseas believing the Aphaedian prophecy was about a baby."

He shook his head. "Don't do that, Thea. Just accept what is. Garbhan's visions are strong. *My life will be taken in the presence of the ley lines.* Sometimes the Elders' words are weaker than other times, but Garbhan has always been an excellent seer."

"You don't know—"

"Don't I?" he interrupted with a harsh laugh. "Did he never do *anything* that made you wonder just how he could know to do it? The right place at the right time? The right precautions to take? They converse with him quite freely."

I stilled, counting back over it all as my gaze fell to the floor.

"You know what he saw when he first met you, don't you, Thea?"

My eyes slowly raised to his. "What did he see?"

His elegant face was hard and cold. "Every atrocity he committed against you was because of me. Because he saw you not as yourself, but as *mine*. He saw you only as my mate."

My chest cracked open. "It's not your fault—"

"It doesn't matter," he interrupted. "I will not allow myself to hurt you further. Go."

He stepped away, gesturing to the door. "Please," he pleaded as he leaned his head back against the wall, eyes falling shut.

But straightening my spine and drying my tears, I said, "One more question."

His brow furrowed in pain as if the request was too much. But he said, "Alright."

"Did you mean it when you said that you'd accept any mate over me?"

"Yes."

He answered so quickly, not an inch of hesitation.

"Why?" I whispered.

His eyes opened, dark with swirling stars. "If I tell you, will you go?" he nearly growled, his words pained as they were dragged through his throat.

My voice was nothing more than breath as I stepped up to him, closing the distance enough to see the rapid fluttering of his pulse in the hollow of his throat, to scent him thick around me. "Yes."

His breath left him in a pained rush. "Because life with a dead mate is an immortal life of hell. It's a burden I would gladly place on anyone's shoulders before yours. I would heap it on my own instead if I could without taking your life."

I didn't ask, but he felt it burning within me. *Why?*

He searched my eyes. "Because I love you so deeply, Thea, and I have for longer than you can even imagine."

His fingers shook as if he fought to restrain himself, but he brushed back a long lock of my hair. "You have been a gift to me for as long as I've been able to have you. My equal—my counterpart—in every way that's mattered. Strong where I am weak, gentle where I am hard. In the immortal darkness that has been my life, your coming was the birth of a violent, blistering dawn."

He studied me long, tears pooling on his lashes. "In another life, my Thea."

"In this life," I whispered.

"I could never be so selfish," he said just as softly. "Not to you."

"It's too late to send me away. It has been for far longer than we've been bonded."

The tears spilled, warming his cheeks.

I laid my hand against his chest. "I love you, Hrokr."

He shuddered, his eyes falling closed. "You said you'd leave," he said, voice strained.

I pressed myself against him, feeling his heart leap beneath my hands. "I lied."

His face was drawn in pain as he pressed himself into the wall behind him.

"Look at me," I murmured.

So slowly, he did.

"Whether it is days or centuries until Garbhan's prophecy passes—whether it is true or not—it doesn't affect how much I want you, Hrokr. How much I want all the time you have left to give me."

His lips parted, but only silence passed between them.

"Do not send me away."

His fingers were so gentle as they gripped my chin, tilting me up toward him. "I don't want to hurt you," he whispered.

"Sending me away will," I whispered back.

He studied my eyes, hesitating as he searched me. But I was sure, and he could feel it within me.

So softly, he bent his head and pressed his lips to my own. He was gentle as he held me, his other hand coming up to cup my face, to hold me as if I were delicate enough to shatter, fleeting enough to fall away.

My fingers curled into his shirt, pulling him closer.

"I've wanted this for so long," he whispered onto my lips. "Wanted it to be *real.*"

"They were all real," I whispered back. "Real to me."

He cradled my face in his palms, his thumbs brushing against my cheeks. "I love you," he repeated, his glittering eyes drinking me in.

"I love *you,* Hrokr."

He kissed me once more, raw and open.

"Let's finish this," he whispered against my lips. "Then I want to lock you in this tower and never let you leave." I felt more so than heard his smile, but when he pulled away I could see it was a brilliant thing that showed his teeth.

I was sure I looked the same even as I asked, "Is there news?"

"Only what you'd expect. Maddox has been very kind in his silence, not shouting at me as he normally does. But he did inform me that Cornelius is not happy."

"We knew he wouldn't be."

The light in his eyes dimmed. "It's more than that. He's reported us. Ivaylo is livid; Ciri is thankfully feigning ignorance."

"How long have you known?"

He shrugged. "Only a few hours. I had more—*pressing* concerns. And the borders are closed. No one can get in or out; information can't get in or out."

"Then how are *you* getting information?"

He grinned something devilish. "I have my secrets." But at my narrowed eyes, he laughed. "The entrance dock in Wylan is unwarded. You've been—the port city with the statues."

I remembered—sailing in on a Valencian vessel. It was an entire lifetime ago.

"The Weathermen are there," he continued. "No one is permitted to cross, but if Garbhan is going to enter—it will have to be there."

"And you think he will?"

"I would," he said.

"It's suicide."

His eyes burned. "It's the only way to get her back."

And I heard more than what he said. I understood. I would do it, too—brave the unbravable if it could bring Hrokr back to me.

I almost felt guilty. Knowing how it felt to be Hrokr's—is there any line I would not cross to bring him back?

But then I remembered all the line's Gar had crossed outside of saving Mavka. Slaying Lord Cadmus, Lady Araceli, Inina, her unborn babe, Orion, *my own mother.*

He deserved to die.

Perhaps it was a small mercy to send him to death. At least there he would find her.

"He'll move soon," Hrokr said, his face gentling further. "Ciro's sources say that Ivaylo called for all of his kings and lesser lords, all the leaders of his Guard. They're all accounted for except for one."

My chest tightened.

"It will be over, right? If he's dead?"

"One could hope," he said softly.

Hrokr gently lifted my chin with two fingers, kissed my lips, and pulled me into his arms. "Let's deal with it. And then everything I have is yours."

CHAPTER FIFTY-SIX
KILL HIM WELL

W e stood outside of the Council Room, having clung to one another the entire walk down. I relished it, enjoying the warmth of his skin against my own.

Inside, everyone was present, but there was an air of nervousness flitting through the room. When they saw him touching me, saw the easy grace with which we held to another—the Council let out a collective sigh of relief.

Hrokr leapt right into business, and I was thankful to be spared the too-soft smiles everyone offered.

I thought I'd cry if I looked at a single one too long.

"Any news?" he asked, crossing the room toward his desk.

He released my fingers, and instead of following him, I perched on the chaise next to Fallon. She raised up, planting a sloppy kiss on my cheek before lying back down. I squeezed her knee, smiling back.

"Nothing that you don't already know," Ciro said, his dark voice belying his stress. "Ivaylo can't find Garbhan. Supposedly, Jaeger cannot either. But if he is his Nock, as you say," he said with a nod to me, "then I'm sure Jay knows exactly where Garbhan is."

"I expected it to take longer," Maddox admitted, running a hand through his long, red hair. "If he's showing his hand this quickly, he knows people will wonder. He's not going to wait."

"He can't charge the Hall on his own," Fallon said.

"Who is to say he'd be alone?" Hrokr asked darkly, perching at his desk. "Thea encountered one of Garbhan's soldiers very early into her stay here. I have no doubt that there are more."

Haizea, so normally quiet, quirked a perky brow. In her light voice, she asked, "So what? You think the Hall will divide?"

"Don't be so rash," Hrokr replied smoothly.

But I had to force the words out. "Am I missing something? He can't be foolish enough to just voidstep onto the deck. He'd be dead in seconds—right?"

"Right," Ciro said darkly. "The Weatherman are instructed to kill on sight."

"It can't be that easy."

Hrokr sighed. "It likely won't be. He's desperate and out of time, but he's no fool. I can't imagine him spending centuries amassing something so intricately secret only to walk through our front door."

"There's no other way he can get in though, right?"

"No," Hrokr said. "There are other avenues, but they're spelled only to my blood. Now that we're mated," he said—and I did not miss the way he said it to further ease the minds of his Council—"it *might* work for you, but no one else."

"He has to voidstep to Wylan," Ciro said. "It's the only way."

I asked, "And if he waits us out?"

"He won't," Haizea said. "If he was going to, he would have been present with Ivaylo's Guard. He's practically announced that he's up to something. It won't be long until the others put the pieces together."

I nodded, chewing on my lip. "What if he voidsteps an army? I saw *many* people coming in and out of Oxcroft. And that was only one keep."

Hrokr nodded. "It's possible."

Maddox cracked his knuckles. "Perhaps we should be there."

Hrokr shook his head. "We can't leave Castle Habrem undefended. The ley lines run beneath, and he needs them to bring her back. This is the first place he'll come."

"He'll have to get through Wylan first, won't he?" I clarified.

From beside me, Fallon gently said, "Not exactly. The ward stops him from voidstepping in. But we are just as free inside as those on the outside. If can somehow manually charge across the ward, he can voidstep anywhere within."

"Why don't we use a more physically barring ward?" I asked.

"Can't," Ciro said gravely. "We need our archers to be able to shoot on sight. Even the seconds it would take to dismantle the ward could cost us."

Hrokr dropped his hands atop his desk. "We split."

"Always a bad plan," Haizea bit.

"Do you have a better one?" he asked archly.

In his dark voice, Ciro said, "Perhaps we should split. Realistically, he should not be able to bypass the Weatherman, let alone half of the Council. He shouldn't be able to make it to Castle Habrem."

Everyone sat in heavy silence.

"Alright," Hrokr finally said. "I can go—"

"You should stay," Fallon interrupted. "With Thea. I doubt you wish to be away from her."

At his silence, she continued.

"You haven't announced a war yet, Hrokr. The people are still feeling relatively easy. It will send a heavy message if you and Thea are both stalking the ward. Let the four of us go, and we can monitor the dock. You and Thea stay here—just in case."

His starry eyes met mine from across the room. I nodded once.

"Alright," he said softly. "Please. Kill him well."

Everyone grunted their agreement.

We all wanted him dead.

Waiting was no peaceful reprieve, even with all of the amenities Castle Habrem had to offer. Hrokr and I stayed in his room, though I spent most of my time on the balcony, watching the happy city of Fairshroud undulate beneath me, as if I could see Gar coming.

I knew I wouldn't.

Hrokr and I took our dinner on the balcony, sitting on the stone floor. As he pulled the dish cover away—revealing rice and fish and steamed vegetables—he asked, "Are you alright?"

I shrugged as he poured us both a heavy glass of wine. "Ready for it to be over."

He nodded, though we both knew an easy victory was too much to hope for.

"There's one thing I can't get over, though," I whispered.

"What's that?"

I stared at the city, the twinkling starlight now shimmering over it, the colors and smells and sounds of the city carrying up to me. "Gar saw me holding the Orb beneath the eclipse. Does that mean he will fail?"

A deep drink from his wine. "I've wondered myself, but I've come to accept that I often not know the Elder's intentions. Perhaps he will fail, but he has failed many times before and managed to do a hell of a lot of damage on the way down."

I frowned.

He sighed, and I felt his apprehension and grief flowing into me before he spoke. "Thea, this could be the time that—"

"No," I interrupted sharply.

This could be the time that I die, he projected anyway.

I stared at him, letting my grief show. "No," I whispered again.

"We'll be at the ley lines if he gets here," he whispered. "It was always going to happen at the ley lines."

"You can't die," I said. "Not yet. We haven't even touched Aphaedia together, and you believe that prophecy to be about yourself."

He shrugged. "You carry my blood, Thea. We are as touching as two people can be. Perhaps you're meant to heal the Hall on your own."

"No," I said again. And then a softer, decided, "No."

"If it is—"

"Please stop," I said harshly, finally turning to face him.

Grief soured his features, but it was a special kind of grief. The final era, as if he had accepted what was to come. As if he were ready now. "Please," he whispered. "Let me—let me say what I need to."

Tears blurred my vision, but after a long moment, I forced myself to nod.

"I want nothing more than an eternity beside you," he said. "I would have loved to do it all. To show you every inch of Valencia, to kneel before you as you healed Aphaedia. To celebrate festivals and weddings and Winter Solstices." A somber smile turned his lips. "I would have loved to marry you in front of Alynthia herself—to raise children and build a home with you, to be your mate in earnest.

"I'm so thankful that we've had this—that you were loving and kind enough to tether yourself to something fleeting. I do not deserve you, Thea. But still, you've given yourself to me anyway."

The tears—too heavy for my lashes—fell.

"If this was all I ever get—a single night of joy in an immortal life of desolation—it was worth it all. You were worth it all, Thea, and so much more." He took a deep breath, his eyes gentling into something bittersweet. "I've spent lifetimes waiting for you. You are more than a friend, more than a lover. More than my mate. You are my life, Thea Starsea. And however much of it is left, it is yours. Wholly."

"I love you," I rasped.

The words were so weak, so much less than what he'd said. But I did not think I could give more without breaking.

But he touched his chest, where my own heart beat within him. Where he felt my love, my fear, my devotion. He whispered, "I know."

He leaned forward slowly, brushing a featherlight kiss to my lips.

We sat outside, standing guard for our city—for ourselves—and shared a meal beneath the stars. And when we ran out of food—out of wine—he held me on the stone floor, his fingers drawing idle patterns in my back.

I prayed desperately our gift would not be so short-lived.

CHAPTER FIFTY-SEVEN

BACK TO REST

I woke to Hrokr brushing hair from my face and murmuring my name.

My eyelashes fluttered as I found myself in his bed, likely carried in from the terrace beyond. "I hate to wake you," he whispered.

I sat up immediately. "Is everything alright?"

He tilted his head back and forth as if to say, *Kind of.*

"What's going on?" I asked, rubbing sleep from my eyes.

"I was waiting for something to arrive," he said, and I noticed for the first time how much darkness was in his eyes. "It's here, and I need to leave. But I didn't want to leave you alone."

"Where are we going?" I asked.

He adjusted the sleeve of his tunic. "It's something I didn't tell you because I didn't want to sour our time together."

My stomach sank.

"It will put you in an uncomfortable position with the Council, and I'm sorry for that."

I searched his colorful eyes. "What's going on?"

A resolve filled him as he rose to his full height. "I will not let him raise Mavka, Thea." A muscle feathered in his jaw. "Not her, and not after what he's done."

Rising on unsteady legs, I grabbed my discarded cloak. "What are you doing, Hrokr?"

"He can bring no one back if the Orb is used."

My stomach turned. "You told your Council—"

"I lied."

The way he said the words—they were a plea, a lament.

"It won't be Orion or Inina," he said, gesturing for me to follow him into the hall. "That would only complicate things with Ciro and Haizea. And while I miss them both terribly, bringing only one back would cause more heartache than either of them would want."

"Then who?" I whispered. My mind raced, recounting his dead.

"I'd choose my mother," he admitted softly. "But her body was long ripped from her grave." As he led me down the steps, he said, "My father."

My mind spun as I followed after him.

"He was a good man if letters and word of mouth are to be believed. He may choose death to return to my mother, but it will use the Orb and give many the chance to say goodbye to a beloved man."

He cast a look back toward me, his eyes searching my own. Beyond words, I wound my fingers with him and squeezed gently.

He breathed a heavy sigh of relief at the touch.

We wound through Castle Habrem, through unknown passages and into the bowels of the building. We neared a crumbling, wooden door guarded by none other than Gyda.

She held a small sack—the size of a head.

Halls.

She bowed in deference to us both, offering me a soft, somber smile.

Hrokr pushed through the door, guiding us both along. Inside, I immediately stilled.

It was a massive, hollow cave. Running the length of it was the most beautiful river I'd ever seen, one that rippled and cast a strange, violet hue.

It wasn't water at all, I didn't think.

"It's ether," Hrokr murmured, striding decidedly down the craggy, rock floor to the left.

The ley lines.

My eyes took in the space, the ley line, the dancing shadows along the far rock wall. Stalagmites and stalactites adorned the otherwise bare space.

And the *power.*

It was overwhelming—something that nearly made me sick to my stomach.

I followed Hrokr down the path, followed him all the way to the end where the cavern bloomed into a wide bulb. A pool of ether formed—still, even though the river connecting to it thrashed.

Five pedestals were assembled in a straight line, each proudly holding an Orb. The dead Orbs flanked the living one in the center, glowing with the aura of the night.

The sky was open to the night above, though domed with glass somewhere above ground.

He reached a hand back, and Gyda silently handed him the bag. Hrokr did indeed produce a skull from it.

Thick lines of tension tightened his back and shoulders, and I wished there was anything I could do to smooth them away.

I knew I couldn't.

He stood somewhere he was once told he'd die. He stood there holding the skull of his dead father, whom he planned to resurrect to stop his oldest friend from raising his mate—who was coincidentally Hrokr's slaughtered fiance.

No, nothing could erase the heaviness of this moment.

He took a deep breath—the last moment of hesitation he'd allow himself.

I watched in numb shock as he marched straight for the center Orb and thrust his hand within its midnight depths.

He stumbled beneath the staggering force of the ether—a force I felt flowing into my own veins through our bond. Hrokr shouldered it, letting the ether sink into him.

Gyda slipped her hand into my own.

He turned away, facing us once again. His eyes were bright, rupturing supernovas bursting in his normally dark eyes. He crouched over the still pool, and—skull in hand—submerged his hand to the elbow.

Nothing happened.

His brow furrowed.

Silence.

He ripped the skull free, glancing over his shoulder.

The living Orb glowed magnificently, and a faint pulse of light glowed within each other the dead Orbs.

All but one.

I could see it the moment realization dawned in his eyes.

Hrokr cursed. And cursed again. He brought his fist to his lips, his body working through great, heaving breaths. He shoved the skull in his cloak and made for the dull Orb.

As he ripped it off the pedestal, Gyda and I shared a strained glance. We raced toward him, and he met us halfway.

Rage devoured his features, making him look sharper—colder. "It's fake."

"What?" I cried.

"It's—" He sucked in a harsh breath; his fingers shook. "It's *fake,* Thea. This is the Orb from Elements. Ivaylo must have known—or Gar got there first, or—"

His movements were sudden. He threw the Orb, sending it careening for the rock wall where it shattered into nothing more than stone and plaster.

When he met my eyes, a thousand thoughts were spinning behind his own. Hands unsteady with fury, he pulled Cadmus's skull from his cloak and handed it to Gyda.

Silently, she stuffed it back in its sackcloth.

"Return it," he said to her.

She nodded sagely. "My heart is with you, my lord," she said.

Even as rage-shaken as he was, he said, "Thank you, Gyda," and offered her a deep glance of thanks.

"And then?" she asked.

He glanced at me. "Return Father to his rest, and then please come upstairs. I'd not like Thea to be far from me—not now. Determine what size of a crew you'll need to begin moving her things to my room."

"Yes, my lord," she said, bowing her head.

He looked to me as if for permission. "Of course," I whispered.

I had no desire to be away from him, either.

Gyda left, her steps the only sound in the cavern for long moments.

He pulled me against his chest, rasping my name.

"What does this mean?" I whispered.

"It means we wait him out," he whispered back. "It means he can drag this out as long as he needs."

"Will he?" I whispered into his chest.

He sighed, the breath tickling my forehead. "I don't know, Thea."

I don't know.

CHAPTER FIFTY-EIGHT

HUMBLE

Hours later, I lay in Hrokr's bed beside him.

Gyda would be working in my room next door, preparing to move my things here. We had received no news from the Cardinal Council, and we hadn't delivered our news about the fake Orb.

There was nothing to do—nothing but wait.

Most of our time was spent in strained silence as he paced about his room thinking. But I'd finally convinced him to lie down.

He'd agreed on the stipulation that I stay near.

"You can sleep, you know," I murmured, propping on my elbow, watching the steady rise and fall of his chest from where he laid on the black duvet.

"I am sleeping."

I rolled my eyes. "I'm serious."

"Not tonight," he said, some of the levity leaving his voice.

"He might not strike today."

"Perhaps he will."

"Hrokr," I said sharply, and his eyes flashed open, a somber smile tugging at his lips. "Sleep," I commanded. "When was the last time you got a full night's worth? You need to be rested if something happens. You can't stay up forever."

He frowned, reaching up to tap my cheek. I captured his hand, holding it to my chest. "I'll keep watch," I whispered.

"You need sleep, too."

"Hrokr," I said again. "Sleep. I'll wake you up at the first sign of any trouble."

His eyes did indeed look heavy. They fluttered closed. "Fine. But at the *first* sign, Thea. Not the third or fourth."

I laughed softly. "I promise."

"Should I bring Fallon home?" he asked.

I poked him in the chest. "There's no need to stress her out. I'll stay right here. I'll go find a book and curl up next to you, alright?"

He brought our conjoined hands to his lips, pressing a kiss to the back of my hand. "Alright," he whispered.

But instead of leaving, I stretched out next to him. He rolled onto his stomach, his breathing evening out almost immediately. I played in his hair and drew idle scenes into the bare skin of his back until I was sure he was sleeping.

I rose from the bed, taking a long moment just to study him in the soft moonlight pouring in through the balcony and painting his alabaster flesh silver.

When I finally found the strength to drag my eyes away, I slipped out into the drafty hall, going only to my room next door.

There was a small, paranoid part of me that expected to open the door and find everything in disarray, scattered with the remnants of an attack I'd missed.

To find the evidence of our defeat before we'd even fought.

But inside everything was normal, nothing packed yet by Gyda.

I went immediately to the bookshelf, searching the titles. As soon as I had my pick, I slipped back into the hall.

The door clicked shut behind me, and a warm hand clamped over my mouth right as a searing lance scratched my back.

My entire body filled with ice as the scent of sweet, sweet citrus and warm leaves washed over me.

I hardly had time to process what was happening before a hand was pressed into my back and I went spinning through worlds. When the world righted itself, I was shoved forward with another sharp nick to my back, staring at a cave of lavender and star-colored purple. Like a river of stars reflecting the cave ceiling.

The ley lines.

The second stab had to have been rowan wood, because suddenly every bit of magic within me was snuffed out, leaving a hollow ringing in my ears.

"It's nauseating, isn't it?" his voice asked from me behind me.

So slowly, I turned.

Garbhan stood before me, wearing for the first time—in my immediate presence, at least—his true face.

Utterly beautiful, as he's always been.

His hair was darker, longer, and tied back in a half-knot, the loose strands brushing his black-clad shoulders. His face was clean-shaven and sharp, and his eyes—indeed not hazel at all. They looked so much like Hrokr's. If Hrokr's eyes were the night sky, Garbhan's were the earth below it. Sage green with a thousand golden stars rupturing inside of them.

"The ether," he continued, nodding toward the waterless river. "The ley lines are too heavy to be around. It will make you feel sick after a while."

I could whisper nothing but, "How?"

His face—cold and regal, now—twisted into a lazy grin.

"How what, love?"

I narrowed my eyes, wondering how I could hate something so deeply—hate it when it had once meant everything to me. "How are you here?"

"Oh—right, of course," he said jovially. I stayed frozen in place as he strolled over to the edge of that purple river lending the cave its light.

But Gar only bent down by the side of the river, brushing a single finger through it. He sucked in a sharp breath, ripping his finger back. From what I could see of it—it was burned.

"This stuff hurts something awful," he said.

It hadn't hurt Hrokr.

But Hrokr had been birthed from those waters.

"How are you here, Gar?" I growled.

He smiled a smile that I knew well. One that crinkled the corners of his eyes. "There are many answers to that question. But I assume you mean, 'Garbhan, how are you here in Castle Habrem while my merry band of self-righteous soldiers stand guard hundreds of miles away?' Is that correct?"

I curled my fingers into fists, scanning the cavern for anything that could be used as a weapon. There was nothing. The entire place was bare rock wall, and I had no options unless I wanted to wield a rock.

I turned my eyes to Garbhan. "You shouldn't be able to be here."

He grinned, long and wide. "Oh, I know."

I began running through possibilities. Had he been in the Hall at the time it was sealed? Was there a blindspot Hrokr didn't know about?

"All the clues are right there, Thea," he said. "It's obvious. Perhaps not to you—but your Hrokr, your *Council*. They should know."

"I don't understand," I whispered.

His smile was almost wistful, now. "You never do," he said just as softly.

We stared at each other for a long, heavy moment—seeing one another through new eyes. Or perhaps he looked at me as he always had. Only a pawn to be captured in a never ending game of chess with my mate.

But I was not a pawn.

I was queen.

"This throne should not be Hrokr's," he said calmly. "I was born for it to be mine."

I flinched—more out of surprise than offense. "What?"

He leaned in, and I did not dare back away. "I have the Stormblood eyes, Thea. I doubt that means anything to you, but it should have been obvious to anyone else. But they were too pretentious to think a bastard-born nobody could be something greater than all of them."

I only shook my head.

"There's a secret entrance to the Hall, warded against anyone that does not carry the blood of storms."

"You're not—"

"I'm not what?" he laughed. "A Stormblood? I am, and one older than your mate, Thea." At my shocked silence, he continued. "I've left a thick trail of crumbs, love. But no one was humble enough to follow them. Garbhan Silas Stormblood. I took two last names. My mother's and my father's. I could hardly wear Stormblood, so I combined them into Silsto for my political work. And, well," he purred with a grin, "you know Silas well."

"How?" I whispered.

He stepped away from me, heading to the rock wall where a burlap sack waited. "I was Lord Arawn's first son, and by every right the Heir to the Valencian throne. That's Hrokr's grandfather, if you two haven't yet made it that far."

"How?" I whispered again.

"My mother was not his bride. She was only a secret lover—but an adored one at that. But Arawn had the Valencian downfall of blind pride." Gar placed a faux-affronted hand atop his dark-clad chest. "He could not allow his heir born to a *mistress.* So he let her stay here, in Castle Habrem, only long enough to give birth. *And then he threw us both out.*"

I stared.

"My mother was barred from her home, her friends, her family, her *everything*—for the crime of being exactly what he'd asked her to be. And when Arawn died, Cadmus was eager to embrace his father's throne."

Heat burned through the cool fear spooled within me. "All of this is because you were denied a *throne?*"

"Because I was denied a *home,*" he growled, full lips curling back from his teeth. "I was a risk—a threat to his *legitimate* son's future. Mother and I were not permitted back in the Hall."

It should be a heartbreaking tale, but not from him. Not from those green and gold eyes full of sour envy.

"I waged war," he admitted as if it were no more than a passing thought. "I fought for the crown that was mine by birth and blood."

"You're sick," I whispered.

"No," he said. "I was *robbed,* and of more than just my throne and crown, Thea. It's almost as if the Elders wished to right the mistakes. Cadmus's heir was born dead, you know?" he purred, grinning cruelly.

Hrokr.

My lips peeled back from my teeth.

"And he'll die again," he continued, not an inch of remorse or sorrow on his tongue. "Here—if the Elders are to be believed. And they've been believable so far."

"Your fight isn't with Hrokr," I croaked. "Hate your father if you must, but Hrokr's done nothing."

Shadows flickered in the depths of his bright eyes. "He killed my Mavka."

I had nothing to say to that—though, *She deserved it,* almost poured from lips. Instead, I whispered, "He loved you, Gar."

He only smiled. "So did you."

"My darkest regret," I snarled.

He laughed, shifting his weight as if he were bored.

My eyes narrowed.

"I'm surprised you've not charged me yet," he chuckled, smirking.

"I'd be a fool to," I said honestly. "You have rowan wood. I'm alone."

"Ah," he cooed. "Don't tell me my nephew has made you soft." *My nephew.* "My Thea would have charged in head-on. Don't think you can take me?" he asked, cocking his head to one side, his dark hair sliding across his cheeks.

"I don't know what I think," I said honestly, studying him.

But surprise lit his eyes. "I see. Are you waiting for someone to come and save you, Little Shadow?"

I bared my fangs.

"And who would that be?" he purred. "The Cardinals don't know to miss you. The humans you parade as your family—returned to their hovel in Mortis Hollow? Sage and Dorin snuggled up in a cozy home in Fairshroud? Or perhaps you've grown fond of Castle Habrem's help. But Hrokr doesn't like prying eyes, does he? There is no staff to even miss you—no one other than Gyda."

A wicked light glinted in his eyes.

"She won't be coming either, Thea. After Hrokr sent her back to the royal crypt, I sent his favorite maid to the Far Away to join the others."

I flinched as he projected the image—Gyda's porcelain skin slashed and stained in scarlet. The sight curled bony fingers around my heart.

"So only Hrokr is left," he said. "And you're waiting for him to wake up and save you."

I wanted nothing more than to throw my body at Gar, to rend with my nails and shred with my teeth. But he had already proven he had tricks neither Hrokr or I had expected. I was already cut with rowan wood, and while I'd fought—and claimed victory—many times without the aid of ether, there was much more at stake this time.

It would be so easy for him to voidstep away from my attack and land directly in Hrokr's bedroom. In only seconds, he could run a blade through my mate's unconscious body.

Ciro and Haizea were in Wylan waiting for Gar, and therefore not in Mortis Hollow protecting my siblings. Garbhan could just as easily return there, taking even more family from me.

Sagira was here, believing she was safe with Dorin in a city I'd vowed would protect her. If Gar got out into the city, he would slay them both the moment he had the chance.

And the people.

I'd always known protecting myself meant protecting the Aphaedian opportunity to return home, but even that duty felt so much heavier now that I'd seen *Hrokr's* people. Whether they carried Valencian blood, Aphaedian blood, or a mixture of the two—those were *our* people above, trusting their lord and lady to protect them.

Gar could so easily charge into the city, leaving bodies in his wake.

As long as he was here antagonizing me, the others were safe. So, no, I would not charge him until I was ultimately positive I could slay him in one blow.

"Don't worry," Gar winked. He shifted his weight again, a caricature of boredom. "He'll be here. That's what we are waiting for."

Everything turned cold within me.

"Will you walk with me, Thea?" Garbhan asked, nodding down the hall toward the little pool. The river of ether rolled beside us.

"Do I have a choice?"

He grinned, chuckling as he took off down the cavern.

I followed him, drawing blood with how hard my nails cut into my palms.

"It's not the eclipse," I whispered.

I still have a hundred years.

He chuckled. "Visions are always true, but not always what we think, Thea."

I side-eyed him, finding his new, beautiful face grinning at me. "What does that mean?" I growled.

"We don't need the eclipse. Not how you'd think."

Silence.

"Do you care to elaborate?"

He rolled his eyes, his easy smile remaining. "You used to be so much more fun."

A thoughtful expression overtook his features. "I'd never considered the eclipses, not until I saw that vision of you holding the Orb beneath one. Do you want to know a secret?"

My breath left me in a panicked, crackling rush. "Sure, Gar."

"In that vision, you were wearing this same set of clothes. Do you think you'll have the same set in a century?"

I felt so cold.

We reached the same still pool Hrokr had attempted to raise his father from. The Orbs were still aligned, though the fake one had been removed. The first soft rays of dawn were beginning to shine through the opening in the cave ceiling, casting a lilac sheen over the Orbs.

Between the fresh dawn and the starlight-glittering of the ley lines, the entire cavern was painted in glimmering purple.

"I'd never thought much of the eclipses until I saw that little vision of you, Thea. And I only *really* thought about them once you'd slipped my leash," he huffed. "Did you know that the year of Hrokr's birth there was an eclipse? An eclipse with the moon *nowhere near the sun.*"

"What are you saying?" I whispered.

"There was an eclipse in Valencia the year of his birth—even though one was not due for another twenty-five years. It wasn't the moon that blocked out the sun, Thea. It was the presence of the Far Away, thinning, blotting out the light to bring him back."

My breath was coming too quickly, my pulse bounding through my veins. He pulled the last true Orb out of his bag, anticlimactically small next to the last living one. "Here," he said, pushing it into my hands. "I want you to be the one who does it."

"No."

"I will kill him, Thea, or you will play with me. Those are your options. Undo what he did. Bring her back to me."

With shaking fingers, I took the Orb from his hands. I couldn't bring myself to move as he pressed a warm, lingering kiss to my cheek. His kiss felt strange—wrong—without the scratch of stubble.

"Go on," he whispered, tilting his head toward the last pedestal for the Orb. On unsteady legs, I stepped away from him. Slowly, I placed it atop the pedestal.

Immediate, overwhelming power flooded me.

Flooded me. I was freezing, starving, and burning alive as it poured from the Orb and into my palms. I could not pull away—it wanted to hold me. I'd felt this power before, swimming inside of Hrokr.

It made sense—this power was what gave him life.

But his otherworldly, overwhelming power? It was a stream, a bubbling brook. This was an ocean, surging into my body, bringing me to my knees. My hands still clung to the Orb, my arms lifted as if in supplication.

I felt her—Alynthia.

The thought was absurd, ridiculous. But I felt space bending, moving unnaturally in the sky. I was connected to the lifeblood of the world. It wound within me, sucking life from the ground, from the sky, from the river of ether. From *me.*

The rowan wood did not matter.

This was much more powerful.

Overhead, the light of the dawn was snuffed out.

An eclipse.

My hundred years... My hundred years of assured safety—my *net*... It was gone. My immortal life didn't feel very immortal anymore.

Especially when that vast presence released me, dropping me to my hands and knees, only to find Gar standing nearly at the end of the Hall, by the pool. But the strangest thing—he had a wooden sword in his hands, trained on nothing but empty space.

I realized and shot to my feet, crying his name—but it was too late. Not only was I too far away, but I slammed into *nothing*, an invisible wall barring me from stepping away from the Orb.

Hrokr voidstepped into the space at the same time Garbhan swung, cleaving and catching both of his legs, cutting one through the bone. Flesh opened at an unnatural angle as Hrokr roared, falling to his knees. Rage lit his gaze, burning through pain as he tried to rise.

He could not. Not only did his wound cripple him, but he appeared to be locked in the same type of cage I was. Rough scratches were cut into the floor around him.

Runes.

Garbhan laid his blade against Hrokr's neck. His free hand waved toward me in a loose arc. "Come here, love," he said, smiling. "Just don't think to hurt me, or he'll be dead."

"Don't," Hrokr rasped, lifting his eyes to my own. There was already so much blood. It was dark and loose, flowing around him in an ever-widening puddle. The blade had to be rowan wood—he was not healing. "I'm going to die here anyway, Thea, just—"

"No," I cried, lurching forward a step. He'd broken the ward around me.

Garbhan laughed something cold. "He isn't wrong."

Gar shoved Hrokr forward, cutting his neck thinly. Hrokr pushed himself up, held only by hands shaking with strain.

Garbhan cast his eyes over his shoulder at me. "Into the ward with him, Little Shadow."

I wanted to cut him, to scream, to tear his heart from his chest.

But could I do it before that blade cut through Hrokr's throat?

Blood pooled around him. His wounds—a human would have been long dead.

"Please," Hrokr rasped, the stars in his eyes guttering. "I'm *dying*, Thea. We knew this, we—"

"Stop," I cried, choking on my broken sobs. "I don't care about him, I—"

"I do," he pleaded, his breath rattling in his chest. "You need a home to come back to. Our people, I—"

"No," I sobbed, stumbling forward a ragged step.

"I meant what I said," he rasped, ignoring Gar completely. "On the balcony. It was *enough*. It was more than I could have ever hoped for, it—"

"It's not enough."

Gar pressed the blade farther into Hrokr, drawing a line of hot blood that had Hrokr baring his teeth in a weak grimace. "Into the ward, Thea," Gar commanded.

Hrokr shook his head gently, not caring that it cut him further.

But I was already running.

I was already crossing that ward, falling to my knees in the hot puddle of his lifeblood. Gar stepped away once we were both instead, letting his blade fall away.

"Don't leave me," I begged, clinging to Hrokr's chest.

He was silent for a long moment as he processed what I'd done. Finally, in a gentle voice, he whispered, "I don't have a choice, my Thea."

I broke into sobs so violent I couldn't catch my breath, clutching him. He dropped his forehead to my own. "I love you. So greatly, I—"

"Don't," I pleaded.

"I love you," he repeated, using the last dregs of his strength to press a cold kiss to my lips. "Live. Love, Thea. I'll wait for you. I'll be there in the Far Away, I'll—"

I threw myself back into him, holding him so tightly I knew I had to be hurting him.

Knowing it didn't matter if I did.

Garbhan scoffed. "The two most renowned Gentry Fae Alynthia has to offer—and both of you have still found yourselves on your knees. Not so mighty without our magic, are we?"

I found enough rage to turn my face toward him, to study his form where it stood tall and proud.

"Maybe it won't be us," I began darkly, "but someone will stop you, Gar. Someday."

He smiled. It was a brilliantly cruel thing. "And who will that be, Thea? If not the Lord of the North and his vicious bride—then who?"

"The Elders—"

"They will not stop me either."

The only sound in the cavern was our labored breathing and Gar's brisk clipping of boots against the stone floor as he left us. He stepped up to the pool, which glowed with the lifeblood of Alynthia. Garbhan reached into his bag, brandishing a brown, age-faded skull.

He closed his eyes for the shortest second, the purple light bathing him in an eerie glow. And then he dropped the skull inside.

The entire river of ether surged, splashing amidst itself. The pool churned and sputtered.

Gar's voice was so quiet when he said, "I'm not going to kill you, Crow."

Hrokr only breathed, his lashes fluttering as he fought to retain consciousness.

"I'll even call Haizea to tend your wounds," he continued, studying the pool beneath him.

Out of the ether, a violet glow began. Garbhan's breath caught in his throat, a ragged sound I heard from here.

He cried out as a head splashed up through the water—dry. She gasped and choked, a tattered cry tearing through her lips.

She was beautiful, made from spun moonlight. Eyes glowing with silver fire, hair the same color. Her skin was blue-pale, ephemeral.

Gar lifted her out of the tub, her naked body clinging to his. "Mavka," he croaked, all pretense of the violent, heart-of-stone warrior gone.

"Garbhan?" she croaked, looking all around herself like a half-drowned faun.

"Mavka," he repeated, clutching her to his chest. Where she touched his skin, it burned him. He did not seem to care. He ripped the cloak from his shoulders, wrapping it around her.

She huddled inside of it, disoriented and terrified. "I'm going to take you home, alright?" he said, studying her face. He was more unguarded than I'd ever seen him.

She only repeated his name, skittish and afraid.

He stood, pulling her close to his chest. Her feet fumbled beneath her, but his arm was solid around her waist.

It was perhaps the coldest thought I'd ever had—but I would bathe in the glow of her death, to slaughter her before him.

And by the look in his eyes—tarnished only by the love of his bride at his side—he met my vehemence. Mavka started as she saw me, saw *Hrokr*.

She said his name—just once. Afraid and disbelieving. "Hrokr?"

The man who'd once been her husband betrothed.

Gar turned to her, fixing the cloak about her shoulders. "Don't move, alright?"

She said nothing, only studying him with moon-wide eyes.

And then he turned away from her. He—impossibly—stepped away from his reborn mate.

"Alright," Gar's chirped, striding toward us. Hrokr and I immediately gripped one another, holding on desperately to weather this together.

I yelped as he broke the ward to dig his fingers into my hair, ripping me away from Hrokr. We clung to one another, drawing blood with our nails. But it was not enough.

Gar dragged me away by my hair, smearing the pool of Hrokr's dark blood. "I wanted to scare her," he admitted, chuckling. I screamed as he drove his rowan blade into my back.

I looked down in dazed horror as it protruded from the center of my stomach before he ripped it back out. Blood poured in a crimson waterfall onto the stones below.

Hrokr screamed but had not the strength to do anything about it.

"Scare her, yes," he continued. "But it is *you* I want to feel it," he said to Hrokr. "Do you know what it's like to have a dead mate? It's hell, Crow. And I have endured centuries of it."

He dropped me unceremoniously, and I gripped my stomach with shaking fingers, pain a stimulant I could hardly breathe around.

Hope was a stupid thing to feel—but I felt it course through my veins all the same.

Words came back to me.

My life will be taken in the presence of the ley lines.

Do all seer's visions come true?

Not always in the capacity we expect.

I'm not going to kill you, Crow.

You are my life, Thea Starsea.

I stared down at my arms, scratched and bloodied with how desperately he tried to hold me to himself. But I had been torn away.

Perhaps the prophecy had arrived already.

"I want you to live a very long life, Hrokr," Gar said softly, "carrying with you every day the pain that you called down upon me. Perhaps then you can understand the madness, the lengths to which you forced my hand."

Gar's fingers again tangled in my hair. As he pulled me toward the ley lines, I clawed at him, but my wound had weakened me greatly.

In an impossible moment, I wondered if it was better to believe that Hrokr was going to die instead of me.

Garbhan had taken his father, his mother. His friends, his family, his peace. Would he truly take his mate, too? Would I wish the pain of a dead mate on *my Hrokr* instead of myself?

Was there any grief I would not bear for him?

But the choice was not mine to make.

Hrokr—rapidly fading—roused enough to shout something wordless from where he lay.

"Please," I begged, clinging to Gar's forearm as he dragged me toward the river. "Please, Gar, please, I—"

"Immortality is so long alone, Crow," he said, cutting me off. "It will take her a while to die, but the lines will indeed take all she has to give."

Hrokr—so broken—murmured, "Please."

Garbhan paused. "Where is the menace, old friend? The rage? Perhaps you should have thought to humble yourself before we made it here."

And then he lifted me, tossing me over the edge.

The last thing I heard was Hrokr's agonized, anguished roar. And the last thing I saw was Garbhan grabbing Mavka—and disappearing into nothing.

CHAPTER FIFTY-NINE

TIMELESS

P ain was too weak a word.

Time did not exist here.

Only a split-second of an eternity of anguish. Alynthia was hungry, and my body an offering rife with life. The ether pulled my blood from my wounds, stole my breath from my lungs. My eyes burned, my bones turned to liquid inside my skin. Blisters formed and split against my skin, my clothes burning into nothing.

I fell forever, the bottom of this chasm deeper than time could allow. I begged death to hurry, willed the Far Away to reach forward and snatch me up.

Only when I felt my consciousness ebbing, blissful death finally coming to take me, did a hand in the dark reach out spindly fingers.

I woke in the dark.

I could hear a soft fire crackling somewhere, but its light and warmth did not reach me. Something was *wrong*. I could feel the urge to flee, the urge to get out of wherever I was. There was no life here.

There was death here.

An absence of magic, a rejection that wanted me gone—and gone fast.

I thought maybe I was dead.

But when a door creaked open, soft firelight silhouetted the last thing I expected to see. A small family of snow-crusted toadstools—

Letti standing at their head.

CHAPTER SIXTY

ḤROKR STORMBLŒD

I'd never known hurt.

My life? It had been easy up until this point.

But when I woke in a bed that still smelled so richly of *her*... When I woke to find my ether returned, my fresh scars still bound in tight woundcloth... When I found my Hall safe, my family alive and well around me... Haizea monitoring my pulse with two fingers pressed to my wrist, Fallon curled at the foot of my bed like a cat, Ciro with his hand on Haiz's shoulder, and Maddox—Maddox with eyes red and swollen with tears, kneeling at my side—

I knew pain.

"Where is she?" I rasped, sitting up.

Maddox's hand shot out, pressing me back into my bed. "Crow—"

"Where is she?" I growled.

And if the swollen void within my chest, the silence where her heart once beat, was not enough—the crumpling of Fallon's features was.

There was a ringing in my ears—one I knew would never end.

The words felt strange coming through numb lips. "I'm going to her."

Haizea's fingers tightened on my wrist. "Don't say that, Crow, don't—"

My eyes cut sharply toward her. It was cruel of me, but she of all people should know how I felt.

I projected the grief—the devastating emptiness—that had come from her when her husband died.

She flinched, dropping my hand as tears pooled in her amethyst eyes. "You can't leave us, Crow."

But Fallon was angry. "And who will lead when you're dead?"

"Maddox," I said sharply, ripping away the blankets to crawl to my feet.

He stood in my path. "No."

"It was not a request, Commander," I hissed, stepping around him.

But his hand reached out to catch my wrist. "We can't find her body."

Her *body*.

I was going to vomit.

I did not feel the hope he wanted me to. "The ley lines wouldn't have left anything."

She was dead. I knew it.

I could feel the silence within me, feel the heavy darkness where her pulse once lay.

"You're not killing yourself," Ciro said softly.

Would it be what she would have wanted? he projected for only me.

I met his ice-blue eyes, wordlessly funneling my pain.

I know, he whispered. *But she wouldn't have wanted you to follow her.*

"She gave everything," Fallon whispered. "The least you can do is live."

I tried not to hear the words. I was not strong enough to bear them.

If only to shut out the pain, I let in the rage. The anger, the malevolence within me that sent shadows skittering like venomous snakes across the floor.

I voidstepped to the armory—but my Council was ahead of me, knowing my thoughts better than I often knew them myself. They appeared around me, worry written on their faces.

I stripped before them—unconcerned with their prying eyes. I selected fresh leathers, my boots, and a cloak. I stared down my sword and knives, narrowing my eyes at the display.

I would not stay in this world without her, not the way Garbhan had spent centuries without Mavka.

But I could stomach a few days if it put him in the ground. And then I would go home to her.

"Maddox," I said, pulling a sword down from the rack. "Hold the Seat."

Sit my throne, be the Lord of the North in my absence.

"No," he said.

I turned, letting everything inside of me out. I felt the foundations of Castle Habrem shake beneath me as darkness descended over the city. Over the Hall, over the world. His eyes went wide.

"Again, Commander. Not a request."

ACKNOWLEDGMENTS

Thank you, Jesus, for letting me do something I love so much with such supportive people around me.

Thank you to my loving and precious husband, Tylor. I truly couldn't have made it to where I am without you. So many hours of talking through plots and world-building. So many circular discussions of character motivation and arcs. Words will never do justice—but I'm so grateful. I love you more than I can say.

Becca Randle—*thank you so much, Becs.* Thank you. And then thank you some more. While not only helping me get through writing these books by being such a loving and magnificent person, your direct support has been irreplaceable. Thank you for making me such a beautiful cover, for reading these stories and letting me talk through every inch of them, and for loving them as much as I do. I love you with all my heart. My biggest thanks is for being my best friend.

Maggie Logan, Emma, and Scarlett—thank you for the support with not just this project but with all the others. And a big, warm, forever thank you to Holly Morse.

Thank you, Karissa Reddick, for taking the time to read this series and offer me so much love, support, and conversation. Having you to talk to about these characters has meant the whole world to me. Thank you, Leilani Villanueva, for being one of the most lovely and kind people I've ever met and for cheering me on with such unending support. And thank you, Jakelin Medina, for loving fantasy as ferociously as I do—for being such a treasured place to celebrate both my characters and those of so many others we love. The three of you truly make my days so bright.

Thank you, Mom and Dad—for everything.

Calvin and Abbey—thank you for being the safest place in the whole world. Thank you for being my family, for being my best friends, and for being my biggest supporters.

And thank you, reader, for spending so much time with me and loving these characters as I do.

THANK YOU

Thank you so much for reading this book.

Be sure to visit haleydbrown.com to keep up with updates for future books in this series and other projects!

Don't forget to leave a review on Amazon and Goodreads so that others can know what it's like to journey through Alynthia!

ABOUT AUTHOR

Haley D. Brown is the fantasy author of the ***Hall of the Hopeless*** series. She was born and raised in Oklahoma and still lives in her hometown with her husband. They are happily raising their four-legged, furry child.

She is a Christian, a popcorn enthusiast, and loves to fall in love with new characters. She has always been a big nerd that preferred the fantasy worlds of books and games to real life, and now works to create worlds and characters that are loved as deeply as she has loved others.

Ingram Content Group UK Ltd.
Milton Keynes UK
UKHW041838140423
420212UK00017B/155/J